*Praise for*

# RACHEL HORE

'Compelling, engrossing and moving'
**Santa Montefiore**

'A wonderfully moving tale of love and loss,
hope and eventual reconciliation'
**Barbara Erskine**

'An emotive and thought-provoking read'
**Rosanna Ley**

'A story that stirs the deepest emotions'
*Woman & Home*

'A poignant story, rich in period detail'
*Sunday Mirror*

'Her women are brave and good, and you
desperately want them to win'
*Daily Mail*

# RACHEL HORE

## *The Dream House*

**SIMON &
SCHUSTER**

London · New York · Sydney · Toronto · New Delhi

First published in Great Britain by Simon & Schuster UK Ltd, 2006
This paperback edition published 2023

Copyright © Rachel Hore, 2006

The right of Rachel Hore to be identified as author
of this work has been asserted in accordance with the
Copyright, Designs and Patents Act, 1988.

1 3 5 7 9 10 8 6 4 2

Simon & Schuster UK Ltd
1st Floor
222 Gray's Inn Road
London WC1X 8HB

Simon & Schuster Australia, Sydney
Simon & Schuster India, New Delhi

www.simonandschuster.co.uk
www.simonandschuster.com.au
www.simonandschuster.co.in

A CIP catalogue record for this book
is available from the British Library

Paperback ISBN: 978-1-3985-0859-0
eBook ISBN: 978-1-4711-2716-8

Typeset in Palatino by M Rules

Printed and Bound in the UK using 100% Renewable
Electricity at CPI Group (UK) Ltd

MIX
Paper | Supporting
responsible forestry
FSC® C171272

*For my mother and to the memory
of my father*

# *Kate's family*

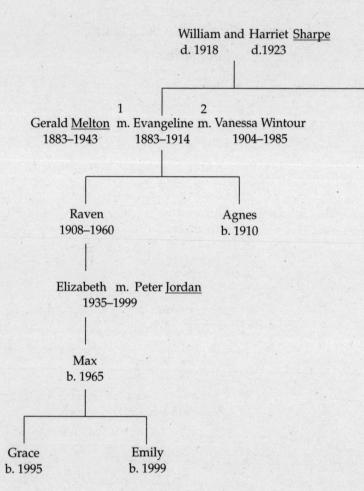

William and Harriet <u>Sharpe</u>
d. 1918          d.1923

        1              2
Gerald <u>Melton</u>  m. Evangeline  m. Vanessa Wintour
1883–1943      1883–1914       1904–1985

Raven
1908–1960

Agnes
b. 1910

Elizabeth   m.  Peter <u>Jordan</u>
1935–1999

Max
b. 1965

Grace
b. 1995

Emily
b. 1999

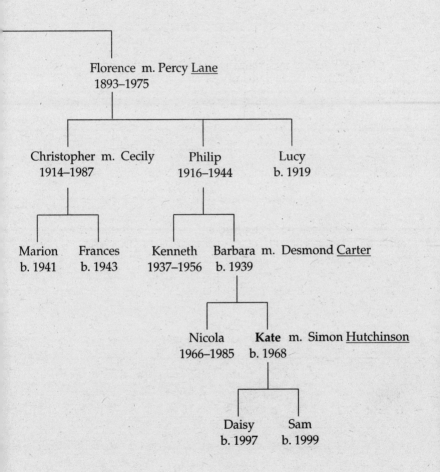

# Chapter 1

*London, November 2002*

'Come on, come on, please answer,' Kate mouthed into the receiver. Her eyes focused on the photo of her husband, Simon, with Daisy and little Sam on the wall of her grey, windowless office as she listened to the distant ringing. Finally she dropped the phone back onto its cradle. Where could Tasha be? Surely Sam wasn't worse or the nanny would have rung her.

Kate reached down, riffled in her bag for her mobile and hit Tasha's mobile number. Straight to voicemail. Damn.

'Tasha – it's me, Kate. Hope you're OK. I need to know how Sam is. Can you ring me at the office when you've got a moment?'

She shoved the phone into the pocket of her jacket, trying to ignore her butterflies of panic. Sam probably just had a bad tummy bug but it had been so horrible seeing him hot and limp this morning, and he'd even thrown up the water Kate had given him. Of course, Tasha was more than competent, but . . . I should have stayed at home with him, she told herself fiercely, rung in sick myself.

*No, you shouldn't,* said an irritating voice in her head. *Tasha can manage perfectly well by herself. What would have happened if you hadn't been at the television studios this morning holding Susie Zee's hand? Susie would probably have refused to appear on the chat show at all and there would have been an awful stink then, I can tell you.*

Kate had to agree that the uncomfortable voice of reason had a point. Susie, a sweet but very needy person, was a singer-songwriter and Kate's employers, Jansen & Hicks, had just published her no-holds-barred autobiography. As publicist for the book, Kate had been shepherding Susie around London media-land for the last week, attempting to protect her from the fallout of her confessed affairs with various famous figures in the music business. Even now Kate had taken a huge risk by leaving Susie in the care of the London sales representative for a book-signing and, crossing her fingers that all would be well, hailing a cab back to Jansen & Hicks's offices on Warren Street. Her plan now was to deal with the worst of the urgent tasks waiting for her and to sneak off home early.

Kate glanced at her watch – twelve fifteen already – and surveyed the horror of her desk. She'd only been out of the office for a morning, and look at it! Towers of new books, tottering piles of papers and magazines, even a heap of plastic toy trolls with Day-Glo hair to promote a children's fantasy title. Why do people just dump things on me any old how? she thought, grumpily, brushing a strand of dark hair off her face and stabbing at the 'on' button of her computer. She wished, not for the last time, that she had an assistant but, alas, she was not high enough up the ladder for that.

The telephone rang now and she snatched it up, hoping it was Tasha.

'Kate? Adam here. Sorry to bother you with another problem, but . . .'

Kate's heart dived. Adam Jacobs was a first-time novelist in need of large dollops of TLC. Normally she would be happy to provide reassurance, but today she just wanted to get him off the line. As she listened to his latest complaint – his local bookshop not stocking his novel – she jammed the receiver between jaw and shoulder and started sorting through the mess. She balanced books in piles by the desk, swept the trolls into a box, stashed papers and circulars into various trays.

'Adam, don't worry, really, I'm sure there's a simple explanation. Whoops!' A pile of books fell crashing to the floor. 'Look, I'll e-mail the sales rep straight away. Yes, yes, yes, I know. Must go, I'm afraid. Bye, now.'

She threw down the receiver, shuffled the fallen books into a pile then started plucking the Post-it notes off her computer screen.

The phone rang again. 'Kate, it's Patrick. Where the *hell* were you?'

Oh my God. How could she have forgotten? She was supposed to have been at that meeting with him and his best-selling crime author! Patrick, the publishing director, was pitching for a new contract and the author had badly wanted reassurance about the publicity side of things.

'I'm so sorry,' she gulped, 'it just slipped my mind. I've been out of the office . . . I know, it's too late, isn't it. I'm sorry. It's Susie . . . No, I know, Patrick – yes, I know it's my fault. Yes. Sorry.'

He slammed down the receiver and she buried her face in her hands, his angry voice still ringing in her ears. If they didn't win a new deal with the author, he had hissed, it was all down to *her*.

*Well, it is your fault really*, said the headmistressy voice of conscience once more. *You shouldn't try to fit quarts into pint pots.*

But I've got too much to do and no one to help me. How can I be everywhere at once? Kate countered.

*You could organize yourself a bit better. Say 'no' more often.*

Kate sighed. Yeah, and then they'll say I can't cope. 'These working mothers, their brains go, you know.' She'd heard Patrick say something along these lines only last week, the bastard. His assistant had left two months after returning from maternity leave because she 'clearly couldn't take the pace any more'. He meant being in the office until seven every night *and* taking work home, Kate presumed.

At moments like that she wished she had a Harry Potter wand. Then she'd magically marry Patrick to a high-flying career girl followed swiftly by a high-flying mortgage and the arrival of triplets who only needed three hours' sleep a night – different lots of three hours. That would fix *him*.

'Hi, Kate. It looks like you're off again,' declared Annabelle, her boss Karina's secretary, materializing at her office door in a cloud of Anna Sui perfume. 'Karina's just rung. She's stuck on the train back from Leeds, so you'll have to go to the James Clyde lunch instead of her.'

Fussy, elderly James Clyde. The last person Kate could handle today.

'Oh that's great – just what I need,' Kate groaned, running both hands back through her dark bob. She simply could not face the celebration lunch for his eighteenth political thriller, due to be held today in the company's private dining suite upstairs. There must be someone else who could go instead . . .

Annabelle understood immediately what was in Kate's mind, for she said hastily, 'There's only me and you left – and I'm busy. *Someone's* like gotta answer the phones round here.'

Something snapped inside Kate. She rose out of her chair and leaned across the desk. Two spots of red suffused her normally pale Celtic complexion and her green eyes blazed with dislike. At five feet five, she just had the edge on little mini-skirted Annabelle. 'Well, you'll just have to answer mine for a change, then,' she snarled. 'And make sure you bring me up any urgent messages. Some of us have real work to do.'

The main course had been cleared away and dessert served: a pretty strawberry mousse patterned with blackcurrant coulis and spun sugar. The select gathering in the small but elegant dining room of Jansen & Hicks included the company chairman, Robert Goss, James Clyde, a portly balding man in his mid-sixties, Clyde's longsuffering editor, Felicity, two sales managers and Kate. So far, Kate had been invited to express her opinions on the following subjects: last Saturday's Chelsea game, about which she knew nothing and cared less; the new décor in the reception area downstairs; Jeffrey Archer's latest venture . . . She surreptitiously looked at her watch – one thirty – and felt for the mobile in her jacket pocket. Could she get away with excusing herself to go and try Tasha again?

But James Clyde chose that moment to ask Kate archly, 'And what *other* exciting projects are you working on at the moment, my dear?'

Kate thought quickly. 'I'm really pleased with the way our book *The Lost Generation* is going,' she told him. 'It's about the highlife of the nineteen twenties. There have been some great reviews already. The launch-party is at the Oxo Tower. And then there'll be the TV series—'

But Clyde's concentration had snapped back to its usual focus – himself.

'That's just what I wanted to talk to you about, Robert,' he addressed the chairman in his reedy voice, jabbing his spoon in the air for emphasis. 'I don't seem to be getting the review coverage I used to. How about leaning on that fellow at the *Sunday Times* book pages a bit, eh?' he chuntered.

Kate remembered last week's conversation with the journalist in question, who was, incidentally, not a 'fellow' at all. 'James Clyde? God, is he still alive?' she'd said.

At this, Robert Goss calmly did what he always did in awkward circumstances. He delegated.

'Well, Katherine? It's true we're not getting notices for James's books. What are you doing about it?'

Kate's hand froze on her water glass. She replayed in her mind another conversation a couple of weeks ago in which she had actually pleaded with the editor of *Motoring Monthly* to photograph the portly Clyde in his silver Lamborghini holding his book aloft. It was the only piece of publicity anyone had managed to get for him.

As her mind spun, searching for the right way to wriggle out of this one, the cavalry arrived in the unlikely form of Annabelle, who sashayed into the room without even a tap on the door.

'Messages for Kate,' she breathed, batting her long eyelashes and brushing against the chairman, she handed Kate a sheaf of yellow Post-it notes before dematerializing again.

The male contingent took a moment to recover from this visitation and Felicity tactfully moved the conversation away from reviews.

Kate sat and looked over Annabelle's childish handwriting, her relief at the interruption quickly evaporating. The top one ran: *Susie, Borders bookshop. Upset. Pl. ring.* Oh well, that was predictable. The next message went, *Yr husband rang. Crisis mtg work. Won't get back for dinner party sorry.* Oh no, something else she'd forgotten! She'd invited Liz and Sarah round with their husbands. Oh hell, not with Sam sick. She'd just have to cancel yet again! The third was a message from Tasha – at last. *At doctor's. But Sam much better.* Thank heavens for that, Kate thought, feeling the tension finally leave her body. But then she stared at the last note and felt her stomach go into freefall.

*Urgent. Daisy's school rang. Daisy has rash – meningitis??? Go to Chelsea & Westminster Hospital.*

Later, Kate wouldn't be able to remember exactly what happened next, though Felicity told her she'd committed the cardinal sin of interrupting one of Robert Goss's shaggy dog jokes. She just remembered arriving down in the lobby, her heart thumping, her body shaking, gazing round wildly. She shoved at the revolving doors – why were they so slow? – and found herself on the pavement. Tube or taxi? Like a madwoman she waved frantically at every passing black cab until finally an empty one stopped. She snatched open the door and threw herself onto the back seat, then explained the crisis to the driver, who nodded sympathetically and swung the cab immediately across three lanes to make it through the right-turn filter light just in time. Kate clutched the strap for dear life as the driver dodged his way south-west through the traffic. There arose in her mind a picture of little Daisy, six years old, blonde and blue-eyed, with that funny lopsided grin that lit up her face. The idea of her ill in a hospital bed with tubes sticking out in all directions was too much after the tension of the day.

After a moment, she searched with her free hand for her handbag to find a tissue to blow her nose. It was then she realized she'd left the bag in her desk drawer. This was just the final straw. How was she going to pay for the cab? She reached in her jacket pocket, pulled out her phone and brought up Simon's office number.

'Why are we putting ourselves through all this?' Kate said wretchedly to Simon later – ten fifteen that evening, in fact. Her husband had walked in through the door of their terraced house in Fulham, exhausted and starving, twenty minutes ago and was now sitting opposite Kate at the kitchen/breakfast-room

7

table shovelling down the Chicken Basque she'd cobbled together last night for tonight's cancelled dinner party. 'Life is like one long obstacle race at the moment.'

Simon put down his fork and looked at Kate from under his blond cowlick. He rubbed his eyes, then reached across to squeeze her hand.

'Poor you,' he said. 'What an awful day. At least the children are all right. They look so peaceful asleep now, don't they? Sam seems to have every soft toy he possesses tucked into bed with him.'

'Let's hope he's not sick in the night, then. Half of them you can't put through the washing machine.' Kate got up to fetch dessert from the fridge – a large bowl of trifle that they'd plainly be eating for the rest of the week. She sat down and spooned out a large helping for him and picked out half a dozen bits of fruit from the jelly for herself. Cream always brought her out in spots, never mind what it did to her hips – she had never lost that last extra half-stone after Sam's birth, and she knew she looked enough of a mess as it was. She pulled her fingers back through lank, tangled hair. Her blouse and skirt were crumpled and she picked at the pink Calpol stains on the skirt, souvenirs of the last seven hours with two sick children.

'When I finally got to the hospital, you can imagine what a state I was in,' she said. As they'd waited in traffic, she had confessed to the cab driver that she had no means of paying him. Amazingly, he had not thrown her out onto the street there and then. 'My kid was ill once like that,' he had said grimly. 'Scared the life out of us, I can tell you. Come on, let's beat this traffic.' And with the determination of a tank driver going into battle, he'd manoeuvred his way through the jams, zipped up and down tiny side streets until they turned neatly into a miraculous space just outside the hospital. 'Here you are, love. Hope she's all right, your little girl. Nah, don't worry about the money. I was on me way home anyway. Just you run along now.' And jabbering her thanks, Kate had torn into the Accident and Emergency reception and through to the bright, toy-strewn children's section.

'I just blubbered something at the receptionist and she had to make me calm down and explain. And then they took me through to a side room and there was Daisy, sitting with her teacher, and oh, Simon, she gave me this huge Daisy smile. I just hugged her and hugged her. The doctor said it was only a rash, but she was being sick with the bug so it was confusing. You can't imagine the relief . . .'

'I know, I know. I'm really sorry you couldn't find me. I don't know why Zara didn't just buzz me on Gillingham's mobile. She knew I was out with him, silly girl.' By the time Simon had got Kate's frenzied call for help the crisis was over. He had accidentally left his own mobile on his desk.

'Poor Tash will have two sick kids to look after tomorrow. It's not really fair on her. Simon, the ends are just not meeting at the moment, are they?' Kate covered her face with her hands.

Simon pushed back his chair and came round the table. 'Poor darling.' She felt his warm breath in her hair as he kissed her. Then he released her abruptly and turned away, his hands diving into his trouser pockets to rattle his loose change.

'Is something the matter?' she asked. Fidgeting was always a sign of anxiety with Simon.

'Perhaps this isn't the best time to tell you, Kate, but it's the reason why I was so late. Staff meeting. Riot Act read. There are no bonuses this year and some people are being let go. No, not me, I don't think – *this* time,' he responded to Kate's sharp intake of breath. He pressed his lips together in what passed as a reassuring smile.

9

They were silent for a moment, both remembering the past. Simon and Kate's thirtieth year had been a testing time. Daisy was on the way and Simon ended up being without a proper job for nearly a year, which had put a lot of pressure on the marriage, more pressure than Kate liked to think about. It was worst after Daisy's birth. Kate developed severe post-natal depression, from which she took many months to recover because, the doctor said, of her psychological history. When Kate was seventeen, her elder sister, Nicola, had been killed in a car accident. Now, the trauma of a difficult birth and the shock of finding herself responsible for a small baby had ripped open emotional wounds that had never properly healed.

Then, just when it seemed things couldn't get any worse, Simon's father, newly retired from his country GP's surgery, had dropped down dead of a coronary on Boxing Day. Simon's mother had been distraught. Simon was their only child and he and Kate found themselves going back and forth from Suffolk for months to be with her.

Things had gradually improved. Simon finally got permanent work, if not with the prospects of his previous job, Kate's treatment started to take effect and the corner was turned.

Kate had been nervous when she'd found herself pregnant again eighteen months later, but her doctor was encouraging and, in the end, her baby blues with Sam were more manageable. She still had patches of depression and went to counselling occasionally. One of the things the doctor had warned her against was too much stress, but 'too much stress' exactly described her current lifestyle. Simon not getting the hoped-for bonus was yet another blow.

'I suppose we should have seen that one coming,' she said.

'Yup. Last month's figures.'

'So we're stuck here.' Kate's voice was wobbly. She looked

round the small room, festooned with the children's paintings. Despite the bright lighting she imagined for a moment that the walls were moving in on her.

'Well, we won't be able to get somewhere bigger in this area, will we?' said Simon, his voice sharp with disappointment.

A lot had hung on the hope of a bonus. Three bedrooms weren't enough now, with Tasha living in. And the single reception room – the knocked-through living room – seemed so small, especially with two children and increasing numbers of large plastic toys.

Kate stared out of the window at the scrubby bit of garden, the bare terracotta pots huddled together in the November chill. She didn't exactly dislike their house, which was in one of the residential roads leading off the Fulham Palace Road, but somehow it had never entirely felt like home. At first it had seemed huge after the tiny flat in Shepherd's Bush she had rented with her friend Claire, but now it had magically shrunk with three adults and two children jostling for space.

Simon had always said they would look for somewhere as soon as capital was available. It never was.

Sometimes Kate felt frustrated at her husband's carefulness with money, but in her heart of hearts she was relieved that he was sensible. Some of his other City friends had got into serious trouble by taking out huge mortgages, then being made redundant and unable to keep up the payments.

Simon started to go through that morning's post in his methodical way. The first envelope contained a bank statement. He cast his eyes over the figures, folded it back into the envelope and tucked it into a letter rack on the dresser. The second envelope contained an estate agent's brochure. He laid it on the table between them and they pored over the prices of local four-bedroomed homes as they had many times during recent months. The difference now, of course, was that they were having to lower their expectations even further.

'We just can't do it, can we?' Kate slumped in her seat.

'Not if we stay round here, darling, no. It's a bit better south of the river, look.' Simon pointed out a couple of properties in Wandsworth. 'Lower council tax, too. Still tiny gardens, though.'

'They're both right on the main road,' said Kate, 'and my journey to work would be even longer.' With one change on the tube from Putney Bridge it took her nearly an hour each way now; Simon, with his direct route, only a little less. 'I can't ask Tasha to work a longer day, and I hardly see Sam and Daisy as it is.'

'Well, we'll only get something significantly bigger if we move even further out. Into Surrey, for instance, near your parents.' Kate looked at him and shook her head firmly. They visited her mother and father, Major and Mrs Carter, once a month for Sunday lunch, and it was always a stiff, claustrophobic affair.

'OK, somewhere else, then. Look, we've had this discussion before and it seems to go round and round.'

'I suppose I could change jobs. Or give up work altogether. But I can't imagine not working. And we've always needed the money, though most of my salary goes on Tasha.'

'You could get something part-time, maybe,' he suggested. 'Did you ask at work?'

'Yes, but Karina hasn't got back to me. I think by her face the answer's no. She wouldn't be allowed any more staff to make up. Anyway, Simon, then Tasha would have to go, and that would be a shame. The children love her.'

As they sat thinking, Kate picked up a pencil and started doodling on a piece of scrap paper. She drew a box house, like children draw, with curtains at the windows, smoke coming from the chimneys, jolly flowers in the garden. She added a little stick woman with a smiley face and two little stick children dancing on the grass with a tiny stick dog

She was suddenly aware of Simon studying her. He cleared his throat.

'You know,' he said, 'I've been thinking a lot about that idea I mentioned a couple of weeks ago. I know it's crazy, but wouldn't it be great to move right out – to the country . . .'

Kate said nothing. She drew the figure of a daddy with a briefcase marching up to the garden gate, a big smile on his face.

'Yes, like that.' Simon laughed. ''Cept you've got the hair wrong. Look, you dope, you can't draw faces, can you? Here, gimme.' Giggling, they both snatched at the pencil, which rolled onto the floor and away under the dresser.

They both gazed at Kate's picture. Kate spoke first.

'Suffolk, I suppose you mean.'

'Well, yes, in that Mother's there and we both know the area.' Simon's parents had moved nearer the Suffolk coast from Bury St Edmunds after Dennis Hutchinson's retirement. 'It's a beautiful part of the world and it would be great for the kids to have a country childhood.'

'It's so far away from London and everyone we know, though. What about our work?'

'Well, I could keep going at Pennifold's. It's an hour and a half from Diss to the City on the train. Not much more than now really. If it got bad, well, I could look around locally, I suppose, though the money wouldn't be great.'

'What would I do there?'

'You'd find something – freelance publicity, or you could train as a teacher. You're good at lots of things. And our friends could all come and stay. We'd be able to get this great big house.'

'Like this one, you mean?' Kate yawned as she waved the picture.

'Yes, but with straighter walls. Now, I'll make us some tea and then we'd better get to bed.'

While Simon stacked the plates in the sink and made the tea Kate sat deep in thought. It had been such a horrible day, even with the relief that her two children were asleep happy and nearly healthy upstairs. But she dreaded work tomorrow. It was the tiredness, she supposed, and the pressure everyone was under all the time. Never seeing the kids, that had to be the worst thing.

'You'd have more energy and time for the family. Think about it,' Simon broke in as he put the milk back in the fridge. 'I get worried about you sometimes, darling. You don't want another patch of the blues.' He put two mugs of tea on the table and ruffled her hair. Then, tidy as ever, he bent to fish out the pencil from under the dresser.

'I'm not saying no to the whole idea of moving out,' said Kate carefully. 'It's just there is so much to weigh up.'

'We need to draw up a chart of pros and cons,' Simon said crisply, reaching for the estate agent's envelope.

'Not tonight we don't,' Kate said in a weary voice, taking the pencil and envelope out of his hand. 'You're not in the office now, and anyway, you're getting way ahead of me.'

'Well, at least we can look at some house prices when we're down at Mother's at the weekend,' Simon said. 'Do some sums.'

'If the children are well enough to go,' Kate said. 'Hope so.'

Then she scribbled something under her picture, laughed at her efforts, and went to pin it up on the noticeboard. She had written *The Dream House*.

# *Chapter 2*

By Friday both the children were their usual perky selves and the Hutchinsons left Fulham for Suffolk at nine o'clock on the Saturday morning. A steady drizzle of rain followed them all the way, but by midday, when they turned off the Lowestoft road, away from the coast towards Halesworth, a pale torchbeam of sun had begun to penetrate the misty cloud.

Kate slowed right down at the speed signs by the new development of detached redbrick homes. Soon the road widened out into the centre of the village. There, two dozen cottages, some thatched, were built around a small green. In the summer, they overflowed with flowers, but now the houses looked shut up, the gardens glum and dripping with rain. Out on the far side, the fourteenth-century church within its walled graveyard rose out of the mist, then they passed the Victorian redbrick primary school, a post-office-cum-stores and two pubs. Each pub vied with the other over offers of real beer, one advertising live music on Fridays, the other home-cooked food every day except Mondays. Kate remembered her mother-in-law, Joyce, telling her the pubs were owned by two brothers. Quite an opportunity to

15

play out old sibling rivalries, she smiled to herself, feeling the cares of the week begin to fade.

'Muuuum, are we there yet?' Daisy asked, as she had asked every mile for the last twenty.

'Yes,' said Kate joyfully, as they turned left down an unmarked lane, her spirits rising. 'We're there.' She parked at the dead end, by the only building in the lane, a large thatched flint cottage with a white picket fence, a coil of smoke rising from the chimney. It was picture-postcard perfect and Kate loved it.

As she jumped out to open their doors, Kate was nearly knocked over by a barking hairy bundle of black and white, Joyce's springer spaniel, Bobby, ecstatic to see his favourite pet humans.

Over bouncing dog and dancing children she saw Joyce walking stiffly up the garden path towards them; Simon's mother was a tallish woman in her late sixties wearing an elegant white polo-neck and a navy skirt, a silver Charles Rennie MacIntosh pendant over the jumper and matching dangling earrings showing beneath her neat short silvered hair.

Joyce put her arm round Simon, who had gone to open the car boot, and kissed him.

He looks like a little boy, putting up with being kissed, thought Kate, not for the first time. As she hugged Joyce, she felt a pang that she could never hug her own mother like this, for Barbara Carter shied away from demonstrations of affection. Even when she had held Daisy and Sam as babies, it had been as though she was worried about dropping them.

'A good journey? All well?' asked Joyce anxiously. Kate nodded, and Joyce turned to open her arms to Daisy and Sam, who were shoving at each other and Bobby to get to Granny first. 'Darlings, I've got you both,' she cried, encircling one with each arm and hugging them to her.

'Granny! We've brang you some chocolates. Can I have one now?' gabbled Sam.

'How lovely. Come on in. Lunch is on the table and after that you can have a chocolate, darling. No, Simon, leave unpacking till later, won't you, dear? I'm sure you're tired and the soup is ready.'

'It won't take a moment, Mother, don't fuss.'

'But it's raining again and you're not wearing a coat.' Indeed, it was starting to pour as Kate hurried the children inside while Simon set about bringing in the bags, a familiar stubborn set to his face. It was strange how Joyce and Simon slipped back into what must be the old childhood pattern – Joyce mollycoddling Simon and Simon sullenly going his own way.

'I'll get you an umbrella, then,' she heard Joyce say from the path. 'Do mind that puddle.'

Kate let them get on with it and, while the children rushed upstairs to inspect every corner, she wandered across the hall into the large living room.

Paradise Cottage was just the place for a cosy winter weekend away. The living room was crowded with big comfortable chintz armchairs around a roaring log fire. The air smelled of applewood smoke and lavender polish, and Kate sat for a moment looking at the old beams, the china dogs on the mantelpiece and the prints and photographs on the walls. She could hear the children's footsteps overhead and the slow tocking of the grandmother clock against the wall. Home, she thought, and Bobby, throwing himself onto the hearthrug in a mock show of exhaustion, clearly thought so, too.

Already, their dark house in Fulham, too near the main road, the long squealing grind of lorries braking, the grim lines of smoke-coughing cars, the dirty rain that tasted of iron and soot, her grey office with the flickering fluorescent light, all seemed to be rushing away into oblivion . . . A log shifted, sighing in the fireplace, sending up a spray of sparks.

'I could live somewhere like this and be myself,' Kate whispered to Bobby, who wagged his tail, but as soon as she'd made this statement the doubts started to rush in. How could you possibly know what it felt like, actually to *live* where you went on holiday? What would she truly miss most about city life? Her work had to come top of the list. It was what she did – it helped define her. Just how much would she miss it, if she didn't have it any more? The thoughts whirled round and round in her head.

Simon is right: we need a list of pros and cons, Kate thought as Joyce put her head round the door to call her in for lunch.

'We've never done Norwich, have we?' said Simon, cheerful over post-lunch coffee. 'It's a bit wet for the beach or walks today, kids. Look, it's only half-past one. Why don't we zip up in the car for a couple of hours? What do you think, Mother?'

'There's a castle,' Joyce said to the reluctant children as she passed round the chocolates. 'And a big market.'

'I'll come if you buy me a treat,' said Sam, then seeing Granny put on her 'cross face' and withdraw the chocolate box from his outstretched hand, he said, 'OK, I'll come.'

Parking was a nightmare in Norwich on a Saturday so close to Christmas, but they eventually found somewhere near the cathedral, which they decided to visit. Joyce led them round the simple Gothic edifice of mellow Normandy stone. Whilst Daisy and Sam ran round the huge cloisters, ignoring Kate's attempts to interest them in the coloured bosses on the vaulted ceiling, Simon went off to inspect the treasury. When Joyce took the children to the shop, Kate strolled around by herself, reading the inscriptions on the tombs of long-dead bishops, trailing her hands over the carved choir stalls, hearing the heartbreaking swell of organ practice stopping and starting above. She found a little chapel tucked away by the great south entrance. The modern glass door bore a whorl of lettering – some words of T. S. Eliot: *Reach out to the silence/At the still point of the turning world.*

That's just where I'm at today, she thought. The still point. Where you can think. And maybe learn the answers to things that you're searching for. Or not yet, in her case.

Following the others into the cathedral shop she found a bookmark with the famous words of the medieval mystic Mother Julian of Norwich: *All will be well and all manner of thing will be well.* Kate bought it on the off-chance the saint was right.

After half an hour, Simon was anxious to move on. 'You'll love the castle,' Joyce told the children. 'There are mummies and a dragon costume.'

'Would it be all right if I met you all in a little while?' asked Kate, feeling guilty about wriggling out of the childcare. On the other hand, it would be nice for Joyce to have the children. They always went to their mother if Kate was there. 'I feel like exploring round here.'

They arranged to meet by the market and Kate watched them go off together, Sam holding Joyce's hand and Daisy her father's.

Kate ambled through the cathedral close and across a main road into a maze of narrow streets as the old cracked bells of the cathedral dropped their dissonant litany into the cool late-afternoon air. For nearly an hour she wandered, utterly enchanted by the misshapen houses, the stone churches, the myriad antique shops and quaintly named pubs. She crossed and recrossed the river, looking at the boats and the old wharves rearing up on either side. In the event, she almost missed the little shop on the corner of two streets. What caught her eye was a striking, Egyptian-patterned plate in orange and black. Next to it in the window, a naked nymph held a lamp aloft.

Kate peered through the hatched glass to see what else was there, remembering pictures from the book about the Bright Young Things she had been working on. She saw Clarice Cliff-style tea services and, ranged along the back wall, Art Deco wardrobes and dressing-tables. The whole shop specialized in art from the 1920s and 1930s.

What drew her through the door was a small glass display case of jewellery. It contained a beautiful link bracelet, each black enamelled square bearing a delicate Russian pattern in red and gold, large plastic red earrings with geometric designs and chunky rings. And crammed into one corner like an after-thought was a large silver pendant, its chain balled up. The oval bore a moulded relief of a young girl with flowing hair. A dove had alighted on her raised palm. Studying it, Kate was struck by a teasing feeling that it was familiar. But she just couldn't put her finger on why.

When she pushed open the door a little bell rang, but for a moment nobody came. Then a door banged at the back of the shop and a tall young man eating an apple slipped in behind the counter. He smiled shyly. Kate moved over to the jewellery.

'May I?' she asked, and when the young man nodded, she reached into the back of the display case and picked up the pen-dant. It was a locket, the size of a fifty-pence piece, she saw, turning it over. No, half a locket. The remaining half displayed a washed-out photograph of a woman's face. Such a shame the piece was broken – the hinge looked as though it had been ripped apart. Kate studied the front again and ran her thumb over the design. The girl was a little rough-hewn but something about her – her serenity, her affinity with the bird she had tamed – touched Kate. The thin chain was still perfect and the clasp good.

Kate looked at the price tag – £25. It was broken, but very pretty. Suddenly she wanted it. It would be a present to herself. She always wore silver, it suited her Celtic colouring. Even her wedding ring was platinum rather than gold.

'Do you know anything about this piece – its history, I mean?' Kate asked the young man, who dropped the apple core in a bin and shook his head.

'You'd have to ask my mum. I'm just minding the shop while she's out,' he said. 'I can't do bargaining, I'm not allowed. You have to pay the price it says.'

Kate was ten minutes late already to meet the others near the market. She had to decide.

'I'll take it then,' she said, and waited while he wrapped it up, inexpertly, in tissue.

Kate couldn't resist unwrapping the package as she went on her way. She slipped the locket quickly around her neck and tucked it under her shirt, where it felt cold and heavy against her skin. Trying to remember the young man's directions, she crossed a main road and hurried on through a striking Art Nouveau shopping mall, its entrance framed by leaves and flowers in stained glass – and out to the bustling market square.

That night, in Paradise Cottage, under the sloped ceiling of Joyce's second bedroom, Kate lay spooned with Simon in the mahogany boat bed and dreamed. In her dream it was a perfect summer's day. She was walking down a path through an Italianate walled garden, a gentle breeze caressing her face. Before her was a gracious redbrick house with tall chimneys and wisteria blossoming rampantly round the walls. There must be three storeys – she could see the skylights in the attics. To the right was a conservatory. Inside, a grapevine in full leaf wound its way up one wall and across the ceiling. The French windows in the centre of the house were ajar, and as she walked up the four steps to the terrace she could see through them into the drawing room beyond, with its faded blue chairs, a polished grand piano, a great carved wooden mantel. She turned back to the garden and stood quietly, taking in the scents of the flowers, the statues, a little tinkling fountain. A distant skirling rose above the gentler notes of the garden birds – the cry of peacocks. As she waited – for what? – the light changed and the lovely sunny day folded into a deep evening gold. The sounds of the birds converged into one low, ringing note. The house was fading, everything was rushing past her . . . She felt a terrible pang of loss.

Suddenly Kate was awake, the velvet darkness pressing on her face. It took her a moment or two to remember where she was. She lay there, listening to the creaks of the wooden beams and the pattering of rain on the roof, thinking about the dream. The beautiful house had seemed so familiar and dear as to feel like home. And yet, she was quite sure she had never been anywhere like it. Perhaps she had seen it in a picture or a film. Had some deeply embedded memory come to the fore because they'd been talking about houses? Perhaps her mind had put together some lovely peaceful ideal of home. Wishful dreaming.

Kate tried to get to sleep again, but she was too wide awake now. After ten minutes of tossing and turning, she thought she'd visit the bathroom and eased herself out of bed so as not to disturb Simon. Her foot connected with a particularly boring manuscript she'd been reading the night before – something she was supposed to finish before Monday – and the pages sighed their way across the rug. A thin line under the door from the dimmed landing light guided her out.

On the way back she slipped into the children's room. They

were sleeping peacefully, their faces golden in the soft light. Sam was as still and cherubic as a warm baby statue. Kate picked up Daisy's toy dog, which had fallen on the floor, and tucked it back in the crook of the little girl's arm. Daisy's eyes opened for a moment, gazing unfocused as though seeing something in another world, then closed again. Kate stood watching them sleep. I love my children most when they're asleep, she thought suddenly. Perhaps it's because they look so innocent and vulnerable. They and Simon are my world, the most precious things in my life. How is it I can leave them every day? Kate sank down on the end of Sam's bed. I don't know if it's the dream or something else that's making me so tender, she thought, wiping her eyes. I cry so easily at nothing at the moment.

She sat there for a while, wondering at the lovely house in her dream, turning over in her mind all the strands of her life, trying to untangle them, to imagine them woven into a new pattern. Finally, shivering with cold but strangely elated, she trailed back to the bedroom. As she felt her way back to the bed, her hand met the bedside cabinet and closed on something cold and hard. It was the locket. The oval fitted comfortably into her palm and she lay down with it under the duvet in the dark, running her fingers over its bumps and edges. Images of her children, the house and the locket went round and round in her head. What should they all do?

'Simon?' she whispered finally, hearing him sigh and wondering if he, like her, was lying awake.

'Mmm?'

'You know we've been talking about moving? I was wondering. I suppose we could get quite a big place here after London, couldn't we?'

'Mmmghhh,' he muttered and began to snore lightly.

Tomorrow, Kate decided, they'd go and look at some estate

agents' windows in Halesworth. After all, just looking couldn't hurt.

When she came to pack up to go home late the next afternoon, Kate thrust the manuscript, unfinished, into Joyce's recycling box, finding satisfaction in this pitiful gesture of rebellion. The locket she slipped into a small zip-up compartment of her holdall for safety. Then, as the waters of everyday life closed over her again, she forgot where she had put it.

# *Chapter 3*

*London, April 2003*

The first Sunday in April, five months later, the Hutchinson family were part of a crowd of spectators lining the banks of the Thames near Hammersmith Bridge. It was late afternoon, the day of the annual Oxford and Cambridge boat race, and the Longmans, friends of theirs whose house backed onto the towpath, had been hosting one of their famous parties.

'Blimey, Kate! Sam'll be in the river in a minute! Here, take Charlie.' Laurence Longman thrust his own son at Kate, who spun on her heel in confusion to see four-year-old Sam, in full Spiderman regalia, wobbling his way along a willow branch out over the murky current. She dashed towards him, heart in mouth, but Laurence got there first. Stretching his lanky body across the length of the tree trunk, he dragged Sam back to safety.

Kate crushed Sam to her, simultaneously gulping with the horror of what might have happened and dizzy with relief that it hadn't.

'I wanted to see! I can't see the boats.' Sam wriggled against his confinement.

'Come on, I'll lift you up – hold on tight!' Kate gasped, hefting him onto her narrow shoulders with Laurence's help. 'Oof, I'll have to stop feeding you.'

'They're coming,' someone shouted, and Kate edged forward to look. There in the distance, through sparkling rainbows of spray, she could make out the shapes of the two boats, almost prow by prow, oars lifting and falling in regular rhythm. A gust of wind blew her hair in her eyes and made them water. Sam bounced up and down on her aching shoulders, pointing and squealing.

'Cambridge are moving into the lead,' remarked a middle-aged man with a radio to no one in particular. Kate watched them toil closer, the nearer boat definitely gaining the advantage.

Sam was wriggling, so Kate helped him down and gripped the back of his costume as he strained towards the river.

The bridge and the towpath were crowded with people of all descriptions, young City types in thick overcoats swilling champagne straight from the bottle, students making do with Fanta, families wrapped up against the fresh spring breeze. Kate caught Simon's eye where he waited further down the bank. Daisy on his shoulders waved a dark blue flag – Kate couldn't remember why they supported Oxford, but they always did. Had Laurence's brother Ted been there? She smiled at Simon and he smiled back – a look of such complicity a rush of warmth spread through her. They had a secret and today they were going public.

Every year, for the last five, they had come to Laurence and Liz's Boat Race Special at their Edwardian house in Barnes, a good vantage point for the famous Surrey bend of the river. Race Day coincided more or less with Laurence's birthday, and Liz, who loved big parties, invited a crazy mix of friends and acquaintances. Today there had been a slap-up buffet and sticky chocolate cake washed down with plenty of fizz before they had all filed through the little garden gate onto the wide muddy path to watch the race. Kate was struck by a sudden sad thought – this might be the last Boat Race party for her and Simon.

'Cambridge will do it!' said Radioman smugly as the boats toiled past, the wind carrying to them the angry barks of the coxes and the grunts of the rowers above the slap and splash of the oars. On, under the bridge. This bend was crucial to the result. 'Rubbish, they are, Oxford.'

'Can we go, can we go?' Sam had lost interest now. Kate waved to Simon and followed her son back through the gate into the chattering throng of guests, where she shortly learned that Oxford had, in fact, won.

Half an hour later, Sam and Daisy safely ensconced in the play-room with Charlie and the Longmans' twin daughters, Lily and Lottie, Kate went out into the garden to look for Liz.

The numbers were thinning out now. Simon was talking to a woman in her late thirties Kate had been introduced to earlier, Meredith something or other, a tall, well-groomed blonde in a charcoal sheath dress – some American colleague Ted had in tow from his bank. Kate noticed with a mild flash of envy that she carried one of those embroidered Miu Miu bags recently featured in *Desira*, the fashion and lifestyle magazine which Liz edited and where Laurence was creative director.

Seeing neither of her hosts, Kate went to the gate to check it was locked; after her scare with Sam earlier she wasn't taking any chances. The key was safely turned so she wandered slowly back towards the house, unrolling the sleeves of her jacket against the sudden cold breeze.

Deep in some anecdote, Simon didn't notice her, and Kate played the old game of pretending she was seeing him as a stranger might, as she'd seen him that night ten years ago when they had first met.

He really did look like Jude Law, she thought, not for the first time, admiring the animal grace of his gestures as he talked, an unlit French cigarette (who had he cadged that from, then?) caught between two fingers. OK, so his nose had a bump in it and his black cashmere sweater and elderly leather jacket were dotted with mud from Daisy's shoes – there was nothing like the rosy filter of love. Though he hadn't narrowed his blue eyes at his wife in quite such a seductive way for a long time. Meredith seemed utterly absorbed in what he was saying. Simon liked the company of women – he got on well with them. Indeed, it was one of the things that had first appealed to Kate about him, his ease and friendliness. She had always been quite shy with men, had never 'set her cap' at anyone in the way, so the story went, that Liz had with Laurence.

That evening at her old schoolfriend Sarah's engagement party, Kate had been standing on her own, wondering why she was the only one of their class whom Sarah seemed to have invited, when a passing stranger had jogged her arm, spilling champagne over her dress. The culprit had moved on, unnoticing. Instead it was Simon who, disengaging himself from a noisy group nearby, offered her a handkerchief, holding her glass whilst she mopped the damp patches, then fetched her a refill, all the while chatting in his shy manner, which turned out not to be true shyness at all, about schooldays and playing football with Sarah's fiancé. As he talked, those half-narrowed blue eyes focused on Kate's, moving to her mouth, and back again to her eyes. Then his fingers had accidentally brushed against hers as he'd lit her cigarette – they had all smoked occasionally then, before marriage and children – and a shock of desire had rushed through her.

During the weeks that followed she realized that while he drew her out of herself and reassured her, in turn, she was a haven for him. Kate accepted him for himself, made no demands that he be anyone except himself. She remembered one conversation driving back from Suffolk after meeting his parents for the first time. She'd tentatively commented that he had not seemed entirely relaxed with them.

'It's Dad.' Simon shrugged. 'He's always after me about something.'

'He did seem anxious that you're happy.'

'Yes, but he wants me to be happy in *his* kind of way. He's never got over me not doing medicine like him. My grades were never good enough. So then he was on about me having a profession – you know, law, accountancy or something, and I just went along with him, I suppose. Scraped into doing maths at university, had fun, got a reasonable degree. Then the City seemed the obvious thing. Dad was pleased, so that was good.' Simon sighed. 'But now he won't let up till I get a partnership.'

'I thought you liked your job, Simon.'

'I like being part of a team, all that stuff, but I hate the pressure. And auditing is hardly exciting. I can't stand the thought that I'll be going through figures for the rest of my working life.'

'But you don't have to, do you?'

'I don't really have anything else I want to do, Kate. I'm not bad at it. I rub along all right with the people. And it keeps the old man off my back. Maybe I'll make a million and retire at forty. Then see what else turns up.' He smiled at her briefly with that lopsided smile that made her heart flip and squeezed her hand.

As she looked at him now, Kate experienced the same tenderness she had felt in those faraway early days. Recently, there had been less of the passion, but was that surprising after eight years of marriage and the exhaustion of running fulltime jobs and two children? Well, now they had made their decision, perhaps they were embarking on a life where they would have more time for one another again . . .

'You're *kidding*!' Ms Miu Miu's husky laugh broke through Kate's reverie. Simon half-turned, smiling at his own joke, the smile faltering when he saw Kate. He slipped the illicit cigarette into his pocket – does he think I'm going to tell him off, like his mother? thought Kate – and held out his hand, drawing her over.

'You've met Kate, haven't you, Meredith?'

'Yeah, hiiii,' the woman drawled, looking Kate up and down. Suddenly the chinos and jacket she thought she'd looked perfectly nice in that morning felt depressingly high street next to Meredith's designer outfit. Kate fought desperately for something to say. She tried, 'How long is it you've known Ted?' but this only caused a frown of impatience to pass over Meredith's perfect features.

Just at that moment Liz appeared in the kitchen doorway, her shock of red curls escaping from their slide, her bracelets jangling, a tray of coffee in her hands. 'Will one of you guys take this?' she yelled. Ted, as lanky as his brother Laurence but more smartly dressed, broke away from a group of earnest fellow bankers, hurried over and relieved her of her burden. As he brought the tray round to offer Meredith coffee, he was nearly knocked flying by Sam.

'Mummy, Daddy, Charlie did throw my mask and Daisy pushed me.' Sam's chubby face was streaked with tears. Simon knelt down and cuddled him. 'Come up, Daddy. Tell them be good,' Sam ordered, so Simon lifted him up, smiled apologetically at Meredith and Kate and went, Spiderman's grubby arms tight round his neck. Meredith smiled politely at Kate, nodded and moved away to join the bankers.

I've been dismissed, Kate thought, feeling put out. She turned away, only to meet Liz emerging again from the back door with another tray – just two mugs on it this time.

'Now, darling, that's everyone fed and watered and frankly I'm done in. Let's take this and find a seat, shall we? I'm sorry, I haven't talked to you all day – well, you know how it is with parties.'

They sat down at a little garden table. Liz reached over a bejewelled hand and rubbed Kate's arm. 'What are you up to then, pussycat? You've been looking sort of faraway today. What mouse are you after?'

They laughed at the old joke. Liz and Kate had known one another at York University, but Kate had always imagined she wasn't extrovert enough for Liz, never appreciating that her tendency to daydream gave her a mysterious allure. It wasn't until they met up again at the same antenatal classes in Hammersmith that their friendship had grown, over strenuous breathing exercises and bouts of helpless laughter at their ridiculous whale-like state.

'If I'm a cat then you're – I don't know – a lioness or a bird of paradise,' laughed Kate now, for Liz was exotic, larger than life with a voice that was made for hailing taxis. Some people were terrified of her. She often spoke out loud the thoughts they only dared think. But Kate had learned that this alarming characteristic was tempered by large doses of tactful good humour.

As they drank their coffee Liz had constantly to disappear to say goodbye to people or sort out problems, and it was a while before they got back together again.

As the last of the other guests filtered out, Simon joined the

31

two of them and they sat round the table, jackets pulled tight against the early evening air. It was starting to get dark but the children didn't mind. They shrieked and sang as they played on the little climbing frame, Kate getting up and down every now and then to rescue Sam or Charlie. Laurence emerged from the kitchen with a pot of tea and pulled up another chair. 'Bit chilly out here now. Shall we get the kids in, in a moment?'

Kate took a deep breath before there could be another interruption. 'Wait. We've got something to tell you,' she said, studying Liz and Laurence. She reached for Simon's hand next to her. He clasped it hard.

'You're not in pig again, are you?' gasped Liz. 'I warn you, having three is no joke. You just can't get round 'em all. Look at my grey hair.' She shook her perfectly red mane at an unsympathetic audience.

'Liz, "in pig" is a revolting phrase.' Kate laughed, though Sam and Daisy were a bit like roly-poly piglets sometimes. 'And no, I'm not having another baby. It's just, you know we were thinking about moving house? Well, we've decided—'

'We're moving out of London,' Simon broke in. 'We had the estate agents round yesterday. The house goes on the market at the end of the week.'

There was silence, then a wail from Liz. 'What do you mean, out of London? Where out of London?'

Kate looked at Simon for encouragement. 'Suffolk,' she said, wincing at another wail from Liz.

'Phew!' Laurence stretched out his long body in the chair and clasped his hands behind his head. 'That's sudden. We thought you'd just come south of the river. Where in Suffolk?'

Kate managed to get out, 'Fernley. Halesworth. Where Simon's mum lives.'

'But that's *miles* away,' shrieked Liz. 'Practically in the North Sea. You can't do that!'

'Didn't we meet up with you there once?' said Laurence. 'Southwold, with the lighthouse in the town?'

'That's right,' said Simon. 'You borrowed that cottage, I remember. Yes, It's near Southwold but not so touristy where Mother is – and the tourists only come in the summer anyway. The rest of the year it's very wild. Halesworth's a nice little place, and Norwich and Ipswich aren't far.'

'Kate, that's awful. I mean *why*, for goodness sake?'

Kate had braced herself for this reaction, but still the force of her friend's distress cut through her. Liz was one of people she'd miss most.

'We're just tired of it all, Liz,' she said quietly. 'Of working all the time. Not seeing the children. Not seeing each other. Hearing the planes and the Fulham Palace Road practically going past our bedroom window all night.'

'And it would be great to have a proper garden for the kids,' Simon added.

'But all your friends are here,' Liz objected. 'And what about the theatres, the exhibitions – everything, really? The country's for holidays. Come on, you're city people, like us.'

'We're not, actually, Liz. Simon was brought up in the country and I've lived all over the place. But the point is, we're stretched to breaking point here. So we've decided, we don't want to be part of the ratrace any more. We want to spend more time as a family. Surely you can see that.'

'But why so far away? It's so drastic.'

'Liz, it's Suffolk, not Mars,' Simon joked.

'What'll you do about your work, Simon? You can still commute, can't you?' Laurence, as ever, was more phlegmatic.

'I'll take the train up from Diss,' Simon said. 'It's very quick now – an hour and a half – and I can walk to the office from Liverpool Street. I've talked to Nigel, remember him?' Nigel was a burly corporate financier who had come to supper once when Liz and Laurence were there, and he'd talked about share issues and the German Eurobond market all evening. Kate had practically slid under the table with boredom. 'His wife Janice has left him, poor sod,' (fed up with the German Eurobonds, Kate imagined) 'so he's rattling about in that big Docklands flat on his own. Says I can crash with him a night or two a week if the journey gets a bit much. And I can work on the train, of course. Take my laptop.'

'But you're going to look for something local, aren't you?' Kate prompted him. This was one of the areas she had worried about most in their plans. Simon seemed reluctant to commit himself to changing his working life in any way. She couldn't blame him. Downsizing to finance-manager level in Suffolk would mean a big pay cut, to say nothing of the loss of his place on the ladder.

'Once we're settled, I can look around,' was all he said now, drumming his fingers on the arm of his chair. 'Kate's got plans, haven't you?'

'Yes, when the children are used to it and we've got somewhere proper to live.'

'Where *are* you going to live?' asked Liz.

'We don't know yet,' Kate admitted and Liz's eyes widened. 'We'll look when we get there, but we're going to stay with Simon's mother for a bit.' When they had broached their moving plans with Joyce she had insisted upon this. And she had adamantly refused the offer of rent, agreeing only to a regular contribution to the housekeeping.

'Rather you than me,' muttered Liz, darting little glances at Laurence, who pretended not to hear. Laurence's mother was also a strong personality. Kate couldn't imagine those two spending one night in the same house without fighting like a couple of tigresses. She was glad it wasn't like that with her and Joyce.

'We'll be fine,' she said now. 'Joyce is happy to have us. There are only three bedrooms, but it'll do us until we find somewhere of our own.'

'We'll miss you.'

'We need a change, Liz, we really do.' Kate fiddled with her half-empty cup and it tottered, spilling over the table. They watched it spread and drip through the slats. Laurence dropped a tea-towel on it. 'Sorry. Typical. I'm getting so stressed with everything. It's all right for you, you seem to feed off it, Liz – the pressure, I mean. But I'm different from you. I need a more peaceful life, time to think, watch the grass grow. I don't know why I came to London in the first place really – just that everybody did, you know, and I followed the herd. Because I studied English then everyone said, "Yes, BBC, publishing, teaching, for you." And the publicity secretary job was the one I happened to get. I just got on the treadmill and I've never got off. It's been fun – I've loved it, don't get me wrong. But I've got other skills, I know I have, and this will be a chance to find out what they are.'

Kate gazed round at her audience. Liz was nodding her head, slowly. 'Maybe I can train to be a teacher,' she went on, 'or I might turn out to be good at gardening or running a business. And I'll make it fit in with the kids, this time.' Explaining it all to them suddenly made it all seem real. Anything was possible. 'And I can always do some freelance work for Jansen and Hicks to start off with, just to keep my hand in. Don't want my little brain to rot, do I?'

Liz smiled. 'Maybe you can write something for the magazine,' she suggested. 'How about a column – *Life Amongst the*

*Turnips*, with a shot of you in dungarees like Felicity Kendal in *The Good Life*?'

'Oh shut up, you!'

'I always wondered how they paid for everything, Tom and Barbara.' Laurence said. 'Didn't have children to think of, I suppose. What are you doing about schools, by the way?'

'We went round a couple when we stayed with my mother at half-term,' Simon answered. 'The village school at Fernley and the bigger one one at Halesworth can both shoehorn Daisy in for September, but Sam wouldn't be able to start until Easter at Halesworth. Fernley primary school's a bit small, but we loved it.'

'It's very sweet,' Kate agreed. 'Just eighty children, and it's near Joyce and the teachers seem so committed. After that, the kids go to Halesworth for secondary school.'

'The buildings are a bit crumbly, that's the only thing I worry about,' said Simon.

'But Halesworth is further away and the other children there won't be so local, Simon . . .'

Kate caught Liz's eye. Her friend looked as though she was about to say something, but stopped. 'Yes, well,' Kate went on, a little defensively, 'we haven't quite sorted out some of the details yet, but we're getting there. I feel so much better about everything now we've decided to go. It'll be a fresh start for us all. And it'll help Joyce, too. She's still so lonely without Simon's dad.'

'Funny reason to move, to make your mother-in-law happy.'

'Oh, don't twist things, Liz. Come on. It'll be a new direction. And I can be with the children all the time. They'll be brought up in the country. It'll be fantastic. And we can get a lovely house, an old house with a big garden – think about it! And we could have animals. Joyce has got a dog – we could get one, too.'

Daisy had wandered over and was leaning against her

father's knee. 'And ponies. Dad, you said we could go riding or get a pony,' she said excitedly.

'Two ponies,' Simon said wickedly, tweaking her hair. 'And a Shetland for Granny.' Daisy giggled at the thought of the dignified Joyce on a little fat Thelwell pony.

'And you can all come and stay with us, can't you?' Kate squeezed Liz's arm. 'In our dream house.'

But Liz wasn't yet to be bought. 'Have you told your parents yet?'

Kate's face went blank. 'No,' she said shortly. 'They're away in Spain. We're seeing them next weekend. I'm simply dreading it.'

# *Chapter 4*

'I don't know which I fear more,' Kate confessed to Simon, as they sat in a traffic jam the following Sunday, on their way to lunch with Kate's parents in Surrey. 'Them being really really upset that we're moving so far away, depriving them of their grandchildren, or them being too wrapped up in themselves to care at all.'

'Whatever, I just want to get this over with,' grumbled Simon, who felt perpetually on edge in the company of his in-laws. 'Sam, give Daisy back her toy, for goodness sake, and stop squabbling, you two,' he shouted into the child-view mirror. Kate reached round to help restore property and peace. 'Damn these roadworks.' Simon smacked the steering wheel and, as if at a signal, the vehicles in front began slowly to move again.

'At least when we get a place of our own it should be big enough for them to visit,' said Kate, as the car gathered speed and made it through the workmen's green light, just in time. 'Maybe they'll be more relaxed then. They could come for Christmas. Just think, real old-fashioned country Christmases in our country home!'

'Yes, it'll be their turn to sit in the motorway traffic,' muttered

Simon, but Kate pretended not to hear. Her mind was drifting back.

'There's no place like home.' Even nowadays, when she watched *The Wizard of Oz* with Sam and Daisy, snuggled up on the sofa, Kate always mouthed the words with Judy Garland, tears in her eyes, just as there had been when she first saw the film as a lonely twelve year old at boarding school.

I've never really had a proper home, she thought to herself now. In truth, her family had always moved around. Her father had been in the army, stationed first in Hong Kong then, briefly, West Germany, before several stints in the Middle East sandwiched with short periods in the South of England. Sometimes they had lived in officers' family accommodation, at other times, as in West Germany, the Carters had rented a furnished house near the barracks. In the Middle East, they had to live in a compound with the rest of the ex-pat families. Kate remembered always living with other people's furniture, other people's choice of décor. Often, her mother did not bother to unpack all their toys, ornaments and books – all the personal things that made a house into a home. What was the point? It would all have to be packed up again before too long so they could move on to the next place.

At one stage, during a visit back to England, her parents had bought a house in Kent as an investment and to make sure they had somewhere to call home when Major Carter's career in the forces was over. They rarely lived in this Sevenoaks house during subsequent visits, because it was leased out to tenants most of the time.

At the age of eleven, Kate and her thirteen-year-old sister Nicola were dispatched to boarding school in Sussex, usually flying out to join their parents in the holidays, wherever they were, and spending many half-terms or the occasional free weekend with their paternal grandmother in her small terraced house in Hastings. The girls had loved those brief holidays by the seaside. Old Mrs Carter, their only surviving grandparent, had been ailing even then, but she was warm and caring, especially towards Kate, and she wrote regularly to the girls at school and sent them little presents. She had died just before Kate met Simon and Kate still missed her.

Major Carter retired from active service in 1984, when the girls were eighteen and sixteen and he still had a good ten years' working life in him. Nicola went off to Cambridge. The girls' holidays were now spent in the Sevenoaks house, which badly needed renovation after years of tenants had made their mark, and Desmond Carter got on the train to London every weekday morning to go to a desk job in the Ministry of Defence. His particular experience in the Middle East made him a valuable consultant and he quickly became absorbed in his job, often working long hours. But then came the tragedy of Nicola's death and everybody's life was turned upside down. It wasn't long afterwards that the Carters sold the Sevenoaks house they had waited so many years to call home but which was now tainted with tragedy. It was while they were packing up to move that Kate's father drove her up to York where, still dazed with grief, she was due to read English at university. Never again did she call her parents' house 'home'.

Simon had turned off the main road now and they were following a winding back route that took them to Epsom High Street, then up a long hill lined with large detached houses to the Downs.

Barbara and Desmond Carter now lived in a Charles Church mock-Tudor development by Epsom Downs station. One of the three spare bedrooms stood cold and empty, the second, the guest room, briefly Kate's bedroom during holidays from university, was hardly used. The boxroom held Des's golf clubs, his regimental memorabilia and his car magazines, none of which Barbara liked cluttering up downstairs.

The car slowed down as they passed the golf course where Desmond played regularly. Barbara kept herself to herself, walking the couple's two miniature long-haired daschunds on the Downs, playing the occasional hand of bridge with some other forces wives locally and driving into Epsom when she fancied a wander round the shopping centre or a visit to the hairdresser. To Kate it seemed an immensely depressing life, but she recognized it was all her parents, still bound up with grief, seemed able to manage.

Simon swung the car into the Carters' housing estate. They were twenty minutes late and Kate felt the usual miasma of misery descend. They passed a dozen ideal homes with immaculate front gardens, the dads washing their cars or tending the lawns and, as the Hutchinsons' Audi rolled onto the drive beside the Carters' polished black Rover, Kate saw Barbara's pale face waiting anxiously at the window, saw her turn to call Desmond, and the front door open. The family marched up the path with red tulips standing to attention on either side.

'You were late. We were starting to worry,' said Desmond as he unlocked the drinks cabinet. In the sparsely furnished living room, where Desmond waged perpetual battle against dog hair, the grown-ups perched on the stiff-backed suite and sipped at little glasses of sherry. Major Carter watched his wife anxiously as, having drunk her sherry in two mouthfuls, she wandered over for a replenishment.

Sam and Daisy had retreated to one corner, by the upright piano that Kate and Nicola used to play, but which was never opened now, the dogs to another. The children were nervous of the snapping tendencies of Ringo and Benjy, who in turn, disliked the sudden, unpredictable movements of young children. There was nothing to play with at the Carters' house, so Kate had brought a couple of boxes of toys and games to keep the children amused.

'I'd better see to the chicken,' said Barbara, gulping down her second sherry. Her husband eased the glass out of her hand as she got up. Kate followed her into the kitchen.

'I just got one of those ready-stuffed ones from Sainsbury's,' said Barbara, a touch too brightly. 'They seem to be all right. There are some roast potatoes in the top drawer of the freezer. Oh, and some peas somewhere. I can't . . .' She stopped, looking confused.

'I'm sure it will all be fine, Mum,' Kate said, tying a plastic apron over her skirt and blouse and setting about the task of Sunday lunch. Her mother leaned against the cabinets, playing with her necklace and looking lost and faraway. Kate noticed a cut-glass tumbler over by the sink and wondered whether, if she picked it up, it would smell of gin.

I'll wait till lunch is over before I say anything about our plans, she decided. Instead, in between shoving a tray of frozen potatoes in the oven, whisking up a packet of bread sauce and unwrapping the supermarket apple crumble waiting on the side, she asked her mother whether she was sleeping any better, about Desmond's back trouble and how his sister Maggie seemed when she came last week.

Barbara, small, thin, but still elegant, her chin-length hair expertly tinted and coiffed in the 1960s ends-turned-out style that she'd always worn, politely answered each question in a toneless voice, only showing some animation when telling Kate about the problem of Travellers camping on the Downs. It was a relief when they could all move into the dining room and watch Desmond carefully carve the chicken.

'How's the house then?' Desmond asked Simon as he lowered himself into his chair, unfurled his cloth napkin, and gave the signal to eat. 'All shipshape?' Desmond always asked his son-in-law this question but today, instead of the usual, 'Fine, actually, Desmond. We had the gutters cleaned last week but the porch needs retiling,' Simon looked over at Kate, who was cutting up Sam's meat, and nodded, raising his eyebrows.

Kate put down her knife and fork and took a deep breath. 'We're planning to move, actually, Dad.' She looked anxiously at her mother, who had been picking at a potato with her fork and glancing at Daisy, as if trying to think of something to ask the little girl. Barbara looked up at Kate, her face suddenly full of alarm.

Kate went on to explain that they were moving to Suffolk. Her father looked puzzled for a moment, then nodded. 'Nice part of the world, if I remember. But what d'you want to go there for?'

Kate stabbed at a piece of chicken and summoned the courage to continue. 'Simon's mother lives there. She's got a cottage large enough for us to stay in while we look for somewhere of our own. Simon will still work in the City but look for something nearby. It would be a new start for us, and it would help Joyce now she's on her own. You remember we thought she might have had a small stroke last year? She's recovered completely, but Simon would like to be nearby in case anything happens.'

In fact, Simon had never said anything about being anxious for Joyce's health, but Kate instinctively felt that her parents would be reassured by being given a practical reason rather than any heavy emotional language about needing somewhere to call home or having more precious time with the children. Kate's parents didn't do emotion. They didn't really do children either, and Kate had always been determined to bring up her children completely differently from the way she and Nicola had been raised.

'I don't know why you protect them so much,' said Simon once when her mother had forgotten Daisy's birthday for the second year running, despite Kate having reminded her twice. 'They were terrible parents. They should never have had children. And now they're hopeless grandparents.'

'But they're so vulnerable, Simon. They've been hurt by everything – losing Nicola, Mum's problems. It would be like kicking them in the teeth to criticize them.'

'Yeah, I know, but I hate seeing you tie yourself up in nervous knots trying to defend them. Oh, I'm sorry, I shouldn't complain. After all, Dad could be pretty annoying sometimes with his lecturing.'

The time her parents' remoteness had come home to Kate hardest of all had been when Daisy was born. Joyce had immediately got the next train from Diss, her bags full of newly knitted cardigans, bootees and little hats, and had bedded down in the Hutchinsons' house for a fortnight, directing operations with Simon fetching and carrying while Kate struggled to tend to the needs of a tiny baby who wouldn't suck. Desmond and Barbara visited twice during this period, staying precisely one hour each time. The second time, towards the end of the visit, Barbara had inexplicably burst into tears. Desmond, his own eyes rheumy, whispered stiffly to Kate that 'the old girl' found the baby brought back difficult memories and gently steered Barbara out of the front door. That time, Kate had cried herself into such a state that Simon, alarmed, called the doctor.

After the metallic-tasting apple crumble, the adults cleared the table and Desmond banged about in the kitchen, inexpertly loading the dishwasher and making a pot of tea. Her mother had vanished somewhere and Kate went into the living room where Simon was on the floor preventing violence breaking out over Snakes and Ladders. She sat down next to the mahogany bookcase, with its ranks of photographs. There was a single picture of Daisy and Sam taken by her friend Claire the summer before, and a small wedding portrait of Kate and Simon. But the other dozen photographs, not to mention the three framed enlargements on the wall above the piano, were all of the same girl, a pretty, laughing, blue-eyed brunette – a little like Kate but not Kate. There she was, full of life, her sister Nicola – as a jolly sun-hatted baby sitting in her pram, playing in a sandpit at three, in school uniform with a thick navy Alice band at twelve, in a white confirmation dress at fourteen, gorgeous in midnight-blue taffeta at nineteen . . . when the photographs stopped.

As familiar as the pain from an old war wound came that double stab of jealousy and guilt. Jealousy that her parents' attention was still, after all these years, focused on Nicola. Guilt that it was Nicola who had died, not Kate. Nicola, whom Kate still firmly believed, everyone had loved best.

When she and her sister were very young, they had had a series of nannies, mostly local women with little English, in whichever country the Carters were living in at the time. The girls only saw their parents for a small part of every day. Barbara, nervous when handling small children, usually found some secretarial or voluntary work deliberately, to take her out of the house, and then there was a range of mess events and bridge parties in the evenings.

Nicola didn't seem affected by this mild form of neglect that constituted the traditional English officer-class way of bringing up children. She was naturally bubbly, charming, self-possessed, and the obvious favourite of the nannies. Kate, on the other hand, everyone dismissed as quiet and stubborn. She badly needed cuddles and reassurance, which she didn't get – except from her big sister. Nicky always guarded Kate. There was one famous incident in Hong Kong, when the amah had slapped Kate hard after accusing the five-year-old girl of stealing from her. Nicola had jumped up and slapped the woman back, then lectured her like a grown-up, threatening her with the sack. The money was later found to have been taken by a visiting child, but Missy Nicola was held in awe after this and Kate loved her for it. And hated herself for still being jealous of her sister.

One thing she found increasingly difficult to cope with was that, whatever she tried to do, Nicola unwittingly took the limelight. Their mother was no more affectionate to Nicola than to Kate, but Kate could see that at least Nicola made some impact on Barbara. Barbara would encourage her to try new things – to ride her bike, play the piano, take ballet lessons, go out with friends. She never showed the same interest in Kate, rarely praised her when she practised hard at the piano and passed her exams ahead of Nicola.

When the girls both went away to boarding school, again, it was Nicola whom everyone liked best. 'Nicky, would you like to take the lead part in the play?' 'Nicola, we need you on the lacrosse team.' 'Nicky, will you come and stay with us at half-term?' At first Kate trailed around after her sister, trying desperately hard to get into a school team, writing to her parents that it wasn't fair that Nicola should go to stay with friends and not her. But after a while, she learned to avoid pain by avoiding Nicola. She made her own friends, but their interests were less high profile – writing for the school magazine, listening to music, outings with the Natural History Club. But still envy twisted inside, though she knew Nicola was hurt by her behaviour. For Kate, though, keeping away from her sister was a survival

46

technique. She loved her sister – indeed, along with the rest of the school, how could she not? But Nicola's continued to be the name on everyone's lips. Nicola became deputy head girl, while Kate didn't even get to be prefect. Nicola won a place at Cambridge . . . Kate was advised not to apply.

But it was Nicola who drove too fast one rainy July night down a narrow country lane after an evening out, the headlights cutting a swathe through the black woods on either side. She misjudged the bend, plunging the car through the undergrowth and into the trees. She must have died instantly, the coroner said.

Hundreds of people attended the funeral. *Golden girl mourned by all*, the local paper said. Kate had never felt so lonely in her life. Her parents, felled by grief, turned in on themselves. They should have reassured Kate that they were glad they still had her, that she was precious to them, but it was as though they had lost their only child. Her mother hardly spoke for weeks after the tragedy, not least because the doctor had dosed her up with sedatives. And her father, alien to the language of emotion as his own father had been before him, could only manage to hug Kate awkwardly, then turn away so she wouldn't see him cry.

Resentful, self-pitying, it was a while before Kate realized she too was mourning her sister. The year of her A-levels was one of the worst of her life. She tried to lose herself in her work, but away at school, cut off from her parents who were, anyway, too self-absorbed to help her, she felt isolated. Many of the staff and pupils were devastated by the loss of Nicola, but the fact that in death Nicola was raised to a pedestal of beauty and perfection made it harder for Kate to grieve. Only in the visits to her grandmother in Hastings was she able to unbottle her grief to someone who really understood and cared, and to cry herself to sleep in the old lady's arms.

Since having Daisy and Sam, Kate had often wondered what her relationship with her sister would have been like if the accident hadn't happened. She concluded that she would probably have grown out of her jealousy. Nicola would have become a happy and successful woman, married, had children. Sam and Daisy would have loved playing with their cousins and their mums would have laughed and cried over their own childhood, healing each other in the process, sharing the burden of trying to get on with their now-ageing parents.

But if Nicola hadn't died, their parents would surely now be entirely different . . . Barbara might not have started to drink, Desmond might have been warmer, bluff and relaxed in retirement. They might have got on well with their adult children, have been close to their grandchildren. If Nicola hadn't died . . .

'Are the children allowed sweets, dear?'

Kate pulled her attention back to her mother, who had appeared with a suspiciously dusty box of mint imperials. Then Desmond bustled in with the tea tray and laid it on the glass coffee-table. He brushed at the sofa, plumped the cushions and sat down.

'Well, we'll miss you, there's no doubt about that,' he mumbled. 'But your mother and I, we'll . . . harrumph, I'm sure . . . When are you off?'

'July probably,' broke in Simon, coming to join them. 'Fits in with Daisy's schooling. And I'll be able to take a bit of holiday to help.'

'I had some lovely holidays in Suffolk when I was a girl,' Barbara said, with unusual vivacity. 'Frances and Marion – you know, my cousins – lived that way. There was someone else we visited, an older cousin. Ooh, Desmond, do you remember me talking about her?'

He shook his head. 'Must have been before we met, darling.'

'A beautiful house, yes – and she had a maid, a real maid with a uniform. I might have some photographs upstairs somewhere. Or did we throw them out when we came here? We got rid of so much.'

'Sounds intriguing, Mum. I suppose she might be dead now, though.'

Kate studied her mother, who was furiously stroking the little dogs in her lap and staring at the carpet. She looked up and smiled at Kate, a smile that carried a flash of charm. Kate suddenly felt an inkling of another Barbara, a Barbara long gone. She wished she had the courage to reach out to her mother and hug her, but she knew that Barbara would shy away from physical contact. That was how it had been ever since Kate could remember. Barbara had rarely been able to demonstrate that she was sad or happy, that she loved or hated. Kate had seen pictures of her mother at twenty and could never believe this was the same woman; she'd seemed so vibrant then, full of the love of life, probably quite a catch for a kind but dull man like her father, handsome in his new officer's uniform at the Sandhurst ball.

What had happened to Barbara after her marriage? Kate's father had always deflected his daughter's timid questions. Old-fashioned loyalty was the name of the game in his book and his love for his wife was tender and unswerving. Of course, Nicola's death was the unmentionable barrier between them all now, a terrible loss that had frozen their family life entirely.

Kate's eyes moved again to the silent ranks of photos, and was struck anew by how greatly Nicola resembled the pictures of Barbara when she was young. Kate was so different, with her pixie face, her jaw-length dark hair, her green eyes and shy smile. She certainly didn't look like Nicola – the pretty, lively, laughing sister. Suddenly, Kate felt a bolt of childish anger charge through her. It wasn't *fair*! No one ever took any notice of *her*! There must have been dozens of photographs of Kate by herself or of Kate and Nicola together in the family albums, but her parents had only chosen to put out ones of Nicola. Why did their only surviving child seem to matter so little to them?

But with the maturity she had only fully gained after rearing her own children, she breathed deeply until the anger ebbed away and sadness and compassion flooded in to take its place. Of course they must love her. It's just they were so wounded by the loss of their other child. As she was by the loss of the sister she too, despite her envy, had loved.

But why would they never talk about it? Therein lay the hell of this situation. She remembered discussing it with a therapist once, and he'd encouraged her to try again to talk to them or to write them a letter. But she'd never found the courage to do that.

Even now she felt her father's anxious eyes upon her. *Don't mention your sister!* Better not let the side down, had I? Kate told herself with scorn, bringing her attention back to the land of the living. Her father's expression softened and she smiled at him. He relaxed.

'So how's that car of yours, Simon? Still running smoothly?' Normal service had been resumed.

'Thank Christ that's over.' Simon slumped with relief in his seat as he pulled the car out onto the Downs roundabout.

'Simon!' Kate half-glanced round to see if the children had heard, but Daisy was recounting to Sam a long fantasy about her toy dog. 'That's my parents you're talking about.'

'I'm sorry. It's just they're such an ordeal. They're impossible! Anyone would have thought we'd just said we were getting a new washing machine for all the interest they showed, not removing their only daughter and grandchildren to the further reaches of the country.'

'Simon, I know, but that's not what they're feeling underneath. I thought Mum looked quite upset actually.'

'I expect she's heading for the gin bottle even now – look, I'm sorry, Kate. It's just I get so upset for you and the kids. They ought to cherish you more.'

'They do their best.' Kate's voice was wobbly. 'Well, OK, they probably don't,' she conceded. 'Anyway, Mum's drinking is much better than it used to be. Dad says she'll go whole days now without anything.'

'Then she has a blow-out on the Gordon's and spends two days with her head down the toilet.' Once or twice, when Barbara's drinking had got particularly bad, she had had an enforced stay in a local clinic. But since she would never even admit to herself that there was a problem, all attempts to persuade her to overcome it had failed.

'Oh, stop it!' Kate looked round again anxiously but, lulled by the motion of the warm car, both children were falling into sleep.

'Don't shout, Mummy,' yawned Daisy. 'Shouting's . . . rude.' Kate leaned forward and fiddled with the air-conditioning to turn up the temperature in the back.

'Well,' she sighed, 'you won't have to see them so often now, will you? Though I suppose we'll have to ask them to stay – when we have a proper house, I mean. It's a good thing I get on so well with your mum, isn't it?'

'Better than I do.' Simon glanced in the rearview mirror then took his hand off the wheel to squeeze Kate's thigh through her corduroy skirt. She accepted this as a silent apology.

'She's so – homey, your mum,' Kate ploughed on. She knew Simon was often annoyed by Joyce. She could smother you with her affection and concern and she sometimes had too-strong opinions about how other people should run their lives – like what time grandchildren should go to bed and how married couples should run their financial arrangements, and so on. Simon had often felt his upbringing to have been claustrophobic, but Kate envied him the interest his father had taken in him and the way his mother worried about his welfare and comfort. Indeed, for someone starved of motherly love like Kate, Joyce was birthday and Christmas rolled into one.

By the end of May, their plans were moving on swiftly. They'd accepted an offer for the house from a couple with a baby daughter. The survey had revealed no particular concerns and they were now all waiting for the mortgage to be granted – no problem there, the estate agent assured them. Their sale was the end of a short chain but, fingers crossed, they would exchange contracts in the next few weeks, well in time for the planned move in mid-July. If absolutely necessary, they could always take Daisy out of school and go down early. Though Simon wasn't able to take any time off before the second half of July.

Kate handed in her notice at work and was touched by the disappointment her colleagues and authors expressed at her going. Susie Zee had actually wept on her shoulder and even James Clyde had written her a dry little note telling her she had 'worked quietly but well'. Thank you, James. Because of holiday due, she would leave in the last week of June.

The three weeks of her notice period turned out to be an oddly disturbing time. On the one hand, she felt no regret at leaving behind the dross – the boring admin tasks, the time-wasting at meetings, the office politics, the more troublesome authors, but she felt unreasonably hurt by the way office life was already moving on without her. No one bothered to fill her in on decisions about 'her' authors any more. She felt awful pangs at the thought of no longer being involved in exciting developments in writers' careers. After all, it was her carefully planned publicity campaign that was really getting Anxious Adam's first novel noticed. And people were still talking about her 1920s party at the Oxo Tower which had been attended by two B-list celebrities and reported in all the gossip columns. Although she remained convinced she and Simon were making the right decision, part of her wanted to shout 'Stop!' and reverse the whole process. This was such a leap in the dark, she thought, a disturbing feeling exacerbated by a conversation with her boss, Karina, about the possibilities of freelance work.

'Kate, dear, you *know* we'd love to use you if such an opportunity comes up. You've got so close to some of your authors, they're going to feel lost without you for a bit.'

'Do you think there'll be anything for me, until you find my successor, or after that, when you're very busy?'

'If budgets for freelancers aren't too tight, Kate, *of course*. It's just you know how rarely we're allowed to use outsiders because of the cost. Somehow we always manage to keep the work inhouse, don't we? But I'm sure something will come up, if not with us then with other companies. I'll mention your name to one or two people, if you like.'

'That's very kind, if you would,' Kate breathed weakly, trying to hide her disappointment at this response. It looked as though it would be more difficult than she thought to carry on working for Jansen & Hicks.

Tasha, the Hutchinsons' nanny, had, been told about her employers' plans early on. After all, she could hardly be expected not to notice the estate agent's sign going up and parties of strangers wandering round the house, commenting on the navy bathroom and the flaking décor. She was devastated at the idea of leaving Sam and Daisy, but in one way it would be a relief, she confided, as her boyfriend, Rob, had been pressing her to go travelling with him and she'd been putting him off because she hadn't wanted to leave the Hutchinsons in the lurch.

Liz, who had no luck at all with nannies, was sarcastic about this. 'I reckon you just got your plans in first. She's been with you nearly a year. Mark my words, come her anniversary, she'd either have slapped in a request for a massive pay rise or gone off with Lover Boy in a flash. The good ones go and the bad ones have to be pushed. Tasha is too good to hang about.' Kate protested that she was being unfair but didn't add that working for Liz must be the childcare equivalent of stone-breaking, for Liz ran a tight domestic ship.

One thing Simon and Kate had agreed about. It would be impossible to try and view houses in Suffolk from this distance.

'It would just be crazy to pack the kids in the car and hare off down the A12 every weekend,' said Simon. 'We're exhausted enough as it is, and the market isn't going to change that much in a couple of months. We'll look when we get there.'

This wisdom hadn't stopped Joyce, who was overjoyed at the prospect of her son's family moving down near her, from sending up estate agents' details and cuttings from the local paper's property section every week. Most of the houses she alighted upon were wildly unsuitable – either huge baronial halls beyond their craziest financial dreams or rather boxy-looking properties on modern housing developments. There was nothing, Kate mused, remotely like the house of her dream. But she and Simon enjoyed leafing through these missives with the excitement of newly-weds building castles in the air.

'Look at Harwood Hall – sixteen bedrooms and forty acres of land! We could have four bedrooms each and a golf course for Dad.'

'What the heck has Mother put this in for! A wet dyke, it says – dread to think what that is – at Brundall.'

'Must be for mooring boats. Look, the photo's just a patch of grass and a ditch.'

'Mmm, only thirteen thousand pounds, though. Perhaps we should think about it. I did a lot of sailing with school. It would be great to have a little mirror dinghy.'

That was the difference between them, thought Kate, with sudden unpleasant clarity. Simon seemed to be treating the whole move as a kind of hobby while Kate herself was making life-changing decisions in a search for somewhere to call home.

# Chapter 5

'Who would have thought we had so much stuff?' Kate said, surveying the wall of boxes waiting in the living room to be stowed in the van. 'Where in this house did we keep twenty boxes worth of books?'

'No idea,' said Simon, shaking his head. 'When I moved here eleven years ago, I got everything in a small Bedford van. One more problem having a wife and two children has added to my life.'

Moving day had dawned at last – a grey drizzly Wednesday at the beginning of July. In the end, the moving chain had all clicked into place, but the Hutchinsons were having to go earlier than planned. Simon had managed to get today, Thursday, and Friday off, but was expected back in the office on Monday morning for a meeting at nine o'clock sharp.

A huge removal van had edged its way down Queensmill Road at eight o'clock that morning into the space Kate had pre-arranged with the council. She had spent the previous week piling into cardboard boxes the portion of their clothes, toys and other possessions that they intended to take with them to

Joyce's, storing those boxes out of the way in their bedroom. Today, the removal men were packing up everything else, including all their furniture, and driving it to a storage depot in Beccles. There it would stay until the Hutchinsons found a home of their own.

'Never mind what we've got already, I'm going to make you buy a whole lot more,' Kate teased Simon. 'Once we find our dream house, this scruffy old suite will have to go, and we'll need proper garden furniture and a formal dining table and chairs.'

'Remind me to leave my credit card in London then,' said Simon waspishly. 'And do you think the kids would notice if we left half their toys behind?'

'Oh yes, they'd notice. Daisy made me promise they'd all go to Granny's and not into store.'

'Good thing Mother's got a huge shed then, isn't it?'

Tasha had taken Sam and Daisy out for the day – London Zoo was the plan. Later, she was due to take them back to the Longmans' house where the Hutchinsons would all stay the night, then that would be goodbye.

Tasha was off with her boyfriend Rob the following Friday for a year abroad. The thrill of it all had not stopped her bursting into tears at various points during the previous week – which had unsettled Sam rather – but she had shown the kids picture books of Australia and promised to send them lots of postcards and bring them back toy koalas. 'No, I want a crocodile,' shouted Sam. 'A biting one.'

Liz had pleaded to be allowed to throw a farewell party for the Hutchinsons, but Kate had stubbornly refused.

'I can't face the fuss, Liz, kind of you though it is. The party at the office was ordeal enough and you gate-crashed that.' The marketing director, Emma, had organized drinks and canapés downstairs at a nearby wine-bar one sultry evening during Kate's final week, and Kate had been overwhelmed at the large numbers of well-wishers from the office who had squashed into the hot little cellar room in pursuit of free food and drink. She hadn't been the centre of such attention since her wedding day and, melancholy after too much champagne, she wept copiously on Simon's shoulder in the taxi home because she was leaving all these lovely people who had insisted on how much they would miss her and had contributed to the generous Habitat token they gave her as a present. The next day they looked at her in the lift as if to say, 'What, are you still here? I thought we got rid of you last night!'

'No, Liz, we'll just say goodbye to people individually and slip away. It's not as though we won't be seeing everyone lots – we will.'

And, indeed, there had been a month of going out for drinks or dinner or Sunday lunch with friends and acquaintances. 'It's a bit like Christmas,' joked Simon. 'There's this kind of desperation to see everyone. As if the world is about to end. We've seen people we haven't bothered with in years of living in the next borough to them in London!'

By July, Kate felt the whole thing was peculiar, like a sort of honeymoon but with kids. Here she was, effectively on holiday, but with lots of help from Tasha, arranging all sorts of exciting things for the children, buying clothes for their new life.

But most unsettling of all was the evening she went out for a drink with her old university friend Claire. Claire was now a portrait photographer who ran a successful business out of a small studio in Greenwich. She lived in a tiny flat there, overlooking the river. At York, Claire had been considered arty and eccentric; after graduation, those attributes had worked in her favour and she had collected a wide and interesting range of friends in the arts and entertainments world. She and Kate had always stayed close, as if Claire were taking the place of the sister Kate had lost. They had shared a flat together when they had started work in London thirteen years before, and the experience of managing on low budgets and buoying one another up through the low periods had proved to be a glue of super strength. The main difference between them was their attitude to relationships. Kate had always wanted to marry and have children, to create the warm family unit that she herself had missed. Claire, on the other hand, had come from a large affectionate Catholic family. In the O'Brien household there had never been a moment's peace, and as the eldest child it was the unspoken assumption that Claire would help with the five younger children. As a result, she was still running.

'Sam and Daisy, I love them to bits,' Claire would sigh, and indeed she was a most generous aunt figure to them, despite having a whole heap of real nephews and nieces of her own. She was always arriving with forbidden sweets and chocolate and was happy to watch endless *Thomas the Tank Engine* videos with Sam and play amusing alternative Barbie games with Daisy, in which Barbie threw off her model clothes and went off to climb Kilimanjaro in kit borrowed from Sam's Action Man. 'I also just love waving them goodbye at the end of the day and going home to my peaceful little flat.'

Claire's lovelife was a constant source of interest to Kate and Liz. Men from all sorts of backgrounds came and went in her life, but not one of them was allowed to move into that peaceful little flat.

One evening at the beginning of July, Kate met Claire in the champagne bar of Kettners in Soho. Claire arrived late as usual and laden down with cases of photographic equipment. She had, she said, been doing the kind of job she hated most – taking stiff little photographs of members of the board of a well-known travel company for their brochure. No creativity involved and too much masculine self-importance. And one instance of groping in the lift.

'Revolting lech,' she remembered, shuddering. 'Why are men like Broadband?' she quipped, slumping down in the chair in front of the glass of champagne Kate had fetched from the bar.

'Because they're always on?' Kate guessed. 'Good thing you were wearing sharp heels then.' She laughed. Claire always dressed in black up to her short spiky hair, black and silver earrings and black eye make-up, and down to her high-heeled boots. 'Oh Claire, it's so lovely to see you. I can't believe we won't be doing this again for ages.' She swung her half-filled glass through the air in a mock toast. Claire laughed.

'*I* can't believe the next time I'll see you will probably be on a boggy heath, me in my walking boots and cagoul.'

The thought of Claire dressed down for a country walk made Kate choke on her champagne.

'Seriously though,' Claire leaned forward and studied her friend with a look of affectionate concern, 'I know it's a bit late to say this, but do you really think you're doing the right thing? At least here, with people you know and love, you're protected. You'll really be out on your own where you're going. And I worry about you.'

'I'll have Simon and the children – and Joyce,' Kate countered. 'And I'll make friends. It's much easier with kids, you know. You meet parents at the schools and the Brownies. And I can always volunteer for the church flower rota if I get really fed up!'

'When did you last go into a church?' For all her individual personal morality, Claire still rigorously attended Mass every Sunday. Simon would engage her in frenzied argument about this every now and then, but she remained firm. Today, before Kate could reply, Claire moved swiftly on. 'It's just that you're in danger of cutting yourself off from your support systems. And it's you who's giving everything up, not Simon. You won't be so much a part of his world any more. It's all more of a risk for you.'

Kate was used to Claire's forthright manner. Indeed, she had always enjoyed the mild bickering that studded their friendship. She felt safe with Claire who had always proved an unswervingly loyal and loving friend.

'What on earth do you mean? I never did work in the City so I haven't ever been part of his world, as you put it.'

'Yes, but he will still have all the sophisticated urban side, won't he?' Claire waved her hand in the air to emphasize her point. 'The excitement of the hot deal, being with the movers and shakers. He's late enough home every night now – think what it's going to be like, especially if he stays here during the week.'

'Half the City have little weekend cottages in Suffolk,' Kate reminded her. 'We'll probably always be entertaining his colleagues to lunch and dinner. Anyway, we'll be a haven for him. When I was working I was often never there to come home to. And he hardly ever had a decent evening meal and both of us would be too tired to enjoy putting the kids to bed if we did come home in time.'

'I know, and I can see how fond of you Simon is. But it is so important for women to be independent. I think men look at you differently when you're completely reliant on them. I've told you about my sister Maura, haven't I? She's mad cos Andy's always moaning at her about what a great time she must be having at home with the baby, seeing her friends and spending his money, while he's out on the road all day.'

'Oh Claire, Simon's not like that . . . and he doesn't drive a van round South London like Andy. It's all different.'

She stopped, feeling a worm of unease but bidding it depart. Claire was away on one of her pet subjects. She just didn't really understand the issues. After all, she'd never done the marriage and children bit. She just overvalued her freedom, Kate thought smugly. Well, Kate did have responsibilities and now, with this move, she was going to be able to attend to them properly. Everyone, after all, talked about making sacrifices for their children, and if moving away from the friends she loved and the places that were familiar was a necessary sacrifice, then she was happy to make it. And so, she knew, was Simon.

'Claire, don't worry, really. After all, if it doesn't work out – but it will – we can always move back. We won't have done anything irrevocable.'

'No, I suppose not. Sorry, I do preach, don't I?' Claire shook herself out of her mood and smiled. 'Oh, I will miss you!'

'And I'll miss being bossed around by you and Liz. What on earth will I do without you both?' And she squeezed Claire's shoulder.

Driving the car down the A12 to Suffolk, Sam and Daisy in the back with a heap of duvets and toys – Simon had gone ahead with the rented van with all their boxes – Kate's thoughts wandered back to this conversation.

Her husband seemed very upbeat about this move and had shown none of the qualms that Kate had. For him, it was merely a logical solution to an awkward domestic situation, and every time Kate had lain awake having a dark night of the soul about their decision, he'd slept on beside her, blissfully unaware of her torment. It was true that he was returning to home territory, but Halesworth was thirty miles from where he had been brought up.

Anyway, he'd lost touch with so many friends from his childhood, he was in many ways starting again. But husbands often didn't seem to mind about this as much as wives, Kate mused. Their emotional needs seemed to be met within the home. And Simon was usually happy to be friendly to those he was with at the time. His best friends at the moment, for instance, tended to be people he had met at Canterbury, where he was at university, and who had moved to London when he did. Before he met Kate he had spent most of his spare time going out for drinks or football matches with them, yet he hadn't seemed to miss this kind of socializing once he had the responsibilities of a wife and family, and he got on well with most of Kate's friends and their other halves. The only friend of hers he was not at ease with was Claire.

'I feel she doesn't like me,' he complained once to Kate. 'I can't seem to say anything right. It's as if she doesn't think I'm good enough for you.'

'She's just always been very protective of me,' said Kate. 'She does like you, I know she does. Only the other day she was saying you're really good with Sam and Daisy.'

'That's a bone women throw to men they don't approve of,' said Simon glumly. '"Say what you like, he's a good father".'

'Well, you are,' insisted Kate. And that was the end of *that* conversation.

By the time evening came, they were all exhausted. They had spent hours unpacking the van and the car and stowing away bikes and clothes, books, toys, endless coats and pairs of wellingtons. Joyce had been overwhelmed by their huge amount of possessions. One of the garden sheds was now piled high with boxes of bits and pieces they weren't sure they could do without but didn't have anywhere to put in the cottage.

It was while she was emptying her holdall of clothes, stowing them away in the pine chest of drawers, that Kate noticed a few links of a chain hanging out of a zip pocket of the holdall. She opened the zip and scooped out the locket. So that's where it went, she thought, having looked everywhere when she wanted to wear it at Christmas. She untangled the chain and laid the pendant in her palm, feeling its weight, stroking the design with her thumb. Then she turned it over and stared at the faded photograph as though urging it to come into focus and reveal its secrets.

On impulse she slipped the chain around her neck and the pendant lay cold in the hollow between her breasts.

That night she dreamed of the house again. This time it was winter. She was standing in the drawing room, a huge log fire blazing in the fireplace. A young parlourmaid was stacking the tea trolley. She wore a calf-length black dress and a little white cap. When she turned to wheel the trolley out she looked right through Kate, who had to jump out of the way to let it clatter past.

Kate was left alone with the crackling of the fire and the slow ticking of an elegant grandfather clock. She wandered out into the hall, which smelled of beeswax. All was dark wood panelling, with the most beautiful carved wooden staircase rising up to a galleried landing above. She started to mount the stairs, then stopped on the half-landing. She could hear a woman crying somewhere above. Terrible, desolate sobbing. And another woman's voice, harsher, speaking to her.

'I hate you. I'll never forgive you, never!' the crying voice broke out in a wail.

A door closed upstairs, there was the sound of footsteps on carpet, then a thin, grim-faced woman appeared on the landing above. Like the maid she seemed not to see Kate. The latter pressed herself against the banisters and the woman, who wore a dove-grey twinset and a pleated skirt, brushed past her. Kate was shocked by the expression on her face – of suppressed triumph. Above her, the sobbing continued.

Just then, far away, she could hear a man's voice and someone was shaking her. 'Kate? Wake up! Kate, why are you crying?'

When Simon tore her from her sleep, her heart was thudding, adrenalin pumping painfully through her limbs. Once again she felt a deep sense of loss, but worse this time – an intense loneliness such as she had felt in the weeks and months after Nicola's death. Burying her face in Simon's warm neck, she cried. In stumbling words she tried to explain, but her account of a dream house and the locket merely confused him.

'How can you say you want to live in a house that doesn't exist? It's crazy!' He yawned.

In the morning, Kate shut the locket in a trinket tin and stuffed it into the top of a cardboard box of books that still had nowhere to go. Later, after she'd found Daisy trying to unpack the box again, she bundled everything back and took the box out to join the others in the shed. She had no idea what the dreams meant or if they really had something to do with the locket, but she had enough to fill her mind at the moment. She had brought with her from the kitchen of their Fulham home, the funny little picture of the dream house that she had drawn so many months ago, and now Simon pinned it to his mother's fridge with a magnet.

'I bet you didn't believe for a moment when you drew this that it would actually come true.' He laughed. '"Be careful what you wish for", as they say.'

'And "In dreams begin responsibilities", don't forget that one,' Kate mock-lectured him.

'Don't I know it,' he said. 'I've just paid out for the rail season ticket and we can't afford to eat until payday.'

'Even dreams don't come cheap these days,' Kate said, studying her picture. Then she smiled. 'But don't worry, this one is going to be worth every penny.'

# Chapter 6

*August 2003*

Simon enjoyed looking round houses.

'This is one of the best we've seen so far,' he said, as they loitered on the gravel drive in front of the third property of the day, a fine Georgian rectory.

Simon's work schedule had proved unusually punishing this summer, and this week towards the end of August was the only one from the original planned fortnight's holiday he had, in the end, been able to take. Joyce had been looking after the children while he and Kate visited estate agents in the area and tirelessly viewed property. But nothing seemed to suit. Now it was the Friday afternoon and Simon's holiday was nearly over. Kate was beginning to despair.

'They've made a nice job of the roof,' he said, taking several steps back and craning his neck to see. He looked down at the particulars again. 'There's certainly enough space, if we made this snug into the playroom. And the conservatory's useful. There's just the question of the master bedroom – isn't it hideous?'

'Sssh.' Kate glanced anxiously at the open door. 'The owner will hear you. I suppose we could change it easily enough.' She turned and gazed over the front garden. 'My real problem is with this road. There are so many lorries. What's the point of moving away from London if we've still got traffic roaring past our door?'

'I expect it's mostly in the daytime, but you're right,' Simon sighed. 'There are the fumes and we'd worry about Sam and Daisy running in the road. Never mind trying to get the car out of that blind entrance at night.'

The rectory was just outside a large village several miles east of Fernley. It had been recently restored to within an inch of its life. However, although the living areas had been suitably renovated – the farmhouse kitchen, the chintzy drawing room, the grand Georgian panelled dining room – the owners had gone astray when it came to decorating upstairs. The bedrooms had been themed in different periods of design. The Art Nouveau guest room was beautiful, if impractical with all the Tiffany-style glass fittings. The simple geometric patterns of the Art Deco room were attractive if dour. The Kate Greenaway nursery for the owner's visiting baby granddaughter was delightful, albeit not right for Sam or the thoroughly modern Daisy. But when the owner flung open the door of the master bedroom, it was all Kate and Simon could do not to gasp in horror.

'This is the one we were really proud of,' said Mr Potts, a thin, sad-looking man who had lost his wife the year before. 'Polly always felt we could really be ourselves in here.'

They stared in silence. Had Polly Potts had a hankering to be Mae West? The ceiling and one wall were one big mirror. The carpet was a field of white fur, the remaining walls were papered in a hideous ultramarine and pink circle design. As for the bed, Kate had never seen such a huge one. Never mind king-size, this one would cater for the Emperor of the Universe.

'A water bed, as you can see,' said Mr Potts, sitting on one corner and bouncing gently up and down, disrupting the pile of furry cushions on the pillows. 'I can arrange to leave it if you like.'

The 1960s theme had been carried through to the bathroom, where a vast heart-shaped jacuzzi had been sunk into a dais approached by three shallow steps. Something told Kate that Mr Potts hadn't used it since his wife's death. This wasn't a bathroom for one.

'Let's walk round the village, see if we can get a cup of tea,' said Simon now. They called goodbye to the lugubrious Mr Potts, inched the car out of the perilous driveway and drove carefully through the village until they saw a pub that advertised afternoon tea. The lounge of the King of Hearts turned out to be shabby-genteel and dusty, but they sank into the comfy armchairs with relief and ordered tea.

'There just doesn't seem that much in our price bracket,' Kate commented a little later, spreading a scone with butter and jam out of plastic pots.

'Oh, I don't know. We've seen thirteen places so far this week. I think we're doing rather well,' said Simon, who had drunk his tea quickly and was now rattling his keys, eager to get back on the road. They had one more place to see at four. 'I just think we need to be looking nearer Diss. The drive to the station adds an hour to my travelling.'

'Well, we'd better find somewhere quickly then,' said Kate. 'I don't want the kids to settle in and then have to change schools again. Daisy's nervous enough about starting at Fernley, and Sam's confused. When Tasha's postcard arrived the other day, he asked if she was coming back to look after him.'

To tell the truth, Daisy and Sam had hardly mentioned their old nanny. Despite having to fall back on one another's company, without the host of friends Tasha had gathered round them in London, the children had been enjoying a wonderful summer. The weather had often been beltingly hot and, once the chores were done, days at the beach had been interspersed with picnics in the countryside and cooler days spent wandering around small market towns. They had visited the otter sanctuary at Bungay, the castle at Framlingham, and the safari park at Kessingland. Next week, Joyce's friend Hazel was having her grandsons, Toby and Joe, to stay, and Joyce had arranged some outings with them.

In many ways it was proving an idyllic period for Kate. She had never had so much free time to spend with her children – maternity leave was tarnished by the memory of her depression – and she was free of the dread she usually felt during family holidays, knowing that soon they would end and the grind and the guilt would start up all over again.

The biggest problem was Simon – or rather, not seeing enough of Simon. Most mornings he caught the seven o'clock train from Diss and often returned exhausted only after the children had gone to bed. The weekends had become even more precious than they had been in London. Only on Saturday and Sunday, it seemed, could they be a normal happy family together.

Kate missed him badly now that she was at home all day, although she was far from alone – the children and Joyce saw to that. And therein lay a second difficulty: she had had to get used to living side by side with her mother-in-law. Of course, living with someone was always going to be different from staying with them for a few days; Kate hadn't expected otherwise. And she knew she was incredibly lucky to have so much help with the children. But she hadn't foreseen quite how irritating Joyce could sometimes be. For a start, her mother-in-law was so relentlessly cheerful. She chatted brightly about trivia, when Kate wanted silence. Joyce even talked to herself, a consequence, Kate supposed, of living alone. 'Now, I wonder whether that cake is ready yet,' or 'What a silly place to put my glasses,' Kate would overhear her say. Most annoying of all, if Kate was elsewhere in the house, reading, maybe, or putting away the children's clothes, Joyce would come and check up on her. 'Ah, just wondered if you were all right, dear,' she would say or, 'There you are. Do you need anything?'

Kate tried hard to fit in with Joyce's routines, but small irritations built up. She hated the way Joyce would stack the washing-up in the sink 'to soak' before adding it to the dishwasher, and would pointedly transfer it all to the machine. And she disliked the fact that Bobby's half-empty dog-food tin sat next to the family food in the fridge.

At the same time, she knew certain of her habits were annoying to Joyce. Kate was lazy about making the beds, she didn't make gravy the 'proper' way Joyce had been taught, and she never drank the last inch of her cup of tea. 'Have you finished with this, dear?' Joyce would ask three times a day for the first fortnight before removing Kate's mug.

Weekends, too, could be difficult. Simon and Kate had to go out together by themselves to achieve any privacy, and their love-making had become an almost furtive affair, indulged in only long after the house was quiet and Joyce, they assumed, safely asleep. It was a mercy at least, Kate often thought, that Joyce had her own en suite bathroom so that there wasn't *that* kind of embarrassing encounter on the landing.

On the other hand, during the week, if Simon wasn't back till late and Joyce was out at her reading group or having supper with friends, Kate found there was too much time to reflect. As the summer wore on she felt increasingly lonely and directionless, and began to wonder whether she had done the right thing in giving up her job and moving away from everyone she knew. A couple of visits to London to see her old friends merely underlined this feeling of loss: their busy lives were going on without her. She often slept badly, haunted by anxious dreams. Never mind, she told herself firmly. It will be better when we find a place of our own.

'Durrants showed me some places near Diss here,' Simon said now, and reached for his briefcase, removing the sheaf of prospectuses the estate agent had given him that morning. 'There's one here I liked the look of.' He passed it to Kate who squinted at it in the half-dark of the pub lounge.

'Oh, but that's a barn conversion,' she said, and threw it on the table. 'It's not what we're looking for at all. I want somewhere old.'

'We've looked at some old places. The one just now. And what about that farmhouse this morning?'

'No, that didn't look right. I'd like somewhere . . . Victorian, I think.'

'Kate, the farmhouse *was* Victorian. Look here, it says 1865. That's mid-Victorian.'

'Oh. Well, it didn't look Victorian.'

Simon rolled his eyes in exasperation and Kate felt guilty. Somehow the image of the dream house had lodged very clearly in her memory. She was aware that she was being unreasonable, scouring the countryside for an imaginary house, and she was too embarrassed to say anything about it again to the oh-so-rational Simon, but she knew that wherever it was they chose, she had to feel in the deepest sense that it was 'home'. The dream, she was growing more certain, had been a sign.

The final house of the day was too dark and there was a large swampy pond in the grounds. Kate shuddered at the anxieties that could cause. On the way back to Fernley they took a different route down a quiet country lane, and drove past a sign for the village of Seddington. Just after the sign they passed a row of poplar trees and Simon pointed at a large brick gateway with wrought-iron gates.

'Wonder what that place is,' he said.

Kate turned to look up the drive, but just then her attention was caught by a line of cyclists toiling towards them.

'Watch out, Simon!' She cringed as her husband swerved and braked. The cyclists sailed past with space to spare.

'I saw them,' he said irritably. 'There was plenty of room.'

'Sorry,' Kate said, leaning back in her seat with a sigh. 'I'm not used to these narrow country roads.' They had forgotten all about the mysterious gateway.

They were in the village now, passing rows of thatched cottages, a pub, an antique shop. To their left was a short cul-de-sac up to the church. A family with two tots on bikes, and with another in a buggy to which was tied an elderly dog started to wobble their way across the road in front of them. This time, Simon slid deliberately to a halt and waved them across. He sat there as they ambled over, his fingers drumming on the wheel.

Kate lowered the window and looked up at the church.

And there she saw her. Outside the lych gate, an elegant old lady with a stick was waiting by a small car parked with its nose pointing down the hill. Kate watched as a middle-aged woman opened the front passenger door, took charge of her companion's stick and black handbag in one hand and held her arm with the other. The older lady gripped the car door, then looked up as she steadied herself. She gazed straight down at Kate. She and Kate stared at one another a moment, and Kate felt an odd shock of recognition. The old lady gravely inclined her head in acknowledgement, then Simon set off once more.

Over the next few months, whenever they drove through Seddington, which wasn't very often, Kate remembered this tableau and looked for the old lady. But it was to be many months before she saw her again.

# *Chapter 7*

*Easter 2004*

'Where has Kate taken the children today?' asked Joyce Hutchinson's friend Hazel. It was the last Friday of the Easter holidays and Hazel had just arrived at Paradise Cottage for lunch.

'Easton Farm Park,' Joyce told her friend, pouring her a glass of wine. 'They're meeting up with Kate's new pal Debbie and her family. No, *down*, Bobby, or I'll shut you in the hall.' The spaniel slouched off to his bed in the corner of the kitchen. 'I'll just shove the quiche in the oven and find something to put on the salad.'

'I took little Joe to Easton last week,' said Hazel, wandering over to look out of the back window at the garden. 'He just loves feeding the lambs. Ooh, doesn't your garden look lovely? Especially the hyacinths. And, look, your lilac's coming out already. Mine's way behind.'

'There, I'll just set the buzzer and . . . Yes, I only noticed it today. It has such a gorgeous smell, don't you think? It used to be a favourite of Dennis's.'

Hazel nodded sympathetically. 'Rodney liked tulips. Two lips in the dark was his joke.'

'Really?' Joyce said politely, though Hazel had told her this several times during their friendship. 'It was because of the garden we chose this house, you know,' she said, taking a gulp from her own glass and staring out at the lilac bush with its emerging dots of white.

Hazel had also heard Joyce say this before but as a widow herself, albeit for twice as long as Joyce, she knew how important it was to remind oneself of these facts; it kept the memories alive.

'Dennis would have been proud of you, you know,' she said gently, seeing a sheen of tears in her friend's eyes.

'How do you mean?' Joyce said hoarsely.

'The way you've picked yourself up and gone on. It was easier for me, I think, having the family near, but you were new to the neighbourhood – you hardly knew anyone. Look at all the things you do now.'

'You mean the reading group and the charity shop? And the church flowers? That's not much really.'

'Six hours a week in the shop is more than "not much". Then you've worked so hard on the house – and it's not every grandmother who would be happy to have a family of four to move in for so long.'

'There's no doubt it sometimes feels very full here,' Joyce agreed, looking round the kitchen as if seeing it with a visitor's eyes. The room where everything had previously had its place and was in that place, had been allowed to slip into the cheerful messiness of a family home. Children's paintings and clay models decorated every available surface, two overflowing boxes of toys and Lego were parked under the front window. On the carefully restored pine dresser, now scuffed, and with felt pen scribbled on one door, Joyce's mother's Royal Albert tea service fought for position with origami boats, snapshots and bits of broken toy. A heap of what looked like estate agents' details had been pushed to the side of the round table, which Joyce had laid for lunch. And the fridge was completely covered in artwork, class address lists and children's party invitations.

'There's just this overwhelming tide of possessions,' said Joyce with a wave of her hand as if to brush it away. 'And you should see upstairs . . . I can't keep up with it.'

'You look tired, dear,' said Hazel. 'Are you taking those pills at bedtime?'

'I had one last night, yes,' Joyce said, rubbing her eyes. 'I still wake so early in the mornings and have to lie there, my thoughts whirling round. I should sleep really,' she went on. 'I'm tired enough after helping with the kids all day. They're dear children, but Daisy teases Sam and Sam kicks her, and then she screams . . . you know how it goes.'

When, a year ago, Simon had asked if he could bring Kate, Daisy and Sam to camp in her cottage for a couple of months, Joyce had joyfully agreed. She had always envied Hazel having her grandsons in just the next village and it seemed such a privilege to have Daisy and Sam with her for a while and then for them to move to a house nearby. She had grown very close to them in the last eight months and she knew that they loved her back. It was just that it was much harder work than she believed possible.

'At least I don't have Toby and Joe with me all the time,' Hazel mused, 'and I couldn't live with Gina now, she's got such strong ideas about everything. And she's my daughter . . .'

'Oh, Kate and I get on well, surprisingly well really, but a daughter-in-law is not quite the same as a daughter, is it? I feel I'm on walking on eggshells with her sometimes. If I make a comment about one of the children not being made to eat up their food, or say something about it being their bedtime, she

76

looks worried, as if I'm criticizing her. But it's difficult to say nothing. I was always taught that children should have regular hours, and it's important that they know the boundaries.'

'I so agree with you. Children today don't seem to do what you tell them. My mother always used to say "Don't contradict me," and "Do what you're told or your father will get to hear about it," and that was that. We shut up and put up.'

Just then, the buzzer on the cooker sounded and Joyce leaped up to turn it off. But when she picked up the oven gloves the phone started ringing in the hall.

'Oh! Would you mind?' said Joyce, passing Hazel the oven gloves and hurrying out to answer it.

Hazel found a heat-resistant mat hanging on a nail and carefully placed the quiche on it on the table. Then she turned off the oven and sat waiting for Joyce to reappear. Her eyes passed over the stack of estate agents' brochures at her elbow. She picked up the top one and her eyebrows shot up. It was a huge thatched farmhouse in two acres of land and with a price tag to match. Extraordinary, what houses seemed to be worth now. Then, hearing her friend coming back into the room, she hastily put the paper back on the pile.

'That was Kate's father,' said Joyce in a distracted voice. 'He sounded a bit agitated. Wants her to ring him.'

'Can he catch her on her mobile?'

Joyce shook her head. 'She's lost the charger. She's been managing without for weeks. He is funny, you know.'

'Who?'

'Major Carter. He's very formal, and he never asks after the children. Isn't that interested. He's very wrapped up in his wife, you see. Barbara is never quite . . . well. She has been depressed for a long time. I told you about that awful business with Kate's sister. Well, you never get over something like that, do you?'

'Children are supposed to outlive one,' Hazel said sadly.

Joyce picked up the slice and started to cut the quiche. The phone rang again. 'Oh drat. Who can that be now?'

While she was out of the room, Hazel took the opportunity to flip through some more of the house prospectuses. Barn conversions, a fifteenth-century manor house, a modern architect-designed bungalow roofed with great solar panels. She let them drop again as Joyce returned.

'One of Kate's friends this time,' Joyce said. 'Claire. Nice girl but wears an extraordinary amount of eye make-up.'

As they started to eat, Hazel asked casually, 'How are Kate and Simon getting on looking for a house, then?'

Joyce swallowed her mouthful too quickly. 'Still no progress. Kate's intent on finding somewhere nearby so the kids can stay at the school, while Simon wants somewhere nearer the station. They just can't seem to agree. And to make it more difficult, Kate has some sort of ideal home in her mind. We all know there's no such thing in reality. There's always something wrong with a place.'

'Have they really found nothing they like?'

'There was one, last month. A Victorian rectory in a village halfway between here and Diss. I drove out to look at it with Kate one day. They put in an offer, but there were other bids and Simon wouldn't go any higher. I could see that Kate really liked it but, no, he knew best. And he was very shirty with me when I supported Kate's point of view. I got quite cross with him actually. After all, it's difficult for me not to have some kind of opinion, isn't it?'

'You have to be ever so tactful,' Hazel agreed, helping herself to more salad. 'Sometimes with Gina and Andrew . . .'

'As you can see,' Joyce motored relentlessly on, 'estate agents keep sending them more details, but Simon's so busy at work he hasn't got much energy at weekends to go out and look. Kate's losing heart a bit.'

'Is Simon coming home at all during the week now?' Hazel asked, and watched in concern as Joyce slowly put down her knife and fork and pushed her plate away, half her lunch uneaten.

'Hazel,' she said, 'that's what's really worrying me at the moment. That long journey is quite a strain on family life. Simon's so caught up in his work, and he and Kate see less of each other than they did in London.'

'That doesn't seem right. What a shame.'

When Simon and Kate had first moved here, he had managed to be on the six o'clock train home most evenings or, at worst, the seven o'clock, unless he had a late meeting or was away on a trip. But as the autumn moved on and it became darker and colder, and there was a bad patch with the trains, he had started staying over at his friend Nigel's flat in Docklands once or twice a week.

'Nigel has moved out and is living with his girlfriend,' said Joyce, 'and is glad to have the rent, apparently. The trouble is it's now four nights a week Simon stays in town.'

'I don't know how people can do that. There was a time in our marriage when Rodney had to work in Chelmsford on a contract and he boarded with a young couple there. I missed him like anything.'

'I'm not surprised. But it is quite a grind, the travelling, and the trouble is, his firm are trying to drum up business in Eastern Europe – you know, all those new countries coming into the Common Market.' Joyce still insisted on calling it that. 'And there's a lot more pressure. I don't know what time he'll get back tonight, but it wasn't until after ten last week, and sometimes he'll go back on a Sunday night if he has an early meeting next morning. He's awfully tetchy at the moment, poor love, but then he's so tired. And it's rotten luck for Kate.'

'She still helps you, I hope?'

'Oh yes, we share the housework and the washing, and take turns going to the supermarket. She has had a bit of work to do for publishers, so I let her get on with that as much as I can.'

'Writing things, do you mean?' said Hazel.

'Press releases, yes, and letters and phone calls to publicize books. She's set up a computer in Dennis's study. Simon is a bit impatient with her. Says she would get more work if she got on the phone to people and sold herself. Then she'll say, it's all right for him, he doesn't know what it's like being here all day away from the stimulation of an office, and so it goes on. They think I don't hear them arguing, but I do. I can't help it, the walls are so thin, and anyway sometimes they just argue in front of me as if I'm not here listening.' Joyce was speaking faster and faster, and her final word ended in a distressed squeak.

'You poor dear,' said Hazel, patting Joyce's hand where it lay on the table. 'It's not really fair on you, all this. Can't you have a talk with Simon about it? Perhaps they should find somewhere to rent until they get a place of their own.'

'I have tried broaching the subject, yes,' said Joyce guiltily, 'but not very hard. I feel mean, you see, when he's having such a tricky time at work.'

But Hazel was right, Joyce thought. She would have to say something to Simon again soon. This situation couldn't go on indefinitely, could it?

The phone began to ring for a third time.

# Chapter 8

'Don't get me wrong, I love it here. Suffolk's beautiful,' Kate was telling her new friend Debbie Samson. 'Though I still can't get used to the slow pace of life.' They were sitting on a bench in the adventure playground at Easton Farm Park, watching Sam and Daisy play on the climbing frame with Debbie's elder children, Natalie and James, while Debbie rocked the buggy, trying to get little Holly off to sleep.

Kate had got talking to Debbie at the school gate the previous September and, like a grateful flower to the sun, had opened up to the other woman's comfortable friendliness. Debbie was nicely rounded, with dark curly hair, dark eyes and olive skin that betrayed her Italian forebears. She had taken Kate under her wing, introducing her to other parents and inviting her along to girls' nights out and a regular weekly slot some of the women shared at a local swimming pool. She had proved a lifeline.

'At first I'd find it maddening,' Kate went on, 'people at the front of the queue in the shops having a good long chat with the sales assistant about the weather and their husband's gallstones while I'd be mouthing "Get on with it" and looking pointedly at my watch. You couldn't see Londoners standing for it!'

Debbie laughed. 'I know, and it still drives me mad.' She peeped over the top of the buggy. 'Oh, that's good, she's away.' Eighteen-month-old Holly had flaked out, exhausted by the morning's activity.

They had seen the lambs at feeding-time first of all. Twenty lusty-looking orphans, all bleating frantically, butted one another and the sides of their pen in their anxiety to get to the bottles of milk the assistant was doling out to the children squashed onto the row of hay-bales.

The chicks and ducklings were next. Holly had stood quivering in silent, round-eyed joy as Debbie tipped a tiny yellow chick into her cupped hands. Then they had watched a dozen piglets running around in the sunshine whilst the huge sow lay snoring in a corner.

'I bet she needs a glass or two of wine after getting that lot to bed at night,' Kate said.

After visiting the gentle great shire horses, their manes and tails gaily plaited to show off to the holiday crowds, and the goats, who ate Holly's bag of goat food, paper and all, the women had herded the children into the café for lunch. Now, four kids' meals, two jars of baby food, two coffees and two packs of sandwiches later, Holly was out for the count and Debbie and Kate could finally have a proper conversation. Debbie and her husband Jonny, a freelance journalist, had moved to Suffolk five years before, so Kate had no hesitation in being honest about her own experiences of being a newcomer.

'You know, I always thought it must be a myth, country people being kinder, but they genuinely seem to be, here,' Kate mused.

Debbie threw back her curly head and laughed. 'I think that's self-preservation, actually. They're probably no nicer or no meaner than anywhere else. It's because everyone knows everyone. They daren't say anything unkind in case it gets back to their victim that they said it. I hated that when we first came,' she remembered. 'How people talked about you behind your back. You'd meet a complete stranger, in the post office, say, and they'd know lots about you and seemed to think it was their right to find out more. Everyone kept asking about Johnny like he was a celebrity or something, just 'cos he writes for the papers. Things are changing, though,' she added. 'The locals are getting used to newcomers' funny ways. Even in the last five years you can see there are more and more people like us moving here from London, demanding fast service and designer this and that. The shops are going upmarket, and you can't get a plumber or a carpenter for love or money, there are so many incomers buying up property and throwing money around doing it up. It's awful for local people, what it's doing to house prices.'

'Well, here we both are, adding to the problem. And on that selfish note, I just wish we had a property to throw money around on,' Kate said sadly.

'Have you seen nothing you like recently?'

'Not really.' Kate felt embarrassed to say that she had a vision of the house she wanted. The dream she'd had only twice sounded rather silly nine months later and in daylight. Since the Victorian rectory there had been hardly anything that they had both liked, and Simon had lost the energy for going round properties at weekends unless Kate was so keen on something that she forced him.

'There must be somewhere you both like, Kate,' ventured Debbie. 'Shouldn't you just take the plunge and go for something?'

Kate thought about it then said carefully, 'You're probably right. We've just reached a bit of a boggy patch about it. Simon's so busy at the moment and I think the estate agents are getting fed up with us. But so much of the nice stuff is going to sealed bids. You have to be really motivated to get it.' She would have liked to say more of what was on her mind to Debbie, but they were still new friends and she felt it would be disloyal to talk about Simon behind his back. She cast her mind back to last Saturday night's argument and sighed.

She and Simon had just been to a potluck supper at the Samsons' house in Fernley village. There had been another set of parents from Daisy and Sam's school there, the Beatons, who farmed locally, and Louise Beaton, part of the swimming coterie, a thoroughly nice woman with thick-lensed glasses, had asked Simon whether the children were enjoying the school project they were currently finishing.

Simon had looked blank for a moment and Kate had been about to break in and remind him that it was about different modes of transport, when he had said with one of his charming smiles, 'You'll have to ask Kate, I'm afraid. That's her department.'

Her department. He meant anything to do with the children. How patronizing! She was furious.

'Well, I'm sorry, I can't keep up with it all,' he said as they walked the twenty minutes home, her arm through his, their flashlight showing up the potholes on the footpath. 'I don't know what they're up to all day at school.'

'That's because you're never there, are you? And you don't seem very interested when I tell you on the phone.'

'That's not true. Of course I'm interested in what my kids do. It's just . . . well, I'm up in Town working to pay for everything, aren't I? And when we speak in the evenings I'm usually knackered. I can't remember everything you say, can't take it all on board.'

'I'm sorry you're up in Town working so hard.' Kate's tone was weary. 'And that you feel you're paying for everything. I'd work more if I could, it's just it's not easy. And there's too much to do with the kids.'

'Well, precisely. So the kids *are* your department now.'

'Simon?' She stopped and dropped his arm. 'You make it sound like I'm second string. That we don't share anything, that I'm not your equal. I hate that.'

'I'm sorry, darling.' Simon hugged her sheepishly, though she stood stiffly, her arms folded over her chest. 'I don't mean that at all. But it's difficult to see how else the division of labour can be at the moment.'

'Does it have to be like that?' She relaxed and they resumed their walk. 'Can't you come home more often during the week? Get a job round here? It's ridiculous. I miss you, and the kids miss you when you're away all week. I don't get to know all the little things about your day, and you don't know all the things about mine. There just doesn't seem to be enough time to catch up at weekends, and you're always tired. I thought we had all these plans to do things together locally.'

'I came tonight, didn't I?'

'Yes, and you enjoyed it, didn't you?'

'It was OK, yes. I wouldn't say I had much in common with the Beatons, though. There's a limit to what I have to say about sugarbeet subsidies.'

Kate couldn't understand why Simon was being grumpy. He had been like this for the last couple of months and she had put it down to exhaustion. But now she thought there was something else. Simon obviously felt on the fringes of her life here. Debbie and Jonny and the Beatons were her friends and he did not share their world whereas she was beginning to do so. He just hadn't settled down here yet – hardly surprising as he was so rarely around. He was always very good with the children at weekends. He would take them out to the beach in all weathers, to the little cinema in Southwold, was even happy to take a turn with the bedtime regime. But it was rare for him to meet the people she saw every day, and he'd had no time or energy to become involved in anything locally. It wasn't exactly his fault, it was just a fact of life. She remembered with a shock what Claire had clumsily warned her about all those months ago. It was coming true. She and Simon were starting to inhabit different worlds.

Now, as Kate watched Debbie cuddling James, who had fallen and hurt his hand, she turned her situation over in her mind. It was partly the fact that one of them was working and one of them wasn't. In London, both of them were contributing to the pot; now, she was Simon's dependent. She had to ask him for housekeeping money and, although he never asked her to account for what she spent, from time to time he would frown when she asked for some extra and, she hated this most when the extra was for something for herself – shoes or a new coat, for instance. It made her feel she had to justify her existence, her right to have nice things, although at the same time, Simon seemed very keen that she wore stylish clothes, especially on the rare occasion when she was invited to something that involved his colleagues. Not only was she dependent on his money, she was living in her mother-in-law's house, relying on her kindness. Not that Joyce would ever see it that way, she hastily told herself.

Her world and Simon's were different geographically and culturally, too, with Simon in the City and herself in the country, and this meant that, daily, they were having completely different experiences. Of course, large numbers of couples lived like this and thought it normal, coped with the stresses. But it didn't feel normal to Kate; it felt as though everything had changed, was falling apart. Suddenly, their marriage, previously a relationship of equals, was becoming a partnership between strangers. Simon was just never there, and when he was, they couldn't seem to pick up with each other where they'd left off.

Suddenly, Kate felt quite panicky. Perhaps they had done the wrong thing in moving; perhaps they should go back to London before it was too late. Was the fact that they hadn't found a house they liked a sign that, deep down inside, they both knew this move wasn't to be permanent?

*But I don't want to go back*, a part of her said with great clarity. *I like it here*. She loved seeing so much of the children. She loved living in the country, watching the changing seasons, even if, as she joked to Liz on the phone, one of the things she missed most was having a lamp-post outside the front door plus the air smelled of pig manure and the nearest cappuccino was five miles away. She was starting to bed down here, to make friends locally. But she really must sort out something else to do, workwise. One of the mums ran a mail-order business for children's clothing, another was making her own soap and selling it through local giftshops and craft fairs. Although neither of these things appealed to Kate, there must be something out there for her, if she thought about it for long enough.

'Do you feel at home here yet?' Debbie was asking her now, James having run back to play, his injury forgotten. 'It took me a couple of years, you know.'

Kate felt a rush of warmth at Debbie's tactful understanding.

'I do miss my friends in London, I can't deny it. We all lead such busy lives, it's not as easy to see them as I thought it would be. I can't always be hopping on the train up to Town – it gets a bit much for Joyce, looking after both the kids for long. Oh, it's not as though people aren't friendly here. They are – and you've been so lovely, Debbie.' She squeezed the other woman's shoulder affectionately. 'But there's nothing like people who know you deep down, is there? You don't have to pretend with them, they know where you're coming from, what's giving you an off day, what makes you laugh. I worry about saying the wrong thing here sometimes.'

Debbie nodded. 'Oh, I know what you mean,' she said. 'It still happens to me. Actually, the worst time was when I said to Laura Simpson – you know, Frankie's mum? – didn't she think Jenny, the receptionist at the surgery, could be such a pain? And it turned out she was Jenny's sister. I've spent the last four years telling Laura every time I see her how nice and efficient the wretched woman is, even though she's sour enough to turn the milk.'

Kate laughed. 'Good thing my friend Liz doesn't live round here. There'd be civil war in no time!'

'Have you been up to see any of your old friends recently?'

'No, but we've spoken on the phone and Liz and Laurence are bringing the family up for a weekend in the summer.' Kate had taken Sam and Daisy up to stay with the Longmans during the February break. From there they'd gone down to spend a night with Kate's parents, an occasion fraught with anxiety, as the Carters weren't used to overnight guests. And she'd paid a visit to her old office. 'I felt I didn't belong there any more,' she told Debbie now. It had been so alienating, seeing someone else sitting at her desk with her authors' books on the shelves. And they'd changed the furniture round. Worst of all, it looked better this way. 'I do miss work,' she murmured, almost to herself. 'God, what I wouldn't give even to go to a meeting and negotiate with adults for a change!'

'Me too,' Debbie said. 'Even a budget meeting with the

managing director droning on about targets I couldn't care less about.' Debbie had worked in market research, which she'd given up without much regret when they moved. Her real interest lay in gardening, she had told Kate. Maybe she'd take a landscape gardening course once the children were a bit older.

'At least there are more women who stay at home round here,' Debbie went on. 'When I go up to Jonny's London parties sometimes, I feel so left out. All these smartly dressed confident women ask me what I "do". How can I really get across to them what life is like here? So I just say, "I spend Jonny's money", and they laugh, but at least then I've got over the embarrassment.'

Kate admired Debbie's air of confidence. Of course, she was lucky that Jonny worked at home and she saw so much of him, but Debbie didn't seem to care what other people thought of her, or to worry about whether she was doing the 'right thing'. It was a real gift to be at home in your own life, Kate thought. Hers felt like an ill-fitting suit at the moment.

The last eight months had been very strange. For a start, she hadn't really known how to organize all these acres of time with which she'd found herself once the children had started school. At the office, she had been used to a list of tasks that had to be achieved, that could be ticked off one by one, even if more kept popping up to take their place. Being at home with two young children seemed an alarmingly unstructured affair. She was lucky that she had lots of help from Joyce, although after eight months of living with her mother-in-law, the strain was starting to show. Joyce was as chatty as ever, but not as relentlessly cheerful. Indeed, sometimes she seemed to Kate quite grim, especially as she surveyed the mess the children created or whenever she had to separate them when they were fighting. Last week she had even lost her temper with Sam.

'You are an extremely disobedient little boy,' Joyce had hissed at him after he had knocked a china goat off a shelf, chipping a horn. 'I told you to put that sword down. If your daddy had done that when he was a little boy, he would have gone straight to bed without his supper.'

Sam had looked so shocked at his grandmother's angry tone that Kate's heart went out to him. Yet Sam *had* been naughty and she felt she had to back up her mother-in-law when Joyce said, 'You're not having any chocolate pudding for tea now,' and turned her back on Sam.

While Joyce wasn't looking, Kate gave Sam a quick hug, but felt powerless to undo the punishment of missing his very favourite dish, though her son's shoulders shook in silent misery. If only she were in her own home and could discipline her children in her own way.

She also felt powerless when it came to Joyce's relationship with Simon. All right, so the woman could be annoying, but Kate felt embarrassed whenever Simon was rude to Joyce, or fell into one of his sullen silences and offered his mother only monosyllables when she asked after his day. After all, they were relying on Joyce's hospitality.

Kate knew that Joyce was very worried about Simon's absence and, if she stopped to look at it squarely, which she didn't want to do, Kate would agree.

She badly missed her husband's company. She missed the way they had been a team. Now she felt she had been exiled from his life – locked in a tower, stationed in a distant outpost, whichever way you liked to look at it. Perhaps he felt the same way about her? And although she was making friends, putting down roots, it was often hard to concentrate on being in Suffolk. Her mind drifted all the time to London, wondering what her old colleagues were doing, how her friends were. She felt she was making a lot of the running in keeping up some of her friendships. Worse, she knew she was right – her old colleagues had moved on, they were forgetting about her. She could be doing more about getting freelance publicity work, but she hadn't in all honesty enjoyed the bits and pieces she'd been doing, such as publicizing the uninspiring novel by a local TV interior-design-show presenter who had proved ungrateful for all her efforts, and a series of travel guides, which had bogged her down in endless administration. And, as predicted, she had to avoid any work that meant travelling to attend publication events – which meant most of the more interesting projects. No, she'd be better off turning her attention to something different.

'Would you like to stay in Fernley, though?' Debbie was asking.

'Oh yes, it's so friendly, it would be great to get a house there,' Kate replied. She loved the little school, especially since Sam and Daisy were so obviously happy there. There was a surprising range to the curriculum, with parents often invited in to share their skills with the children. Mrs Smithson, the headmistress, was a calm and experienced teacher and manager, and knew instinctively how to treat each individual child. Sam had shown some early signs of dyslexia and she had immediately arranged some special exercises for him, which had made a great difference to his progress.

The only problem was to do with the facilities. The school buildings were originally Victorian and had reached the stage where some major repair work was required. Mrs Smithson had been chasing the local authority about the matter for some time now.

'We must introduce you to some more of our friends locally,' said Debbie. 'And you and Simon should come along to the belly-dancing,' she added, a twinkle in her eye.

'Belly-dancing? Are you joking?' said Kate. 'Is this some local coven?'

Debbie laughed. 'Hardly. The vicar's wife runs it – she's a dance teacher. It's at the church hall in Seddington on Friday nights. It's really funny who comes along. All ages, all sorts, all sizes!'

Seddington was a couple of miles away towards Halesworth. Fernley's vicar was also vicar there. Although Kate sometimes took the children to St Felix's Sunday School at Fernley, when there were services – Simon had refused point blank to go – she'd never been to Seddington church and had had no idea about all this other life that clearly went on there.

'I'll let you know, Debbie,' was all she said now. Belly-dancing, indeed!


Kate, Sam and Daisy returned to Paradise Cottage at four o'clock. The children were tired, and they showed it in the usual unhelpful way of misbehaving. Daisy kept calling Sam a 'weedy baby'. Sam kept hitting her with his toy sword until Kate took it away from him, then, at tea, he stood on a chair and threw his drink across the table at his sister. It missed and milkshake splashed all over the curtains. Kate bundled him up to his room. Then she went down to apologize to a tight-lipped Joyce.

'Don't worry, dear,' the older woman said. 'It's just I don't remember Simon ever doing anything like that when he was a child.' Kate thought Joyce had a rather rose-tinted view of the infant Simon – she knew more than enough about his stubborn streak if he didn't get his own way – but she didn't like to say anything. She brought Sam down to say sorry, then they settled the children in front of a video cartoon while Joyce made her a cup of tea.

'You look done in, dear.' She patted Kate's hand. 'Why don't you let me put them to bed tonight?'

'Joyce, I couldn't. You've had more than enough of the children this afternoon.' Was that the light of martyrdom in her mother-in-law's eyes, or a genuine desire to help? It wasn't easy to tell.

'They're quieter now,' Joyce said, almost pleading, 'and I could make my peace with Sam. Why don't you have a break – take Bobby out for a walk?'

Kate looked out of the window at the gorgeous golden evening. It would be wonderful to be out in the fields by herself. The temptation to skip the strung-out chores of children's bedtime was too much to resist.

'Thank you,' she told Joyce. 'And I'll ring Dad and Claire later. I need to escape.'

'A change of air will do you good,' said Joyce, and little did she know how true this would prove.

# Chapter 9

Kate hauled back Bobby, who was straining, rasping, on his leash, and swung the gate shut behind her. She looked up at the children's bedroom window. A small face was squashed against the glass in a halo of steam, the soft mouth spread, limpet-like in a parody of a kiss. Sam. Kate raised her hand and wiggled anemone fingers in an answering wave.

'Bobby, come *here*. Don't pull, you wretch,' she hissed. Taking the three-year-old spaniel out was not exactly a break, she thought crossly, then felt chastened. It was certainly a change from getting Daisy and Sam in and out of the bath. Real-life bedtime was never like the ads. Poor Joyce . . .

Ouch! Kate, preoccupied, had hardly noticed where she was walking and now it was through a patch of stinging nettles. Bobby had led her the 200 yards down to Fernley Lane and left along the rough verge towards his favourite rabbit-chasing place, the cornfields. She felt another flash of irritation. The farmer had just ploughed and after yesterday's rain the fields would be a quagmire. She should have worn her wellies. Hard luck, dog. 'It'll be through the village to the woods for us today, matey,' she said sternly and dragged him round. Bobby sat down in the road and looked at her, resentment in his eyes. She frowned at him and pulled. Badly trained animal. Over-indulged surrogate child. All this was true, unfortunately, but his soulful eyes could still melt the hardest heart. She wouldn't drag him all the way to Ketley Woods – that would be no pleasure for either of them. What should she do? She looked about for inspiration.

After a moment, a half-hidden notice across the road caught her eye. There, almost eclipsed by a huge holly bush, was a little opening between two hedgerows. Was it another way down to the woods?

'C'mon, Bobby!' Kate tugged. 'Rabbits!' she breathed in mock excitement. And this time when she pulled he came, sniffing the air joyfully. That was it with men, she thought, as she unclipped his lead. Mention food and off they go.

She grinned, the warm golden evening beginning to work its magic. The dry earth lane twisted and turned its way between the high hedges. It was like a maze, Kate realized with a growing feeling of excitement. She was being drawn on an adventure to she knew not where. The glowing disc of the dying sun poured liquid light on the chestnut earth, the knobbly roots of the hedge and the foliage shiny from the recent shower, and the air was filled with a heavy woody fragrance with high notes of spring flowers. There was Bobby, darting to and fro ahead, snorting and snuffling, occasionally raising his head to look at her with a look of doggy ecstasy. If only life here could always be like this.

She strode on, listening to the birdsong, feeling the tension gradually leave her shoulders. The path seemed to be curving away from the direction of Ketley Woods, uphill. Where was it taking her? It was widening now, and then suddenly, on the left, a high wall reared up. It was crumbly in places, the patterning in the bricks recognizably Victorian. The tops of trees loomed above. Occasionally the wall bulged or was breached where roots or branches tried to reclaim the space.

On she walked as if in a dream, the sun losing all its heat now, the light flickering from gold to silver to the colour of running water in the shadows of the great trees. A slight breeze picked up, lifting her fine hair. What might be over the wall? Kate wondered. There was something familiar about it.

Where was Bobby? It was a while since she had seen his feathery flag of a tail. She called. Silence, then Kate heard a single bark. She quickened her pace around the next bend in the path. No Bobby. Then something caught her eye. She stopped and looked.

A little door in the wall. A wooden door rounded at the top and with Gothic wrought-iron bars and a little slip latch. It was open slightly, shivering on its hinges in a sudden breath of wind. Could he have gone inside? 'Bobby?' she called. She made out another, more distant bark, this time definitely from the other side of the door. What should she do? She reached out her hand and pushed the door gently. It swung open and Kate stepped into the wild and beautiful garden of her dream.

Transfixed, she stood looking around, the door swinging to behind her. This was the same garden, the same house. No, the trees were taller, the walls more crumbly, the flowerbeds were overgrown, the greenhouse practically a ruin. It *was* the same garden, but many years on. There was evidence that the lawns were mown and the shrubs pruned, and of course the lovely Italianate features were still there, but the fountain wept no more, the gravel was scanty and the statues were half-covered in yellow lichen.

Kate was overwhelmed with shock. She raised her eyes to look at the house. Yes, that was how she remembered it. The wisteria, just coming into flower, covered more of the house.

The grapevine in the conservatory was gone, though. The house itself looked deserted. All the windows were closed, the curtains drawn across some of the upstairs rooms. Kate walked up the gravel path to the flagged terrace. She could see the familiar silhouette of the scrolled chaise longue through the French windows. Perhaps she could go and see . . . Then she came to her senses. She was trespassing. She must find Bobby and leave.

To convince anyone inside that she wasn't a creeping intruder, Kate marched noisily round the side of the house, rattling Bobby's lead and calling for him. The building was really quite extensive. This must be the kitchen, this the scullery, here some outhouses and, beyond, the kitchen garden. 'Bobby!' she called out. She heard a couple of yaps, then a steady volley of barks and whining noises. Kate ran round a gravel path to the front. And there, in the porch, was Bobby.

He was scraping at the huge wooden door, whining and yelping.

'Bad dog, come here. This isn't our house.' Surely if there was anyone in, they'd have come out by now to find out what the noise was all about. But there was nobody. 'Come *on*, Bobby.' He wouldn't budge. They looked at each other, Bobby waiting to see what she would do next. She reached out to grab his collar and she heard something. A cry. The spaniel barked and they both listened. There it was again. Definitely a weak cry. Kate inspected the bell pull on the right of the iron-studded door. She dragged it down. A clang sounded deep within the house. Then came the cry again but no footsteps.

Kate looked in vain for a letter box. She peered through a diamond-paned window to the left of the door, but a great vase on the inside sill blocked her view. Retracing her steps out of the porch, she gazed through the window of what appeared to be the dining room – it was so cluttered with furniture and bric-à-brac that only the huge table gave away its original function. Nothing moved. Hurrying back to the front door, she tried and failed to turn the iron handle. She went to investigate the room on the other side of the hall, pressing her face up against a window and squinting. The library. Walls of books and, again, junk everywhere. The door to the hall was ajar. She could just see the dark panelled walls, the hall as full of furniture and curios as the other rooms, and – it was like a kick in the stomach – a newel post of the great carved staircase from her dream. At the bottom she could see a shape. It moved slightly. An arm lifted.

Kate went back to the front door, put her mouth against the crack and shouted, 'Hello. Don't worry! I'm coming!'

She jogged back round the house to the scullery door. Solid wood. Locked. She'd have to break a window. How did they do it on the telly? She shivered at the idea of pushing a cloth-covered hand through the glass and instead took a rock from the nearest flowerbed.

In the end it was the work of a moment. There was the sudden, shocking sound of shattering glass, which set Bobby jumping and barking. She stood on a small broken chair she found in the kitchen garden, eased back the casement window, laid down an old builder's sack against the shards of glass, and hoisted herself through onto a work surface.

'It's all right,' she called out. 'I'm here.' She scrambled down onto the floor with care and made her way through the warm half-darkness in the direction of the hall, and there before her at the foot of the stairs, lay the figure of a very old lady.

'Oh, thank God, thank God,' the lady whispered, as Kate knelt down beside her. She was on her back and Kate pulled off her jacket, folded it and slipped it between the woman's head and the rug. She was so light and trembling – she must have been terrified lying here alone, Kate thought. She looked into the faded blue eyes, which were welling with tears, and even in the gloom could see the pain there. 'I've . . . broken something – my hip.'

'Don't worry, I'm here.' Kate spoke clearly to make sure she was heard. 'I need to ring for an ambulance.'

The woman's eyes squeezed closed as if against a wave of pain, and she gestured to the back of the hall.

'Where are we? I need to say an address.'

'Seddington House,' the woman breathed, then grunted as another wave of pain engulfed her. Seddington, the sister parish to Fernley. Kate remembered suddenly where she'd seen this lady before – outside the church there last summer.

Kate found a light switch, though the soft glow of the chandelier in the sunset was no more effective than candlelight. She used an old telephone on a console table in a corner. *Miss Agnes Melton*. That was the name on a doctor's appointment card lying by the phone.

The man on the 999 switchboard located the village of Seddington on his map and Kate answered his questions as best she could. She was told not to move the patient, but to keep her warm. Kate climbed the straight flight of stairs to find a blanket.

The galleried landing was carpeted, like the stairs, with a long Persian runner, bare boards on either side, and ran off in corridors to left and right. There was a door almost opposite the top of the stairs. Kate opened it and peered inside.

Right first time. Agnes Melton's bedroom. Once more, furniture was squeezed in against all available wallspace. Pictures, mainly landscapes in oils or watercolour, filled in the gaps. The surfaces were covered with china ornaments, a dressing-table set, vases of dried flowers, a wash basin and ewer . . .

Kate turned her attention to the single bed. It was neatly made, and a woollen travel rug lay folded across the foot. She grabbed it, but as she turned to leave the room, she noticed a photograph on the chest of drawers by the door and froze in surprise. It was a formal portrait of an Edwardian lady in a lacy white dress, very young, very beautiful. Although, in the photographic style of the time, she was not smiling, she looked as though she very much wanted to. But her face. How could it be? Kate stared a moment more, her mind spinning. Then she hurried back down to the great panelled hall. Above the front door, a stained-glass rose window cast patches of sunset onto the carpet and the wall below.

'Stupid fool that I am,' murmured Miss Melton as Kate tucked the blanket around her. 'Dropped my . . . special necklace alarm. In there.' She nodded towards the half-open door of the library. 'I needed pills – upstairs. Fell down. Broken my bally hip. Summers will be furious. Get me put in a home.'

'Don't talk, you'll exhaust yourself. The ambulance will be here in a moment.' Kate's voice was soft. She lifted Agnes's hand and began to stroke it. Gradually, the tension left the woman's face and her eyelids fluttered closed. She must have been very lovely once, thought Kate, with her fine eyes, her small heart-shaped face, high cheekbones and forehead. Her hair, still abundant, was swept up into a French pleat, and her face was framed by the high collar of a pretty cream blouse.

As she sat and stroked the woman's hand, the eyes opened again, the look was direct.

'I know you, don't I? Who are you?' Agnes asked.

'Kate Hutchinson. I've seen you at a distance, I think,' Kate said, 'but we've not met.'

'Kate,' she breathed. 'No, I don't know you. But you look like someone . . .' Then, after a moment, 'Talk to me, Please.'

'Yes,' Kate said, then felt tongue-tied. 'It'll be all right. I mean, the ambulance will be here in a minute.' Then, seeing an irritated frown cross Agnes's face she hurried on, 'Yes, I – that is, we, my children and my husband, live in Fernley. The next village along.' Don't be stupid, Kate, Miss Melton would know Fernley. 'We are living with my mother-in-law, Joyce Hutchinson. We've only been there since July. We're looking for a house, but we haven't found one yet.' She stopped. I'm babbling now, she thought.

Agnes's eyes were closed. 'Go on,' she whispered.

'Daisy and Sam go to Fernley School. Daisy is six. She has wavy fair hair like Simon, my husband. She's very good at reading and she likes animals. Sam's dark and more like me – "a late developer", Dad used to say . . . I'm sorry, I'm being very boring, talking about my family like this, and you in such pain. Is there anyone else I can ring for you?'

Agnes shook her head and gave a feeble gesture with her free hand. 'Summers is away. Go on with what you're telling me,' she commanded.

Kate wondered who Summers could be and where the ambulance was. Should she ring again? She'd wait a moment or two. Her mind moved on, searching for a new subject.

'Have you lived here long?' she whispered. Agnes nodded once. 'Since you were a child?' Agnes nodded a second time.

'It's a beautiful house,' Kate sighed. 'It must have been heaven being brought up here.' That was obviously a stupid thing to have said as Agnes's eyes snapped open and her gaze was angry.

'I'm sorry,' Kate rushed on. 'It's just my family used to move about so much . . . I think I must ring again and see if the ambulance has got lost.'

She laid down Agnes's hand and went to the phone. The man

assured her that the ambulance was in the area and would be there in a moment.

Kate put the phone back in its cradle and tried to give Agnes a little more water. Then she went to draw back the bolts on the front door and turn the key in the lock. The door opened easily. Bobby was lying in the porch but sat up expectantly. 'Stay there, good dog.' He slumped down again with a moan. Kate looked out across the gravel drive. A hundred yards down, through a garden of trees and shrubs, two great gateposts rose out of the gloaming. The wrought-iron gates stood open. As she watched, an ambulance turned into the drive, blue light flashing. Bobby got to his feet and let out a volley of barks.

'Shut up, Bobby.' Kate hurried back in. 'Miss Melton, it's here, the ambulance.' She crouched down again by the old lady's side, suddenly feeling she didn't want her to go away by herself in the ambulance.

Miss Melton seemed to sense this and gripped her hand. 'Kate Hutchinson,' she said in urgent tones and locked Kate in her stare. The ambulance pulled up in front of the door. Blue light strobed across the floor. 'Kate. You must go home now . . . I'll be all right. Come and see me, won't you? Come and see me. Tell Summers that . . .' Doors slammed, footsteps marched. Kate never heard what Miss Melton wanted her to say. Whilst the paramedics were busy, she found a bag and collected a few items for the old lady to take to the hospital. Up in the bedroom she glanced at the photograph again. Yes, the eyes that met hers could have been her own. It was almost like looking in a mirror.

After Miss Melton had been safely lifted into the ambulance and driven away – to the hospital near Great Yarmouth, one of the paramedics said – it was another hour before Kate was able to leave.

She had told them about the broken window and they said

she should call the local police station, so she did and then rang Joyce to explain what had happened and to say she wouldn't be home for a while.

'Is Simon back? Perhaps he could come and fetch me,' she added. But there was no sign of him yet, although it was a Friday and after nine. 'Don't worry, I'll ask for a lift.'

She did her best to sweep up the glass in the old-fashioned kitchen, then went to the library where Miss Melton had been sitting to make sure the electrics were turned off. By her armchair, a single standard lamp was burning. Kate stared round at the walls of books that faded off into the darkness, guessing that there must be valuable editions tucked between the collections of nineteenth-century literature and the annals of local history she could make out on the nearer shelves. She picked up the book Miss Melton had been reading: *The Dead Secret* by Wilkie Collins, and closed it at the bookmark. Then she looked under the armchair and found the dropped alarm, a special necklace that should be worn all the time and pressed to summon help in an emergency just like this one. She sat down in the chair, suddenly tired and troubled.

Headlights swept the shelves and wheels crackled over the gravel. A security light flooded the concourse. Kate went out to see what was happening. A creaky old orange-and-white Volkswagen van swung in a half-circle and parked as if used to doing so every day. As she waited, a hand on Bobby's collar, a tall rangy man in his mid-thirties with an unkempt mane of toffee-coloured hair jumped out, slammed the door, raised his arm to her in greeting and went round to open the rear door of the van. He pulled out a toolbox and walked over, smiling in an easy manner. She let go of Bobby, who trotted round the newcomer, sniffing interestedly at the paint on his jeans and sweater.

'I'm Dan,' the man said, putting out his hand and shaking Kate's. 'I work here sometimes. The constable rang me. Poor Miss Melton.' He shook his head. 'The very time her housekeeper has to go away. Lucky you were passing. How is she?'

Kate explained, all the while appreciating that he didn't seem to question her presence there. Everyone seemed very accepting of the situation. In London there would have been hordes of police nosing about asking her questions.

'Who is Summers?' she asked. 'Miss Melton mentioned that name.'

'Marie Summers, the housekeeper. She's in Ipswich tonight. Her sister's sick.'

Kate took Dan through into the kitchen to show him the broken window. She watched as he fetched a piece of hardboard and some wood from an outhouse and nailed up the gap. He worked quickly and efficiently, without talking. Kate thought about Miss Melton, the pain she must be in. Was she on the operating table even now?

Dan was finished.

'I'll get some glass in the morning,' he said. 'Now, I'll just set the alarm and then, if you're happy, I'll take you home.'

It was ten o'clock before the car pulled up outside Paradise Cottage.

'Here.' Kate scribbled Joyce's telephone number with a stubby pencil Dan produced. 'Please – let me know how Miss Melton is. I promised to visit her.' She looked at Dan. 'I so hope she'll be all right.'

She and Bobby got out. She waved to Dan and went in through the gate. When she turned her key and opened the front door, she could hear the sounds of a furious argument.

# Chapter 10

'Look, Mother, I don't want to talk about it,' Simon was shouting. 'I've had a hell of a week and I just want Kate to come home and to sit down for a bit of peace and quiet.' He looked up as Kate closed the front door and walked into the kitchen. 'Oh, there you are. What the heck have you been up to?'

Kate flinched and tried to take in the scene. Simon, tired, grimy and still in his coat, had scraped back his chair and half-risen before slumping down again. She caught a brief glimpse of Joyce's face, crumpled with misery, before her mother-in-law turned back to the sink and furiously started doing the washing-up.

'What a welcome! What's going on, Simon?' Kate said gently, bending to kiss his cheek. He shrugged but rumpled her hair.

'It's my fault.' Joyce turned round, her hands wet and her eyes full of tears. 'I was intruding. Come on, dearie. I'll make you a cup of tea. You must be done in. How is the poor lady? Simon was all for coming out to get you, but I said I thought you were being brought back. I hope I did right.'

Kate looked from mother to son and back again. She felt like crying herself, walking into this after all she'd been through already this evening.

'It was fine,' she said as calmly as she could. 'A guy called Dan gave me a lift. I think he must be the handyman. Anyway, he's going to find out how Miss Melton is in the morning. I'll make the tea, Joyce, then I think I'd just like to have a hot bath and go to bed. Simon, do you mind? You look tired, too.'

Just then the phone rang. Joyce picked up the receiver. After a moment she passed it to Kate. 'Your father. I told you he rang earlier, didn't I? He rang again a couple of hours ago,' she whispered.

Kate took the phone from her, wondering what could be wrong.

'Kate? At last.' Her father's voice was high-pitched with relief. 'Look, it's about your mother. She's all right now, thank God, but I'm afraid she has to stay in hospital for another of her little rests.'

'Oh no, Dad, what's happened? What's going on? You didn't tell me this was coming.'

'We thought we had her drinking under control recently, but this time she took some old pills of mine. I was prescribed them last year when I had trouble sleeping. There weren't many. We were lucky – the hospital washed her out. But she can't come home for a bit. I thought you'd want to know.'

'Dad, that's terrible. Poor Mum. I'll come right away.'

'No.' Major Carter's word was instant and firm. 'Wait a bit until she's more herself. I don't think she wants to see anyone at the moment. She won't speak to me, even. She's . . . she's gone inside herself. Look, I'll telephone you again when we've sorted her out a bit. Then you can come.'

'But Dad, I ought to be there, surely?'

'And you will be, but not right away. We need some time.' His tone was sharp through the weariness. 'I'm sorry,' he said, more softly.

So there she was, pushed away again. Kate put the phone down and stood there, deep in thought, the others watching her. Perhaps she could get in the car tomorrow morning and go? No, her father would be angry. He and her mother were just two people shut away against the rest of the world. Unfortunately, the rest of the world included their only daughter.

She explained in broken words what had happened.

'Your poor mother. And your father. Oh darling, I'm so sorry.' Simon hugged her.

'Come on, dear, here's your tea,' said Joyce. 'Let's bring it through to the other room, shall we, where it's comfortable. Then I'll run a bath for you.'

'Were the children all right?'

Joyce sighed. 'Sam flooded the bathroom being silly with that crocodile your old nanny sent him. You know, I wonder whether a little slap occasionally wouldn't do him any harm. It never seemed to have a bad effect on Simon.'

'No,' said Kate shortly.

Later, Simon and Kate climbed into bed and lay there in each other's arms.

'I hadn't realized your mother had got so bad again,' he said.

'I wish we'd encouraged them to come and visit more. They've only been that once.'

'Well, when your mother's better, I'm sure they can come again.'

'If we had a big enough house, it would be easier . . . Simon?'

'Yes?'

'What were you arguing about before I came in?'

'Oh, Mum was having a go at me. Not getting home often enough, not seeing enough of the kids, not getting on and look-ing for a house. Actually, she's starting to get quite antsy. Says she loves having us but we ought to find somewhere of our own.'

'Well, we should. It's too much for her. We've been here far too long. And I'm not sure that she and I see eye to eye on the upbringing of children. Oh, but I saw the most fantastic house today, Simon. Miss Melton's. Do you know, you're not going to believe me, but I think it's the one I saw in my dream.'

Simon turned and looked at her with an exasperated expression. 'You must have seen it before, then. You couldn't just dream about it without having seen it. Or a house like it. Unless you've been reading the kids too many fairy stories.'

She laughed. 'Maybe. But it gave me a most peculiar feeling, though.' A thought struck her and she got out of bed and went and rummaged in her jewel case. Then she remembered. She'd packed the locket away in a box for the shed. She got back into bed. Then there was the photograph in the woman's bedroom – oh, everything was so confusing.

'Will it be all right if I go and see Miss Melton this weekend? If she's OK and allowed visitors, that is?' she asked him.

'I don't see why not. What are the children up to tomorrow?'

'I ought to get Sam some new shoes. Then Daisy's got a riding lesson at half two. We'll have to see what time visiting hours are.' Kate rolled over and stroked Simon's face, then nuzzled her head into his neck.

'Mmm,' he said, his eyes closing. He didn't move away, but nor did he respond. She felt rather hurt, though she told herself he must be immensely tired after his week, as he usually was. They lay there for a few minutes in silence, then Simon disengaged himself and reached over to turn out the lamp.

'Goodnight, darling,' he murmured, yawning and pulling the duvet up over his shoulders.

'Goodnight.' Kate stared at his back in the darkness.

Despite feeling stretched thin with tiredness, her mind was alert and she lay awake turning over all the disturbing things that had happened that evening. Miles away, her mother lay in a hospital bed. Was it just a cry for help, taking those pills, or had she really wanted to die? She'd gone inside herself, Kate's father had said. Barbara had never tried anything like this before – what could have brought it on? Hadn't her father been able to gauge that things were coming to some sort of a crisis?

The thought of hospitals brought her to Miss Melton. She hoped Dan's call tomorrow would bring good news – she badly wanted to see the old lady again, not least to unravel the mysteries about the house and the photograph. There must be some family link somewhere – which made her think of her mother once more.

And then there was Simon. She reached out and touched his hair in the darkness. He didn't even stir. The poor darling was exhausted. They must find somewhere to live very soon, even if they had to rent. And she must talk to him again about his work: they couldn't go on living their lives like this, at a distance from one another.

How strange her new life here was turning out to be, how troubled. Before they'd moved, she'd thought certain things were going to be quite simple – that she and Simon would have more time for one another, that they'd find somewhere idyllic to call home. She'd been more worried about the children settling in, about missing her friends or about determining a sense of direction for herself. Yet the children seemed very happy with their new country environment. And she was missing her husband even more than her friends or a job.

Thirty miles away, Miss Melton slept deeply, the monitors by her bed flashing their regular message of reassurance. In her dream, she was a tiny girl again, her nanny calling.

'Agnes, Agnes! Come out of there, you'll wake her.'

Agnes stood by the four poster-bed, wondering why her mother was asleep in the afternoon. As Nurse swept into the room, her mother's eyes opened, she smiled and reached out her hand.

'Come on, darling. Come and cuddle down with me.' And little Agnes climbed onto the high bed and snuggled down in the damp warmth of her mother's embrace, safe and secure against the world, the scent of lily-of-the-valley all around her.

That afternoon, an age ago, was the last time she'd felt safe for a long, long time.

# Chapter 11

'Wake up, Mummy. Mummy, wake up! Daisy, come here, Daddy's home! Daddy, can we go in the garden? We've been watching telly for hours and now we want to go out.' There was a sudden draught as Sam lifted the end of the duvet and burrowed up between his parents. Simon rolled over and tickled him and the duvet slid off. A shivering Kate grabbed it. Daisy came to join the fray, shrieking with joy as her daddy pretended to bite her tummy.

'You'll have to get dressed first, darlings.' Kate yawned, when they all lay tickled out and panting. 'And have breakfast.'

'But I'm not hungry,' howled Sam. 'Garden, garden. Bobby wants to go out, too.'

'OK, well why don't you see who can get dressed the quickest?'

The children raced out and Simon pulled on his dressing-gown to go and make tea.

'Seven o'clock,' he moaned, peering at the clock. 'You'd think they'd give us an extra hour in bed at a weekend, wouldn't you? Where did we go wrong?'

At nine thirty promptly, the phone rang. Joyce had gone out, so Kate answered it.

'Kate? Hello, it's Dan here. Sorry if it's a bit early to call at the weekend. I thought you'd like to know that I rang the hospital and Miss Melton is doing fine. They've set her hip and she's had as good a night as can be expected. She's very woozy this morning, but she's eaten some breakfast.'

'I'm so relieved. It's really kind of you to let me know.'

'I don't know if you still want to go and see her? The hospital is close on an hour's drive. They reckon she'll be well enough to see people by tomorrow afternoon. It'll be good for her to have visitors, in fact, they said. I won't get there before four so it would be great if you could go.'

'If you don't reckon I'll be getting in the way of anyone else. Have you managed to speak to the housekeeper yet?'

'Marie? Not yet. Her daughter's ringing her – Tina something. Do you know her? She lives in Fernley.'

'That might be the mother of the girl who cleans for us. I can never get used to everyone being related to everyone else round here.'

'The only relative of Miss Melton I know is her brother's grandson. Max Jordan, his name is. I've only met him once. Mrs Summers'll have to ring him as I don't know the number.'

Kate wrote down the directions to the hospital and thanked him, saying she'd go about three thirty the next day, after she'd taken Sam to a birthday party at the church hall.

Shortly after she'd put the phone down it rang again. It was Claire. She didn't seem as chatty as usual, but you could never tell with phones, could you? Kate had seen her once or twice when she visited London, but Claire herself had never ventured beyond the M25 to visit Kate. Now, it seemed, she was suddenly free this weekend and wanted to come.

'Claire, it would have been lovely to see you but you're right – it's too late now, isn't it? I'm sorry I missed you yesterday. What about next weekend?'

But, no, next weekend was no good. Claire mentioned someone called Alex possibly being around and said that, no, she wasn't certain she could bring him. He might be around the following weekend, too, so she'd better not fix that up. June might be all right, after the fifteenth, possibly. It all sounded very unlike the Claire Kate knew, the Claire who was always in charge of her life.

'Well, if you won't tell me any more about this mysterious Alex and you can't come until mid-June, why don't you hitch a lift with Liz?' She suggested. 'They're all coming down at the end of June and she'll probably have a space in the car. I can fix up the B & B for you if you like. Oh, and you mustn't forget your walking boots and cagoul!' But Claire's laugh wasn't as ready as usual.

On Sunday afternoon, Kate followed Dan's directions to the hospital; it turned out to be a functional-looking two-storey modern building on a main road into Great Yarmouth. She was directed through several corridors to a small side-room off a large bright ward, where Miss Melton was propped up on a pile of pillows. In her pink brushed-cotton nightdress and with her white hair falling about her shoulders, only her pointed face and her faded blue eyes marked her out as the same person Kate had rescued on Friday night. But the nurses had obviously taken trouble with her. Her hair was brushed and Kate imagined she was wearing her false teeth – her face didn't have that caved-in look. Indeed, the old lady seemed surprisingly alert considering she had recently undergone an operation and was presumably taking something for the pain.

'Thank you for helping me. Don't know what I would have done, how long I might have lain there.' Miss Melton's voice was not much more than a hoarse whisper.

Kate didn't like to think of that either. She just said, 'It's funny, but in a way I believe it was meant to be. Something was drawing me there that evening.'

'What do you mean?' Miss Melton's question was sharp despite the hoarseness, and her eyes piercing, as if she were Kate's old headmistress asking her to explain herself after Kate had made some particularly woolly statement in an English lesson. Kate told her about the dream. That sounded foolish enough so she didn't tell her about the locket. She didn't want Miss Melton to think she was completely bonkers and, anyway, it might have been pure coincidence that she'd dreamed while wearing the locket.

After she'd finished, Miss Melton was staring into the distance. 'There *is* a kind of atmosphere about the house, you know.' She sighed. 'A sad one, I'm afraid. When I'm dead and gone . . .' She broke off in a fit of coughing and it was a moment or two before she could swallow some water and recover. She directed her intense gaze on Kate again. 'When I'm dead and gone, whoever comes next should sell all the rubbish and throw open the windows to blow the ghosts away!'

She stopped and studied Kate's face. 'There, I didn't mean to scare you. It's just that, when you asked me about my childhood . . .' She closed her eyes. 'Just let me say that I had some happy times there, very happy times. But that was all too long ago now,' she muttered, opening her eyes and staring round the room. There was silence for a moment, then she seemed to come to herself again. She smiled at Kate. 'What about you, my dear? Where were you brought up? Are your parents living?'

'Yes. Though my mother is unwell,' Kate said carefully. She was still getting used to the idea of Barbara's brush with death. She explained about the telephone call of two nights before and about her peripatetic upbringing.

'You don't sound close to your father and mother. Oh . . .' The old lady seemed to be in some pain now. She pushed a button on a pad on the bed and a nurse appeared and helped her change position. When she'd settled again, Kate said she thought she must go soon.

'Of course, dear,' Agnes said, her eyes closed. 'Tell me about your parents first.'

So Kate told her about her mother and father, and then found herself talking about Nicola.

'She died in an accident when I was seventeen,' Kate said. 'She was two years older.'

'Oh my dear,' said Agnes, opening her eyes wide. 'How very terrible.'

Kate stared out of the window, remembering. 'She had only just passed her test. Dad had bought a little runaround car for us to use and it was her second time out in it. We don't know exactly what happened, but she was driving down one of those narrow Surrey country lanes in the dark. She came off the road and crashed into a tree.'

Miss Melton's clear blue eyes were full of sympathy. 'I'm so sorry, my dear,' she said. 'I, too, lost people close to me when I was young. You never forget them. The years pass and you never forget.' And she closed her eyes tight. Kate wondered if she was drifting off to sleep, but then Agnes looked directly at Kate and smiled.

After a minute, Kate whispered, 'I'm sorry, I must have worn you out. I ought to go now. They'll be wondering where I am.' She stood up, then thought of something. 'Miss Melton . . .'

'Agnes, dear.'

'Agnes.' She stopped. 'In your bedroom, when I fetched the blanket, there was a photograph near the door.'

'Yes.' Agnes nodded. 'My mother. She died when I was three.

You're very like her, you know.' And she smiled. After a moment she said, 'You said your father's name is Carter. What was your mother's before she married?'

'Lane,' said Kate. 'She was Barbara Lane.'

'My aunt married a man named Lane,' Agnes said softly. 'She was my mother's sister and was ten years younger. I wonder . . .'

As Kate made her way down the stairs, she met Dan coming up. He paused, leaned against the wall, one arm stretched up the handrail towards her. Comfortable, strong. Kate explained that she was sorry, she felt she'd tired Miss Melton. Dan smiled, creasing the faint crow's feet at his eyes.

'I'm sure she was pleased to see you. I won't be staying long, just to say hello. Marie Summers came yesterday in the end. She was in a state when she heard, but she wanted to go straight away. She was going to check the house this morning and ring the grand-nephew.'

'I'll see you soon then, maybe,' said Kate.

'Yes. Come and see her again.' His blue eyes were warm as he stood smiling, waiting for her to pass.

That evening, Simon had booked them in for dinner at the Five Bells, a gourmet pub-restaurant five miles away. It was lovely to be going out, Kate thought, just the two of them.

'You don't have much fun after all those places you used to go in London, do you, darling?' he said as the waitress left them with their menus.

'Well, I must admit this is a real treat.' Kate looked round at the old beams, the collections of Toby jugs, horseshoes, farming implements that could have doubled as torture instruments and the inevitable hunting prints – 'the unspeakable in pursuit of the uneatable' was not a joke to be made too loudly round here.

'That chap Tim Beaton we met last week recommended this

place,' Simon said. He was in a good mood this evening. He had enjoyed a bit of gardening with Daisy while Kate and Sam were at the party, and then Bobby had taken the three of them on a muddy walk in the fields after Kate left to see Miss Melton and Joyce had put her feet up.

'Meet anyone interesting at the party?'

'Actually, yes,' she said. 'Sebastian's dad's a bit of a dark horse. Runs an antique shop in Saxmundham. Knows a lot about local history, too. He was telling me all about Dunwich. Did you know it was a huge port in the Middle Ages, before a lot of it fell into the sea in a storm? They say you can still hear the old church bells on a stormy day.'

'Get him to scare the kids with a few stories of Black Shuck, did you?'

'You mean the devil's dog with eyes like hot coals?' Kate shivered. It was a local legend.

'Don't worry, Bobby'd see him off,' laughed Simon and took a long draught of the local bitter that had just arrived with Kate's very unlocal Chardonnay.

'Bobby would see anyone off if he smelled like he did this afternoon.'

The spaniel had not distinguished himself by rolling in a manure heap. Simon, Sam and Daisy had had a fabulously messy time giving him a bath with, it turned out, Kate's Jo Malone bath oil. Now he smelt of horse poo with grapefruit high notes.

'So how did you get along with the old girl this afternoon? I haven't had a chance to ask you.'

'She wasn't too bad. Surprisingly alert. It's a good hospital and the nurses seem very caring and respectful of her. It's funny, you know. I wonder whether we're related.' And she told Simon about the photograph and the coincidence of names. 'I must ask

**117**

Mum. Not that I can at the moment, though.' She sat tracing circles on the tablecloth with her finger. Simon grasped her hand and held it tight.

Their food arrived and looked delicious. Kate had monkfish and Simon a very hearty steak and kidney pie. They ate hungrily and in silence, Kate trying out in her head different opening sentences to the matters that were on her mind and rejecting them all. Perhaps now, when they were sitting companionably together, wasn't the time for heavy discussion about their pressured lifestyle.

They had nearly finished eating when Simon's phone suddenly trilled. He ferreted around in his jacket on the back of the chair, pulled out the handset and gazed at the screen. A smile passed over his face and was quickly commuted to a frown. He pressed a couple of buttons and stuffed the mobile back in his pocket without looking at Kate. All he said was, 'Work.'

'On a Sunday night? Who?' said Kate.

'Oh – er, Gillingham. After some figures, I guess.'

The plates were taken away. Coffee arrived.

After furiously stirring in two sugars, Simon rested the spoon on the saucer and steepled his hands, his elbows resting on the table. He looked at Kate and seemed to choose his words carefully.

'We're having another difficult time at the office. I'm sorry I'm so late all the time. I know it's hard on you, and I know I don't see enough of the children.'

Kate relaxed. He was opening the conversation for her.

'It's certainly not how I thought it would be here.' She played with her cappuccino, making snowy mountains of the frothy milk with her teaspoon. She put the spoon down. 'I'm frankly in limbo,' she said. 'And you seem so far away . . .'

Simon gave a heavy sigh. 'I just have a lot on my plate right now.' He began to fiddle with the sugar bowl on the table beside him.

'Is there anything I should know about? Are you frightened of losing your job, is that it? Whatever it is, don't worry, we can sort it out.'

He looked at her in silence. 'No,' he said finally. 'Nothing like that. It's going pretty well, in fact, much better than last year. I'm enjoying it – more than any job I've ever had, I'd say. Gillingham says I might be up for promotion soon. No, it's still this European thing. Just too few heads to do too much work. It doesn't help having Mother nagging me, though. I could really do without that.' He looked at his watch. 'We ought to get back, really, oughtn't we? I must be up early tomorrow. There's an eight-thirty meeting.'

While they waited for the bill, Simon looked at Kate, then reached over and stroked her cheek. 'Don't worry,' he said. 'We will start looking for a place of our own again – when things settle down at work. I just need to get through this next bit with the Frankfurt trips. I know it's not been fair on you. I'm sorry.' He stopped. 'I do love you, you know, Kate.'

Kate gave him a watery smile and rubbed her face against his hand. 'I know,' she said. 'I don't think I could bear it all if you didn't love me.'

He smiled but his eyes were troubled.

# *Chapter 12*

On Tuesday, when Kate phoned her father, it was to hear better news.

'They're sending her home tomorrow. Giving her some pills to cheer her up, poor old thing, but it'll be good to have her home. Dogs are missing her like billyo.'

'Oh, that's wonderful, Dad! But are they sure she's ready?' asked Kate.

'The doctor said something about counselling,' grunted Major Carter, 'but I said we'd see. She needs a holiday, I reckon. I'm booking up that place in Spain again for the end of the month. She likes it there now she can take the dogs. Golf was good, too.'

'Oh, I was going to ask you to come and stay round here again.'

'We'd like that, yes. We'll see how it goes. She might find the kids a bit much at the moment, though.'

'Oh.'

'Not that she isn't fond of the children, don't get me wrong,' he added hastily. 'They're bright little things.'

'Yes, Dad.' Kate sighed. If only her parents would get to know Sam and Daisy better – it would be good for both sides.

'But your mother would love to see you. I don't suppose there's any chance of you popping down sometime? By yourself, I mean?' Kate felt a rush of relief at the invitation.

'That would be great, Dad, I'd love to come. I'll have to talk to Joyce, though. Simon's away for a few days in Germany, but she won't mind managing them for a night. Would tomorrow be all right?'

Joyce had sighed, but had agreed to look after the children, and the next morning, after Kate had delivered Sam and Daisy to school, she insisted on making Kate a Thermos of too-weak coffee ('just in case you need a break from the driving, dear') and waved her off in the car.

Barbara was much better than Kate had feared. She was a bit disconnected because of the anti-depressants but, back home, distanced from her usual misery by the excitement and the medication, she was actually quite chatty.

'I don't know why everyone's making so much of it all,' she said, while enjoying the unaccustomed attention. The door bell and the telephone hardly stopped ringing. The doctor came, the next-door neighbours brought flowers, Kate's jolly, unmarried Aunt Maggie, her father's sister, came up from Sussex for afternoon tea.

'It was just an accident,' Barbara insisted to Kate that evening as Desmond was clearing up in the kitchen after supper and making coffee. Ringo and Benjy were curled up together on their mistress's lap as if to stop her leaving again. 'I thought the pills were the paracetamol. I had such a headache, you see.'

Kate forbore telling her mother that you never take so many paracetamol at one go either; she was reluctant to do anything to affect her mother's unusual cheerfulness. She still wished she had accepted the suggestion of counselling, but their generation could be so suspicious of it. All she could get Dad to agree to was that he would ask Mum to consider it. Now she steered the conversation on to the other question to which she so much wanted an answer – the mystery of the photograph at Seddington House.

'Mum, you know you said you had holidays in Suffolk when you were little, was that staying with family?'

'Yes. My brother and I were sent to stay with Uncle Chris and Aunt Cecily. Where was it – began with a W. Wood something.'

'Woodbridge?'

'That was it. And they took a house by the sea in Southwold one summer. Nineteen fifty-four, it would have been. I was sixteen. They were still getting over those awful floods. Everything was a terrible mess, I remember.'

'Christopher's name was Lane, wasn't it, like yours?'

'Yes, that's right. You remember Chris and Cecily, don't you? I visited Chris once or twice in hospital before he died. No? And their daughters, Marion and Frances, coming to your wedding?'

Kate frowned uncertainly. 'Just about,' she said.

'They're my first cousins. Marion is two years younger than me and Frances four. '

'And what did Grandad do? Wasn't he a civil servant before the war?' Kate was fascinated. It was a long time since they had talked about the family tree and her mother seemed unusually animated, remembering the distant past. Kate's grandfather had died in the D-Day landings and her grandmother when Kate was ten or eleven. Kate remembered Barbara telling her Grandad and Grandma had married very young.

'Yes, his name was Philip and he was Chris's younger brother. There was a sister, Lucy, as well, but I don't remember meeting her much. She moved to New Zealand when she married.'

'Mum, did you ever meet anyone in the family called Melton?'

'Melton . . . Yes, that was the name I was trying to remember. When we drove back from seeing you last time, we went through a village and the sign reminded me.'

'Was the village called Seddington?'

'Yes. My grandmother was called Florence. She had an older sister, Evangeline, who had died. Once or twice when we stayed at Woodbridge, we visited a lady Chris said was a cousin, her daughter. Do you remember? I told you. She was the one with the maid – a proper maid with a uniform. It was a big house with tall chimneys. Full of antiques. I found a picture somewhere. Desmond,' she told him as he came in with the coffee, 'it's Melton – the name of my father's cousin that I was trying to remember. Could you dig out the album again? I want to show Kate.' Barbara nodded to herself. 'Agnes Melton. Yes. Aunt Agnes, I was told to call her. Though she wasn't my aunt at all.'

When her husband returned, Barbara flipped through the black pages of the shabby little photograph album he handed her. Kate watched with stirring awareness. She hadn't seen that album before, had she? Maybe she had, long ago, when she was a child.

The picture on the page her mother showed her was blurred, but instantly recognizable. It was a snapshot of a house taken from the end of the drive, a teenaged boy – Barbara's elder brother Kenneth who had died as a soldier in the Suez crisis – standing on the grass waving. The high chimneys, the light reflecting off the diamond-paned windows – it was the house of her dream.

'And so we must be related!' Kate told Agnes.

It was early Monday afternoon, a week after Agnes's accident, and Kate had driven over to see her. Debbie was having Daisy and Sam to tea and Kate didn't have to pick them up until six.

'Well, that explains so much,' Agnes said, nodding in wonder. She was sitting upright in the bed today although, she'd grumbled to Kate, the nurses had been trying to get her up and walking about. 'With that blasted thing.' She had nodded grimly at the Zimmer frame parked at the other side of the bed. Kate gathered the walking experiment had not been successful.

' Which makes us, Kate – well, let's see . . . first cousins twice removed.'

'I never understood how that worked. What does the removed mean?'

'It means that you are two generations away from being my first cousin. The children of each of a pair of first cousins are second cousins to one another, but those children are a generation removed from their parents' first cousin relationship.'

'I see, so if all of those second cousins go on to have children . . .'

'That new generation will be third cousins to one another, but second cousins once removed to each other's parents. Personally I always liked the phrase "kissing cousins", which is a general term used when everything gets too complicated to work out. You and I shall be kissing cousins.' She held out a hand to Kate and the young woman clasped it. They sat for a moment, beaming at one another.

'But I still can't get over how like my mother you look,' the old lady went on. 'It's uncanny. Especially since I remember Barbara and she didn't take after our side of the family.'

'Yes, it's funny how looks can skip generations. And then some children seem to be mini-versions of their parents. I can never meet our friend Laurence's parents without smiling;

124

they're so tall and thin like their three sons that their conversation at family events goes on above the heads of everyone else!'

'I looked very like my mother, although my hair was lighter than hers.'

'I know you said your mother died when you were little. That must have been awful for you. Had you any brothers or sisters? Did your father marry again?'

At first Agnes did not respond. She seemed to be thinking. And what she was thinking about made her sad. Finally she said, 'I'd like you to know about it all. There's been no one else to tell. Not my brother – he's been dead many years. I have a great-nephew. Summers says he's coming to see me, but he's not turned up yet. Sent those, though.' 'Those' were a large arrangement of hothouse flowers on a table in a corner of the room. 'Lives in Norwich. No, it's too long a story for today. Go on, off you go, you've got to fetch your children. Pass the tissues, would you? Then find the nurse for me. I need to get up.'

Agnes was clearly in some discomfort, but it wasn't just physical. It was as though Kate had accidentally touched some nerve, for her mood had changed. Kate gave Agnes the fruit she'd brought, then when the nurse arrived, quietly slipped away.

As she made her way back to the car, Kate thoughts turned, as they often had over the last few days, to her mother's photograph album.

'Have I seen this book before?' she asked her parents, but they didn't know. They weren't the kind of family who pored over photographs of the past together. Maybe she had once found this little album and turned the pages of this other world, a world where her mother was young and smiling, where Kate's lost Uncle Kenneth stood waving in front of a house from a dream. And it had stayed in her subconscious all these years . . .

*

The next week, when Kate got to the hospital, it was to find that Agnes's housekeeper had already arrived. Marie Summers turned out to be the person Kate had seen helping Agnes into the car outside the church the previous summer. She was a pleasant woman, clearly fond of her employer, and she insisted that Kate stay.

Agnes asked after Simon and the children, then cross-questioned Mrs Summers about the state of Seddington House. Yes, Dan had started painting the kitchen, yes, the police had been round to discuss security and new alarms were being installed. Kate gathered that Mrs Summers often stayed at the house but, that with Agnes in hospital, she sometimes asked her son Conrad, who was perpetually out of a job, to be there instead. Agnes seemed to approve of this. Dan would be visiting later in the afternoon.

After a while, Mrs Summers got up and said goodbye, but by that time there were only ten minutes before Kate herself had to go and pick up Daisy and Sam.

'It sounds as though the house is being properly looked after while you're away,' she said to the old lady.

'Yes, it's a great worry. All those things I've collected over the years. I had a friend from the auctioneers at Ipswich to look at everything several years ago. She seemed to think it was all very valuable. I should have got rid of it all then, but I couldn't face it. It's all I've got in life. Memories and old things. I lost everyone, you see. And now I'm stuck in here.' Agnes's tone was fierce. She stared out of the window at nothing.

'When did you start collecting?' Kate tried a new tack. Agnes became quite animated again.

'Oh, I've always been a magpie, ever since I was a child. My father encouraged me. First shells and stamps, then coins, then, one day, when I was nine or ten, I found a miniature of a lady in a blue dress in a junk shop. Eighteenth century, it turned out.

Very pretty, but damaged, so it cost next to nothing. And so my passion began. But it was only after the war – Hitler's war, that is – that I got serious. Father had died, you see, and I had nothing else to do with the money.'

'Did you ever . . . consider marriage?' Kate was nervous of upsetting Agnes again.

'I had my chance,' sighed Agnes, 'but I ruined it. I'll tell you about it one day. But I'm tired now. And you must go.'

As Kate was gathering up her things, Agnes said casually, 'Max called in on Saturday.'

'Did you say your great-nephew lives in Norwich?'

'That's right. Barrister there. Had a wife, don't know what happened to her – he says it didn't work out. Don't think he likes hospitals. He didn't stay long.'

'Well, it's good he came, though,' Kate said, and Agnes nodded thoughtfully, something of a gleam in her eye.

It was now the second half of May. Kate nearly didn't make it to see Agnes the following week. Monday, she spent the day in London, meeting Liz for lunch and seeing the Braque exhibition with her old schoolfriend Sarah in the afternoon. Sarah's children had both started school and she chattered happily about how nice it was to have some time for herself, though it was a shame that her husband, Jamie, *would* work such long hours at his computer consultancy.

'Do you miss London?' Sarah asked, as they sat over a sandwich in the gallery restaurant.

Kate finished her mouthful, trying to arrange the confused emotions the question evoked. 'It was horrible getting off the train at Liverpool Street station and being struck by the noise and the crowds and the pollution. And the tubes are still awful. I don't miss any of that.'

'What about the shopping? And the exhibitions, and the theatre? It must be so quiet down in Suffolk.'

'It's busier in the summer. I went to a lovely organ recital last week, and there are always little art exhibitions.'

Sarah wrinkled her nose. 'Surely nothing like we've just seen.'

'No. I suppose I do feel a sort of bereavement coming back here.'

'Oh?'

'It's hard to explain. It's like I'm a ghost coming back to see my past life. I feel forlorn that everybody is happily going on without me. That I'm shut out.'

'Well, you can't have your cake and eat it,' Sarah said sniffily.

Kate hadn't really expected her to understand. Sarah had always been a practical girl who got on with the job in hand and dismissed 'the path not taken' as morbid nonsense. Kate wished she could have seen Claire today as well. She would understand. Mysteriously, Claire wasn't answering her phone at home and her mobile was on voicemail.

At six, Kate met up with Simon for a drink. He seemed harassed. Another trip to Germany was coming up and his team were working day and night to get the presentations together.

'I'm off on the plane on Wednesday morning, and I've left my damned passport in Suffolk.'

He didn't have time to come down to fetch it, so Kate eventually agreed to bring it up the next morning, together with his dinner jacket, which she had just had cleaned.

When she got home at ten o'clock that evening and started rummaging through Simon's bedside table for the passport, she found his building society passbook attached to it with an elastic band. Although the account was in his name, Simon had always been careful to explain that the money was a nest egg for both of them. They had a few other investments, of course, and the proceeds of the sale of the Fulham house were in an account that paid out monthly interest, which Kate used to give Joyce some housekeeping money. Still, Kate thought she'd check just how much extra they had. She faintly remembered that Simon had said, 'Oh, eleven thousand or so,' when she'd asked six months ago. But when she ran her eye down the figures, she frowned. The £11,300 that was recorded had dwindled in the past six months to £6,010. Where had all the money gone?

On impulse, she picked up the phone and dialled the number to Nigel's flat. After ringing for a while, a recorded voice clicked on. Perhaps Simon was still at the office. She rang his direct line there but it switched immediately to voicemail. She tried his mobile. It rang three times, then went dead. Eventually she left a tetchy message on the flat number to say she'd meet him at twelve and went to bed.

'But where's it all gone?' she asked Simon the next day in the Starbucks coffee shop by his office.

'Life is very expensive here at the moment,' said Simon, not looking at her. His coffee was pushed away untouched. 'There's my season ticket coming up for renewal, then I'm paying Nigel. And there was the optician's bill last month – and it's not cheap eating up here, you know.'

'Yes, but that doesn't add up to five thousand pounds. And you've been doing so well at work. There was your salary rise at Christmas, and the bonus.'

'The bonus wasn't that much, Kate.' As an accountant rather than one of the dealers, his rewards were modest. 'And we put it in the pension pot, remember?' Simon was on edge now, looking at his watch, tapping his foot.

'But you could have told me about this.' Kate prodded the passbook on the table before her.

'What d'you want me to do, ring up the wife for permission every time I write a cheque? For God's sake!'

Kate flinched. This was so unlike Simon. 'I didn't mean . . .' She was lost for words.

'No, I know. Look, we can't talk about this now.'

'I suppose you've got to get back to work.'

'Yup, sandwich lunch with Gillingham *et al*. Three-line whip. C'mon, darling, I'm sorry I was sharp. Everything's so stressed at the moment. Let me put you in a taxi.'

Outside on the street, he rattled the coins in his pocket and said, 'Let's have another look at that old farmhouse outside Diss this weekend, eh? That one with the huge kitchen. Durrant's rang this morning. The owners have reduced the price.'

He kissed her on the cheek and helped her into a cab. A quick wave and he had gone. Kate sat there as the taxi pulled away, stunned at how he had just brushed her off – had refused to discuss something as important as their finances and then just dispatched her like a parcel. Suddenly she remembered the house he'd mentioned. It had been too small upstairs and too isolated, they'd decided. Had he really forgotten? What was going on?

On Wednesday night, Marie Summers rang to tell Kate that since Agnes was now out of the surgeon's care she was being moved back to Halesworth the next day to the community hospital there.

'It's a nice place and it'll be easier for us to visit,' she said comfortably.

On Friday afternoon, Kate drove into Halesworth and parked outside the hospital, a pleasant redbrick building in spacious grounds. But when she reached the little room Agnes had been allocated, it was to find the old lady was asleep.

'She didn' have a good night,' whispered the young West Indian nurse, who had accompanied Kate. 'The pain was botherin' her, my dear. And she was worryin' about something. So Doctor gave her some pills after lunch.'

Kate sat by the bedside for a while, watching Agnes. Her sleep wasn't restful – her lips were moving without sound, her face contorted in a frown. She looked very, very old now and, without her teeth, her face looked all caved in. There was hardly a scrap of flesh on her, thought Kate, noting the thin wrinkled skin hanging over the proud cheekbones. How old was she? Well over ninety, surely. And yet the sharpness of her mind and the strength of her spirit belied her age.

Kate was surprised at her feeling of tenderness towards the tiny figure in the bed. It was such a strange coincidence, the way they had met, and such a short time ago, but already, she and Agnes seemed to have formed a strong bond, the same as she had used to feel with her Hastings grandmother. It wasn't just the fact of their being family, though that was part of it. Although there were sixty years between them, they were kindred spirits. Was it because they were both wounded birds? Kate didn't yet know the full extent of Agnes's emotional wounds, though losing her mother so young had had an obvious effect, but she hoped as she got to know her cousin better, that she would learn something of the secrets she guarded.

After ten minutes spent deep in thought, she left the bottle of elderflower cordial and the copy of *Mansfield Park* she'd brought on the bedside table and got up to go.

'Hello, you've found her then.' Dan had put his head round the door. He looked at Kate appreciatively and she automatically smoothed her hair.

'Oh, hi. Haven't seen you for ages,' she said, a touch shyly.

'No. I went to the other place every week, but not till late most times. Thought I'd get here early today. I needed some parts from the garage, so it seemed sensible to drop in here first.'

'Bit of a wasted trip for you, I'm afraid.' And Kate explained about the sleeping pills. As they walked down the stairs together, she asked him about his work.

'I help out at Seddington a couple of mornings a week,' he said. 'Do a bit of gardening, repairs – that sort of thing. Wish I had more time to go there. That garden needs a lot of looking after.'

'Maybe Miss Melton will be home before too long.' Kate paused on the bottom step. In front, Dan swung to face her. His blue eyes looked deep into hers.

'I hope so, Kate, I do hope so.' Then he said, 'Whatever happens, meeting you has made a difference to her. She talks about you a lot, you know. I gather you're cousins or something. It's so amazing that you found each other like that.'

Kate smiled. 'Yes, it makes you believe in destiny or something. And she's made a difference to me. Now she's nearby I want to bring the children to see her – do you think she'd like that?'

'I think she might. Why don't you do that?'

The next morning, by the time she got back from taking the children to school, Kate and Simon's credit-card statements had arrived. Kate opened hers. No surprises there. For half an hour, she prowled around, wrestling with her conscience. At ten o'clock, when Joyce went out with Bobby, she took Simon's envelope into the kitchen and steamed it open. She couldn't believe her eyes. Simon owed £4,000 on his card. She read the list of entries. £430 for some dental treatment, yes, but over £1,500 to City restaurants? £700 to British Airways? She resealed the envelope but the operation didn't look convincing, so she ripped it open again. She could always pretend she'd done so in error. But in the end, when Simon came home, she didn't even bother to do that.

'Look, it's all right, Kate. God, you're so suspicious What's got into you lately? It's just I lost my business credit card. Really stupid – can't think how it happened – and the new one didn't come through straight away. Then Zara had to fix up some German flights at a moment's notice, so I got her to use my personal card. I've got the new company one now so I just have to claim this little lot back. All right? Satisfied?'

I want to be convinced, Kate said fiercely to herself, but her feeling of uncertainty grew. Why was Simon becoming so distant? There were times when he seemed to be miles away and would jump when she spoke to him. He was rarely unkind, just absent.

May turned to June. Kate took the children to EuroDisney at half-term; it turned out to be an exhausting affair, especially since they wouldn't sleep thanks to all the E-numbers they consumed and the high-pitch level of excitement. Simon had been supposed to come too, but a week before they were due to leave, he was dispatched to Germany again – Munich, this time. Joyce was reluctant to take his place on the basis that it would be too tiring so Kate, disappointed, bit the bullet. While it was lovely being on her own with the children, she missed Simon dreadfully, not least because he always took responsibility for tickets, passports and finding seats on trains.

The Carters came back from Spain and settled into their normal routine. They talked about coming up to see the family in Fernley, but kept putting it off. Then one of the dogs developed kidney trouble and Barbara didn't want to leave home.

Simon was working as hard as ever, with regular trips to

Germany and sometimes further afield. He remained remote and hardly touched Kate. Money was a subject they avoided. Simon seemed to be spending more on clothes – two Armani summer suits, a pair of handmade shoes. Well, it was important for presentation, Kate thought. But Simon had always been so careful with money. She couldn't quite shrug off the feeling that he was hiding something, but he avoided all her attempts to talk seriously about money or moving or changing jobs. She drifted through her days with a sense of disquiet, not daring to face what was happening to their relationship.

Her greatest comfort every week was going to visit Agnes.

# *Chapter 13*

*June 2004*

On the sixth of June it was Kate's thirty-sixth birthday. Joyce offered to collect the children from school, so that Kate needn't hurry back from visiting Agnes. Early in the afternoon, Kate arrived at the hospital to find that her cousin had a little package for her wrapped in tissue paper and tied with a blue ribbon. When Kate unfolded the paper, she found a string of large pearls with a diamond-studded clasp.

'Agnes, they're beautiful. But I can't accept them – they must be so valuable.'

Agnes smiled proudly. 'Well, who else would I give them to? They were my mother's, but I've no use for them now. Go on, put 'em on.'

Agnes was sitting up in a wheelchair by the window today. She was wearing a blouse and skirt and someone had put her hair up for her. Only her socks and slippers and a greyness about the face gave away her status as a patient.

Sitting opposite, Kate slipped the pearls round her neck. They lay warm on her collarbones, and when she looked in the mirror over the little sink they seemed to glow. She stared at herself.

With her slightly parted lips and her dark hair tucked behind her ears, she fancied she could pass for the portrait in Agnes's bedroom – if it weren't for her own air of sadness.

She turned back to Agnes, who seemed to think the same for she said, 'I've always believed they were the ones my mother wore in the photograph.'

'What was her name, your mother?' asked Kate, taking advantage of Agnes's cheerful mood.

'Evangeline. My father was besotted by her. People don't know their Longfellow any more, but Father had written on her gravestone, *When she had passed, it seemed like the ceasing of exquisite music*. She was buried with the baby boy that had never breathed.' Agnes stared out of the window, where the rain was falling in torrents. Kate waited, hoping she'd go on.

'People talk about bereaved lovers being heartbroken. I think my father just wanted to die. For weeks he shut himself in his room. Then one day, he signed up for the army and was sent to the trenches. For my elder brother Raven and me it was like losing both our parents in one stroke. I was too little to understand. I was used to them being away sometimes and I loved my nurse. But for Raven it was terrible.' Agnes shook her head as though the memories of ninety years ago were fresh upon her. 'But when Father came home a year later, he found he could go on with life again.' She looked at Kate. 'You asked once whether he married again. Well, he did and I can remember the day he broke the news . . .'

*Suffolk, July 1927*

If, as a small child, Agnes Melton climbed on a stool and peered out of the window of the highest attic of Seddington House, she fancied on a clear day she could see over the tops of the poplar trees that marked the garden's boundary with the road, across the rolling woods and fields of Suffolk, to the wetlands and the sea beyond. Her brother, Raven, had always sneered at this idea, and said that the line of distant blue was just part of the sky, but to be able to see the sea was vital to the romances that the lonely little girl wove about herself, and so she persisted in her belief. Today, as a willowy sixteen year old, no longer in need of the stool, it was still possible to imagine that the house's site on the gentle slope of a hill gave them a vista of the coast three miles away.

The attic had always been one of her favourite places on a sunny summer's day, and when she could escape from her governess, Miss Selcott, Agnes could either be found curled up with a book on the old swing seat in the rose garden or up here playing with her dolls in a den she'd made of the old iron bedstead and the broken furniture. It was warm and quiet in the attic, and Agnes would lie and listen to the buzz of the flies on the windows, the screeches of peacocks and the distant sounds of the life of the house, and fall into a daydream that, instead of being an ordinary-looking (for so she saw herself), motherless little girl, she was a great beauty and queen of all the lands around, that the dolls were her ladies and confidantes and that Alf, the gangly gardener's boy, was the latest of a line of princes who came to ask for her hand. Down at the harbour at Southwold, she imagined, bobbed a fleet of tiny ships bearing her ensign, only awaiting a fair wind and the swell of the tide to launch them across the sparkling seas in search of riches and adventure.

The attic was also an excellent lookout when her father was expected home from one of his all-too frequent trips to London, and this was why Agnes had come up here today. He would take the train to Halesworth to be met by Lister in the car. The child used to stand, teetering on her perch, where she could see the road, and when she spotted the silver Bentley, tiny in the distance, turning the bend and tipping down the hill, she would jump down in a clatter of falling furniture and, with a shriek to Raven, race harum-scarum down two flights of stairs and out of the front door in time to see the car nosing in at the great iron gates.

Little Agnes knew that Gerald Melton was the most wonderful father any girl could wish to have. He would wave frantically at his daughter as she stood jumping up and down on the doorstep, then, when the car drew to a halt and Lister strode round to open the door, he would step down stiffly, with the help of his stick, and open his arms to her.

'How do, little princess. Haha!' And he would envelop her in the folds of his greatcoat and squeeze her tight. She would rub her nose in his tickly tweed waistcoat with its familiar smell of warm wool and tobacco and know that everything was all right again. 'Well, damn it, I'm sure I had some little somethings somewhere,' he would groan, patting his pockets. 'Don't say I left 'em on the train.' And a pantomime would ensue whereby she would search all his pockets and his briefcase and the car until they found whatever he had brought with him this time – a little ornament for her collection or a dolls' tea-set or a necklace of shiny red beads.

In the meantime, Raven, loitering on the steps behind the servants, always too superior for such displays of enthusiasm, would slouch over to let his father ruffle the blue-black hair that gave him his nickname, and to snatch whatever packet Agnes held out to him. Then he would lope back inside to open his present in private. Gerald Melton would look after him in puzzlement; his only son, handsome and intelligent though he was, was a sulky enigma to him. It was Agnes he felt at ease with, this friendly child who teased and flirted with him, who took him inside and asked about his trip as a wife would have done, and helped him into a chair in the drawing room, and loosened his tie and ordered tea.

*Like a wife.* The other reason Gerald could bond so well with his little daughter was that she had such a look of Evangeline – her hair was wavy and lighter in colour, but the blue eyes, the full lower lip, the beguiling expression were the same. Any other grieving widower might recoil from such a constant living reminder of the woman he had loved and lost, but Gerald found the thought that Evangeline lived on in her daughter a comforting one.

It hadn't always been like this. Soon after his wife had died giving birth to their third child – a stillborn boy – the Great War had broken out. His excuse for joining up was his officer training at Sandhurst, but in all reality he was so heartbroken at the loss of Evangeline he was reckless of his own life and immune to the needs of his children. When he'd been sent home with a shattered leg and a dose of mustard gas, a year later, he had been forced finally to spend time with Raven and Agnes. However, by then, the damage to his relationship with Raven had already been done. The youth was eventually packed off to Bellingham's, a public school where, as far as Agnes could gauge, he had lied, cheated and charmed his way through something by way of an education. Gerald Melton had been hurt by his son's obvious resentment, was at a loss how to deal with his dark moods. But he had been drawn to Agnes, so sweet and sad and lost, Agnes, who would climb into his lap and tell him she was so sorry for him and that she loved him.

Agnes had always recognized the nature of this close bond with her father, and now she was sixteen was looking forward to filling the gap in the household left by the death of her mother thirteen years before. Although her head was currently full of

Tennyson's poems and the novels of the Brontës, and her day-dreams were of romantic trysts, she had as yet no admirers and felt marriage must still be years away. In the meantime, she could take over the running of the house for her father. She would learn to negotiate with Cook and look after the accounts – but only if she could get round her rival for the role, her governess Miss Selcott.

When Raven had first gone away to school, Agnes had missed him terribly, but she enjoyed a steady friendship with Diana, the Rector's only child, and in the school holidays, both girls followed Raven around like lambs; he would organize their games and make them perform terrible dares like walking on the garden wall or soaking poor Alf with the garden hose.

In termtime, with Raven away, first at school and latterly at Cambridge, Miss Selcott ruled Agnes and Diana with a rod of iron. There were lessons from nine o'clock until one every day, then a rest after lunch followed by physical jerks – the governess was a keen proponent of regular exercise – followed by a nature walk, weather permitting, or silent reading in the library if not. Both Agnes and Diana were good and dutiful scholars, and, if they didn't actually like their governess, they did not mind any of this. What Agnes did mind was the transparent way in which Jane Selcott sought the attentions of her employer, and her never-ending efforts to show that she was superior to the rest of the staff of Seddington House.

Cook, the redoubtable Mrs Duncan, knew her place – as mistress of the kitchen and, in the absence of a housekeeper, the guardian of the household accounts. She also knew Miss Selcott's place, and that, Agnes sometimes overheard her telling Ethel, the maid, was *not* to order her, Mrs Duncan, around. From time to time, Miss Selcott would try to alter a menu or comment loudly to Lister about the quality of Ethel's dusting and a genteel kind of low-level warfare between the governess and the rest of the servants would rumble along for a while.

As she grew up and became more aware of downstairs politics, Agnes sometimes wondered how on earth Seddington House ran as smoothly as it did. It was partly down to Mrs Duncan's natural authority and efficiency, she decided, partly down to Lister the butler's phlegmatic nature, and partly down to Ethel's tact and good humour. Alter any ingredient in the mixture and the household might descend into crisis.

Recently, though, the natural order had begun to change. Mrs Duncan had started to show Agnes the housekeeping accounts and Mr Walters, the elderly gardener, would occasionally ask her opinion about a new rose or the quality of the vegetables. Though still utterly loyal to Gerald Melton, for whom they had the greatest respect, it was as though the staff were gently telling Agnes it was time for her to take up the role of mistress of the house.

Up in the attic, Agnes rested her forehead on the glass, deep in thought. Suddenly, a tiny movement caught her eye: the distant shape of the Bentley gliding down the hill. She whirled round. Checking in the chipped wall mirror that her brown locks were neatly tied back – Miss Selcott had dismissed as nonsense her timid request to have it cut into a fashionable bob – she hurried down the stairs to meet her father.

After dinner that evening, Agnes would normally have been expected to leave the table to go and sew or read, by herself or with Miss Selcott, in the drawing room. On this occasion, however, Miss Selcott being great friends with Diana's mother, the Rector's wife, had gone across to the rectory for a meal, and so the family dined alone. Unusually, when the meal was over, Mr Melton asked Agnes to stay. There was a tension hanging in the air. This was partly because of an argument between father and son about Raven's college bill, which Miss Selcott had apparently found screwed up in the library grate. Raven, it appeared, owed a massive £85 for wine and spirits. He was also unable to satisfy his father on the matter of his academic achievements, and eventually confessed he was due to sit penal exams on his return to Cambridge in the autumn. Strangely enough, Mr Melton wasn't as angry as might be expected on hearing this: there was something else on his mind.

When Lister had cleared away all the plates and brought the port to the table, he lit the candelabra and drew the curtains against the darkening sky. Then he left the room, closing the doors behind him,

Mr Melton leaned forward in his seat and looked from one of his children to the other.

'I have something to tell you both,' he said, and smiled. 'During the course of my business in London, I have met a gentleman called Wintour. He is of an old Sussex family. They are,' he waved his hand as if in dismissal, 'distantly related to the Duke of Westminster. A family of good standing if not wealthy. I have dined with him at his house in Hampstead on several occasions over the last year. He is, like myself, a widower, and he has a daughter, Vanessa.'

Raven was staring morosely into his port, but at this he looked up and winked at his sister. Agnes felt a sense of panic as she listened to her father's words.

'Miss Wintour is a sweet girl of some three and twenty,' Melton went on. 'She's been educated by an excellent governess and her father has brought her up in exemplary fashion with the help of his elder unmarried sister. She was launched into society in her nineteenth year, but sadly, soon afterwards, she became ill with a strange malady that sapped all her energy and has hence lived a sheltered existence for the last two or three years. Thankfully, the doctors have now pronounced her completely healed.

'I visited her a number of times in her convalescence and she has proved a very sweet and attentive companion. She has been very interested in my business, in our home here and in you both, in books and, I am flattered to say, anything else an old buffer like myself has to say—'

'Oh Father, you're not an old buffer,' broke in Agnes. 'You're only forty-four. And you haven't got any grey hair, not like Diana's father . . .' She trailed to a halt and stared at her hands, clenched in her lap. She was dreading what her father had to say, but gabbling would only put off the awful moment. She looked up at him, his neat black hair, his dear sensitive face, and was struck suddenly by how handsome and charming he was. Perhaps, she thought with a shock, he hadn't been short of admirers in the years of his widowhood, despite his health. He was studying her, understanding clear in his sad dark eyes.

He reached out and patted her arm and said gently, 'Thank you, Agnes. Your support matters to me so much, my dear. Well. This is what I have to tell you both. I am delighted to say that Miss Wintour – Vanessa – has agreed to marry me.'

There was a silence. Outside, a nightingale began to sing. They sat and listened to the liquid song, not daring to meet one another's eyes. Agnes felt her world tilt on its axis.

Raven spoke first, but his tone was sneering. 'Well, I say, that is some news. Congratulations, Father.'

'Yes,' stuttered Agnes. 'Congratulations.' Then she burst into tears.

'Darling,' said her father, reaching out for her. 'Come on, don't cry. Vanessa's so sweet, you will love her. I feel so lucky. A beautiful wife and a beautiful daughter.' He laughed, then

**143**

looked solemn once more. 'We've had so much trouble, haven't we? I can hardly believe that she loves me – you know, a man twice her age. But she does.'

Agnes only cried harder than ever. Gerald threw his napkin on the table and edged his way over to put his arms around her, resting his cheek against hers. 'My little girl,' he cried. 'What is the matter? I'd never do anything to hurt you.'

How unprepared she'd been for the force of the emotion that rushed in. 'Mama . . . You've forgotten Mama,' were the only words she could say between the sobs. How fresh still, after thirteen years, was her loss.

Raven stared at her, his expression wild.

'I'll never forget your mama,' whispered Gerald into her ear, stroking her hair. 'I've missed your mother every moment of every day. Why do you think I went away to the war but to get away from the memory of her?'

'This makes me *sick*!' burst out Raven. 'You left *us*. Don't think I don't remember. And now you've got *her*, you won't want us here any more.' And he ran from the room, the door slamming shut behind him.

'Wait! Raven! Come back!' shouted Gerald, limping over and opening the door, Agnes close behind him. What they saw was Raven hauling the front door open, to reveal the startled figure of Miss Selcott standing on the step. 'Come in, come in,' cried Raven, bowing extravagantly, and Miss Selcott edged past him warily. 'Join the party. We're just congratulating my dear Papa.' And with that he walked out into the dark.

'Congratulating?' Miss Selcott said as she peeled off her gloves, looking from Agnes's tear-streaked face to Gerald Melton's anxious one.

'My father is getting married again,' Agnes murmured, then swayed, feeling faint. Mr Melton reached out to steady her.

**144**

The governess quickly recovered her own composure, carried on removing her gloves and nodded to her employer.

'Congratulations, sir,' was all she said. Meanwhile, Agnes made her way upstairs, feeling that she would never get over this shock.

The old lady's story had drifted to a halt. She sat now, her eyes closed.

Kate, who had remained silent throughout this narrative, apart from the odd whispered question, now asked, 'And what was Vanessa like?'

'I'll have to tell you another time!' Agnes said. 'I'm tired now. Wish they'd bring me some tea.'

'Oh my God, look at the time,' cried Kate. 'I'll never be forgiven if I'm late for my own birthday tea. Daisy's made the cake. Thanks so much for these . . .' She fingered the necklace. 'And thank you,' she bent and gently kissed Agnes's cheek, 'for telling me so much. I do want to hear more.'

'Next time,' Agnes promised tiredly, and fumbled on the bedside table for the bell to summon the nurse.

# Chapter 14

The following weekend, Kate took Daisy and Sam to meet Agnes.

When she'd aired the idea with Simon he'd been unsure. Would the children be frightened by the hospital, the other patients?

Unexpectedly, Joyce had been of the firm opinion that it was good for children to go, and so, armed with a packet of sweets as bribery for good behaviour, Kate took them both. She asked Simon to come, too, but he said he would rather stay at home for a bit of peace and quiet. And, to tell the truth, she was secretly glad. Sometime, when Agnes was back in her own home, it would be nice to introduce Simon to her. He would be on edge in a hospital.

In the event, the children behaved beautifully. Agnes asked them about school and what they liked doing best. Sam was allowed to be pushed about in the wheelchair by Daisy.

'They're darlings,' Agnes told her the next time Kate came. 'Do they get on well?'

'Most of the time,' said Kate. 'There's the usual fights and I suppose they have different interests, but they have the same sense of humour and Daisy can be really sweet the way she looks after Sam sometimes.'

'After I was eighteen I never saw my brother again,' said Agnes suddenly, as if stabbed by an old remembered pain.

'What happened? Did he die?' Kate asked tentatively.

Agnes shook her head. 'Not till nineteen sixty,' she said. 'But after what happened, Father never spoke to him again. Raven never even came to Father's funeral. And I couldn't forgive him for that.'

Kate wasn't sure what her elderly cousin meant by 'after what happened'. She simply asked, 'You were telling me about Vanessa. Were they married in Seddington church?'

'No,' said Agnes. 'Her family arranged the wedding, so it was in London. I don't remember ever seeing Father so happy as he was that day . . .'

*Autumn, 1927*

Gerald Melton and Vanessa Wintour were married one Friday in October in the baroque church of St James's Piccadilly. The groom's side of the church was pitifully empty – just Raven, Agnes, their Aunt Florence and her husband, Lister and a few of Gerald's London business connections, including his friend William Armstrong, whom Agnes knew and who shared her interest in collecting. Vanessa's side of the family, however, seemed to have taken the divine instruction to 'go forth and multiply' too far. Although Vanessa herself was an only child, her parents had both come from huge families, and their sisters, and the brothers who had survived the war, had all in their turn given birth to many children, and they all filled most of the left-hand rows of pews.

Vanessa had never looked prettier to Agnes's mind. She was possessed of a wispy fragility that was accentuated by fine wavy blonde hair, a pink and white complexion and light blue eyes. Agnes could see how her father had been so quickly captivated. There was something about Vanessa that begged you to look after her.

For Mr Melton was now a different man, younger-looking, light of spirit. If Vanessa was in the room, his eyes would hardly leave her face. If she was absent, he would talk about her. 'Of course, Vanessa will have her own ideas about the decorations,' he would say when a discussion arose about the peeling William Morris wallpaper in the drawing room. Or, 'Vanessa thinks we should entertain our neighbours here more often. We must see if Mrs Duncan might not be persuaded to, ah, spread her wings a little in the matter of menus.'

Vanessa seemed so sweet-natured, too. She had come down to Seddington on several occasions over the summer, once with her aunt, another time with her father, and she had taken great pains to befriend Agnes.

'It's ridiculous, of course, that I will be your stepmother. You must be my sister, my darling sister. I've always wanted one, you know. It's been so lonely since Mama died and I got so ill.'

They were lazing together on the swing seat in the morning sunshine, Vanessa lying with her head in Agnes's lap, one trailing foot gently rocking them to and fro.

Agnes ran her fingers through Vanessa's blonde bob and smiled. 'I always wanted a sister, too, though I know I'm lucky having Raven. I've got my friend Diana, of course, but it's not the same.' Diana was, in fact, none too pleased at Vanessa's arrival on the scene. She no longer had the Meltons to herself, and she privately agreed with her mother that Vanessa was 'too pretty for her own good'.

Vanessa reached up to hug Agnes. 'Oh, we shall be such friends, you and I. We shall have such fun!'

And Agnes felt as though her heart would burst with happiness.

'Don't ever *ever* think I would try and take the place of your mother,' Vanessa continued. And Agnes believed her. Vanessa seemed in awe of the sacred memory of Evangeline, without being cast down by the figure of her sanctified predecessor. And having Vanessa in no way disturbed the girl's memories of her mother – it *was* rather like having a delightful elder sister. At the same time, she realized that her own position in the household was changing. She would have to give way to Vanessa now, who as the future Mrs Melton was to be the new mistress, but Agnes minded less than she had thought she might.

Vanesssa was enchanted with Seddington House – 'It's so much bigger than our cottage in Petworth' – and wanted to meet all the neighbours. So the Fortescues at Fortescue Hall, the Waverleys at The Gables and the Forsters at Halesworth Grange obliged, curious to meet this exotic butterfly who had finally melted the widower's frozen heart. Vanessa was the centre of attention at these gatherings. She would profess how delighted she was by everything, would charm the old men and flatter the women, play with the children and pet the animals.

Not everyone succumbed to Vanessa's spell. The Rector's wife was naturally suspicious of physical beauty, and there was no doubt that Vanessa's occasional impatience with the simple customs of the household rubbed Mrs Duncan up the wrong way. 'She's artful, that one,' Agnes overheard Mrs Duncan saying to Lister one day. 'I caught her in the library. She didn't see me. Going through Mr Melton's private bureau, she was. Looking at his papers.' Agnes puzzled over this, but concluded that Vanessa must have had her father's permission to look for something.

The staff were also bothered by rumours of change in the

household. Miss Selcott was still in residence and directing Agnes's reading, but she announced that she would be leaving shortly after the wedding, taking lodgings with the Rector's family and tutoring children from local families. After all, Agnes was now a young woman and there was much discussion about her future. Whatever was in store for her, she wouldn't need a governess.

In September, the housemaid Ethel, and Alf, her sweetheart, were married in the village church and Mr Melton paid for a bountiful reception for them at the new village hall. As a married woman, Ethel's services were no longer required at Seddington House and so a farm labourer's daughter, Ruby, was brought in to be trained up as her replacement. There was talk that she would also be expected to attend the new Mrs Melton.

The most important person Vanessa was failing to charm was Raven.

When she first arrived at Seddington, only Agnes went out to the front with her father to greet Vanessa and her aunt as they stepped down from the car. After introductions and embraces, they swept into the hall and almost right past Raven who was loitering in the shadows by the stairs. Only Agnes noticed the shock that passed over his face as he took in Vanessa's china shepherdess looks. Then the usual sullen shutters came down.

'Oh, this is my brother Raven,' gabbled Agnes, pulling him forward. 'We always call him Raven – he hates his real name, Arthur.'

Vanessa put out her hand to Raven and dimpled prettily at him. He took it briefly, then nodded at Aunt Evelyn and slipped round the newel post and up the stairs, two at a time. After a moment they heard a door slam upstairs.

'Well, really!' started Aunt Evelyn.

'I'm sorry, he finds this hard,' stuttered Agnes.

'Poor boy,' whispered Vanessa, and Agnes was surprised to see her baby-blue eyes well with tears. 'I know how you both feel, you see,' she appealed to Agnes. 'Losing our mothers.'

After that, Raven did his best to be staying with friends when Vanessa came, or else just went to another part of the house. Mr Melton was furious about it, but what could he do? Raven was perfectly polite to Vanessa when they had to meet at meals or in company, but otherwise he kept his distance.

After the wedding, and the reception at a nearby hotel, Gerald swept his new bride away on a three-week honeymoon, travelling in Italy.

When they returned to Seddington House, the Meltons threw a Christmas party for their neighbours. It was the first time for many years that there had been any sort of entertainment there, and Mrs Duncan and her staff were worn to a ravelling with the cooking and the preparation, despite the recruitment of extra help. Ethel came in every day for two weeks for light kitchen duties, looking palely fragile – it was known that she was already expecting a child. Alf himself was busy, for Vanessa insisted on a huge Christmas tree covered with candles in the hall, then that he deck the reception rooms with boughs of holly, pine and mistletoe from nearby woods. A great yule log was dragged in to burn in the drawing-room grate.

If the vast buffet lacked the glamour of London haute cuisine, it was the very best of hearty country fayre. There was roast beef, a huge ham, a variety of game, fish and pies, an array of vegetables, salads, breads, mousses and aspics. Then came a spread of trifles, fruit pies, mince tarts, custards and creams. Lister had plundered the cellar for the remainder of the fine wines laid down before the war and spent hours with Mr

Melton negotiating with his London wine merchants to build up a new stock.

The night of the party, the second Mrs Melton appeared to her guests at the top of the stairs, a vision in shimmering eau de nil silk studded with sequins and with a short train. It exactly complemented her complexion and set off her hair. She looked ravishing and Agnes saw that even Raven could not take his eyes off her as she swept down the staircase to greet everyone and wove her way through the throng like a lively little bird, stopping for a moment to converse with each and every one.

The rector and his wife were there, of course, with Diana, who had an admirer in tow – the new young curate, fresh from theological college in Oxford. He was a little spotty, Agnes thought, and more than a little earnest, but he seemed most solicitous of Diana, though he was clearly hurt to see the way his inamorata's glances would frequently rest upon Raven.

Raven really was very naughty where Diana was concerned, Agnes thought – such a tease, encouraging her when Agnes knew he considered her friend to be too serious and too plain. What was the point of this behaviour? Everyone except Diana could see that a relationship between the two would be disastrous. Agnes made up her mind to have a tactful little talk with her friend soon.

Raven, who had miraculously scraped through his penal exams, had a friend from Cambridge staying, a dapper young man wearing a white tuxedo and with a transatlantic accent. His name was Freddy Irving and his family currently lived in Chelsea. Raven was hazy about his background, but it was known that his father was very wealthy. Freddy had a man-of-the-world air and a kind heart, so Agnes, just turned seventeen, ducked the attentions of a bluff farmer's son, who had opened a conversation with her by asking if they could smell their pig farm from Seddington House, and practised flirting for the first time.

'You must find us very provincial after London and Cambridge, Mr Irving. Do you go to parties every night or do you sometimes find time to attend to your studies?'

'If someone goes to the trouble of giving a party, Miss Melton, we feel it is our Christian duty to attend, do we not, Raven?'

Raven smiled and took a drag on his Turkish cigarette. 'Never let it be said that we don't do our duty. Unless, of course, it's someone frightfully dull and then we feel it's a veritable act of charity to go.'

'And,' she paused a moment, 'are the girls very pretty in Cambridge?'

'Damned pretty,' Freddy sighed. 'If only I could get one to even look at me.' He rolled his eyes theatrically. 'But,' he went on, leaning towards her, 'not as pretty as here.' And Agnes giggled deliciously.

She laughed at Freddy's stories about undergraduate life and teased him about his flippant attitude. She didn't feel seriously attracted to him, nor, she thought, he to her, but it was heavenly fun all the same. She had begun to realize that there was something about her that was engaging to men. Freddy seemed animated by her attentions and the farmer's son continued to hover and pass compliments if in the slightest way encouraged, which she felt tempted to do merely for the sensation of power it gave her.

She hoped she was looking quite pretty this evening. Vanessa had taken her to a dressmaker in London and she knew the very pale blue dress her stepmother had ordered suited her newly shingled dark-honey hair. Her father had taken her aside the evening before and presented her with one of her mother's diamond pendants, which now flashed at her throat, together with matching clip earrings. She would treasure them for ever, she had whispered through her tears, and her father had hugged her tightly.

Freddy, it turned out, was an accomplished pianist, and after supper, cajoled by Vanessa, he perched himself at the newly tuned Bechstein grand and played the requests of the different generations – Scott Joplin, Ivor Novello and Strauss. There wasn't really room to dance, but some couples tried anyway. Raven leaned against the mantel, watchful, a glass of wine never far from his hand.

Much later that evening, when all the guests had gone and the servants were clearing away the last of the debris, Agnes went looking for her father to say goodnight. She found him in the library in deep conversation with Mr Armstrong. They didn't even notice when she looked round the door, so she closed it again quietly. She stood for a moment in the hall, waiting for Lister and Alf to carry through a borrowed table, then followed the sound of gramophone jazz music into the drawing room. There, Freddy and Vanessa were dancing the Charleston together. Raven was sorting through a pile of records, talking animatedly.

'Let's try this one. I got it from Levy's last week. It's Fletcher Henderson. Everyone's wild about him.' And a thrilling new sound filled the room. Freddy and Vanessa swung back and forth. Raven changed the record again – Louis Armstrong's 'Hot Seven' this time. Then Duke Ellington. Finally, exhausted, Vanessa fell back into a chair, flushed and laughing.

'Come on, the night is yet young,' Freddy gasped, and this time he grabbed Agnes and tried to take her through some steps.

'I'm sorry, I'm terribly stupid about this.' Agnes laughed. 'No one's ever shown me, you see.'

'Raven and I will demonstrate then,' said Vanessa, regaining her energy and returning to the fray. 'Come on, Raven. I've never seen you dance.'

'I don't like to,' he stuttered, but she gently took his hand and steered him round the floor to a popular number by Duke Ellington. 'One, two, one two. No, like this. And round, come on, swing me,' and she twirled and bobbed with surefooted grace.

Raven was absorbed with getting the steps right, one, two, one, two, swing. His sullen expression was gone utterly. Much later, looking back, Agnes would imbue this moment with the significance it deserved. But at the time she was merely relieved that her brother and stepmother seemed finally to have become friends.

The few months that followed were the strangest time that Agnes could remember. On the one hand, they were blissfully happy. Although Vanessa accompanied her bridegroom frequently to London, there were periods as long as a fortnight when the couple were down at Seddington. These were times when Agnes would get up in the morning not knowing what the day held, although she knew it would be something fun.

On the other hand, Vanessa, it was becoming clear, required constant entertainment. Unlike her stepdaughter, she was never happy to sit quietly and read or embroider. Agnes would spend long hours looking over her growing collection of miniatures, old coins and other curios, which she displayed in a set of locked drawers that Mr Melton had ordered from a local cabinet-maker for her birthday. Her father would give her pieces to put in it and sometimes accompanied her to Norwich to a coin dealer there. Otherwise it was a matter of looking through curio shops for inexpensive items that interested her.

She had once shown Vanessa her collection. Her stepmother's

enthusiasm had been no more than polite. 'Oh, you are so clever, Agnes. Such pretty things.' But that was as far as her interest went. No, Vanessa loved the new and the vital, not the old and the still. Music, dancing, chatter, outings, parties. And these were rare in rural Suffolk in winter.

There were frequent trips in the car, especially if Raven was home, to see friends at Fortescue Hall, at Aldeborough, at country houses up and down the coast. Winter was clearly a difficult time for Vanessa; it was too cold and inclement to do anything outside, the gardens looked wretched at this time of year, and anybody truly society-minded had made their way up to London.

Agnes's father worried about this. 'Do you think she's happy here?' he asked Agnes one day late in February. 'Our life must seem, well, a little dull.' He paced the library, a deep frown on his face, but before Agnes could reply, he sighed and said, 'I think we will be returning to London at the end of the week. It'll be more . . . suitable for her there. She pines for her friends, you know.' Then he smiled and said, 'And Vanessa is trying to persuade me that you must join us soon. Spread your wings, meet other young people. You're becoming cooped up here, you know.'

'But Father, I like it. It's . . . well, I know who I am here.' But, still, she was surprised to feel a flutter of excitement at the idea.

But late in Febrary, Vanessa seemed to have a recurrence of her nervous illness. She lay on the deep sofa in the morning room half the day with the gramophone playing 'Oh for the Wings of a Dove' over and over, waving away offers of food and weeping. Agnes could hardly get a word out of her and Gerald Melton was beside himself with anxiety.

'She has delicate nerves,' the doctor said. 'She must be very careful with herself and rest a great deal.'

Thankfully, after a few weeks of this, Vanessa recovered and her high spirits returned. Even the sad news that Ethel had lost her baby failed to diminish the family's relief.

'And that's when our lives took another new turn,' Agnes told Kate. 'Vanessa's recovery really began when Raven was suddenly sent down from Cambridge. It seems his college had finally had enough of him. He just came home and hung around Vanessa and was insolent to Father and the servants. Father was furious with him. Finally we all went up to London and Raven took a job. But the damage had already been done.'

'What damage do you mean?' Kate asked quietly.

'To the marriage, of course,' Agnes snapped. 'You see, Raven had developed a crush on Vanessa.'

Kate opened her mouth to ask more, but just then Mrs Summers arrived and Kate got up to go.

'Mr Jordan telephoned this morning,' Mrs Summers told Agnes. 'Says he'll be along at the weekend.'

'He only came last weekend,' said Agnes in an acid tone. 'Must be getting worried about me! Perhaps you should meet him soon, Kate,' she added. 'Max is Raven's grandson.'

# *Chapter 15*

'When Kate finally met Max Jordan, on a boiling hot Saturday two weeks later, it was completely by accident.

The Longmans had arrived the previous night and were staying in a borrowed cottage in nearby Blythborough. Claire had come with them, a pale, listless Claire, and was sleeping in the tiny boxroom. Kate had just manoeuvred Liz's large car with five chattering children in the back into a just-vacated space in the overcrowded car park at Walberswick Beach, turned off the engine with a sigh of relief, and pushed her sunglasses up on top of her head.

*Paaah! Paaah!* There came two angry blasts of car horn and a silver Range Rover slid to a halt in front of them. A bespectacled male face frowned at them through the driver's window.

'What have we done?' Kate asked Liz, who was unclicking her seatbelt next to Kate, and checking her reflection in the vanity mirror.

'Looks like you nicked his space,' Liz said drily. The other driver threw open his car door and strode round to Kate's open window. He was a good-looking man of about forty, with a wing of black hair that fell across his high forehead. In his light linen suit he looked overdressed for the beach. He had to stoop to speak to Kate through the window.

'I don't mean to be difficult, but I was waiting for that space. I've been driving round for several minutes.'

'I didn't see you,' she gasped, eager as ever to make amends, whether or not she was in the wrong. 'Really I didn't. I'm so sorry.'

'Well, you can't have been looking,' came the clipped response.

Liz's eyes lit up. She could never say no to a fight. She leaned forward in her seat and, in a voice that made editorial assistants quake in their fake Jimmy Choos, boomed, 'You heard what my friend said, she didn't see you. And, look, we've got a carful of children. There's only yourself. I'm sure there's plenty of space up the road.' As the poor man, clearly taken aback, opened his mouth to reply she intoned, 'And mind what you say in front of the children. You'll spoil their holiday.'

The wide-eyed children in fact looked as though their holiday was made, but the frustrated man obviously decided that discretion was the better part of valour and retreated with a shrug. His car's wheels spun in the sand as he swung it into reverse and they all watched as he wove a perilous way backwards out of the car park. Kate realized she was gripping the steering wheel tightly.

'Sorry,' said Liz. 'I was probably a bit hard on him.'

'The car park is not usually quite this crowded,' grumbled Kate.

Behind them, the incident already forgotten, the children were scrambling out. Daisy hauled open the rear door and started passing out buckets, spades and beach towels to her eager servants – even Sam was doing what he was told today. Lily, Lottie and Charlie were here and this was the first time they'd all seen each other for a whole four months. Lily and Lottie, willowy blonde twins, had been born a month before Daisy, and lanky Charlie, who took after Laurence, was five weeks younger than Sam.

A familiar black and white spaniel appeared and dived straight into the picnic bag.

'Bobby, get off the sandwiches!' shouted Daisy. 'Mummy, I don't want the one with dog lick.'

In hot pursuit of Bobby came Joyce, who had driven Laurence and Claire down in her car. The Hutchinsons' Audi was in the garage with a sick carburettor, and Simon had, as usual, left his old banger at Diss station at the beginning of the week. They had partly chosen Walberswick today because dogs were allowed on the beach in June, which wasn't so on the even more popular and hygiene-conscious Southwold beach up the coast.

Kate was furious because Simon hadn't come home last night. Damn him – he'd known about this weekend for months.

'There's a pretty tricky project going on here,' he had said when she'd tracked him down on his mobile earlier that morning. 'I'll be on the two o'clock though. See you at home later.' He rang off.

'You'd better be there, stranger,' hissed Kate to the dead receiver. It had taken hell on earth to get their party booked into Southwold's Crown Hotel restaurant that evening.

Arms full of beach bags, rugs, windbreaks, buckets and spades, they picked their way like a line of refugees over a little bridge, across the mudflats and down to the beach. The tide was coming in, the deep blue of the sea reflecting the deep blue of the sky. A fresh breeze blew and seagulls shrieked. Despite her worries, Kate's spirit soared.

They struck camp at the base of a sand dune, then after the children had been suncreamed to within an inch of their lives, Joyce asked if she could go and look round the gift shop.

Claire, wearing her usual urban outfit plus sunglasses, refused even to remove her boots. She huddled up on a rug with an Ann Tyler paperback, but deigned to agree that it was a beautiful day and that she was not unenjoying herself.

Liz peeled off her elegant wrap-around dress to reveal a simply cut one-piece costume. It was probably worth hundreds, thought Kate with envy, and Liz wouldn't have had to pay a penny. Whether the swimsuit would ever meet seawater was another matter.

Laurence, who loved all boyish pleasures, rolled up his jeans and went to supervise Sam and Charlie, who were throwing stones in the water for Bobby to chase. Bobby, being a dog of little brain but much enthusiasm, couldn't understand where the stones were disappearing to, but played his part with much excited diving and worrying.

Daisy, in pink bikini, followed elegant Lily and Lottie, who were picking their way through the pebbles on dainty feet, looking for shells.

The women talked. Liz moaned about the magazine group's new chief executive. She was clashing with him over the direction of *Desira*, which he wanted to make less exclusive to broaden the advertising. Then she moved on to the latest nanny and how she'd found her journal – 'Liz, you didn't read her private diary!' – and Kate choked with laughter at Liz's indignation.

'Inga complained about my cooking, of all the cheek! All she gives the kids is burgers and fish fingers. And she says I'm mean because I don't lend her my clothes. Apparently, her last employer gave her the run of her wardrobe. Well, I couldn't look her in the face after that. She's going to go as soon as the agency come up with someone suitable.'

On Liz's interrogation, Claire, who had been quiet up to now, took off her sunglasses and, whirling them round in her hand in agitation, finally let them into the mystery of why she had been so difficult to get hold of. His name was Alex. Yes, he was single; no, he didn't have any ex-wives or children.

'Mmm, new rather than second-hand – what's wrong with him then?' wondered wicked Liz.

Nothing, apparently. 'He's a tenor. With D'Oily Carte. He's just been working so hard he's never had time for serious relationships. We met cos I had to photograph him for a pro-gramme.' Claire burrowed in her bag and drew out a folded brochure. Liz snatched it from her and scrutinized it, then handed it to Kate. *Alexander Weinberg*, the programme said, *is a rising young star . . .*

'He looks gorgeous, Claire,' Kate said, taking in the hand-some Slavic features, the cropped dark hair, the discreet earring. Claire had accentuated the air of Wagnerian moodiness in her photograph. 'So, how long has this been going on? And why have you been so elusive?'

'Since March, actually.' Claire blushed for no apparent reason then looked miserable again.

'You really like him, don't you?' Kate said gently.

Claire nodded. 'That's the trouble, though,' she said, and started throwing pebbles at a large stone three feet away, miss-ing every time. 'I don't know how much he likes me. He pours all his energies into his work, you see.'

Like someone else I know, thought Kate, cast down in sudden gloom.

'I never know when I'm going to see him,' Claire said. 'His schedule is so punishing. I never thought I'd let any man run me around like this.' She laughed, but not with much amusement. 'I'm only here now because he's gone to America for three weeks. Sad, aren't I?'

Liz gave Claire's shoulder an affectionate rub and thought it time to change the subject. 'Ted saw Simon for a drink last week.'

'Oh, he didn't say. How is Ted?' Laurence's puppylike banker brother was always on a search for true love. Unfortunately he would go too deep too quickly and would usually frighten the woman off.

'Single again, poor Ted. Meredith, that glamorous American you met last year, didn't last long, then I thought he'd make a go of it with one of the young secretaries, but she decided to go off round the world rather than hitch up with him. Then,' Liz counted on her fingers, 'there was Tricia. Met her in a bar – I never asked what sort. She was a real laugh, but turned out she had a string of boyfriends. Just out for a bit of fun with Ted's money. Last month there was another banker, Aruna. I think they had a one-night stand. He was crazy about her. Kept on sending her huge bouquets. She wasn't very impressed. In the end she told Human Resources he was harassing her. That really hurt but at least he stopped. Silly Ted. Born a romantic, die a romantic. Laurence doesn't know what to do with him. Ha, that's just given me an idea for the magazine. The male Bridget Jones phenomenon. Ted would look great with his big soulful eyes.'

'Yeah, like Bobby,' said Claire. 'Go away, dog,' she shouted, brushing sand off everything. 'No, I don't want your gobby old stone.'

'Mummy, Mummy, can we have ice creams now?'

'Later, Sam, after lunch.'

'Oh, but Charlie and me are hungry *now*.'

'Yes, but it's only eleven o'clock. We'll have lunch in an hour. Have an apple.'

'Mummy, Mummy, Daisy and us want ice creams.'

'Ice creams after lunch, Lily. Lunch in an hour. Have an apple,' recited Liz.

'Oh, but . . .'

'Anyone else who mentions ice creams won't get one at all.'

'Icecreamsicecreamsicecreamsicecreams.' They ran off chanting to join Laurence who was making a huge fairytale sandcastle. With its Disney turrets and winding stairs, it was so beautiful that other people's children were starting to crowd round to watch. He looked over at Liz and gave a mock bow, as if to say, 'I did it all for you.' She smiled imperiously at him. Anyone who didn't know Laurence and Liz well might consider that Liz wore the trousers in their marriage. But Kate knew that Laurence offered calm and reliability. And Liz was so strikingly like Laurence's mother in height and temperament it was a fact too obvious to mention.

'How is your mother, Kate?' Liz asked.

'Up and down, Dad says.' Now a normal routine had returned, so had something of Barbara's depression. At least she was still taking her medication and had kept off the drink since her overdose. 'I'll go down again later in the summer, and maybe they'll come for a visit in the autumn,' she went on. 'Who knows, we might have a house of our own for them to stay in by then.' Kate knew her voice sounded strained.

She lay with her eyes closed, soaking up the sun, while her mind prodded the tight little knot of anxiety she'd been worrying at all morning. It was to do with her conversation with Simon, earlier. She'd suddenly realized something – that she'd had to pussyfoot around him. What would seem to most couples a reasonable demand – that he spend time with her and their children – was clearly becoming unreasonable to him, an annoyance even. She sensed that not only had they now got used to his periods of absence, but that absence had become normality. They were living two separate lives. Her husband was beginning to slip out of her reach.

*

The morning passed beautifully. The children splashed in the waves. Kate, who loved sea-bathing, swam, while Sam jumped up and down on the beach shouting in anger at her to come back. Joyce returned, finally, having had several coffees in the gift shop after bumping into her friend Hazel.

They all sat on the rugs and ate sandy sandwiches and cake and apples. Then Laurence took the children off to buy ice creams from the van. A flock of sea birds flew across the sun.

When the children ambled back with dripping 99s, Laurence pulled his copy of the *Guardian* out of Liz's beach bag and asked if anyone would mind if he took the ferry over the harbour to take a nose round the bookshops in Southwold. The ferry was, in fact, a little rowing boat that could take ten people the twenty yards over the fast-flowing river. The harbour was a collection of rusting little craft interspersed with the odd yacht on the far bank. The others said, of course, and they would pick him up outside Southwold church at three thirty.

After he'd gone, the children set up a clamour to go crabbing.

'Please, Mummy, there's some children on the bridge and they've got lots and lots of crabs in a bucket,' Sam shouted.

'I don't see why not,' said Kate. 'There's a shed at the harbour where we can buy bait and nets.' She and Joyce collected up the remains of the picnic to put in the car. Claire said she'd stay and look after the rest of their property and read her book.

They bought five shrimping nets at the tiny shop, plus lines with a wood handle at one end and a piece of fatty bacon at the other. Daisy stood watching a group of youths dipping their lines in the river and landing black crabs as big as her hand.

All kitted out, they marched back to the little bridge and the children paid out their lines into the stream.

'I got one! I got one!' shrieked Lottie immediately. A tiny grey crab was dropped into one of the buckets.

'Me! me!' squeaked Sam, and an even tinier one fell out of the net onto the bridge.

'Quick, Bobby'll get it,' Liz shouted and Kate knelt down and swept it into the pail just in time.

The others had less luck. Charlie could never land any of his. In his excitement he would jiggle the rope and back the crabs would fall. Bobby barked and barked. Once he upset the bucket and crabs went in all directions. Joyce put him on his lead but he just got entangled in everyone's legs.

'I'll take him for a walk up the river,' she said and dragged him off through the car park.

'Can we go over to the harbour, Mum?' asked Daisy. 'The boys were getting really big ones there.'

The women looked at each other. 'Well,' started Kate, 'we can go and look.'

When they got there, the children started to dip their lines.

'It's not very safe,' breathed Liz. The bank was built up and it was a sheer six feet down to where dark currents swirled.

'Just for a few minutes. If we keep with the little ones it should be OK,' said Kate.

'Quick, the bucket, I've got two!' shouted Daisy. Into the pail they went.

'Look, Mum, look! I've got one,' shrieked Charlie.

'Lottie! You're too close to the edge.' Liz pulled her back.

One by one, they all caught crabs. It was true, these were much better than the ones at the little bridge. Kate, hoping Sam wouldn't notice her holding the back of his T-shirt, watched the crabs in the bucket, clambering over one another in their slimy black armour. She shuddered.

The ferry boat was on the far side now, a queue of people

disgorging onto the jetty, another queue ready to board. The ferryman helped out a young couple with a baby in a buggy, then handed in a succession of adults before settling down and picking up the oars.

Just then, in a streak of black and white, Bobby reappeared. 'Oh, you've come over *here* now, how exciting, how exciting,' he snuffled at the children. He wagged his tail and stuck his nose in the bucket.

'*No!*' shouted Charlie, and dived at Bobby. The spaniel jumped sideways. Kate grabbed at him. Too late. He scrabbled at the side then somersaulted into the water. One of the children laughed. Daisy screamed.

'Bobby!' screeched Joyce, loping up panting. 'Quick, get him someone.'

Poor Bobby was treading water, fighting against the current. Kate swiped Sam's net and lay down, poking the net end towards him. He was out of her reach and starting to drift away. At one point he vanished under the water, then bobbed up again choking and sneezing.

'Here, let me.' It was the man from the car park. He took the net from Kate and lay down, batting at Bobby. Useless. 'Get a boathook from the hut. Quick!' Kate ran to the shed where they had bought the nets and gabbled at the woman serving. The woman looked blank for a moment, then rushed out in the direction of another shed and returned with a long boathook.

'Here, take this. There's a lifebelt by the path. I'll get it,' she said.

Kate ran back with the hook. Bobby's flailing was getting weaker; he could hardly keep his nose above the water. The man passed the boathook hand over hand across the water and, after some fumbling, jabbed it under Bobby's collar. Caught. But how to get him out?

The shed woman arrived with the lifebelt, assessed the situation and ran back up the bank, shouting to the ferryman. He paused in his rowing, swung round in his seat and looked at Bobby, then turned back and said something to his passengers. He dipped hard with one oar and pulled the prow round.

To Joyce and Kate it seemed a long moment before the boat drifted alongside the exhausted dog and the ferryman shipped his oars. A burly man leaned over the side, put one arm under Bobby's chest and tried to pull him up. The ferryman disengaged the boathook and felt for the dog's back legs. In a moment they dragged him, sneezing and yelping, into the boat. They could see him crouched in the bottom of the boat, coughing up water. The ferryman rowed in strong quick strokes for the shore.

Liz gathered the children and they all went down to the jetty. Bobby was shivering and spluttering, but he was alive. Joyce hugged his sodden body to her. 'You silly, silly boy,' she sobbed. 'You're all right now. Thank you, thank you.' She beamed at the circle of people. The ferryman gave a wave and pushed off in his boat once more.

Kate turned to the man from the car park, who was brushing at the mud on his suit with a handkerchief, though with little success. 'Thank you,' she said in a low voice. 'You were brilliant.' The man gave a modest smile, then looked at her more closely and his face changed.

'Ah, it's you. Yes, um, sorry about earlier,' he said abruptly. 'I felt bad about . . . maybe you didn't see me after all.' He put out his hand. 'The name's Jordan, by the way. Max Jordan.'

The name was familiar, but she couldn't think how. She clasped his hand and then it was as if a shot of electricity ran through her. 'Kate Hutchinson,' she replied. 'I know who you are.'

He stared at her, still holding her hand. Yes, thought Kate, his eyes are the same as hers, but a more intense blue.

'Kate Hutchinson,' he repeated. 'Was it you who rescued my Great-aunt Agnes?'

# Chapter 16

'Of course, I must thank you for everything,' continued Max, releasing Kate's hand. 'Rescuing my aunt and coming to see her so often. And I gather we're somehow distantly related? That's an incredible coincidence.' He stood shaking his head. 'Why Aunt Agnes will insist on living in that old pile still, I don't know. Something like this was bound to have happened sometime. Really, at her age, she should be in some sort of sheltered housing or a home.'

Kate thought he seemed nice but a bit patronizing, although Mrs Summers had said almost exactly the same thing when Kate bumped into her on one of her visits a few weeks ago. It had been one of those periods when the doctors thought Agnes might be well enough to go home soon. But Mrs Summers had said it differently, her anxiety for her employer born out of long acquaintance.

'This whole thing has really shaken me, Kate,' she confided. 'I don't want her coming back to that big house, I really don't. She couldn't get upstairs easily before, and what'll it be like now? Though we could get a stairlift, I suppose . . . And it's murder to clean – all that stuff everywhere and I'm not allowed to move anything, oh dear me, no. It's my job on the line saying this, but she'd be much better off in one of them bungalows in the village with a nice new kitchen. I could go and clean for her there. But she keeps saying she won't go. It do worry me, Kate, it do worry me.'

'Have you been visiting your aunt today?' Kate asked Max now. 'How is she?'

'Bit miserable, to tell the truth. They've suddenly moved her onto the main ward – say they need the room. She's not her usual self. Wants to get out of there. Well, it's the best place for her at the moment, I reckon, until something else can be arranged.'

Kate was shocked. She'd only been to see Agnes a couple of days ago and there had been no mention of this being about to happen.

'Oh, poor Agnes, I'm not surprised she's upset. She'd hate being on a ward with lots of strangers. Are you very close to her? Is there anything you can do? I mean . . .'

'I can't gauge how much she minds. I only met her for the first time a few years ago, after my mother died. It sounds ridiculous but Mum had never met her either. Apparently there was some sort of family rift that no one ever talks about. Some scandal about my grandparents' marriage. I wrote to Aunt Agnes about Mum's death and visited her once or twice . . .'

'Kate, I'm sorry to interrupt, dear.' Joyce, with a sodden and chastened hound on a lead, looked panicky. Kate introduced her to Bobby's rescuer.

'Mr Jordan, I can't thank you enough. Bobby means so much to me. Since my husband died, you see . . . Kate, I ought to go and get Bobby looked over by the vet. He's not himself. But what about Laurence? Oh dear, how are we going to manage the cars?'

'I'll leave you to it then,' said Max. 'Hope to see you again sometime. Good dog you've got there.' He ruffled Bobby's wet fur, gave him a quick pat and walked off through the car park.

In the end, Liz took her children and Claire to pick up Laurence at Southwold church and return to their cottage in Blythborough. Joyce, Kate and the Hutchinson children took Bobby for an emergency once-over at the vet's in Halesworth.

It was quarter past four when Joyce's car turned into the lane up to Paradise Cottage. Kate's heart leaped with relief when she saw the blue Fiesta outside. Simon was home, though he couldn't have been there long if he had caught the two o'clock.

The vet had declared Bobby to be fine, but said she would keep him in overnight for observation, so it was a subdued party that got out of the car and trouped indoors.

'Daddy! Daddy!' the children shouted. There was no answer, but there was a sound of running water so they ran upstairs to look for him. The answerphone light was winking. Kate listened to a message from the Crown Hotel requiring her to ring and confirm the size of her party.

She reached for the receiver. Where was the number? The phone book had vanished. Well, it must have been the last call they'd made that morning before they left. She pressed the redial button and waited.

Two rings, then, in a perky American accent, *Hi, it's Meredith here. I can't talk to you now, but leave your name and number*. The beep sounded but Kate just stood there, her mind working. Then she realized she was listening to silence and replaced the receiver.

'Wrong number,' she said to Joyce. Very wrong, she thought. And yet she knew, with a flash of insight, that something at last made perfect sense.

So this is it, Kate said to herself later, sitting in the bar of the Crown Hotel, watching Simon embrace Liz and Claire and clasp

172

Laurence's arm and clap him on the shoulder. This is how it feels to know that your husband is having an affair. This is how countless women have felt over the centuries. What do I do? I don't want to be here. I don't want to think about what next. I just want to run away and cry.

But she sat there, a fixed smile upon her face, laughing when the others laughed, trying to ask Liz and Laurence sensible things about their work, hearing about the American tour Claire's Alex was currently on. And she watched Simon.

Her husband seemed his usual self. Except she couldn't say she knew what that was any more. It was like looking at him as she had at the beginning of their relationship, noting the careful way he dressed, the way his blond hair – sparser now – fell down over his forehead. Then the filter changed and he looked so immensely familiar that she felt a stab of pain. She could see her children in him. Daisy's eyes, Sam's mouth. This man belonged to her, they had forged their beloved boy and girl from their joined flesh. He was part of her. She was part of him. Is that what the one flesh of the marriage service meant?

The waitress came to announce their table was ready and the party moved from bar to restaurant. Kate hardly noticed what she ate or drank. Ashes in her mouth, yes. But as the evening went on, and everything seemed normal, she began to wonder whether she had got the situation wrong.

Meredith is in banking too. Why shouldn't he have phoned her?

*But on a Saturday afternoon, at her home, as soon as he'd got back from a long week at the office? Oh, come on.*

But he loves me – he's always telling me he does. He wouldn't betray me.

*OK, so why has he been so quiet and withdrawn recently, so absent from our relationship? Isn't that one of the classic symptoms?*

He's been working hard. He's totally exhausted.

*Yeah, right. And what about the mystery of the missing money? That's another sign.*

It's been an expensive time recently. And there was that confusion over the lost credit card.

*You'll have to do better than that, Kate . . .*

Kate sighed. Perhaps she should look at it differently. Suppose he had slept with Meredith – did that matter nowadays? It didn't have to mean the end of everything. They could make it up, they could change things.

*No and no and no,* her heart cried. *We can't. It's broken.*

But perhaps she had got it all wrong . . .

On and on, her thoughts whirled.

Then came another bolt from the blue.

Claire said to Simon, 'What did you think of the play the other night?'

The others glanced at him, puzzled. Claire looked at Kate, a long look with a note of apology in it. Simon picked up a book of matches and began to fiddle with it. 'Not bad. Not one of his best, though. Pretty difficult subject for a play, I thought.'

Claire explained to the others. 'I saw Simon at the National Theatre, didn't I? A week ago.' Her tone of voice was artificially bright.

'Yes,' said Simon. 'I don't usually go to the theatre,' you've certainly barely been with me, Kate thought, 'but a colleague had tickets and asked me to go.'

'You didn't tell me you were going out to the theatre,' she said in a small voice.

'I think you'd know his colleague,' said Claire to Laurence. Again, Kate was bewildered. Why was Claire doing this? 'Ted's old girlfriend. You know, the American woman. Meredith Something.'

Someone moved the conversation on. To other London productions, thereby wending its way to Suffolk and what there was to do culturally there. Music festivals, Jill Freud's summer theatre.

'So how have you been spending your time, Kate, when the kids are at school?' Laurence asked. 'Not lying around eating chocolate, I hope.'

Kate explained about the friends she'd made, Debbie and Louise, and about looking for somewhere to live. 'I work a bit, do the domestic stuff, look after the kids. I don't know,' she shrugged. 'The time just seems to disappear. Oh, but I've found some family nearby.' She went on to explain about Miss Melton. 'It's curious, but she's become a very good friend. I wish I'd met her before, before she was ill, I mean. She doesn't seem old – she feels things so deeply. She's a very strong person but she is very vulnerable, too, as if a lot of sad things have happened to her. We connect. And she lives in this amazing house stuffed with antiques and interesting ornaments and books. I'd love to have a proper look round one day if she ever goes home and invites me.'

'I think Kate would like us to put in an offer for her house,' joked Simon, obviously trying to restore normality to proceedings. But his attempt was foiled.

'I think Kate would like you to put in an offer for *any* house,' said Claire, her face pale. 'And live in it.'

Liz looked at her. 'Claire,' she said, 'what is the matter with you this evening, darling? You've hardly eaten anything and now you're being bitchy. That's not like you, sweetie.'

Claire turned pale suddenly and gasped. 'I'm sorry,' she said. 'I guess I'm just upset about something. Oh, about Alex. Excuse me a minute.' She got up and rushed off in the direction of the toilets.

'Well,' said Laurence, 'this definitely isn't our usual cool Miss O'Brien.'

'I'll just go and find her,' said Kate, and squeezed behind Simon's chair. 'You go on and order coffee.'

When the door to the Ladies swung shut behind her she was confronted by the sight of Claire being copiously sick into a basin.

An ageing matron shut her handbag with a loud click and bustled past. 'Well, that was a waste of a cordon bleu meal,' she muttered to Kate, shooting a disgusted eye at the mess.

Kate watched her leave, stunned into silence by such tactlessness. Then she went over to the towel-holder and started pulling out wadges of paper towel.

'Here,' she said. Claire seemed to have stopped being sick for the moment. She buried her face in the tissue while Kate swilled out the basin.

'I'm so sorry,' Claire sobbed, her pale face tragic and running with mascara. 'I couldn't help it, about Simon. I was so angry for you. I should have told you on your own, but I haven't seen you by yourself. It's . . . you see, when I saw him at the theatre he was kissing her. Really kissing her, I mean. I didn't know if I should say anything, but this evening, playing Happy Families like he does, with you sitting there unhappy, I just saw red. Perhaps I should blame the wine. And I feel so ill all the time.'

'Why, Claire, what's the matter?'

'I'm pregnant, aren't I? I didn't want a baby. And Alex doesn't want it. I don't know what to do. I love him – I've not felt this way about anyone before. I think I'm going mad.' And Claire threw herself into Kate's arms, sobbing wildly.


Later that night, Simon and Kate lay side by side, not touching, in the darkness. The silence between them was like an electric charge. Each seemed to be waiting for the other to speak first.

Kate had no idea how she had forced herself through time and place to be here. Back in the Ladies at the Crown, she had tried to comfort Claire, but her mind was in shock about Simon. It was almost as though she hadn't really believed it until it had been confirmed by somebody else. And seeing Claire, who had always been so strong and independent and honest – though her honesty had not been the best part of her tonight – now so lost and vulnerable, Kate felt like going to pieces too.

After a moment, the door to the toilets had creaked open and Liz had appeared. She took in the scene in a moment. It was she who bullied the gist of their stories out of them, mopped up their tears and told them to pull themselves together.

'I'll deal with Claire when we get back to the cottage,' she whispered fiercely to Kate as they filed back to the table behind their friend. 'You and I can have a chat tomorrow morning.' She stopped and gripped Kate's arms and studied her face. 'You OK?' she murmured. 'Oh, that stupid, stupid boy. I could kill him for you!'

Kate managed to curve her mouth in a smile. 'I'm OK,' she breathed, meeting Liz's gaze. Liz's anger was definitely as good as a shot of Scotch and certainly better than sympathy at this moment.

When they got back to the table it was to find that the men had paid up and were ready to go. No one said anything on the way back to the cars.

When they pulled out of the tiny hotel car park, Simon asked in an uncertain voice, 'So what was that all about then?'

'I think you know what it was all about,' spat Kate. 'Meredith.'

He looked at her but said no more. They followed the Longmans' car the few winding miles towards Blythborough where the great church of the marshes towered above the borrowed cottage. Joyce's cleaner, Michelle, had been babysitting the Longman children and Kate and Simon had promised to drop her off home.

They pulled up behind Laurence and Liz's car and Liz got out and hurried up to Kate's car window. 'Look,' she said, 'I'll just get Michelle. I'll give you a ring when we get up in the morning.' She nodded at Simon but did not speak to him.

Lying in bed, Kate turned over phrases in her mind. In the end, the one she selected was, 'Is it true, Simon?'

'Is what true?'

'That . . . you're having an affair with Meredith. That's where all the money's gone, hasn't it? On her.'

Silence. Then, a strange barking sound. Kate was astonished. Simon was crying.

'Such a mess,' he said in a cracked voice. 'I don't know what to do.' He rolled over and tried to hug her but she shoved him away. The action unleashed her anger.

'How could you?' she shouted. She hammered blows on him. 'I hate you, I hate you. You've spoiled everything.' She was crying herself now, great uncontrollable sobs tearing her insides out. He lay there curled up, his arms protecting his head, waiting for her to stop. Suddenly exhausted, she rolled back over and buried her head in her pillow, crying and crying.

'I love you, Kate,' came Simon's muffled voice. 'I'm sorry this has happened but I do love you. And Daisy and Sam. But I'm so confused. It's so powerful. I'm just overwhelmed. I feel I'm being torn in half.'

'But you let it happen. How did it start, Simon, eh? Did she force herself on you, drag you away to her lair and lock you up? And she knew you were married and had children – I met her, remember Liz's party? How could she do this to us?'

'She's very intense, Kate. She just fills you up. It's difficult to think of anything else. You can't understand. Oh, I'm not putting this right . . . Our banks were working on a deal together. We'd been talking, working together for weeks. And then the deal went through. It was brilliant, so exciting. The gang went out to a restaurant to celebrate. I suppose we had a lot to drink. It was late and she and I shared a taxi. And it sort of went on from there . . .' He trailed off.

'When?' was all Kate said.

'Huh? I don't know. Three, four months—'

*All that time and she hadn't known – or had she?* Already her mind was whirling back. Suddenly she was seeing so many things in a new light – his grumpiness, his reluctance to make love, his lack of interest in finding a home . . .

'What are we going to do now?' she whispered.

'I don't know, Kate, I don't know. I'm in such a muddle.' Again he reached out to her, but again she shoved him away.

This has happened before, thought Kate suddenly. Something made sense now.

It was back when Daisy was tiny and she'd been so ill. It had seemed to go on for months, Kate wrapped up in the needs of this tiny baby who cried all the time. She knew now she had pushed Simon away; when she saw him, it was like through the wrong end of a telescope. She hardly noticed the effect she was having on him, so absorbed was she in herself and Daisy. He still couldn't find work, but he would be out of the door at eight o'clock every morning, going to see the head-hunter, using the desk facilities he'd rented, going round the agencies. There were a couple of months when he got some contract work and then he'd stay late or go out with his mates. Often he didn't come in until after she was asleep. He would climb into bed to find his wife sleeping and baby Daisy lying between them, her big eyes staring at him in the light from the street-lamp outside.

A business trip, he said. The job meant he had to go to Singapore for a week to see some customers. Funny to send someone new on a short-term contract, Kate thought, but she wasn't interested enough to ask.

Looking back now, she wondered. Had he really gone by himself? And why couldn't she speak to him at the hotel? There was no one there of that name, they said. She had pushed her suspicions out of her mind – she couldn't cope. He came back and he seemed quiet. But then he often was at this time. Then his father died and Kate woke up to the fact that Simon needed her. It was the start of her recovery and the renewal of their relationship.

What had gone wrong this time?

She remembered her conversation with Claire, the week they left London. Perhaps she and Simon had grown apart. But was it her fault? It was she who had given up everything to move here, her job, her friends, all that was familiar to her. She who was holding the fort, bearing the brunt of the childcare, keeping them all together. And she had failed even to do that. What on earth was she going to do now?

'Don't do anything hasty,' advised Liz the next morning. Laurence and Simon had taken the children out and Joyce had gone off to fetch Bobby. She and Kate and Claire were sitting in the sparsely furnished front room of the Blythborough cottage. 'It might all just blow over.'

'I can't bear to think that it won't,' Kate answered. 'It's like I'm staring into an abyss. He's hardly looked at me this morning. Or talked to me. Daisy knows something's up, I'm sure she does. She won't do anything I say and keeps being rude to me. And Joyce keeps giving me these looks. I'll have to tell her. I'm sorry,' she choked. 'I can't stop crying. Sorry, Claire.'

'No, it's me who's sorry,' said Claire. 'I shouldn't have said what I did last night. It's just made things worse, hasn't it?'

'It's right that it should come out in the open, though. And I know you were trying to support me.'

'My over-developed conscience. I always thought telling the truth was best, but it isn't always, is it? It's more complicated than that . . .' She trailed to a halt and fumbled for a tissue to blow her nose.

'Claire and I had a long talk last night,' said Liz.

'I'm going to have the baby.' Claire put her tissue down and smiled shakily. 'I couldn't not, could I?'

'Not you, Claire, no.'

'I don't know what Alex will say, but then it's not his decision,' she said fiercely. 'It'll be my baby. I won't ask him for anything. We'll look after ourselves.'

Liz sighed. 'And we'll help you. Come on, let's go and get a bit of fresh air. Then we'd better go and meet the others.'

After a walk on the heath, Liz and Claire went back to make some more coffee while Kate took a look at the church. The morning service was long over, though one or two elderly ladies were piling up hymn books and notice sheets and removing wilted blooms from the flower displays. There was a narrow stone spiral staircase at the back by the south door and Kate made her way up. She found herself in a tiny chapel with large windows and rush matting on the floor. It smelled of damp, but it was warm in the sunlight and peaceful.

Kate sat on one of the wooden benches and focused on the simple altar. She could hear her watch ticking, it was so quiet.

Here she was somehow relieved of her anxiety. She closed her eyes and breathed deeply.

*All will be well and all manner of thing will be well.*

Somehow, she would get herself through all of this.

# *Chapter 17*

The rest of Sunday passed in a confused blur. After saying good-bye to their visitors Simon and Kate went back to Paradise Cottage for one of Joyce's huge high teas. Simon was trying very hard to behave normally to Kate, while she could barely bring herself to look at him. At one point he muttered to no one in particular that perhaps he ought to go back to London this evening, but the children's wails and Joyce's indignation put paid to that. He and Kate would have to endure another night of agony alone together.

During the evening, Kate had a phone call. It was Dan.

'Miss Melton's asking for you, Kate. She's not too good at the moment, to be honest. A bit depressed about going onto the ward. I think something's on her mind, too. Anyway, I said I'd give you a call.'

'Dan, thanks. I'm a bit tied up here, to be honest. I'm not sure I can. Oh, and there's a problem. The car's in the garage and they're waiting for the part.'

'Well, I do have to take something in for her Tuesday, so I could give you a lift in the afternoon, if that would help.'

Frankly, Kate didn't feel like doing anything or going anywhere at the moment. 'Look, that's really kind of you, but I don't know. I'll ring you, OK?'

There was a silence at the other end. Then, 'I'm sorry, it seems I've called at a bad time,' he said softly.

'No, it's not that. Well, yes . . . It's a bit complicated, Dan. Just things here.'

That night, as they undressed for bed, Kate tried to talk to Simon, but she just kept crying and crying.

'Do you want me to come back tomorrow evening?' he asked, trying to put his arm round her. She pushed him away.

'I don't know.' She looked up at him. Suddenly rage surged through her. 'No, don't bloody bother,' she hissed.

He flinched but nodded. 'I'll definitely be back on Friday. It's Sports Day, isn't it? I'll try to get back during the week, but we need some time to think.'

'To think. That's what you call it, is it? I suppose you'll be seeing *her*.'

'No. I don't want to see anybody. I just want to think and I bet you do too. Kate, I'm sorry, I know it's hard for you, but it's hard for me, too. This whole last year has been hard for me, if only you knew.'

Like hell, thought Kate. She banged her hairbrush down on the chest of drawers and glared at him, her expression murderous.

Simon went out to the bathroom. When he returned he was carrying some blankets. He picked up his pillow and his clothes for the morning. 'I'll sleep on the sofa. Otherwise neither of us will be good for anything,' he said, looking away.

When a puffy-eyed Kate went downstairs at seven o'clock the next morning, he had gone.

'It's a perfect summer's day,' said Joyce, coming in from the garden, having unlocked the shed for Mr Brierly from the village to retrieve the lawnmower. Kate was too down to notice the weather when she left for school with the children at half past eight. When they arrived, the little huddles of parents round the gate seemed larger than usual. She hugged Sam goodbye – Daisy just tore off yelling 'Bye, Mum,' over her shoulder – then looked round for Debbie, but she must have missed her. She waved at Louise, who was ambling across the playground towards her, looking even more distracted than usual.

'You've heard, have you?' she said.

'Heard what?' Kate asked.

'Apparently Mrs Smithson has had a letter from the council about the building repairs. They're going to look at closing the school.'

'No!' Kate must have paled suddenly, because Louise grabbed her arm to steady her. Not this on top of everything else.

'I suppose you're talking about what I think you're talking about.' It was James Galt, father of Sam's friend Sebastian, a slight, dapper man with a neat greying beard. 'Can you believe it? I've just been to see Mrs S. She's in an awful state. Says it oughtn't to have got out like this. She was going to write to parents.'

'But that's terrible. Why shut the school? It's so good. Sam and Daisy are so happy here. And they'd been building up the numbers, hadn't they?'

'Not fast enough, apparently,' went on James. 'I suppose we ought to have seen it coming. The authority has been looking at one or two other village schools and reaching the same conclusion. We'll have to get the children into Halesworth.'

In her misery about Simon, Kate was quick to anger. 'But we can't just let them tell us what to do! What do they know about the school and the way it works – its importance to Fernley.'

'Probably nothing,' sighed Louise. 'It's just numbers, isn't it?'

'Like the way they closed the library three years ago,' said

**185**

James. 'There was some consultation, but in the end it came down to pounds and pence – it was either the library or one of the local museums, they said. I suppose the museum folk all shouted louder than us, not that I can blame them.'

'This sort of thing is just killing our communities—' started Louise, but they were interrupted by the appearance of Mrs Smithson herself.

'I know, it's simply dreadful,' she said. Kate had never seen anyone actually wringing their hands before. 'Out of the blue like this. They say that someone will be down to talk to us and listen to our suggestions, but I didn't like the tone of the letter. Very peremptory. We've been telling them about the terrible state of the roof for years, but I never thought it would come to this.'

'We can't let it happen,' said Kate. 'We must be able to do something.' She looked around at the circle of faces in disbelief. The mood seemed to be of defeat already. 'You are going to fight it, aren't you?' she said to Mrs Smithson.

'Well, we'll do what we can.' She shrugged. 'We're having a governors' meeting tonight. It's just that one feels so powerless. The buildings are very old now, and I can't argue with the fact that we need a new roof. It's ridiculous to have buckets in Miss Hawkins's classroom every time it rains. I've seen this happen to other schools, but I thought we were safe, with our numbers. What can we do? At least the children will get educated some-where, and I expect the staff will find new jobs. After all, they'll need to take on new teachers at Halesworth because of us.'

'But the school is at the heart of Fernley,' Kate pointed out. 'What will be left apart from the church? I suppose it will be the post office after this. And the pubs.'

The others nodded, but it was despair that Kate saw in their faces, not anger. She couldn't believe their acquiescence. It was the life of their community they were talking about, after all.

'We mustn't go down without a fight,' she told them. 'There must be something we can do.'

'Let's go away and think about it for a bit, shall we?' said Miss Smithson. 'I'd better go back and teach your children!' Her mouth smiled but not her eyes. 'I expect the governors will get a letter out to all the parents straight away.'

'Would the authority give us a breakdown of the figures, do you think?' said Kate. 'At least then we could get an idea of what we're up against. And perhaps the governors could ask whoever it is from the department to come to a meeting and give us a few facts.'

'Yes, yes, all that,' said Miss Smithson. She looked at Kate as if she had thought of something, because she smiled suddenly. 'What was it you did in London?' she asked.

On the walk back to Paradise Cottage in the sunshine, the shocks of the last two days suddenly hit Kate. Joyce, watching for her out of the window, caught sight of her daughter-in-law's tear-streaked face and hurried to open the door.

'Where have you been? What's happened? Are the children all right?'

'The children are fine, just fine. Well, I hope they will be.' Kate started to tell her about the school, but this merely unplugged a deeper misery and soon she was sobbing uncontrollably.

Joyce helped her onto a chair and sat down at the table next to her, putting her arms around her. This was such a motherly gesture, one she'd always missed, that Kate buried her head in her mother-in-law's shoulder and cried harder than ever. Bobby came and jabbed his nose into each lap in turn, but Joyce pushed him away.

'Oh, Kate, dear. This can't just be about the school. What's the matter? I know everything seems very difficult for you at the

187

moment and I know I don't always help. But is there something wrong between you and Simon? Of course it's none of my business, but I can't sit here and pretend that that wasn't a miserable weekend.'

Kate sat up and rubbed her eyes. 'I don't know if it's me who should be telling you . . .' She stopped. Simon's mother would surely feel her first loyalty was to her son, no matter what he had done.

But already Kate had gone too far. Joyce sat upright in her chair. Her eyes did not leave Kate's face, so Kate told her the cold facts of Simon's affair.

When she'd finished, they sat there in silence, then Joyce said, 'I don't know what to say. I wouldn't have believed it of him.' After a moment, her bewildered expression was replaced by one of fear. She said, 'What are you going to do?'

'I don't know, I don't know.' Kate began to cry again. 'And I don't know how serious he is about her. I don't know what he wants to do. I do still love him. I can't just tell him to go. And there are the children to think of. Anyway, this is his home more than mine – you're his mother. It's me that would have to go. I'd have to find somewhere . . .' She finished, 'I couldn't go without the children.'

There was silence again. Then Joyce said carefully, 'I know he is my son and I will always be there for him, but Daisy and Sam are my grandchildren and I'm fond of you, too. What he's doing is very wrong. I can try and talk to him, but I don't know whether it's going to be any use. He won't listen to me, he never has done . . .' She trailed to a halt, the enormity of the problem coming home. After a moment she decided. 'You must stay here,' she said. 'If it comes to it, Simon will have to find somewhere else. It's not right that the children lose their home. But maybe it won't come to that. Maybe he'll see sense. Oh, don't give up on him, Kate, don't. We had difficult times in our marriage, everybody does, but you can get through.'

'Yes, but your husband has to be *there* to do that,' Kate snapped. 'I feel like a widow most of the time anyway – sorry, Joyce, that was tactless of me. Oh, I wish we could turn back time. We should never have left London. I suppose we've led such separate lives we've got used to being without each other.'

'It's so different now, isn't it? My parents were apart for most of the war, but my mother never looked at another man, though we missed Dad so much. She used to say he wasn't the same after he came back, but she didn't complain. So many men never came back – she knew she was one of the lucky ones.'

'It's hardly like the war though, is it?' Kate instantly regretted her sharpness. 'I mean, we see each other every week. I'm sorry, Joyce, I didn't mean to be rude, but we can't make these comparisons. Things are just much more complex than they were sixty years ago.'

'That's just what Hazel was saying last night. We didn't use to go into a shop and have to choose between thirty different jams. Or have to decide between a dozen different Directory Enquiries firms when the old one used to work perfectly well . . .'

Kate sighed impatiently. Joyce had such a grasshopper mind these days. Her mother-in-law took the hint. 'I'll make us both some coffee,' she said and started bustling about, fumbling the cups and spilling the grains. She stopped, the decaff jar in her hand and turned round. 'You know, if you and Simon want to go off on a little break, maybe next weekend, I'm very happy to look after the children.'

'Thank you, but I don't know whether he would. He's very strange at the moment. And I'm not sure I could face a whole weekend, just the two of us. He's got to want to come back. I

can't make him . . . I don't even know whether I want him back.'
And with that she burst into tears again.

'What are you going to do?' Debbie asked.

They were sitting at the wooden table in Debbie's sunny
cottage kitchen the next morning, drinking tea. Kate added two
sugars to hers and Debbie pushed a packet of chocolate biscuits
towards her. Down on the floor, little Holly upended a box of her
big sister's doll's-house accessories on the quarry tiles and
plumped herself down happily to sort through the little figures
and furniture, gabbling to herself. Jonny had just drifted into the
kitchen, his olive skin and dark hair and eyes reminding Kate just
how like brother and sister he and Debbie looked. She had often
noticed how married couples grew to look like one another. Did
she, Kate, share Simon's facial expressions, his turns of speech,
his gestures? She'd never thought to consider such a bond
between them before and now it was with a pang. Would that
bond, too, dissolve? She watched Jonny run his fingers back
through his wavy hair in the same way Debbie always did, as
they discussed the news about the school, but then, perhaps sensing dark whirling currents of female emotion, he helped himself
to a handful of biscuits and vanished upstairs to his desk.

'I just don't know what I'll do,' Kate said now. Why does
everyone expect *me* to be doing something? she thought angrily.
It's Simon who's been doing things. 'It's like I told Liz on the
phone last night, one minute I feel so angry I'm shaking, the next
I cry till I'm as weak as a baby. Last night was awful. I lay awake
just going over and over the last few months, trying to see where
it all went wrong. I hate him for what he's done but that doesn't
mean I don't still love him.' Kate looked up, dark circles making
her eyes appear huge in her face. 'Suppose he doesn't want me
any more? Suppose he goes off with her? What will I do?'

Debbie put down her cup and made to say something. Then she appeared to change her mind.

'Kate, it may not come to that. It's early days yet. But if that is what happens, you will survive. Honestly. You have friends here – I'm here for you – and it sounds as though Joyce is ready to help. It's a most awful crisis but people do get through it.'

'I don't even want to see him at the moment but I'll have to at the weekend. He'll want to see the children. And I guess we need to talk.'

'Yes, you do.'

'I know we haven't seen enough of one another over the last year, but many couples manage that, don't they?'

'Well yes, but every marriage is different, I suppose is the answer. I mean, look at Jim and Janet next door. Jim's away a lot with his work but Janet told me once that they made this agreement when she was pregnant with their first, that he would work hard to earn the money and she would devote herself to the children. They talked it all over in great detail, how Janet would feel, whether Jim would see enough of the kids and so on. But Jim had an awful upbringing – his mum left when he was seven – and he said he couldn't bear to think of anyone but Janet looking after his children.'

'Jim's a salesman, isn't he?' Kate asked.

'Yes, his firm have a lot of foreign contracts. Janet says they both get fed up sometimes, but what is life-saving is to go away together by themselves several weekends a year . . . I'm sorry, I'm blathering on here. Their situation really is completely different.'

'No, it's just all too late for me – for us – isn't it? I didn't see it coming.'

'Kate, isn't it more complicated than that? You not seeing one another enough might not be the only reason for him . . . doing this. There might have been other things in your marriage – or from before you met. And you have to think very long and hard about whether it's just a slip-up on his part and whether you can get back what you had.'

'I know, I know. And the children. I can't think what this will do to Sam and Daisy, they love their daddy so much. And my mum and dad will be horrified. They don't need any more trouble . . .' And Kate dissolved into tears once again.

At lunchtime, Kate was forcing down a sandwich when Dan rang again.

'Hi, Kate, I've been out all morning. I'm on my mobile. I might have missed your call?'

'No, Dan, sorry, I forgot,' said Kate. Joyce was semaphoring in the background, so she said, 'Hold on,' and put her hand over the receiver.

'If you want to get out to see the old lady, dear, I can collect the children. Hazel's got her grandsons visiting – we can go round there, I expect.'

'Thanks. I suppose I ought to see Agnes.' She spoke into the phone. 'Yes, I'll come, Dan, if you don't mind picking me up. Yes, half two will be fine.'

After lunch, Kate looked so exhausted and tearful Joyce sent her to bed for an hour. She awoke soon after two, and by the time she had washed her face, slicked on some lip gloss and brushed her hair, Dan's van had pulled up outside.

'Here,' said Joyce. She thrust a bouquet of large yellow roses from the garden into Kate's hand. 'For Miss Melton, hoping they'll cheer her up.'

Kate buried her nose in the gorgeous blooms. 'Mmm, I'm sure they will. They certainly do me.'

And, indeed, as she opened the front door and waved to Dan,

she felt her spirits lift just a little. It would be good to go somewhere different with somebody new and have to think about someone else's troubles. No, that didn't sound quite right, thought Kate, but what woman would not feel cheered by going down the garden path to meet Dan leaning easily against his car smiling?

Which thought only made her want Simon.

# Chapter 18

'Lovely garden your mother-in-law has. Her cottage is picture perfect.'

There was something very comfortable about sitting next to Dan in the untidy old van, windows open and Classic FM floating out.

'Yes,' Kate replied. 'I always say it's like the Seven Dwarves' house, or the Three Bears' cottage. She's collected all those bird-tables and nesting boxes from around the country. It's what she used to do with her husband, you see, take holidays where you could visit gardens. Like the garden at Seddington House – that must have been magnificent in its heyday.'

'Miss Melton's grandfather had it laid out at the end of the nineteenth century. There was a full-time gardener once and an assistant, and now there's just me. Oh, and a local firm comes in with a tractor mower once a week.'

'What else do you do – apart from helping Miss Melton, I mean. If I'm not being nosy.'

'Of course you're not.' They had stopped at a junction, and Dan glanced at Kate as they waited for a break in the traffic. 'I have what they call a mixed portfolio. I paint – that's what I like doing most. And I run a gallery in Halesworth with a friend. We show local artists, mainly. That's where I was this morning, framing pictures.'

'Oh?' said Kate, with interest. 'Do you ever show your own work there?'

'Sometimes. I've got some drawings up at the moment, in fact.'

'I'll have to come in and see them,' said Kate.

'That would be great.'

'It's special seeing work by people you know, don't you think?'

'It can be dangerous sometimes. What happens if you don't like it? Does that change your opinion of the person who created it?'

'By their works shall ye know them. Yes, there is that risk.' Kate chuckled. 'But I'll take it.'

'And then there's my motorbikes,' he added.

'Your motorbikes?'

'Yes, I buy old ones and restore them and sell them. And I do a bit of stunt riding.' Dan grinned. 'When the police aren't looking!'

'It sounds safer to have the van. Do you camp in it?'

'It's done a lot of travelling, good old soul, been round Europe.' He patted the dashboard affectionately. 'Now it's mostly useful for carting stuff about.'

'Hope you're not meaning me,' Kate teased him.

'Yup, stuff like you,' he agreed and laughed.

When they got to the hospital, they found a space easily in the car park.

'I'll come in and say hello and give her this from Marie.' From behind the seat, Dan lifted out a leather shopping bag, which appeared to have clothes in it. 'Then I'll drive down to the town. Pick you up here about four?'

Kate thanked him and Dan looked at her as if wondering whether to say something else.

'Just a word of warning,' he said finally. 'Well, perhaps "warning" is too strong a word. That nephew of hers is about.'

'Max? I bumped into him at the weekend.' She explained about Bobby's drama.

'Yeah, he's not a bad bloke. Trouble is, he rubs Miss Melton up the wrong way. Treats her like an old person, if you know what I mean.' He was choosing his words with care. 'My view would be he's too aware that he's her closest relative. He's hardly been to see her at all until she had this accident. Now he's around half the time asking me and Marie questions about this and that . . . Miss Melton's solicitor said he could have the keys to the house.' He stopped. 'I'd better shut up. I get over-protective about her and, after all, it could just be real anxiety for her on his part.'

Kate nodded. After Max's help with Bobby she felt she owed him the benefit of the doubt, too. It didn't sound as if it had been his fault that he hadn't got to know his great-aunt earlier. The family row, whatever it was, had not been of Max's making.

They asked directions to the ward. Kate was relieved to see that it was bright and airy, with a dozen beds. Agnes was, fortunately, alone. She was sitting in a wheelchair next to her bed, staring into space, a stale cup of tea untouched on the tray table in front of her. Someone had left an old copy of *Woman's Weekly* next to it. That wasn't touched either. Huddled up in a blanket, despite the warm weather, her face looked shrivelled, vacant. Kate was struck again by how she now often looked every one of her ninety-odd years. A butterfly of unease fluttered in her mind.

It took a moment for Agnes to recognize them, but when she did, the vitality rushed back.

'You found me then,' she quavered as Dan placed the bag on

the bed and pulled up a chair for Kate. 'Don't know why they've put me in here with all these poor old things.'

Kate kept her eyes on Agnes and hoped the other occupants of the ward hadn't heard this.

'It's good to have people to talk to,' Dan said. 'And it's a nice bright room, this. I won't stay now. I have to get a few bits and pieces to deal with that rotten window in the library. I'll fetch Kate in an hour, Miss M., and come back later in the week.' He winked at Kate and strolled off down the ward, his rangy figure attracting admiring looks from the two young nurses on duty.

'Good boy, that one,' croaked Agnes, then cleared her throat and spoke more strongly. 'I wish he'd make a success of something. Did you know he gave up a career in London?'

'Really?' said Kate, surprised. 'I don't know much about him, but he certainly doesn't strike me as an urban animal. Have you known him long?'

'Only since he came home looking for work a few years ago. Summers knows the family. She engaged him to clear the front garden while he was studying and then we kept finding other things for him to do. I think he only comes out of kindness now, you know. He always seems very busy . . . whatever it is he does. Kate, it's lovely to see you. And what wonderful roses. Ask Nurse to bring you a vase, and a proper cup of tea, too. I was asleep when they brought this. It's disgusting.'

Kate went over to the nurses' station to cajole one of them into carrying out Agnes's orders, then sat down at the bedside. Agnes pulled Dan's bag over and started rummaging around amongst the clothes. Kate took the chance to look round at the 'poor old things'. The cubicle curtain was drawn between Agnes and the bed on her left, but in the bed on the other side, a nearly bald lady lay asleep. Opposite was a huge woman crippled by a stroke. She sagged against the pillows, her eyes unable to focus, her mouth hanging open. Her equally large husband, a man in his seventies, was sitting by her side, coaxing her to drink from a child's beaker. He caught Kate's eye and twinkled at her. 'I come every day to see my Maureen,' he confided. 'She looked after this ol' bugger –' he jabbed at his chest to indicate himself as the old bugger '– every day for fifty years. Never a cross word. Now I look after her.'

Kate didn't know what to say, though her father's ever-patient tending of her mother passed through her mind. There were so many quiet faithful acts to see in the world if you only looked. She gave him a smile and turned back to Agnes. The old lady had wrestled a small envelope out of the bottom of the shopping bag and put it on the tray in front of her.

'Kate Hutchinson,' Agnes said, fingering the envelope. 'I'm telling you all this because I think you understand me. I don't believe I've got much time left.'

Kate opened her mouth to object but Agnes waved her hand impatiently and went on. 'No, I don't think I'm going to get home again. It's not because they've put me in here. I just feel it to be so.'

'Agnes, don't. I know it seems—'

Once again, Agnes shushed her. 'I know we've only got to know each other a little time, dear, but we're family and we see eye to eye. There are things that you've said about yourself that make my heart go out to you. We're birds of a feather. I wish we had met before. However,' she went on, 'we'd better get on before my great-nephew turns up. You met him at the weekend, I hear. What d'you think of him?' She didn't wait for Kate's answer. 'Well, never mind, it's not his fault he is who he is. This is the key,' she handed the envelope to Kate, 'of a cupboard in the library. It's behind a set of the *Domesday Book*. I want you to read what's inside – then you'll know who we're looking for. I want to find him, you see . . .'

Kate took the envelope wonderingly, but before she could ask who 'he' was, the young West Indian nurse Kate remembered from an earlier visit arrived with a vase and two mugs of tea. She and Agnes had clearly taken to one another, for Agnes didn't seem to mind being mothered by a girl a quarter her age. After the roses had been arranged, the nurse tidied up the bed and left them once more. Agnes started to talk again, but then she looked past Kate to the nurses' station. 'Oh damn, *he*'s here. I can't say any more now. Take the key and read, then we'll talk.'

Kate rose from her seat and turned to see Max marching down the ward. He was wearing a grey suit and light blue tie today, his dark hair neatly slicked back, and was carrying a bunch of pink carnations. He nodded to Kate then bent and kissed his great-aunt on the cheek.

'Nice to see you sitting up in your chair, Aunt,' he said, speaking in the slightly too-jolly voice people use for young children and those in their second childhood. 'You look well today. I expect Kate here has been cheering you up.'

'I'm just off now, actually,' said Kate. 'I have to meet someone.' They stood there awkwardly, as if unsure of the protocol around a hospital bedside. Max's tall businesslike presence filled the little cubicle. His aunt, huddled in her chair, seemed diminished in comparison. Kate said, rather gushingly, 'I must thank you so much again, Max, for saving poor Bobby.'

'How is he now? That was quite an adventure he had.'

'Back to his normal bouncy self, I'm glad to say. Joyce is so relieved.' Kate gave her apologies to Max as charmingly as she could, then squeezed Agnes's proffered hand and hurried off down the ward. Was it her imagination, or did Max's gaze follow her all the way?

*

Downstairs, she walked into the car park to see whether Dan was waiting yet. She couldn't see his van, but then it was still only twenty to four. She returned to the reception area and sat down to wait in the cool quietness.

Usually she was soothed by her visits to Agnes. The old lady was almost Kate's grandmother's generation, but this wasn't quite like snapping back into the motherly relationship she had had with her grandmother – no, Agnes was more of an equal, a very good friend. Despite the gulf of experience between their generations, they had something important in common, more than the ties of blood. Perhaps it was the currency of grief? But today, Kate felt disturbed by her visit. It wasn't just the mysterious task Agnes had entrusted her with – Kate felt for the envelope in her trouser pocket – though that was troubling enough. Nor was it Max's slightly oppressive presence, or finding out that Dan didn't fit into the handyman pigeonhole she'd made for him. No, it was that the grip of Agnes's fingers on hers had seemed weaker, her normally upright pose slacker, her attention beginning to wander, as though the knot that tied her to life was gradually loosening.

She couldn't lose Agnes now. She needed her, her strength of will, her links with her family's past, with Seddington House. She wanted to find out the rest of Agnes's story. Talking to the old lady was like immersing herself in a different reality to her everyday life, one from which she herself gained strength. She could forget her anxieties about Simon when she was with Agnes, but now that she had a moment of peace, all this morning's misery came flooding back. She sat there, the tears rolling down her cheeks, uncaring of the curious looks she was getting from passers-by – weren't people used to tears in a hospital, for goodness sake? – when someone sat down on the banquette beside her. It was Dan.

'What's happened?' he whispered, the expression in his blue eyes both tense and tender. She looked away, not able to bear his sympathy. 'It's not Agnes, is it?'

Kate shook her bowed head quickly, wiping her eyes with the back of her hand. 'No. Agnes is . . . as you said. And Max is there, so I came down early.'

'What's the matter then?' he said. 'Come on, let's go and find somewhere to have a cup of tea.'

They drove into town and found a little café and Kate sat and told him about Simon having an affair, and how he was pushing her away, about how lost she sometimes felt down here, how she missed her work and her friends, about the threat hanging over the school and how she just felt so muddled and angry and didn't know what to do. Dan listened. He didn't try to comfort her or to make bright suggestions or to volunteer his own experiences. It was a relief to lay it all out like this. Eventually, they sat there, comfortably silent. Kate had told him how relieved she was that Joyce wanted them to stay, and now she had run out of words.

'So here you are,' Dan sighed, his eyes fixed on her face, 'like Ruth amid the alien corn, if I remember my scripture lessons right.'

Kate thought about the implications of that. In the Old Testament story, Ruth had gone with her husband to live in his country, as was the custom. Then her husband died. She was supposed to return to her own people but instead she chose to stay with her lonely mother-in-law, Naomi. 'Your country will be my country, your people, my people,' Ruth had told Naomi. Well, she wasn't sure she could feel like that about Joyce, but the two of them had certainly been thrown together. And at least Kate's husband wasn't dead. And she had her darling Daisy and Sam. Ruth's story had a happy ending – she had married a wealthy farmer and was able to look after Naomi in her turn.

But what does Dan mean? We haven't got to that stage yet, Kate told herself fiercely. It's going to be all right with Simon – isn't it?

The waitress appeared with the bill, which Dan paid, and Kate's mind snapped back to the present. The key! She decided to confide in Dan, whom she instinctively trusted.

When she told him all about Agnes's strange request he seemed quite animated.

'It's nearly five. Do you have to get back right away?' he said. 'We could go to the house now.'

Kate rang Paradise Cottage but heard only the answerphone. The family must still be at Hazel's. She left a message to say she'd be back in an hour and then they walked back to the van.

'Thank you, Dan,' she said simply. 'You're a good listener.'

'That's got me into trouble plenty of times,' he said mournfully, and she laughed.

'Agnes said you used to work in London.'

'Yes, in advertising – Jones Kline. I was a designer there. '

'What sort of thing did you work on?'

'Toothpaste, toilet cleaner, weedkiller . . . yes, I got all the glamorous accounts. Stuck it out for nine years then I just lost the urge to get up in the morning. The design bit was all right. I just hated London, hated the office politics, missed Suffolk, my home ground.'

'Where did you study design?'

'Norwich. That was all right, I could still live at home, get in on my bike every day. But London turned out to be where the jobs were.'

'Couldn't you have gone freelance once you got back here, or worked somewhere local?'

'Could have. I just felt I had other things I wanted to do. The painting mostly. I did a part-time fine art course a couple of years ago. That's what I should have done in the first place, but everyone was telling me I needed to train for a proper job.'

'I remember what that feels like. And haven't you ever . . . I don't know, settled down? I mean, didn't you need to pay for things?'

'You mean am I married, don't you?' Kate felt herself blushing, but Dan was smiling. 'I was. For four years. We met at college. She came to London at the same time I did and we got married as soon as we could get a deposit together for a flat. But she changed – or I did. We were too young, really. Gabby loved London and she did well at her job, but she turned out to be a party animal. She started to say I was being boring – I probably was. I didn't want to go to clubs, do cocaine and stay up half the night like her. In the end we just seemed to pass on the doorstep. Then she found someone else . . .'

'Poor you,' whispered Kate. 'I know what that's like now.'

'Yes, but by then what we'd had was long gone. It was a bit of a relief, in a way, when she said we should split. She and her bloke bought me out of the flat and I rented somewhere else and tried to make a go of it. It didn't work out. Now, here we are . . . Looks like Marie's son Conrad is out.' And Dan swung the van round in a shower of gravel in front of Seddington House.

'Excuse me a moment,' he said, reaching his hand across Kate to rummage in the glove compartment, which was a glorious mess of cassette tapes, bits of string and glucose sweets. What long, sensitive fingers he has for a practical man, Kate thought, intensely aware of him leaning across her, his shoulder briefly brushing hers. Then, as his hand closed over a bunch of keys, she noticed something else – bits of Polly Pocket toys. Did Dan have a child?

'We'll have to go through the back of the house, I'm afraid,' he said now, winking at her. 'No Lady Muck for you, sweeping through the front door, my dear.'

'What do you mean, Lady Muck? When have I put on airs and graces?'

'Ah, don't think I haven't seen you looking. You fancy this house, don't you? Well, who wouldn't?'

'Where do you live, Dan?'

'Down in the village. Cottage with the blue door, near the pub. Bit of a garage round the back to do my bikes and a shed for the painting. It was my dad's house, but he got married again a few years ago and moved into his wife Sally's bungalow in Wenhaston.' He opened his door to get out. 'My mum died, you see. When I was ten.'

'I'm sorry,' said Kate softly. 'That must have been shattering.'

'It was the end of my childhood,' said Dan. 'She was so ill, but I never thought she'd die. You don't believe your parents can die when you're only ten. But she did. So then there was just me and Dad. And now Dad's got Sally. I'm glad for him really. She's OK. Organizes Dad, but he likes that. Mum used to organize him, you see, tidy up after him, get his meals on the table. Everything was a right muddle when it was just Dad and me.' He laughed. 'Anyway, he gave me the house so I'm grateful for that.'

Kate listened to his footsteps as he went round to the back of the vehicle to get out his tools then she pushed open her door and jumped down. She stood looking up at the house. Pink-edged clouds were reflected like swans gliding on the diamond-hatched windows. The place looked even more shut up than it had on her first visit. The curtains of the library were closed now – was she just imagining the air of desolation? She turned and looked across the front gardens.

'I've been keeping the hedges cut, and spraying the worst of the weeds,' said Dan, as if reading her thoughts. 'Marie checks on everything and dusts, and Conrad often stays. Otherwise, there's not been much to do, apart from finishing the kitchen. Oh, and the library window. I'll deal with that tomorrow.'

They walked to the left, round to the kitchen door. Dan picked out a large iron key and a smaller brass one for the mortice lock. The door opened easily; he hurried in to switch off the alarm, and Kate followed him through the kitchen to the hall beyond and the library.

The warmth, the muffling of their footsteps and the half-dark reminded Kate of going into a marquee on a hot summer's day. The stuffy air smelled of soft furnishings and old books, which also deadened sound. A bluebottle buzzed tiredly somewhere in the room. Dan walked over to the windows and worked the cords of the burgundy velvet curtains one by one, then pushed the casements open. All at once, the room was flooded with light, fresh air and the twitterings of birds. Kate looked around. The chair in which Agnes had sat had been pulled back into line. Her personal alarm, its cord neatly coiled, lay on the table next to a pack of cards and the Wilkie Collins. It was as if the room was standing to attention, ready for Agnes to walk back in.

Kate started to scan the shelves. Eventually, at waist-level, half-hidden by a chair to the left of the fireplace, she saw what she was looking for: a row of slim leatherbound volumes. Each spine bore the name of a different English county in gilt lettering, and the series title, the *Domesday Book*. She began to take the books off the shelf, but all that was revealed was the wallpaper behind. Puzzled, she persevered. Perhaps there would be some lever or handle – but no. She replaced the books and started feeling up and down the sides of the shelves. Still nothing. She walked over to the fireplace and examined that closely. Again, no clue.

'Here,' said Dan, coming up to stand behind her. 'Let's look at that key.'

She pulled the envelope out of her pocket and extracted a golden key two inches long. Strangely, it had no tines – the operational end was octagonal in shape, and hollow.

'Let's take the books out again.' They piled the volumes one by one next to the fireplace.

The tiny keyhole was behind the volume entitled *Surrey*. It could have been an imperfection in the elderly Strawberry Thief design to anyone not looking closely. A false wall! Kate pushed in the key and turned it. The whole shelf swung open. There behind was a low rectangular safe about the size of two stacked box-files. It had a combination lock. 'Oh no,' cried Kate. 'What do we do now?'

'Look at the envelope,' said Dan.

Kate turned it over and over, then realized that where she had torn it open, she'd ripped through a number. 1910.

'I think that's when Miss Agnes was born,' whispered Dan, close but not touching, his breath warm against her cheek. Kate felt an urge to lean back against him, to feel safe in his enfolding arms, and resisted it. 'Try it,' Dan said, meaning the code.

Kate turned the dial back and forth with care. Something clicked. She pulled open the safe door.

To one end inside was a pile of flat, velvet-covered boxes. Kate picked up one and opened it. She gasped. It contained an exquisite diamond necklace and matching earings – Edwardian, she guessed, from the design.

'Why doesn't she keep it in the bank?' said Dan, shaking his head. 'Must be worth thousands.'

Kate closed the box. 'I don't think it's this she wanted us to look at,' she said, and replaced the jewel-case with the others. 'It's these.'

On the right-hand side of the safe was a pile of notebooks, five in all. Two were child's exercise books, the others were covered in patterned cardboard. Kate opened one at random. *December 1943*, ran the top line in classic dark blue italic. *Father still very ill. The doctor says it's his lungs, the mustard gas. He coughs horribly, on and on and on, though there's nothing . . .*

'Her diaries.' Kate pulled the rest out. There was something else in the safe, half-tucked behind the pile of jewel-cases, a thick manila envelope sealed with sticky tape. Kate turned it over. It was addressed: *To my son from his mother, Agnes Lavender Melton.* Her son! Agnes had a son! Was it this that Agnes wanted her to know?

Just then they heard wheels crunching over gravel. They turned to see through the window a silver Range Rover roll to a halt next to Dan's van. A smartly dressed figure got out.

Max surveyed the frontage of the house as he slammed the driver's door and locked it. In a moment a key rattled in the front-door.

Kate and Dan looked at one another.

'Quick. He mustn't see all this,' Kate said, worried. She stuffed everything back in the safe, shut the door and the bookshelf and dropped the key into her handbag.

'Hello?' called Max from the hall.

When he opened the library door and peered round, the two of them were piling the volumes of the *Domesday Book* back on the shelves. A palpable air of guilt hung in the air, and Kate felt as if she and Dan had been caught in some terrible kind of *flagrante delictum*.

How on earth were they to talk themselves out of *this*?

# Chapter 19

'What the hell?' Max started. 'What are you doing in here? Who's given you permission to touch things?' He stared at Kate, then at Dan. Dislike snapped through the air between the two men.

'I work here, Mr Jordan, *if* you remember. I have a key,' said Dan, deliberately.

Max looked him up and down. 'I wasn't aware that your duties included thumbing through my aunt's private collections, Mr Peace.' Dan Peace – Kate hadn't known his surname before. The glares he was giving Max now were anything but peaceful. 'We really need to improve the security here,' Max said, as if to himself. 'Until everything's sorted out . . .'

'Max, your aunt asked me to look for something for her here, some papers,' Kate said, trying to sound firm but merely seeming defensive. The scene must, indeed, look very suspicious to Max. The handyman and an unknown woman claiming to be her cousin who'd wormed her way into Miss Melton's affections, going through her possessions in her deserted house. In his place she'd be annoyed, too, though his air of arrogance wasn't necessary.

'Really, it is all right,' she tried to assure Max. 'Ask your aunt.'

She was reluctant to show Max the little key. Her instinct was that Agnes wouldn't want him to see the diaries, and if he knew the existence of the jewellery he would surely be even more accusing. Damn! How were they going to get the diaries out of the safe now that Max was on to them?

'I *will* ask her,' he said shortly. 'And advise her against letting near-strangers into the house. I don't mean to sound churlish, but I must ask you both to go . . . immediately.' He went round the room closing the windows and dragging the curtains across any old how. Dan and Kate heaped the last books back onto the shelf and he ushered them out of the room. Dan reset the alarm and secured the back door while Max stood over him – Kate could sense Dan's humiliation. Then Max showed them out of the front door before locking that. They all stood outside, at a loss as to what to say next. It was Dan who eventually spoke.

'Well, I'll be back in the morning to mend the windowsill. I hope that's all right by you, Mr Jordan.' Max appeared to examine Dan's tone for sarcasm but didn't seem sure.

'Do you need to go into the house for that?' he asked. Dan stiffened and shrugged then turned away.

'I—' Max stopped then. He took off his glasses and regarded Kate and Dan gravely for a moment, before returning them to his nose. 'I think you should know I spent some time talking with my aunt today. I believe I've persuaded her that it would be sensible to give up this house. Clear it out. Sell it or rent it out. She doesn't seem totally against the idea.'

'But Max,' Kate gasped, 'surely the hope of coming home to this house is what is keeping her going! It's where she's lived all her life. Her treasures are here! She might lose the will to live if we take this away from her and give her . . . some modern bungalow.'

'A residential home, is what I was recommending. There's a

suitable one I've visited quite near the hospital. The Lawns. They've a place available.'

'I know it, Kate,' said Dan quietly. 'It's a new building, but attractive. Classical style. And there's a big front garden, lots of trees.'

'But it won't be here, will it?' cried Kate in passion. 'It won't be Seddington House with all her beautiful things and her memories. You'll be uprooting her.'

'It would be for the best,' Max said, his voice stern in response to her emotion. 'I talked to the doctor. Her walking isn't good now and there's a shakiness that wasn't there before. It's possible she's had a very small stroke. She can't come back here with all these stairs. She'd need full-time care. What if she fell again?'

'I didn't know about the stroke,' said Kate humbly. She realized that the doctors wouldn't tell her. Max was the next-of-kin. 'She seemed a bit frail today, I admit. Does the doctor say she can come out soon?'

'The doctor won't commit herself at the moment. They're running tests. But if the damage is contained . . .'

'Max. I . . .' It would be stupid to alienate this man any more. She must speak calmly. 'I know you're Agnes's nearest relative, and that you have her best interests at heart, but I don't think you really understand about her. I mean . . .' She watched Max take in a sharp breath, then blow it out through pursed lips before he spoke.

'I can see that you've got to know her well in a short time, and I know she's very attached to this place. But somebody has to make some tough decisions here. The Lawns have a place for her, and as soon as the doctor gives the go-ahead . . . I'm sure I'll be able to talk my aunt round. Then we'll get the valuers in here and try and sort the old pile out.'

'I just think you're wrong, that's all,' said Kate in a low voice.

'She's unhappy enough being in a hospital. She'd rather have someone come in here to help Mrs Summers, I know she would.'

'Well, I think it's just too risky. Sorry.' And with that, Max smiled and patted Kate's shoulder. 'Come on,' he said. 'It'll be all right. It's what happens when people get old. They need to be where they can be looked after properly. Now, I need to be getting back and I think you should too.' He nodded at Dan and they went to their separate vehicles without saying another word.

'Oh Dan,' said Kate, slumped in her seat as the van bumped its way down the drive. 'Perhaps he's right. But I think Agnes would go straight downhill if she knew she couldn't come home.' She stopped. 'You don't reckon this is Max being greedy, do you? That he thinks it's all already his?'

'I think he is genuinely concerned about her, even if he doesn't understand her. As for the rest, well, he could hardly ignore the fact that he's likely to get all the dosh at some point.'

'But what about this child – her son?' Kate remembered suddenly. 'I wish we hadn't had to leave the papers behind.'

When they pulled up outside Paradise Cottage, Dan killed the engine and sat back in his seat. He looked at Kate and smiled. Then he touched her hand in a tender gesture.

'If you give me the key, I'll rescue those papers for you. Assuming Mr Suspicious isn't hanging around, that is.'

'Oh Dan, thank you. Don't get caught though, will you? I wouldn't like you had up as a diamond thief.' She tipped the key out of the envelope into his hand.

Dan laughed. 'I could always take Marie Summers with me. She'd see him right. But I reckon he'll be back in Norwich tonight. Got a legal practice to run, hasn't he? Can't always be popping down to look after his inheritance!'

211

'You don't like him, do you?'

'I think he's straight, he's got Miss Melton's interests at heart. I . . . just feel he's judging me, that he's made up his mind before knowing anything about me. I hate that.'

'I do, too, but I think it's just an unfortunate manner. Perhaps we're making judgements about him, too.'

When she got inside, Daisy, Sam and Bobby greeted Kate as though she had been away for a week. 'Come in the living room, Mummy. Play with my trains,' whined Sam. But Daisy wanted to show her mum her reading book. Kate realized they must sense her misery, her distractedness, and immediately felt guilty.

'Let Mummy sit down, then she can cuddle both of you,' Joyce said, rolling up her embroidery and picking up pieces of thread from the floor. 'They've had a big tea and both of them played football with the boys. And the garage rang to say the car's ready. Oh, and Daisy, you'd better give Mummy her letter.'

The letter was the one promised by Mrs Smithson the previous morning, but Kate wasn't quite expecting the precise nature of its contents. It was signed by a Mr Overden, chairman of the board of governors, and explained the situation regarding the school, but then went on to say:

*Following a conversation with the County Council Education Department this morning, a representative has agreed to find a date to come and address us all. After consultation with Mrs Smithson and some of the parents, we have decided to appoint a Save the School Committee. Any parents who are interested to help, please would you contact me.*

All well and good. But then there was a handwritten message enclosed with the letter.

*Dear Kate*

*You were so inspiring yesterday morning in the school
playground, encouraging us to be positive, that after some
thought and consultation, we would like to ask you, nay to beg
you, to join the Save the School Committee. I and other
parents I have spoken to agree that with your experience of
the media and your obvious commitment, you are just the
person to help. You are right – we must fight for the school.*

*I do so hope that you will not let us down in our time of need.*

*Faithfully yours,*

*Gwyneth Smithson*

'Oh, but I can't do this, can I?' She passed the letter to Joyce, who read it quickly.

'Don't be silly, dear.' Her mother-in-law was brisk as she passed the letter back. 'You've got children at the school. You want it to stay open, don't you? And you do know about how to get publicity.'

'Yes, but that's for books. I don't know how the education system works. And I don't really know people round here.'

'Then it's a good way of getting to know them, isn't it? And it would be excellent to have someone fresh instead of the same old blokes from the board of governors and the parish council. You said this morning, didn't you, that people seemed defeatist. Here's your chance to stir them up a bit.'

'But I'm not the stirring kind of person.'

'Nor are most people until something like this happens. Think of all those cases of people who start charities after some tragedy happens to them, and they organize appeals and get on the telly. Kate, this is something useful you can do. It may help you to be doing something. And it's for Sam and Daisy, after all.'

'What's for us, Mummy. Mummy, are we having a present?' asked Daisy.

'No, dear, your mummy's going to help do something important in your school. Aren't you, Kate?'

'I'm feeling bullied, but I'll think about it. We could at least have this meeting with the guy from the council and see exactly where we stand. For all we know, it might just be a question of some fund-raising. We could start an appeal – that shouldn't be too difficult.'

Despite her natural reluctance to push herself forward, Kate was already thinking of ideas.

But then her mind snapped back to thoughts of Simon. Suddenly a great wave of misery swept over her. Why hadn't he even called her since he left?

The call she had waited for came at ten o'clock that evening. Kate had been out for a drink with Debbie and the phone was ringing as she walked in. Joyce must have gone to bed. She threw her cardigan over the newel post and grabbed the receiver.

'Kate. It's me.'

'Simon. Where are you?'

'The flat, just got in from the office. Well, I stopped for a curry with Gillingham.'

'Oh.'

Neither of them seemed to know what to say next.

'I think – I can't be home till the weekend.'

'Can't you? But it's Sports Day on Friday. You said you'd be there. Sam will be really upset if you miss the fathers' race.'

'I know, I feel terrible, but no can do. Too much going on here. Look, maybe we could get away somewhere Saturday night, you and I? I mean, if you'd like to.'

'I . . . don't know.'

'It's important we have a proper talk.'

'Yes.'

'So I'll see you Friday night.'

'Are you sure you can't come before then?'

'Look, the pressure's on here. I'm working late all this week and the trains are up the spout with the Ipswich tunnel works. I'd be tired and that wouldn't help. Kate – I want to see you. Don't get me wrong. I – I want to make a go of things. With us.'

'Oh.'

'I've made a mess, I know. Kate, please, could you book us somewhere for Saturday night – ask Mum to look after the kids? We'll have a quiet time by ourselves in the country somewhere. Would you?'

'Oh, Simon.' Kate sighed. 'Yes.' She was still angry with him, but her main feeling was relief. He was coming home. Perhaps it was going to be all right.


After a night restless with dreams about Simon and Agnes, muddled up together, Kate was glassy-eyed with weariness. She couldn't remember taking the children to school, just arriving at the school gates. She kissed them briefly and watched them run into the playground, planning to slip away without speaking to anyone. But halfway to the school doors, where his teacher waited, Sam stopped and turned back. He put out his arms and hugged Kate's legs, rubbing his face in her stomach.

'I love you, Mummy. Don't be sad,' he said, then released her and blew her a kiss before racing off once more for his classroom.

Those few extra seconds were enough for Mrs Smithson to spot Kate and come hurrying outside.

'Did you get my letter, dear? Will you be able to help?'

Kate looked hard at Mrs Smithson. She, too, bore the evidence of sleepless nights. Her short fair hair looked greasy and ruffled and one eyelid twitched. In her head she heard her father's voice: 'Mustn't let the side down, must we?'

To Mrs Smithson, she simply said, 'If you think I can do it, yes, I'll do it.'

# Chapter 20

'He's suggested we go away Saturday night. Did you mean what you said? Could you manage with Daisy and Sam?'

Joyce was driving Kate down to Halesworth to fetch the family car from the garage before going shopping.

'I was going to that concert—' Joyce broke off. 'No, of course I'll help. I said I would and it's important. You get off as early as you like and I'll hold the fort. Don't worry about me. Where are you going to stay?'

'I don't know yet. I was going to look on the Net for hotels. We haven't been to the North Norfolk coast yet. Maybe Burnham Market way if we can get a room on a Saturday this time of year.'

Joyce nodded. 'It is beautiful up there. You might get a cancellation. Kate, I probably shouldn't say anything, but I'm so glad you're doing this, giving it all a chance. Simon can be difficult at times. His father . . .' She stopped, noticing a stubborn expression cross her daughter-in-law's face.

'Don't go counting chickens, Joyce, please. I don't know how I feel about things yet. I won't until I see him. Till I know what he thinks.' Kate pulled at the hem of her skirt where a loose thread had puckered a bit of the embroidery. 'We'd better just

217

see how it goes,' she ended lamely, not taking to the idea of discussing her deepest feelings with her husband's mother. The embroidered flower began to unravel altogether.

On the way back home in her own car, she thought of Dan repairing the library window and, on impulse, turned down the road that led to Seddington. She wanted to read some of the diaries before she went to see Agnes next.

Good, she could see his van parked there and the library windows were open. There was a bicycle there, too. She pulled up alongside the van, switched off the engine and got out.

'Hi,' called a voice and Dan scrunched round from the direction of the kitchen, wiping his hands on an old tea-towel. Before she could answer there came another voice: 'Daddy. Daaadeee!'

Dan turned and put out his hand. A tiny girl with ruffled blonde hair trotted round the corner and placed her hand in his. When she saw Kate, she stopped and pressed her face against Dan's arm, but peeped sideways at Kate, looking her up and down.

'Hello, who's this?' Kate said gently. A child, he did have a child. Why hadn't he said?

'This is Shelley,' said Dan. 'Shelley, come on, lovey, say hello to Kate.'

'I didn't know you had . . .' Kate said.

'She's not exactly . . .' Dan said at the same time.

'No, you go on,' said Kate.

'This is my . . . girlfriend's little girl. She's two, aren't you, Shelley?'

'Mmm,' said Shelley. 'Big girl.'

'Oh,' said Kate, prickly. His girlfriend. He hadn't said he'd got a girlfriend. Or a little girl who called him Daddy. But then, so what if he did? What was it to her? Still, she was unaccountably crestfallen.

'Linda had to go to work this morning – she's a receptionist at the health club. Her mother usually has Shelley, but she's at the doctor's today. So I've got her. Right nuisance she is when I'm working, aren't you, Shelley, darling? Won't leave the toolbox alone.'

'I'll stay a bit and help you with her if you like,' said Kate. 'I only stopped to get the diaries, but after that I was going home.'

'That's kind. I've nearly finished now. Just got to find some primer in the shed.'

'Will you come with me, Shelley? We can play in the garden.'

But the little girl shook her head vehemently and hid her face behind her hand. Dan reached down and scooped her up to perch in the crook of his arm. She sat there as though she belonged, peeping at Kate through her fingers.

'Look,' he said, reaching into his pocket with his other hand, 'here's your key. You might as well find the stuff, put it in the car.'

'No sign of Max this morning?'

'Nah. I wouldn't have noticed anyway. Too busy looking after this rascal. Eh, are you a rascal, Shelley? A nice little rascal?'

Shelley giggled and kissed him, then nuzzled into his neck, from where she surveyed Kate as if to say, 'He's mine.'

'Anyway, Conrad's here as well, keeping an eye on things,' Dan told Kate.

'Ah, the bicycle,' she said.

Just then, there was the sound of a door opening and shutting and a burly young man traipsed round from the direction of the kitchen. Marie Summers's son Conrad was in his mid-twenties but his muscular frame was already over-padded with fat, and his hair was receding. He grinned bashfully at Kate.

'Hello,' she said. 'I'm not staying. Just come to pick up something Miss Melton wanted.'

He nodded shyly then said to Dan, 'I'm off now. Job interview this afternoon. You'll lock up, will you?'

'Of course, Con,' Dan said, and he and Kate watched the young man mount his bicycle and wobble off down the drive.

Kate took the safe key Dan held out and walked round to the back door. This time she lingered sadly as she entered the house. Perhaps, with Max's plans to sell up, this would be the last time she saw it. To her it had become so dear, her dream house. In some part of her mind it was hers. *But you're wrong, Kate. It was never yours and it never will be.* It would be way beyond their pocket, even if she and Simon did patch up their marriage and get round to buying a home. She tried to see Seddington House as a prospective purchaser might. It would attract a lot of interest although there was serious clearing out and modernization to be done. After all, who would want a library these days? Or an old-fashioned formal dining room? And there were sure to be hardly any bathrooms.

The white-washed scullery was much as it must have been when it was newly built. There were two huge stone sinks on one side, with a wooden draining board that looked as though it had been scrubbed down by generations of skivvies. As a concession to the times, a washing machine and a chest freezer were both plugged into the single old socket.

The kitchen was a hotchpotch of elderly wooden cabinets and more recent Formica-ed surfaces. There was a stainless-steel sink under the windows where Kate had climbed in that first time, a bright new fridge-freezer and a modern Rayburn in the original fireplace. The vinyl floor and the surfaces were clean, but anyone coming into this house would want to throw most of it out and install something state-of-the-art. There was a particular Smallbone farmhouse-style kitchen Kate had been looking at in a magazine last week . . . No, she told herself, don't even think about it. This house was beyond their means. Not with, what – eight bedrooms? she reckoned. And two acres of land? And all the fittings required to bring it up to the standard of a comfortable family home.

She hurried along a little corridor, past the closed door of the dining room and into the hall. There she stood looking round, remembering that perfect spring evening three months ago, when she'd found Agnes at the bottom of the staircase. The hall didn't get the sun till later. She stared around in the half-gloom, noticing all the things she'd failed to see then – the carved oak hallstand, adorned with a jumble of ancient hats, coats and umbrellas, the clutter of ornaments on a matching chest, blue and white china in a mahogany display cabinet, a Romanesque bust wearing a feathered cavalier's hat on a pedestal, Turkish rugs . . . The panelling was festooned with English eighteenth-century landscape paintings and a large still-life of some long-dead squire's bloody trophies of a day in the field.

A door at the back of the hall clicked open loudly in the draught, making Kate jump. She moved towards the room and, struck by a sudden whiff of beeswax, was propelled back into her dream. Here must be the drawing room. She pushed open the door and peered round. Yes. The faded blue chairs, now threadbare, the chaise longue, the huge carved mantel, she recognized. But the room was crowded with furniture she hadn't seen before; the grand piano of her dream had been pushed into the far corner and was joined by a harpsichord and a spinet. A gilt console table bore a huge Gothic-arched church tabernacle, guarded by little statues of saints. Along the right-hand wall were ranged several museum cases with felt covers. Feeling she was trespassing now, Kate tiptoed over and lifted the felt.

Underneath was Agnes's collection of miniatures – vivid personalities as bright as when they were painted, glowing at her across the centuries. She thought she identified the damaged picture of the lady in the blue dress that had inspired Agnes's passion for them.

Hearing Shelley's cooing voice in the hall, Kate dropped the felt and hurried out, pulling the door shut behind her. Again, she remembered the dream, where she'd followed the maid. The maid! Her mother had commented on there being a maid, even after the war. How strange to be standing here, where her mother had stood so many years before!

In the library, she found Dan at the window stirring the contents of a paint pot. Shelley was deep in some private game, rolling from side to side on a little sofa.

'I'll just get the papers then I'll be off,' Kate said. She piled the *Domesday* volumes on the floor, and it was the work of a moment to retrieve the diaries and the brown envelope from the safe.

'Are you going up to see Agnes again soon?' Dan asked, looking up from his painting.

'Maybe later in the week,' said Kate. 'I don't know when I'll see you.' She was still feeling prickly about the girlfriend. 'But I'll let you know about these . . .' She waved the packages. 'Bye, Shelley.' The child looked up from her rolling and smiled.

I must just walk away now, Kate told herself as she left by the back door. Even though I may never see this place again. And she stashed her papers in the boot, got into the car and drove down through the gates without another look.

When she got home, Joyce hadn't returned, but the answerphone light was flashing. There were two messages, one from a mail-order firm telling Joyce some plants she'd ordered were now in stock. The other was from her father.

*Hrrrmm. Kate. Dad here. Just to say we're fine. Er. You won't find us in today, of course. We're off to Sevenoaks, as usual. Meeting your aunt Maggie for tea at some National Trust place, and back this evening. Our love to everybody. Bye.*

Sevenoaks! She'd forgotten the date for the first time ever! It was the anniversary of Nicola's death. Her parents always went to put flowers on the grave. And Kate hadn't thought what the date was for days, what with everything else that was going on. They would think she didn't care. She sat down on the stairs, her face in her hands. It was nineteen years ago today. She hadn't gone to the grave herself very often over those years. It was partly because she hated going with her parents – couldn't stand the grim atmosphere, the fact that they couldn't speak their grief. But she'd always phoned them first thing on some pretext or other. And today, she'd forgotten.

She leaned her head against the newel post and let her mind slip back to nineteen years ago. But instead of imagining, as she usually did, the horror of the crash itself, she was given a gift – a vision of Nicola at a party, the night before she died, in her dress of midnight blue that sparkled with sequins at the hem and the neck, her dark curls gathered in a topknot. Laughing as she danced or chattered, a centre of attention wherever she went in their schoolfriend's lovely manor house deep in the Surrey woods. And Kate felt a rush of longing, of loss.

She had always remembered that party as one of those night-mares of teenage misery, and not just because of the tragedy that followed. A boy called Pete, the glamorous wild boy of Nicola's year, was there. Kate had fancied him like mad for ages, but had lived in terror of anyone knowing – until Nicola had wormed it out of her. But it was Nicola whom Pete had chatted up that evening, getting her drinks, asking her to dance. Kate, awkward in a dress she had really grown out of, had trailed about feeling

223

miserable. At the same time, she was painfully aware that Nicky was trying to help; her sister kept calling Kate over to speak to Pete, said that she herself was tired, so would he dance with Kate instead? Kate, her sister's very glowing presence rendering her dowdy and tongue-tied, could have died with embarrassment.

Now, finally, Kate was able to view that evening through new eyes. Her sister had merely been trying to be kind. And even Kate's memories of Pete had now been placed in perspective. Her friend Sarah had bumped into Pete recently and told Kate he had had a troubled life so far – drug dependence, drifting from job to job and relationship to relationship. It was probably a good thing Kate and he had never got together, two fragile souls, and she now felt pity for him rather than resentment.

*Your place is with the living.* Where had that phrase come from, drifting into her head? She just had to get on with the here and now.

Feeling stronger, she got up and went to make herself some tea. Then she spent a frustrating hour looking up hotels on the Internet. The Hoste Arms in Burnham Market was full, as were the next three or four hotels she tried. Finally she found Chapelfield Hall, which wasn't near the coast, but which attracted her because of its swimming pool, and was relieved to find when she rang that they had a double room for Saturday. She switched off the computer and walked back towards the kitchen, deciding to ring Liz for a natter.

'She's up with the CEO, Kate,' Liz's friendly assistant Rosie told her. 'I'll tell her you called.'

As Kate put down the phone, her eye fell on the little pile of Agnes's books she had stashed under the console table when she had come in. That's what she'd do next.

*

*To my son from his mother, Agnes Lavender Melton.* Kate, curled up on her bed, turned the envelope over and over. It was sealed with sticky tape. Had Agnes intended her to open it and read it? Surely not. Perhaps she should have left it in the safe.

She dropped the envelope on the quilt and reached for the diaries. The two grey exercise books were dog-eared with yellowing pages. One had *Agnes Lavender Melton* inked on the cover, with a squirly signature device like Elizabeth I's snaking down. Inside, the girl had made a title page with a skull and crossbones centrepiece: *Private, Keep out* was coiled around it. The wording read: *Secret Diary. Agnes Lavender Melton, aged ten years, six months and three days. Seddington House, Seddington, Suffolk, England, The Wide World, The Universe.*

She flicked through the pages. The entries were short.

*Tuesday, 24 May 1921*
Ethel called me at seven o'clock. I had porridge for breakfast and did my lessons. Diane is taken sick, her mother fears it is the inflooenser she is so hot but Miss Selcott says it is a chill from not wearing enough undergarments and playing on damp grass. If she dies I will ask to read at her funeral because we found such a beautiful poem about a bird dying that everybody would be comforted.

*Thursday, 26 May 1921*
Diane better today but her mother sent word to Miss Selcott saying she must be excused lessons. Miss Selcott let me read *Ivanhoe* all morning because she had such a headache. Father telephoned to us on the new telephone that Mrs Duncan is too frightened to use to say he will be home tomorrow for lunch. No boiled fish then, I told her. Hooray.

*Friday, 27 May 1921*

Father is home!!! He has brought us a gramaphone. It is mahoganny and we played Grieg's 'Butterfly' and songs by Caruso. Tomorrow Aunt Florence and our cousins are coming. Mrs Duncan says Alf has found some of the strawberries are ripe so we can have strawberries and cream and Dundee cake for tea!

*Sunday, 29 May 1921*

Yesterday was lovely. Christopher, Philip and Lucy are such sweet children. I was allowed to hold Lucy on my knee and read to her. Aunt Florence is so pretty but Miss Selcott says her hat was unsuitable and that she is too interested in her appearance. Ethel came over all giggly when Miss Selcott told her she would pour the tea, but Aunt Florence said she would. Then Aunt Florence got all sniffly because of Mamma being dead and not pouring the tea. And that made Philip cry, too. So Father took him outside to see if there were frogs in the pond and there were. I wish our cousins could come more often but they spend a lot of time up in London, Father says, where Uncle Percy works for the goverment.

*Saturday, 6 August*

Raven has come home for the holidays and Miss Selcott has gone to stay with her mother for a month. Mrs Duncan said good riddance but then she saw I was listening and slapped her hand on her mouth. So we are free! Raven says he hates school. The food is awful and he loathes rugby. Otherwise he says it is OK and some of the chaps are good sorts. His voice is all funny. Sometimes it's deep and then it goes all squeaky, but he pinches me when I laugh so I have to remember not to. He has already annoyed Father with a frightful report. Father said Mamma would be ashamed of her son's behaviour but he won't tell me what Raven's done. And Raven went upstairs and wouldn't let me in his room. I still think Raven is lucky. He can remember Mamma properly. I wish I could. I try to imagine being a baby again and see if I can see her face, but I can't, I just can't. Mrs Duncan said Mamma wore lily of the valley as her scent. Sometimes I go into Mamma's dressing room and sniff her old clothes and it does makes me feel close to her. I think I can remember the smell from long ago. I have found an old photograph in one of the attics with Mamma, Father, Raven and myself all in a room with vases of flowers. She looks so jolly and I look so happy sitting on her knee. I keep it in my den now upstairs.

*Sunday, 7 August 1921*
There was a huge thunderstorm last night and Raven came in. He gets frightened by thunder. He came into my bed all shaky and I cuddled him and told him everything was all right. He smelled lovely, of soap, and his skin tasted salty when I licked his arm. We went to church and Diana's father made us pray for the Unemployed. Father says a lot of families in Suffolk are suffering because the farmers can't get enough money for the crops. Raven said they should eat the crops then but Father said it wasn't as simple as that and some people in England are angry because they fought in the war and now they don't have jobs.

The next entry wasn't until three and a half years later.

*Saturday, 3 January 1925*
I have decided to keep a diary again this year, then at least I can write down my reading. I have spent this Christmas

227

holidays devouring the novels of Thomas Hardy. I didn't like *Jude the Obscure* because of the children hanging themselves. This has given me bad dreams. But I did like *Tess of the D'Urbervilles* though Alec D'Urberville must be one of the worst villains. I can't imagine letting any man do that to me when we weren't married and I just cried and cried when Tess died at the end. It's as if Alec killed her but nobody blames him. Next I shall try *The Return of the Native* though Father says I will find it bleak. When I have finished all of the Hardys in the library I shall start on George Eliot. I don't know what we should do about poor Raven now Father has gone back to London. Mrs Duncan says she can't tell him anything, he won't listen to her. He has been riding to hounds several times with our neighbours at Fortescue Hall, but he told me he and his friend Paul often lose the others on purpose and spend the time in hostelries. He does smell all beery when he returns. He has made a crystal set using the bedframe as an aerial. Sometimes I go into his room at night and we cuddle up in the bed and take turns with the earphones and can hear the servants talking in the kitchen. We heard Mrs Duncan say Mr Silfield the organist has run off with the schoolmaster's wife and it's a terrible scandal. I wonder where they have run to? Mr Silfield is quite portly so I can't imagine him running very far. Raven says if we lived in a city we would be able to hear orchestras and see plays in the theatre but here in the country we're stuck listening to Mrs Duncan gossiping and Lister complaining about his back. Miss Selcott's mother is ill so Miss Selcott isn't coming back until next week.

*Monday, 5 January 1925*
Miss Selcott has telegraphed to say that her mother has died and that she won't be returning until Saturday. Father says

Raven and I must write to her to express our condolences. Poor Miss Selcott. Father says it is very hard when your parents die whatever age you are and now Miss Selcott will be all alone in the world except for one old aunt and we must be kind to her. He was eighteen when his mother was carried away by the typhoid and Grandfather died the year that Raven was born. I have tried to make myself cry for Miss Selcott but I think her mother was very old and very ill so perhaps it is after all a blessing. I have finished all the Hardy novels we have now. My favourite was *The Mayor of Casterbridge*. I am halfway through *Adam Bede*. It is terrible that poor Hetty let her baby die. I would want to die too if something like that happened to me. It seems so unfair that the women have the babies and then their lives are ruined and the innocent babies suffer so much misery or die. I wonder if Mamma knew she was dying and cried about leaving us? Was she able to say goodbye? I can't ask Father because it will make him upset and Raven won't talk about it. I don't think Lister will know that sort of thing and Mrs Duncan has only been cook since Mr Duncan passed away on the Hindenburg Line.

*Saturday, 10 January 1925*
Raven went back to school on the train two days ago. He looked so miserable. I went to his room the night before and I lay next to him on the bed and we talked and talked about what he would do. Father wants him to go to Cambridge when he finishes at Bellingham's next year and is going to engage a tutor for him in the vacations to help him catch up with the work. He doesn't want to go or to read law but he hasn't got anything else he wants to do either except to write books and Father says that is not a proper job. I told him

maybe it is a good idea not to drink but to study hard, be a success and then he can do what he likes but he got sulky and said I was too young to understand. Diana has come every morning this week. We have sat in the attic and read the poems of Alfred Lord Tennyson to each other. It gives me divine shivers down my spine to read *Oh rare pale Margaret* and *Mystery of mysteries/Faintly smiling Adeline* and of *Serene imperial Eleanore*. I wish someone would write a poem like that about me but Agnes just isn't a romantic name. Unless you say it the French way – 'An-yes' – but Raven has spoiled that, too. He says it sounds like 'onions'. Diana and I wish we knew men like Lancelot though Diana's mother has told her it is better to marry a plain-looking man then you know where you are with him. It is cold and foggy and we've had the lights on all day it's so dark. My head hurts from the gas and from too much reading in bad light.

*Friday, 16 January 1925*

Miss Selcott has been back for a week in a black crêpe dress that makes her look like a miserable crow. She is very pale and sniffs and can't concentrate on our lessons but snaps at us if she spots us making any mistakes. Diana has overheard her mother telling her father that Miss Selcott's mother left no money, only debts, so she will always have to work and have nowhere of her own to live unless some man takes pity on her and marries her. That wouldn't be nice, being married to someone who pities you. I will never marry unless the man worships me passionately and I love him almost but not quite as much. I went to visit Mamma's grave yesterday. The snow-drops Father planted are just beginning to show green otherwise the graveyard looks very wintery and grim and I feel sad to think of Mamma lying there under the earth.

*Saturday, 17 January 1925*

Father returned from London just before luncheon. He has brought a friend, Mr Armstrong, with him to discuss business. Mr Armstrong has no children and his wife is an invalid in a sanatorium. He buys and sells all sorts of exotic things and he talked at luncheon about the ships coming up the Thames with their cargoes of spices and tea and beautiful cloths. He has promised one day to take me round the docks and the warehouses and to visit the markets at Billingsgate and Smithfield. Father asked me to show them my collections, so we spent an interesting hour talking about my coins and miniatures – I have five miniatures, now that Father gave me the portrait of the girl with the doll for Christmas. Mr Armstrong knows all about art and says I am unusually well-informed for a young girl. He looks forward to entertaining us in London when I go for the Season. Father did not look pleased at that. I think he would like to keep me here always because of not having darling Mamma. I have only been to London three times. Aunt Florence likes to fetch me and Raven out to tea at Brown's Hotel and go shopping in Oxford Street where we can see all the new buildings going up. Once we drove past Buckingham Palace but the King was not at home because there was no flag, Aunt said. I have finished *Silas Marner* and have begun *Middlemarch*. I do not know why Dorothea is so fond of Mr Casaubon, he is so old and dry. I must have a love-match like Father and Mamma even though their love was so deep that he is lost without her and can never marry again.

Famous last words, thought Kate, as she closed the exercise book with a sigh. What a lonely childhood the young Agnes had had, cut off from the world, learning about life from Victorian

231

fiction and the servants' gossip. How much she must have missed the mother she couldn't remember. Her father, often absent, was the centre of her life – and poor damaged Raven, who already seemed to be drifting beyond her reach. Dreaming about love, Agnes was, at fourteen, at the stage where she needed a mother figure more than ever, but it seemed that there was no one to guide her. Aunt Florence was too far away and probably too caught up with her own young family. And soon Agnes's fragile bubble would be burst by her darling father's infatuation with Vanessa . . .

Kate had picked up the second exercise book to read on when she heard Bobby barking and the door downstairs open and close.

'Kate? Hello, dear.' Joyce's infuriatingly bright voice rang up the stairs.

Kate dropped the exercise book on the bed with a sigh of frustration and, slipping into her shoes, loped downstairs to help bring in the shopping.

# Chapter 21

Kate wasn't able to read any more of Agnes's diaries until after the children had gone to bed that evening. There was one interruption after another.

First of all, after lunch, the phone had rung.

'Mrs Hutchinson – Kate – it's Gwyneth Smithson here. I wonder whether you've time to pop into my office before school ends this afternoon? I just want to show you this letter Mr Overden and I have drafted. And I need to check, would you be able to make a meeting next Thursday evening? That's when the clerk from Education can come and see us.'

'One moment, Mrs Smithson,' said Kate and put the phone down on the table. 'Joyce?' she said, putting her head round the kitchen door. 'You wouldn't be able to look after the kids next Thursday evening, would you? Or would you like me to ask Michelle?'

Joyce dried her hands on a tea-towel and came to squint at the calendar hanging in the hall.

'I'll give them their baths first and get them in their pyjamas,' Kate put in quickly, feeling guilty that her mother-in-law was having to babysit so soon after having the children for the weekend.

'Well, I've got no plans that evening, so, yes,' said Joyce.

Kate mouthed her thanks and picked up the phone again. 'Hello? Yes, that Thursday should be all right.' Her voice sounded more breezy than she felt. Who knew what next week would bring at the moment? Would she still have a husband, for a start?

'This is the list of parents who've volunteered to help,' said Mrs Smithson later that afternoon. Good, Sebastian's father and Debbie were on the list, and Stuart from the post office. More of a mixed blessing in Kate's eyes was Jasmin Thornton. Jasmin, the mother of eight-year-old twin boys, was a bossy woman with an Alice band, too-pale make-up and a voice sharp enough to shatter bottles at fifty paces. She was always highly organized – the twins' lunch boxes with their home-made organic avocado and chickpea rolls and chocolate puddings were the envy of those mothers who cared about such things, and if costumes were called for, Jasmin's boys were the stars of any show with her imaginative and beautifully turned-out creations. On top of these achievements, Jasmin held down a job as partner of a solicitors' firm in Ipswich. How did she fit it all in?

Kate had to admit that, although Jasmin made her feel inadequate she would be incredibly useful with her list of contacts and her formidable organizational abilities.

The letter, inviting parents to attend the meeting the following week, was a no-nonsense call to arms. A Mr Keppel from the Education Department would be in the hot seat and there would be plenty of opportunity for questions. It was hoped that all parents would attend.

'We've invited the vicar, as well,' said Mrs Smithson, 'and some of the parish council. We need all the help we can get.'

'We surely ought to get the committee together to start work the week after,' said Kate. It would be important to get their defence in motion before the school broke up for the holidays.

Mrs Smithson nodded. 'I'll ask Peter Overden if I should ring round with a few dates. And I'll make sure we all get copies of the accounts for that. All this makes me feel much brighter, you know, Kate, actually doing something.'

Joyce was out for the evening at a friend's birthday supper in Woodbridge, and by the time Kate had given the children tea, taken and fetched Daisy from Rainbows, heard both of them read and put them to bed after Sam's latest delaying tactics, she was glad to have the rest of the evening to herself.

First she tried to ring her parents, but they weren't back yet. She left a message hoping that they had had a good day and promised to ring them soon. Next she tried Liz again, but a new nanny answered the phone and said in a weary voice that her employers were out. Then Kate stood by the phone, dithering. Should she ring Simon? The problem was solved for her when she realized he had left a message while she had been on the phone just now, so she rang him back.

'Did you find somewhere for us on Saturday?' he said.

'Yes, finally. Chapelfield Hall – do you know it? Near Norwich.'

'Heard of it, yes. The de Vere chain, isn't it? Or Arden?'

'Arden. I tried to get somewhere smaller and less corporate, but everywhere's booked up.'

'I'm sure it will be fine. Look Kate, I've got to go to Germany again on Monday – for the whole week. There's a series of meetings with a new client and for some reason they need me there. Just thought I'd warn you now.'

Kate sighed angrily. 'Well, if you have to, you have to. The timing's not great, though, is it?'

'No, it's pretty awful actually. But, look, I've booked a fortnight off in August. Let's take the kids somewhere.'

'I think we're getting ahead of ourselves,' said Kate quietly. 'Let's just see how the weekend goes, shall we? The children would love a holiday, though.'

When she put down the phone she couldn't deny that her spirits were rising. Perhaps all would indeed be well. She picked up the calendar, lying on the table by the phone. It was school Sports Day on Friday, of course. She'd already had to break it to the children that Simon wouldn't be there for the fathers' race and Sam had stomped off to his room in a tearful rage. Anyway, it meant she wouldn't be able to see Agnes on Friday. Tomorrow? She frowned. She had arranged to go with the children to Debbie's after school and she had got to get her father a birthday present in the morning. She would have to see if she could fit in seeing Agnes as well. Otherwise, her visit would have to be postponed until Monday.

Kate made herself some coffee and brought Agnes's books into the sitting room where she pushed Bobby off his illicit seat on the sofa and curled up on the space he had left warm. She picked up the second of the exercise books and quickly leafed through. It covered the years 1926 and 1927 and Kate saw that many of the entries formed a record of the young woman's reading and the development of her collections, which were obviously becoming more extensive in these years. Mr Melton's friend William Armstrong was mentioned often. It seemed he was a collector himself, and he often sent Agnes coins and curios that had come his way.

There was much talk of Raven. Whether because of Agnes's pleading, or to please his father, or for some other unfathomable reason, Raven appeared to have given more attention to his schoolbooks than before. The tutor Mr Melton engaged for his son turned out to be an inspirational choice – a fellow officer from his regiment in Flanders who had been a teacher before the war, turning to writing and tutoring afterwards.

Captain Garland was a kindly man, a bachelor, and Raven in some measure responded to his charisma and his high expectations. Nevertheless, the man confided to Mr Melton that Raven was by no means suited to institutional life, nor was he a natural scholar, though he had an extraordinary facility with words and his love of modern culture was distressingly strong. The captain, himself soaked in the Greek and Roman classics, and an impressive mathematician, clearly had little regard for contemporary literature and 'that corrupt music they call jazz'. His quiet good influence, however, paid off – Raven was admitted to Gonville and Caius College, Cambridge in Michaelmas 1926 to read jurisprudence.

By Christmas, however, it became glaringly obvious that the stringencies of law held no interest for Raven in comparison with the louche charms of a small group of friends whose aim in life seemed to be to read one another their poetry and to enjoy themselves on their extensive personal allowances. And when it came to money, alas, Raven was unable to keep up.

Agnes recorded several tempestuous exchanges between her brother and her father on the subject of Raven's expensive lifestyle. The entry for Easter Sunday, 1927 was typical of these.

After church, I was reading old copies of *Punch* in the library, when I heard raised voices, then Father threw open the door and showed Raven in. They both looked furious. They didn't see me in the chair by the window and Father lectured poor Raven about his allowance and how he couldn't keep wiring him more money. Raven's eyes were all glittery, as if he wasn't there really and Father shouted that he just didn't listen, did he? And then suddenly, Raven turned and opened the door and walked out of the room. A moment later he pounded over the gravel past the library window. He would be heading for the summerhouse, which is where he likes to be by himself. Father saw me then, but he said nothing and went away. When I went out to find Raven to tell him luncheon was to be served he wouldn't speak to me but came in late to the meal, and the rest of the day passed with us all very subdued.

Surprisingly, Kate thought, there was no entry for the dramatic announcement of Mr Melton's engagement, nor for some days afterwards. Was the event too momentous for Agnes to translate into words? Perhaps the shock rendered mental activity impossible.

Her question was partly answered by the following entry:

*Thursday, 4 August 1927*
It is suddenly announced Father is bringing Miss Wintour to visit tomorrow with her aunt, Miss Evelyn Wintour. They will be here for some days and the household is in uproar. Mrs Duncan believes that the best spare bedroom would be the most suitable for her; the aunt will have to make do with the smaller room next door, looking out on the kitchen garden. Ethel has been running up and downstairs with brooms, beeswax and bedding all day, and Mrs Duncan is most jittery about menus. She interrupts my reading every five minutes with some new way she's read of cooking potatoes, though in truth it is impossible to concentrate I am so nervous. Will I like her? Will she like me? Worst of all, will she try to be my mother? I can't call her 'Mother', I just can't. I won't and I hope she doesn't ask me.

I don't know what Raven thinks about it all. These days he never gets out of bed before noon and, since Father broke the news, is often away all afternoon and again in the evening, dining with friends or tooling around the countryside with Roddy Spalding, his college roommate who lives at Woodbridge, in Roddy's motor. I went with them once, to Walberswick, and we had such fun on the beach and fishing for crabs in the stream then fish and chips at the Bell.

As soon as she heard Vanessa was coming, Miss Selcott asked permission to take her vacation early. I don't know where she will go. Last year she stayed with her old aunt in Worthing, but this year she says she will take in some mountain air. I think it is too sad to stay by herself at some boarding house, but a holiday will be good for her. She has been very quiet and pale just lately. Diana says her mother thinks Miss Selcott has not been the same since her mother died, that grief has made her act strangely sometimes. She keeps washing her clothes and hates the dark. Poor Miss Selcott. Surely she will never find a suitor now, even if there was one to be had since the war took so many. Even Captain Garland didn't want her. Raven's horrible trick still makes me shudder. I'd have died of shame if I'd been Miss Selcott . . .

Puzzled, Kate leafed back through the diaries. She found the reference to the 'horrible trick' buried in an entry about Dickens for August two years before. Raven had forged a love letter from Captain Garland to Miss Selcott, scented it with lavender and left it on the governess's bed. It invited her to meet the captain in the rose garden that afternoon. Raven had engineered his tutor's appearance there at the appointed hour and a scene of hideous embarrassment to both parties – the captain being terrified of ladies – had ensued. Raven had had his allowance docked for that cruel escapade.

*Saturday, 6 August 1927*
Vanessa has been here a whole twenty-four hours now and I can hardly express my joy! I fell in love with her instantly. She is so interested in everything, and so kind. I wish my hair was as pretty as hers. She wears it in a shingled style that goes so well with her Clara Bow cloche hat, and makes her blue eyes look huge and surprised. She is very svelte, quite quite fragile. I worry that she is not strong. She is so sweet to me and says we must be sisters and best friends, that it's ridiculous that I could ever be a daughter to her.

And Father looks so proud and manly when he's with her. His face is transformed with love and happiness. Now that I have met Vanessa I am so happy for Father. He has been so worn down with grief all these years, as Diana's mother says, and he deserves to have love and happiness.

It could all have been so good, thought Kate, closing the third book with its patterned cover. If Vanessa had been the right kind of woman, life for the Melton family could have improved dramatically. Agnes would have had a mother-figure to guide her through the difficult passage to adulthood, through the trauma of first love and to the safe haven of a happy marriage. Maybe Raven, too, would have benefited from sensible female advice – though perhaps it was already too late for him. And for Gerald Melton? A happy home, a companion in life, maybe more children. But, as Agnes had said, it was all to go so horribly wrong.

It was getting dark outside. In the corner of the room, the grandmother clock softly struck ten. Joyce wouldn't be back for at least another hour. Kate yawned and flicked on the TV head-lines – more terrible news from Iraq. At a quarter past ten, feeling weary, she turned the television off and went to let Bobby out into the garden. Then she made some hot chocolate. She'd sit and read a little longer, maybe until Joyce was home, then she'd go up to bed. She picked up the next of the patterned notebooks and opened it at the first page . . .

# Chapter 22

Vanessa's mysterious illness in the spring of 1928 lasted for some weeks, a period of anxiety for the household, who all had to bear the routine of looking after the demanding invalid and obeying the fussy requests of Agnes's father, who stayed at Seddington more than everyone was used to and who couldn't disguise his deep concern for his new wife.

Vanessa rarely seemed in the mood for conversation, but she was pleased when Agnes offered to read to her to pass the time. The girl tried out some short stories by Thackeray and Dickens, but Vanessa complained that they made her head ache so. In the end, it proved, the only literature tolerable to the sensitive head of the invalid was gossip from the *Daily Sketch* and snippets from *Punch* or *Country Life*. When Vanessa heard speculation about the coming London Season she seemed to brighten for a while, then would sink back on the sofa under her blankets looking wistful. What hastened her recovery was Raven's return from Cambridge. He devoted his days to her, playing music, chatting and laughing, inviting round friends to cheer her up. There came a time when she began to eat better and the pinkness returned to her complexion. The doctor seemed pleased with her progress and advised her to walk regularly in the garden and even to take in sea air.

Then, one sunny morning in late spring, when Gerald Melton was away, Vanessa refused her usual breakfast in bed and swept downstairs to join Agnes and Raven at the table, her eyes sparkling, the pallor of the previous weeks completely gone.

'Darlings, I'm thinking we should all go to London.' She dimpled at their surprised faces. 'We need cheering up and, Agnes, we really must introduce you to a few of the right kind of people. I know Gerald wants to keep you locked up down here, but I believe a girl should have her chance. I will speak to him sternly and tell him. Do say you'll come – both of you.' She glanced from Agnes to Raven. 'It's no good us kicking our heels in the back of beyond. It's deathly here. *Everybody* who's anybody will be up in Town.' She gave a little wriggle of excitement as if anticipating the fun.

Behind her, Lister gave a sort of snort, which he quickly turned into a cough but only Agnes interpreted it as anything more than evidence of a mild cold.

'We'll stay in the flat, of course.' This was Gerald's pied à terre in Queen's Square, Bloomsbury, where he lived during the week. 'Though I will speak to your father about finding somewhere bigger and a little more *fashionable* if we are to entertain. And, Agnes, we must arrange that you have something decent to wear, darling.'

The next week was a whirlwind of activity. Agnes's father was so delighted to see his wife returned to full health and vivacity he couldn't refuse her anything, even suggesting that Agnes's Aunt Florence be called upon to help with launching Agnes into society. Before long, Agnes found herself installed in her own little room in Queen's Square with a growing wardrobe of exquisite costumes suitable for every possible occasion: cocktails at the Ritz, dinners, dances, luncheons with girlfriends and shopping in Harrod's. Her favourites were a green silk dress

243

with cap sleeves, a pretty sequinned pattern across the front and matching satin shoes, and a beige pleated coat trimmed with fur. How they were all being paid for, Agnes had no idea – it seemed impolite to ask, though she noted how quickly Vanessa's plea to live somewhere 'more fashionable' was dropped from family conversation. And one by one, invitations addressed to *Miss Agnes Melton* in black copperplate italics from people Agnes had never heard of started to tumble onto the mat.

Agnes watched in amazement as a new Vanessa emerged, as if from a chrysalis of illness. It was as though, in Suffolk, they had seen the black-and-white version, and that here, now, was Vanessa in glorious colour, dashing around, gossiping on the telephone, ordering the cook about, reducing Jeanette, the new French maid, to tears with her long lists of errands. Her little black address book was full, it seemed, of friends and family, who were delighted to hear she was back in Town. Agnes had been led to believe that Vanessa had had a sheltered up-bringing, but she seemed to have an astonishing ready-made network of society matrons, happy to add Agnes and even Raven to their invitation lists. She no longer seemed like an elder sister.

Agnes enjoyed her days exploring London. She went shop-ping with Vanessa in Oxford Street, marching past the sparkling new shopfronts of Regent Street to gawp at London's first traf-fic lights in Piccadilly. Sometimes Mr Melton would take her to the Victoria & Albert museum or Raven would escort her to a gallery. Mr Armstrong was as good as his word and spent a day showing her the docks and warehouses, and then they made their way down the Isle of Dogs and walked under the river to Greenwich to see the Observatory. He wore a black armband these days, as his wife had sadly passed away the previous autumn. Once, Agnes went to visit Aunt Florence, Lucy and the boys. Florence was pregnant with her fourth child, but soon after Agnes's visit she suffered a miscarriage and decided to retire to the country for a rest, so Vanessa was left in sole charge of entertaining Agnes.

It was the luncheon parties Agnes liked least. 'You must meet some other girls,' Vanessa insisted, and promptly invited half a dozen young women to luncheon one Tuesday.

As she stood in the drawing room surrounded by six pretty girls, all strangers to her but friends or at least acquaintances to one another, Agnes felt like quietly slipping out to her bedroom; surely none of them would notice. The truth was, she was shy with other girls. She couldn't think of any contribution to make to the small talk, the arch, heartless comments about awful boys and messed-up dance cards, of country-house parties and hunt balls. How had she ended up on the edge of this strange new world? The other girls clearly thought her a little boring and seemed embarrassed if she talked about a book she had read or the latest exhibition at the Academy. And they all seemed to have been to school or finishing school with one another and knew the same network of families. Only the desire not to disappoint her stepmother made Agnes endure the hellish ritual of 'Do you know So-and-so?' and 'Are you invited to Such-and-such?' over clear soup, little cutlets in white paper frills, and pink jelly with blobs of cream on top.

The dances were a little better, not least because she responded well to male company and loved dancing, but there was always that stomach-churning moment at the start when, self-conscious in green silk-satin or pink taffeta and too much make-up, she was stuck tongue-tied, alone with her chaperone, waiting for some man, any man, to come and mark her card.

In fact, as it proved, she was rarely short of partners. Her gold-brown hair and blue eyes were considered *à la mode* and the liveliness and intelligence of her expression made people look at her twice. But, innocent as she was, even she wondered how many a matron of noble lineage would be happy to see her darling scion link up with a bluestocking girl of no connections and modest wealth, and was not surprised that her list of faithful suitors was consequently short.

One constant was Andrew FitzClement, a lanky youth of Anglo-Irish extraction with sandy hair and an earnest face, who made a point of dancing with her at least twice at each party. He would chatter about his time at Oxford and how he would like to stay in London and make his way as a photographer rather than go back to administer the family estate outside Cork. He seemed lonely and probably sensed a fellow soul in torment in Agnes, but he was irritatingly self-absorbed and she failed to summon up any more feeling than gratitude to him for his attentions and refused all his invitations for dinner or the theatre.

Then there was the silent and intense Michael Clayton, saturnine son of a retired diplomat, himself starting out in the Foreign Office. He was a natural dancer, and drew her effortlessly round the floor in foxtrot or waltz under the sparkling chandeliers until, flushed and breathless, she would collapse into a chair laughing.

One hot moonless night he led her out into the dark garden in the middle of Eaton Square. He lit a cigarette, the glowing point throwing into relief his clever-looking face, and asked her, 'So, do you know these people well, the Fox-Chomleys?' Mrs Fox-Chomley was their hostess this evening, a statuesque woman in her late forties who looked as though she'd be as adept at leading a cavalry regiment into battle as she clearly was at organizing this coming-out ball for her youngest daughter, Elspeth.

'She's some distant cousin of my stepmother's,' said Agnes, crushing leaves from a bush so that a sharp smell of privet mingled with the stink of smoke.

'I was engaged to the elder sister,' Michael said in a bitter tone. 'Amelia. But she's marrying some blighter she met at a soup kitchen, can you believe it?' His laugh was harsh, mirthless. 'She's not as pretty as you,' he said, more gently and, tossing down his cigarette, he put out his hand to stroke her hair.

But Agnes tensed up, then panicked, as he pulled her face to his and his hard tongue invaded her mouth. She shoved him away. 'I don't even know you,' she gasped, 'and I won't be second best, I'm sorry,' and she ran back inside to bright lights and safety.

So the days and nights slipped past in a muddled dream – but what of Raven?

Raven Melton often declined invitations to the balls and chaperoned parties though sometimes he accompanied Vanessa since Gerald disliked late nights and rich food. Raven had other fish to fry. For a start he was locked in combat with his father. Since the legal profession was obviously of no interest to his son, Gerald Melton had spent many evenings closeted with him, pacing up and down, discussing the possibilities of the future. Finally, it was agreed, with significant reluctance on Raven's part, that they would accept William Armstrong's kind offer of a place as a commodities broker. It would be a starting position, of course, but if Raven showed an aptitude for the work and applied himself, there would be opportunities for advancement.

'Three months,' the young man muttered. 'I'll give it three months.'

'Six,' demanded his father. 'You've got to give it a proper chance. And if you want to leave then, you'd better come up with some respectable plans.'

So Raven walked out into Queen's Square every weekday morning now, with bowler hat and umbrella, off, as he put it bitterly to his sister, 'to count beans'.

Agnes was momentarily puzzled, as she thought William Armstrong invested in tea and spices, but she conjured up a picture of Raven literally upending sacks of pulses on the floor and measuring them into piles . . .

Predictably, he hated it. 'He says I'm surly,' Raven spat, when Armstrong's deputy, Ivan Plater, gave him warning one day. 'I'm not surly, I just ignore him, vulgar man.'

The second time, a couple of weeks later, Mr Plater complained to his boss and Raven was summoned before Armstrong. One more 'incident' and Raven would be dismissed.

In the meantime, Raven was out every night. Sometimes, Freddy or Roddy came up from Cambridge and they dined at some hostess's mansion before going to a dance. More often he met a growing circle of other friends, writers, artists, musicians and poets – unknown for the most part – at clubs and parties from which he only returned in the small hours, sometimes meeting Agnes on the stairs, brother and sister like bleary-eyed ships in the night. Occasionally, if Gerald was out, and Agnes was taken care of, Vanessa would accompany Raven on these bohemian outings. In the mornings he would be roused by the maid to stumble off late, pale and irritable, to his office in the City while Agnes was allowed her beauty sleep.

Then, one Wednesday afternoon in mid-June, Agnes was resting in the flat alone – Vanessa had gone out to luncheon – when she woke suddenly, aware of Jeanette answering the door. It was Raven.

She heard him asking for Vanessa, then he walked into Agnes's room without knocking and threw himself into an easy chair.

'That's it,' he said. 'I'm never going back. And Father can put up with it.'

'What's happened? What have you done?'

'I punched Plater, the bully.' He explained that in the last few weeks Mr Plater had taken delight in goading him, showing him up in front of the other men. Finally, today, Raven had had enough.

'Oh, Raven. Father will be absolutely furious. What are you going to do?'

'Get a job on a paper. Write. Live in a garret, I don't know.' He got up and paced around the room in great agitation. 'Anything that isn't beastly, hideous business.' He dragged both hands through his luxuriant black hair. His eyes were sharp points of black light. Agnes was startled by his deep anger, his energy.

He tapped his fingers impatiently on the chest of drawers. 'What are you doing now? This evening, I mean.'

'Well, nothing really. There's a dance at the Cowan-Wilkeses, but I told Vanessa I had a headache.'

'Do you? Have a headache, I mean? Come out with me. Now. I can't stay here waiting for Father to get home.' He opened her wardrobe and started pulling out dresses. 'Here, get this on.' A frilly georgette frock in pale green with gold and white trimming landed on her bed. 'And a coat – it's raining out. I'll see you in a moment.' And he left her, sitting up in the bed, while he went to get changed himself.

'Raven, where are we going?' Agnes wailed, adjusting her hat and struggling to keep up with Raven's long strides as he pulled her towards Southampton Row. Queen's Square had turned to shiny slate in the rain and the air smelled of lead. 'My stockings are getting splashed.'

'Here!' he shouted, waving his umbrella at a cab, and

instructed the driver to go to Green's, in Cork Street. 'It's a viewing,' he said to Agnes. 'A sculptor I've met – his first exhibition. I told him I'd try and go. Interesting stuff, I think you'll find.'

Raven was unusually talkative on the journey down to Green Park, mentioning this painter or that poet he hoped would be there, and saying that it was time Agnes saw a bit of life that wasn't one of those 'stuffy dances' where you couldn't get much to drink and had to be polite to boring women.

People seemed to be queuing to get into Green's when they arrived but it turned out the sculptor, a small thin man with a beard, dressed formally in a black suit, was insisting on the courtesy of greeting anyone who came through the door. After passing over her coat to an attendant and enduring with surprise the sculptor's garlicky breath, only thinly disguised by peppermint, as he kissed her cheeks, Agnes was propelled forward by the pressure of those in the queue behind. She and Raven entered the crowd like swimmers, making their way past vast hewn blocks of stone like icebergs, to the far end of the room where there were fewer people and where the smaller pieces were displayed. Raven introduced Agnes to a stout fiftyish lady dressed all in purple, a Mrs Proudhart, then waved at someone across the room and disappeared back into the throng.

'What do you think of my nephew's work, Miss Melton?' Mrs Proudhart's voice quavered with emotion as she gestured to her right towards several blobs of bronze welded together like a clump of toadstools. She fixed Agnes with an intense gaze. 'Is he not a genius?'

'His work is certainly very . . . challenging,' said Agnes, hoping she was saying the right thing. She had been profoundly moved by some of the works of Henry Moore she had seen, but in truth, these strange objects aroused in her only a faint repulsion. She was more attracted by a sudden glimpse of some framed drawings on the far wall.

Fortunately the lady nodded vigorously. 'It is time,' she intoned. 'No more statues of generals on horseback. This is the new age. We must feel our way forward.' And she stroked the sculpture lovingly as though fondling poisonous toadstools was a perfectly normal thing to enjoy.

Fortunately they were interrupted by the arrival of a balding man in white tie and tails. He was in a somewhat agitated state.

'Allow me to present my husband,' murmured Mrs Proudhart. He nodded briefly at Agnes.

'We must be away now, Martha. We'll be late for the Bleesdales,' he barked.

Agnes took the interruption as an opportunity to get a closer look at the drawings. They were mainly charcoal sketches, studies of female forms in various poses. There was something poignant, exhilarating about them and they appeared to have been drawn effortlessly by someone utterly sure of their craft. Each was initialled in a bold hand *H.F.* She stood back and looked for a notice of the name. Ah, there it was: *Harry Foster*.

As she moved along the group of drawings, studying each one, she became aware of a man glancing at her from where he stood at the edge of a laughing, gossiping group. She took care to give him no hint that she had seen him but, after a moment, he peeled himself off from his companions and wandered over to her, his hands in the pockets of his navy suit.

'Something about these interests you in some way?' he asked, slightly diffidently.

Agnes turned and looked at him through lowered lashes. Gradually, her eyes widened and she met his gaze. His was an interesting face, not classically handsome, but his brown eyes were warm against his pale skin and his mouth turned up at the corners as though he were perpetually amused about something. She noticed the shadows under his eyes, the beginnings of crows' feet at their corners, and a slight hollowness to his mobile face. She opened her mouth to speak, but he broke in first, offering her his hand.

'I'm sorry, I've startled you,' he said. 'Here, I'm Harry. Harry Foster. The artist, dontcha know.' He waved at the array of pictures.

Agnes gasped and blurted out her own name, looking from the drawings and back to Harry Foster. 'I'm sorry, I didn't know. I mean . . .' She stopped. 'They're very good. You make it look so easy. Do they take you long to do?'

He laughed. 'Not at the rate per hour I have to pay the ladies to sit,' he said. 'Seriously, though. I make many sketches each time. Only one or two are usually any good. Or none, sometimes. I'm working on a bigger piece now. Oils. But it's a long-term project so I have to keep doing these crowd-pleasers to pay the rent.'

'I love them,' she said firmly. 'They're so . . . I feel uplifted by them, free.'

'Thank you,' he said quietly, studying her.

'This one here,' Agnes said, indicating a nude, 'the curve of her back is so beautiful. She's like a lovely crouching animal.' Although they were now studying the drawings, she was strongly aware of the warmth of Harry's presence beside her, his faint scent of sandalwood and Russian cigarettes.

'That's just what I thought about her, too. She's a shop girl, you know. I spotted her in a cinema queue. Agnes Melton,' he said suddenly. 'Say, are you Raven's sister? He talks about a little sister, but I didn't think he meant one that was all grown up.' He looked her up and down appreciatively and her face glowed with embarrassment. She knew her shingled hair made her look

252

older than many girls of her age, and she was glad she'd taken the time to put on a little powder and lipstick for she didn't like to admit to this man possibly ten years her senior that she was only seventeen.

He offered her a cigarette from a silver case, which she took, although she rarely smoked, and while he was engaged in lighting it she noticed his graceful movements, his long slim fingers and, as he bent over the lighter, the springy chestnut hair that matched his eyes.

'I'm glad you came over,' she said. 'I don't know anyone here. And Raven's just gone off somewhere or other. Do you know him well?'

'No, hardly at all. He's a friend of Tom's. Tom knows everybody.'

'And who is Tom?'

'Chap over there with the snorty laugh. Works for the *Sketch*. Miss Melton, Agnes, I'm glad I had to rescue you,' he said. 'Though I never saw myself in the role of knight before,' he added. 'Can I fetch you a drink?'

Agnes shook her head, not wanting to lose him for even a moment.

'Do you know Mr Proudhart?' she asked.

'My fellow exhibitor? Only met him for the first time tonight. Don't know why Raoul – know Raoul Green? runs this place – put us together really.'

'I hate them,' Agnes said in a low voice. 'These . . . lumps,' she said fiercely, nodding at the toadstools. 'He has no soul.'

'So you're passionate about art, are you?' Harry said, teasing, his eyes sparkling at her.

'I don't know anything really,' she admitted, feeling her face grow warm. 'I am rude, aren't I? Sorry.'

'Not at all. If he weren't my fellow sufferer on this occasion,

253

I might feel freer to hold an opinion myself. Doesn't do to bite the hand that feeds me, though. Tell me, Agnes, if I may call you Agnes, what are you doing later, you and Raven?'

'Me?' Agnes was surprised. 'I don't know. Raven hasn't said. Dinner somewhere, I expect, though we don't have any invitation. Look, there he is!' Raven was making his way towards them through the crowd, his eyes shining, his normally smooth hair ruffled.

'Good to see you, Harry! You've met Agnes, I see. Your pictures are going well – I saw a lady just now brandishing her chequebook. Gone for one of the saucy ones, I expect. Look, I've just been talking to Tom. Freda Brett-Jardine's having a party later. Why don't we go to Previtali's and mosey on there afterwards.'

'Well, why not? Agnes, are you game for it?' Harry asked her, an expression of lazy amusement in his eyes.

She had felt her heart flutter in fear at the thought that this might be the end of their time together, but now all was arranged, she believed she would burst with happiness. Dinner, with this wonderful, fascinating man, and then a party. She nodded, her eyes bright as they locked on his.

'Let's get our hats and coats,' said Raven, not seeming to notice his sister's unusual behaviour. 'We'll find a cab with Tom and meet the others there.' And he grabbed Agnes's hand. On impulse, she offered her other hand to Harry and he gripped it. The warm pressure of his touch was the only thing she was aware of as they made their way towards the door.

'It is the most extraordinary night of my whole life so far,' Agnes sighed. Later, much later, she lay awake on cool sheets, giddy with the effects of drink and dancing, her ears buzzing from loud music and voices, remembering Harry's body brushing against hers as they danced, his breath warm in her ear. She knew without doubt that she was in love. When she finally left him, standing on the stairs outside the party, she had felt bereft, hardly noticing the ride home with Raven through the quiet streets.

The dinner at Previtali's had passed in a kind of dream. Raven and Harry had ordered for her and dishes had come and gone with her hardly having tasted them, though she sipped at her wine. Their party was a noisy one. Tom was a lively fellow, a bluff, red-faced man who regaled the table with his journalist's stories. They were joined by Raoul Green, a lithe Jewish-looking man, and he brought another half a dozen people with him from the viewing, including a Mr Beales who seemed to own a publishing company, and two glamorous-looking women who took little notice of Agnes but giggled a lot and had to take frequent trips to the powder room, knocking into other diners' chairs on the way and apologizing too loudly to their annoyed occupants.

Agnes didn't mind their rudeness. She was just content to sit between Raven and Harry, listening to Raven describe to Sam Beales some stories he was writing and answering Harry's questions about what she had been doing in London. She gauged that he lived alone, using a bedroom with a north light as his studio.

'Where do you come from, Harry?' she asked.

'Cambridgeshire,' he replied. 'Though I don't go back there much now.' He toyed with the grilled fish on his plate. 'My father didn't like my becoming an artist. No money in it. Certainly not respectable. Fortunately, my older brother was happy to take over the business when he retired, so they've tried to forget about me.'

'That sounds very hard. Aren't they pleased to hear how well you're doing?'

255

'Maybe if I chose religious subjects or painted pretty land-scapes. But my mother is very pious – we're Catholics, you see – and the priest has told her I paint pornography, though I don't think he's ever seen one of my pictures, just read a review some-where, I expect. I . . . anyway, I've disgraced myself in a whole variety of ways, so it seems better to keep away.'

'But aren't you very lonely without your family?'

'Lonely?' Harry gave her a curious look as the dishes were taken away and ices placed in front of them. 'When you are a stranger amongst your own family then you can feel the loneli-est person in the world.'

Agnes leaned towards him and whispered, 'I sometimes wonder whether Raven feels like that. Father is going to be furi-ous when he hears he has thrown over his job.'

'Have you, Raven?' Harry raised his voice to break into the noisy conversation on Agnes's other side. 'Have you really left the City?'

'The City has left me! Thrown me out, rather. An occasion to celebrate, don't you think?'

While the others all laughed and drank, unthinking, to Raven's newfound freedom, Agnes sat quietly. She was imag-ining the reception they were going to get on their return.

The rain had stopped now. The air was muggy and it was get-ting dark. As they drifted out of the restaurant, the girls squabbling about what to do next, she pulled Raven aside. 'Don't you think we ought to go home and face the music? Father and Vanessa won't even know where I am.'

'Jeanette will have told them you're out with me. Come on, I promised Freda I would show up. Let's go.'

And when Agnes found herself sitting close to Harry in the cab, she forgot everything but the exhilaration of the present moment.

\*

256

Freda Brett-Jardine lived in a top-floor flat in one of the white terraced streets off Kensington High Street. It was utterly unlike any of the opulent venues frequented by Agnes in the past few weeks. For a start, there was a winding staircase covered in elderly carpeting, up which they had to climb three floors, Harry pulling Agnes by the hand, Raoul's girls complaining all the way. They could hear the unmistakable sound of Louis Armstrong's trumpet growing louder as they went and at the top was waiting the most extraordinary-looking woman Agnes had ever seen.

Freda Brett-Jardine was as dark as an Egyptian, her exotic beauty highlighted by kohled eyes and a gorgeous floaty dark gold dress and jacket, both embroidered with black swirls, like an Indian sari Agnes had seen in a book. She could have been any age between twenty-five and forty-five. Her expression was one of boredom. Even when she smiled, it did not touch her eyes.

'Darlings, you came! Raven, Harry, Raoul, it's wonderful to see you. I was just giving up on you all. No Vanessa? Well at least I'll have you for myself tonight.'

Agnes's eyes widened at her brazenness, but Raven ignored the comment. He introduced everybody else, but Freda's eyes passed vaguely over the rest of the party and returned to Raven. She hung onto his arm as she led them into the flat and straight through to the drawing room where two or three young men in white ties loitered stiffly, clearly waiting for everything to start.

'Freda's husband was an antiquarist,' whispered Harry in Agnes's ear, as she stopped to look round in delighted amazement. 'Travelled all over the East.' The walls were covered with hangings, the floors festooned with Turkish rugs and great cushions, the ceiling was oxblood red, as were what she could glimpse of the walls. Bright-coloured throws disguised sofas and archairs. Huge chests, cupboards and carved decorative pieces in dark Indian wood completed the transformation of a shabby Kensington apartment into a boudoir of a maharajah. Agnes breathed in the heady scent of incense and some mysterious sweeter smell wafting through it.

More people arrived – an elderly man in an ancient black suit, several informally dressed young men, a plain and very talkative young woman in a shapeless cover-all garment with them. Agnes asked for a lemonade when someone offered her a drink, but when it came, it had a strange taste and she sipped at it with caution.

'Where is he now?' she shouted in Harry's ear over the wail of the gramophone, careful not to trip over the snarling head of a tiger rug by the fireplace. 'Mr Brett-Jardine, I mean.'

'Nobody knows. Maybe he was eaten by this fellow,' Harry shouted back, nodding at the tiger. 'Or, more likely, Freda traded him for a native. Exotic tastes, our Freda.'

'What do you mean?' she asked, puzzled. Then 'Oh,' as the penny dropped and she blushed.

Harry laughed. Agnes laughed too. She was beginning to feel dizzy. From the drink – which certainly wasn't just lemonade. From the seductive roll of the music, the heat, which was oppressive despite the open windows, the smoky spice in the air. And from happiness. Around them, as the room filled up with laughing, chattering strangers, she could hear snatches of fascinating conversation.

'And she's thrown him out again . . . this time she won't have him back, I'm sure.'

'Elegaic yet contemporary, a tour de force . . .'

'Bankrupt, my dear, and since the police raid . . .'

Someone changed the music. Ambrose's orchestra. A few

couples were beginning to dance, dreamily, forcing the talkers to move back to make room.

'Shall we?' Harry whispered, relieving Agnes of her drink and taking her into his arms. She clung to him in the small space as they jostled with the other dancers.

There followed more drink, loud conversation, more dancing. Gradually Agnes was no longer aware of what she was saying, or to whom. She laughed and flirted and danced until the room started to spin.

'I've got to get some air,' she said to Harry. He drew her out of the flat onto the landing. It was cooler there, and she began to feel better. She leaned against the wall and, after a while, looked up at Harry, smiling.

'Phew. I must look a sight,' she said. 'My hair everywhere.'

'No, you don't,' he said, reaching out and touching her face. 'I must paint you. You look . . . so lovely. Like Tennyson's lily maid in your gold and white and green.'

'*Lancelot and Elaine*,' she breathed through soft parted lips. 'You know Tennyson.' The air between them altered, became thin, charged with possibility. An eternal moment eventually passed and the spell broke. He bent and kissed her. She kissed him back, and at her response he kissed her again, then he pulled her towards him and pressed his mouth hard against her open lips.

'Agnes!' Raven's voice was harsh. They broke apart. Raven glanced briefly at Harry as if he were no one. 'I think we should go. I'll say our goodbyes and get the coats.' He turned and went back inside.

'I'm sorry,' Harry said. 'I shouldn't have done that.'

'Yes, you should. Yes, you should, Harry,' Agnes said fiercely. 'Don't mind him.' Suddenly she felt miserable. She would lose him. 'You . . . m-may paint me,' she stuttered.

Harry studied her, then kissed her again. Then he reached into his pocket and brought out a wallet, from which he extracted a card. 'It's the middle bell but it doesn't always work, you have to knock. Come when you can,' he said. 'I don't have a telephone, I'm afraid, but I'm usually in late afternoon. Or send me a note.' Then he waited, wordlessly, as Raven re-emerged, helped Agnes on with her coat and swept her downstairs. As they reached the first landing, she looked up and her eyes met Harry's where he was leaning over the banister. At his smile, a rush of desire coursed through her. She gazed at him, her heart plain on her face, until Raven pulled her away.

They hardly spoke a word in the taxi. Raven smoked and stared out of the window into the night. Agnes's eyes fluttered closed, then she opened them again as the world raced round and nausea threatened. It was after 2 a.m. when they reached home. A flustered Jeanette, great circles of tiredness round her eyes, opened the door to the flat, showed them straight into the drawing room and pulled the doors shut on them. Vanessa was huddled up in an armchair, smoking furiously. She had clearly been crying. Gerald was leaning, one arm on the mantelpiece, his face like stone. He ignored Agnes. All his rage was directed at Raven.

'So you're home. Where in God's name have you been with her? We've been frantic with worry. And what's all this I hear from Armstrong? You've got some explaining to do, my boy.'

'Gerald, you must listen to me,' wailed Vanessa. 'He's not a child. He's got to find his own way. Make his own mistakes.'

'Let me deal with my son as I see fit!' shouted Gerald. Then his voice softened. 'I'm sorry, my dear. Why don't you see to Agnes?'

'We'll get you something comforting to drink, darling,'

Vanessa whispered, ushering Agnes out of the room. 'No, *va te coucher*, Jeanette,' she told the maid, who put down the tea-cloth she was clutching and staggered gratefully to her room.

Vanessa made her stepdaughter a tisane and helped her to bed. There Agnes lay for a long while, drifting in and out of sleep, thinking about Harry and Raven and Vanessa. Something was worrying her there. Mrs Brett-Jardine's voice echoed in her head: 'No Vanessa? No Vanessa?' Why should Vanessa have been there? Eventually, there came the sounds of doors opening and closing and the flat fell into darkness and silence. In the morning, she was briefly roused from sleep by the front door slamming. When she finally awoke, it was mid-morning and Raven had gone.

The closing of the front door and Bobby's yapping woke Kate and she sat up, stiff and cold, and looked at the clock. Eleven fifteen. She grabbed at the exercise book that was slipping from her lap.

'Hello, dear, you still up?' Joyce put her head round the door.

'Just about,' yawned Kate. 'Did you have a good time?'

'Ooh yes. And I met a friend of Lillian's who knows you. Marion someone. Says she's a cousin.'

'Marion? Of course, her family had a house in Woodbridge. I didn't realize she still lived round there. She came to our wedding, Mum says, though I don't really remember her.'

'Well, I've got her phone number, dear, in case you wanted to give her a call sometime. Very keen to hear how your mother is, though I didn't like to—'

'Thank you. I will ring her. She might want to know about Agnes.'

'Now I'm off to bed, dear. Anything you want?'

'No, I'll go up myself in a little while, thanks.'

When Joyce had gone upstairs Kate looked at the open book. She had read most of the entries before dozing off into a dream in which she could vividly recall the strange sculptures in Green's, the exotic smells of Mrs Brett-Jardine's drawing room, the touch of Harry's lips . . .

She picked up all the books and arranged them in date order. There was only one more after this. She opened the final book to check. It was the journal that began in 1943 with the words *Father still very ill*. Either Agnes hadn't written a diary for fifteen years, since 1928, or there was a volume missing. As she gathered up all the books to take them upstairs, Kate wondered what those fifteen missing years had brought to Agnes Melton.

# *Chapter 23*

*July 2004*

'There's the sign – Chapelfield Hall.' Simon turned the car right off the main road, through a pair of stone gate-posts and down a gravel drive with coniferous parkland on either side.

'It looks like something from the set of *The Addams Family*,' breathed Kate, as they rounded a bend and a dark Gothic edifice rose into view. 'Ravens and all.'

'Well, common or garden crows. And the odd pigeon. But it is imposing, isn't it? Looks good, Kate!' And they grinned at one another in childlike excitement. Simon freewheeled the car gently into the large car park to one side of the hotel and they sat for a moment listening to the clicks and whirrs of the cooling engine as if, suddenly, neither had the reserves of energy for the task before them.

It was early Saturday afternoon. They had had a quick salad lunch with Joyce and the children before setting out for this hotel ten miles outside Norwich.

'It's just north of the city,' she had told Simon that morning. 'Right in the country. And it's got a pool and a gym.'

And a golf course. But she didn't mention that in case he thought he'd drag her round for a game. She loathed golf.

In fact, though, Simon had been most attentive since his unusually prompt return on Friday by the five o'clock train. The children had been all over him, proudly showing their Sport's Day stickers, Daisy for being first in the egg and spoon race, Sam for being third in the obstacle race. Joyce and Kate had finally managed to get them off to sleep at nine, then Joyce had deliberately disappeared into the kitchen to tidy up by herself, leaving Simon and Kate contemplating one another in the sitting room. Simon wouldn't sit down. He paced about sighing, rattling the coins in his jeans pocket, rearranging the ornaments on the mantelpiece, or going to one of the windows to peer out as if he were suddenly intensely interested in the garden. Finally, Kate suggested they go for a walk, and they let themselves out into the twilight leaving a resentful Bobby behind.

In the event, it wasn't much of a walk. They just followed the road down towards the village and stopped in the deserted adventure playground. Sitting side by side on the swings, rocking gently to and fro, Simon shuffling the bark chippings with his brogued feet, they finally began to talk.

Kate told him briefly about her week, the news of the school, about Agnes, whom she had not had time to see since reading her journals, and what Max had said about the old lady going into a home. Simon was quiet, though he seemed very concerned about the school closure and questioned her about what exactly Mrs Smithson was recommending. When Kate trailed to a halt, he stood up and went and put a hand against the metal swing-frame, shoving it hard, as though testing it for its strength. Then he said, 'I saw Meredith last night.'

'Simon, you said . . .' breathed in Kate.

He turned round sharply, and she could see the emotion working in his face.

'I told her it was over. I wouldn't be seeing her any more.'

'Oh,' she said, and stood up abruptly, then didn't seem to know what to do with herself.

'C'mon.' Taking her arm in a clumsy movement, Simon guided her over to sit on a wooden bench at the edge of the playing area. He squeezed her to him, dropping kisses on her hair, her forehead. She raised her face and he kissed her mouth, hard and hungrily. It was then she realized he was crying.

'Don't,' she said, and started to cry, too.

He pushed back the strands of her hair that had tumbled over her face and whispered, 'Sorry, I'm so sorry, darling,' over and over again, and she kissed him quickly then buried her face in the warm living comfort of his chest.

They sat there for a few moments until she said, 'I've got to move. I've got a crick in my neck.' She found a more comfortable position, with his arm round her shoulders and, after a moment, said quietly, 'What did Meredith say when you told her?'

Simon's voice sounded half-choked. 'I said I had to put my marriage first and my children. That you were all too important to me. She was – angry. I – I don't think she's accepted it really.'

*And you, Simon, have you accepted it?*

'But you've told her, firmly, that it's over – and that you won't see her again? Simon, I must know.'

'No. I mean, yes.' His expression was unreadable.

At that moment, a couple of teenagers pushed the park gate open and shuffled in; a gangly boy of about fifteen in a black T-shirt and camouflage trousers and a plump girl with ragged blonde hair and her tummy bulging through the gap between crop top and trousers. He was carrying a tin of lager and a pack of cigarettes. They went over and sat on the swings where Kate and Simon had sat a moment ago, and talked and giggled and smoked, casting sly looks in the Hutchinsons' direction.

Finally, Simon got up and put out his hand to Kate. 'Let's go.' They nodded at the teenagers, and walked back up the road in the gloaming to Paradise Cottage.

In bed, later, Kate's doubts came crowding back, though Simon reached out and caressed her shoulder.

'No,' she said. 'I can't. Not yet.' And they lay awake together, the moonlight illuminating the gulf between them.

It was after they had collected the key to their hotel room that the problems started. Simon had carried their cases up many ashwood-railed stairs, through several sound-muffling fire doors, over the corporate carpeting of endless corridors lined with bland prints, to reach the door of 312 at the very back of the hotel.

Kate got the door open on the third attempt with the electronic key card. It was a standard four-star room, no doubt exactly like most of the others in the hotel. The only troubles were: 'Oh no, it only has a shower. No bath. I did ask for a bath.' And, 'Well, the view's not great. Are those really the dustbins?' They looked at each other and sighed.

'Come on.' Simon picked up their bags again and they trouped downstairs to reception, only to learn that, no, it wasn't possible to change the room, they were full that night because of a golf tournament. So back upstairs they had to go. Simon wearily dropped their luggage onto the rack by the wardrobe.

'I'll make us some tea,' Kate said, finding the kettle and the tray of cups and tea bags in a cabinet with the mini-bar under the television. While she boiled the water and dunked the tea bags, Simon sat on the bed armed with the remote control, flicking through the Ceefax pages looking for the sports results.

'Surely there isn't any football in July.'

'Oh, a couple of friendlies. And there might be some athletics . . .'

Kate grabbed at the remote control, but Simon was too quick for her. 'Simon, don't be horrible, we haven't come for this. Look, here's your tea and then let's go out. We could walk down to the village.'

'I suppose,' said Simon, pressing the standby button with a sigh. 'What time's dinner?'

'I've booked a table for seven thirty. We could get a swim in first if there's time.'

'Fat chance – I'm knackered,' said Simon, lying back and closing his eyes. Kate looked at him in alarm. What were they doing here, making small talk, misreading each other's moods? Then Simon opened one eye. It twinkled at her merrily.

'Oh, you,' she said, and slapped his leg playfully. Then they sat side by side on the bed like an elderly couple, drinking their tea.

'It's so quiet without the kids, isn't it?' Kate said. 'I keep expecting Sam to throw open the door with a bang, demanding a drink or help looking for something.'

'Or that the phone's going to go, with Gillingham demanding three impossible things before a nine o'clock briefing meeting.' Simon laughed.

They were quiet again. Then Kate put down her cup.

'Why did it happen, Simon? What's gone wrong with us?' Her voice was wobbly.

Simon drew his knees up and slowly began to take off his shoes. 'I don't know. I've been going over it and over it. It's just we haven't seen enough of one another, have we? You've been . . . losing focus, fading. I spend all my time living on adrenaline. The excitement is at work. It's like a fix. And Meredith is . . . was . . . a part of it all.'

'And I'm just on the edge.' Kate felt drained of energy.

'It's different with you,' Simon said earnestly. 'You're more restful. It's like coming home when I'm with you.'

'But you never come home, Simon, that's the whole point. You're supposed to be living in Suffolk, with me, with Sam and Daisy. But you're not really, are you? You're still mentally in London. You haven't made the switch.'

'No, I suppose not. But Kate,' Simon turned and tried to put his arm round her, 'I do still love you. And the kids. I want to sort this out. Really, I do. I'm not seeing her any more. I'm not.' Again, his face looked strange, racked with stress, the effort of holding back tears. His skin had a grey pallor and his hair was lank. He was starting to look old, Kate thought.

'You say that, but I can't take it in yet, can I? I keep thinking of you with her . . . It's not the same. It can't ever be the same. How can I trust you now?'

'I can see that. But we can build trust up again, Kate, we can. Believe me.'

'I want to. But it hurts, Simon. It really really hurts.'

In the end there wasn't time to walk down to the nearby village – they both fell asleep, exhausted by emotion. When Kate woke it was half past five. She turned to look at Simon, still deeply asleep beside her. His colour looked better now but he didn't stir when she got up to go to the bathroom. She watched him for a few minutes, then wriggled her feet into her shoes and quietly let herself out of the room.

Her aim was to walk round the hotel grounds, but when she reached the front porch she saw it had started to rain quite heavily, so she turned and made her way to the bar area where she sat down and ordered some tea.

She looked about her. A couple who might have been in their mid-forties were sitting close together at a table in the corner to her left, finishing glasses of lager. The woman's face, though not pretty, seemed lit by some inner joy. Her hair was beginning to show grey, but it was well cut. She made the best of herself, as Kate's grandmother would have said. The man was lean, but his otherwise abundant hair was receding and his face was beginning to slacken. He sat thigh to thigh with her on the leather sofa. They were looking over some photographs, talking animatedly and laughing, comfortable with one another. When they stood up to go, the man put out a protective hand, then collected the cardigan she'd forgotten on her seat. They linked arms as they left the bar, she leaning slightly into him. Just an ordinary couple, thought Kate. No one would give them a second glance normally. Yet she envied the way they seemed so at home with one another, so utterly trusting, like two musical instruments playing in harmony.

Will that be Simon and me in ten years' time? she thought and couldn't see it, somehow. Their own piece of music had struck chaos, as if a petulant pianist was crashing his hands down on his instrument.

Her eyes teared up and she turned her attention to her tea. When she looked up once more it was to see a man standing at the entrance to the bar, hands in pockets, his shoulders slumped, an unhappy expression on his face as he gazed round, looking for someone. Goodness, she realized it was Simon! Suddenly he saw her, for he waved and smiled as he made his way amongst the tables towards her.

'Should we ask for a different table?'

'Where? There isn't one.'

Dinner that evening was turning into a disaster. There was nothing wrong with the food itself – a marinaded salmon starter, followed by slivers of roast duck – but the presence of a birthday dinner (pink balloons printed with *30 today* attached to every chair) hotting up around a long table in the middle of the room,

269

and a noisy 'murder-mystery' gathering at another on the far side (Kate had even come across the 'body' on the stairs when she slipped out to the toilet) meant it was hard for the couple to concentrate on what each other was saying. What is more, the golf tournament meant that the rest of the tables were quickly filled by groups of loud-voiced men in Pringle sweaters demonstrating just how Duncan or Jeremy missed that crucial hole-in-one at the thirteenth. This was hardly the ideal place to have a serious talk about a marriage.

But since tea in the bar, which had evolved into pre-dinner drinks, Simon's conversation had become cryptic, as if he were working himself up to saying something that he didn't quite have the courage to come out with yet.

For instance, while they were still in the bar Kate had brought up the subject of Fernley school again and asked Simon if he would have a look at the accounts when they got them; he merely said that perhaps it wouldn't be their problem after all. Kate thought he meant that the school would close whatever line they took and was puzzled by his nonchalance. And when she broached the sensitive subject that maybe they had over-stayed their welcome at Paradise Cottage, he simply agreed with her and said, of course, they must do something about it.

That got Kate chattering away about looking at houses again, but she quickly detected that Simon was not interested. Instead, he was looking through his wallet as if he had to find something important in it. Worst of all was his reaction when she took a deep breath and embarked on what she felt was the crux of their difficulties – the fact that they spent so much of their time apart.

'Debbie was telling me about friends who made a real effort to go away for weekends together. Maybe we should plan to do that more. Maybe Joyce wouldn't mind looking after Daisy and

Sam, and, now they're older, they might be able to stay with friends sometimes, anyway.'

'It's a good idea, except I wouldn't see the kids much then, would I?' sighed Simon.

'It would all be OK if you didn't work in London, wouldn't it, Simon? That's what we've really got to do, isn't it, to get you a job locally. Something less stressful. Then you'd be home every night.'

For the first time that evening, her husband was suddenly animated. He leaned forward in his chair and said quietly but deliberately, 'Kate, you just don't seem to get this, do you? I don't *want* to work locally. I like my job. I want to go on doing it. I'm a success at it, finally. I'm about to get a promotion. I love the travel, and I like the other people I'm working with. It's pretty cut-throat sometimes, but it's exciting and I'm part of the team. I don't want to get a poxy finance manager's job in some firm in Ipswich that makes widgets or organizes crates going on boats. I'd hate it.'

Kate was stunned by the force of his emotion, but couldn't stop herself from going on. 'Well, there are surely accountancy firms in Norwich or Ipswich? Or you could re-train.'

'I could, but I don't want to. I'm sorry.'

They stared at one another across the table as if contemplating the damage his words had done. Simon looked calm – too calm, thought Kate.

'Don't you care,' she whispered, 'about us? Won't you change anything?'

'I . . .' Simon seemed to lose courage. 'Of course I care,' he said savagely. He stood up and grabbed his jacket. 'Come on,' he snapped, 'or we'll miss our table.' And he stalked off, not even looking back to see if she was following. Kate remembered the attentive husband she'd seen earlier in the bar and her spirits plunged still lower.

Later, in the dining room, as the laughter at the birthday table reached hysterical proportions, Kate and Simon both turned down dessert and ordered coffee.

Simon had been trying to explain again why his job was so important to him.

'And we haven't even got on to the subject of money. You don't realize what a cut in salary I'd have to take if I did something down here.'

'Yes, I do. But we've got lots of capital towards a house, and surely we could get together a big enough mortgage for the rest on a lower salary. You forget, I'm going to bring in some money at some point, too. When I find a job.'

'Yes, of course,' said Simon absently. Then he took a deep breath and said, 'Look, I've got something very serious to ask you about.'

A feeling of panic spread through her, but he read her thoughts at once.

'No, no, it's not about Meredith. It's about where we live. Kate, it's just not working for me here, out in the sticks. I know you're going to think this is silly, and I suppose it is really, but I want us to move back to London.'

'What?' The adrenaline rushed through to her fingertips like an electric shock. 'Are you crazy?'

A great baying of laughter from the birthday party drowned his next words. *Exactly, it's ridiculous!* cried a voice in Kate's head as she tried to cope with the enormity of Simon's request.

He tried again. 'Kate. I'm just not as at home here as I thought I would be. I know you'll say I haven't really tried, but I suppose I just haven't wanted to try.'

'No, you haven't, you haven't tried', she cried. 'How long have you felt this? Why couldn't you tell me before now?'

'I suppose I haven't really recognized it until the last couple of months. It was partly going round all those houses. You were so picky, and then I began to realize that I wouldn't feel at home in them either, in any of them. I just couldn't see myself out in the country, wearing cords and a tweed jacket, chatting to the neighbours about crop spraying, having to drive to get a newspaper – to get anywhere and to see anyone. Becoming provincial and growing older. It would feel like giving up on life.'

'But it isn't like that!' Kate protested. 'Wait until you start making friends and having things to do round here. You would start to care.'

'The difference between us, Kate, is that I don't want to start to care. I'm sorry. We've spent so many holidays in the area and I guess I saw it all through rose-tinted spectacles. I just don't want to be here all the time. I miss London. I never thought, brought up in the country as I was, that I would be like that. But I always wanted to get away. I've become a city person.

'And there's something else,' he went on. 'You've got to understand. Kate. It's as if I'm living two lives at the moment. I've thought about it, and I'm sure that's why everything has gone wrong for us. When I'm at the office, all I can think about is work, the people there, the excitement of the deals, the projects I'm involved in. I don't think about home and you and the children. We need to redress the balance.'

Their coffee sat untouched, growing cold.

'I can see all that,' Kate burst out. 'But why is it so different from when we lived in Fulham?'

'Work and family all felt . . . more integrated when we were in London. It was a shorter journey from the office to home and I felt that with you working as well, we were like a team, that you were going through the same sort of problems as I was, holding it all together. Now, I'm only with you at weekends,

273

aren't I? And it feels like I'm slaving away while you're having a jolly time at home all week with the children.'

'You know it's not like that,' Kate snapped.

'But that's how it *feels* – and I want it back the way it was. Please understand.'

'But I don't want to go back,' she almost shouted. 'I don't want it to be as it was – that's why we moved. And you can't ask the children to move again, it wouldn't be fair. And, anyway, we wouldn't be able to afford a nice house in a reasonable part of London any more. Simon, I like it here. I've grown into it. I'd miss the people now – Debbie and Agnes and Dan – *and* your mum. I've stopped thinking about London so much. It still feels strange visiting, but I've been able to put it all firmly in the past.'

'Don't you still miss Liz and Sarah and Claire?' Simon demanded.

'Of course I do, but we manage to see each other. We're still friends. And I don't want to work the same hours I used to, Simon, you know that. Surely I'd have to, to help pay for everything, and we'd be back where we started.'

There was silence between them, Kate shoving crumbs around on the tablecloth with small angry movements. On a nearby table a golfer with a loud Midlands voice was reaching the end of some shaggy dog story. Kate shot him such a look that he faltered for a moment and lowered his voice.

Simon leaned forwards and covered her hand with his. 'Poor old you,' he said, pressing his lips together in a woeful smile. 'I'm really messing you around, aren't I? Come on, let's get a drink in the bar and sleep on the matter.'

He summoned a passing waiter and asked him to put the bill to the room. Then he led Kate through the maze of tables and out across the hall.

They stood in dismay at the entrance to the bar, peering in vain amongst the throngs of middle-aged men for empty seats. Through the open French windows beyond, they could see the rain beating down on the metal tables on the terrace.

'Let's check out the mini-bar then,' Simon said simply, and they headed for their room.

Later, in bed, they lay spooned together, and Simon's hand slid down across her breasts.

I must, Kate told herself. I've got to try and make things normal between us. But she was so tense that his touch failed to rouse her; and in the end he turned away, angry at her rejection, but repeating again and again that it wasn't her fault.

Kate rolled onto her stomach and watched the red figures flicker past on the bedside digital clock. She couldn't sleep – the afternoon's nap had put paid to that, and she had too much to think about.

She couldn't go back to London, she just couldn't. She was dug in here now, putting down roots for the first time in her life. So were the children. It would be cruel to move them again, just as they were settled. Yes, as Simon said, children could be amazingly resilient, but she remembered her own experience of being moved about from posting to posting, how hard it was to make new friends in a new place. No, she wouldn't do that to Sam and Daisy. Even if they were forced to move schools to Halesworth, at least their schoolmates would be with them.

There was everything, too, that Agnes represented. She felt so involved with Agnes, as if the old lady's family were her own – which of course they were. This was family ground and she wanted it to be her ground, too. But what would happen to herself and Simon if she refused to move? Their relationship seemed so fragile. Would he stay with her? He had already dealt one damaging blow to the ties that bound them, ties that, a year ago, she had taken for granted. It was he who had been the one keen to move to the country, and that had appealed to a deep longing inside her, a longing for a place to belong. She remembered the drawing pinned to Joyce's fridge – the dream house with the dream family – was that all it represented now? A dream that vanished, forgotten, in the harsh light of day?

When she finally fell asleep, it was to keep waking as the hot-water pipes clunked, voices echoed in the corridor, doors slammed and extractor fans throbbed. The duvet was too hot and she couldn't get comfortable. Then, with the dawn, breakfast started up in the kitchens below. By the morning, she was exhausted.

One night away wasn't enough, Kate thought miserably over breakfast. Simon, who hadn't slept well either, seemed to be preparing to go back to the children already, looking at his watch and talking about checking out. She knew he must have a lot to do, getting ready for the coming week away, but surely they should make time this morning to walk and find a pub for lunch before driving back. Had he always been like this – tense, anxious to move on to the next thing?

'So you'll think about what I said last night, will you, Kate?' he asked now. 'About moving back, I mean? I'm sorry, I feel I've let you down in so many ways, but I'll make it up to you, honestly, I promise. Will you think about it?'

'Of course I'll think about it,' she snapped, 'but you know what I feel already, so what's the point?'

'Don't be cross, darling,' he said, trying to stroke her hand on her lap. She snatched it away. 'No, I can see why you're cross. On top of everything else.' His face sunk into sullen introspection.

'It's no good you feeling sorry for yourself,' she hissed.

'What?'

'Nothing. We'd better go and pack, I suppose. Since you think we need to rush back.'

'OK, we'll stop for lunch if you like. That pub near Beccles you liked the look of.'

'But you want to get back.'

'Not if you don't.'

'But I won't enjoy lunch if I know you'd rather be back home.'

And so the bickering went on.

In the end, Simon agreed it wasn't fair on his mother to turn up for lunch since she wasn't expecting them, and they stopped for a ploughman's en route but ate hurriedly and in silence. 'Anyone looking at us could tell we were married,' Kate grumbled as they got back into the car. She remembered the title of a book she'd once read: *Married Alive* . . .

As they drove in silence back towards Fernley, Kate had an idea. 'Can we go through Seddington?' she asked.

'Seddington? That's out of our way.'

'I just want to show you the house, that's all.'

Simon glanced at her with a slight frown, then shrugged his shoulders. 'Whatever,' he said, and turned off the main road past Halesworth. But when they stopped before the gates of Seddington House, it was to find them padlocked. The wall was too high, the line of trees the other side too thick, to think of scrambling over, so Simon stood peering through the bars whilst Kate kicked at the gravel in disappointment.

Eventually, Simon said, 'A handsome place. I'd like a proper look another time.' And they climbed back into the car and headed for home.

That night, deep in exhausted sleep, Kate dreamed that Agnes was trying to tell her something, but she couldn't hear the words.

*

A few miles away, in the hospital, Agnes lay oblivious to the curtains around her bed, to the whispering voices, to the faint glimmer of the new dawn. Her lips moved. Her eyelids fluttered, then her face fell still as she sank deeper into her dream. She was once more a little girl, a toddler, encased in stiff layers of flouncy white cotton. She teetered at the top of some stone steps – one, two, one, two, she counted them – in a beautiful garden. The air was warm, the light coming through the trees threw dappled patterns upon the grass.

'Come on, Agnes. Come on, darling!'

She looked up in amazement and gasped with joy, the tears prickling her eyes as she stared into the laughing face of . . . 'Mamma!' Yes, it was her mother, as beautiful and warm and loving as Agnes had always known she would be!

'Mamma!' Her lovely face, her outstretched arms – just waiting for her. Mamma, calling for her.

'Jump, darling, come on, jump! I'm here, I'll catch you. You'll be safe. Come to Mamma. Come on, jump!'

And Agnes jumped joyously into the outstretched arms.

At five o'clock in Paradise Cottage the telephone rang out in an urgent, continuous tone, but when Joyce stumbled out of bed to answer it she only heard white noise. There was no one there.

# Chapter 24

Kate was dazed and headachey the next morning. Simon dragged her out of bed at six to drive him to the station because he didn't want to leave the car in the car park there for five nights. They hardly spoke on the way, Simon clearly caught up already in the urgency of his schedule, Kate unable to think of anything to say that wouldn't be cross and hurtful.

At the station, she got out to wave him off and, as she watched him disappear onto the platform she felt a terrible sense of something slipping away from her. On the way home she could hardly drive straight for weeping.

At the house, it was to find Joyce was upstairs getting dressed and the children quarrelling about who should get the free toy in the new packet of breakfast cereal. 'No one shall have it then,' she said furiously, and whisked the piece of plastic out of reach as they squealed in frustration.

After dropping them off at school, she hurried back home, head down so that she wouldn't have to meet other parents and swap cordialities about the weekend. Joyce had gone out with Hazel for the day, so Kate was glad to find she was by herself.

Later that morning, she was putting away the supermarket

shopping in between bundling washing in and out of the machine when the telephone rang.

'Kate, is that you? It's Max here. Sorry, I'm on my mobile and you're all fuzzy. Look, I've got some bad news.'

'Agnes,' said Kate at once. She suddenly knew what the dream had meant.

'Yes, I'm afraid so. She had a stroke very late last night – a massive one. I got down as quickly as I could, but she passed away at dawn this morning. I'm sorry . . .'

Her first reaction was shock. The tears welled up and she couldn't speak. After a moment she began to shake.

'Max. Sorry . . .' she whispered. 'I . . . Poor Agnes.'

'Are you all right?' he asked. 'I'm sorry to tell you like this. I didn't know if I should ring you before, but they said at the hospital there wasn't anything anybody could do, she never regained consciousness. And it took me a while to track down your number.'

'Yes, I'm OK. I suppose it would have been no good being there. I'm glad you were. Thank you.' She cleared her throat. 'Oh, poor Agnes. Max, I should have gone to see her. I was supposed to go on Thursday or Friday. I was going to ask her something.' Now didn't seem the time to tell him about the diaries.

'I suppose it's right that her time had come,' he sighed. 'I thought about what you said – you know, about her going into a home. I still think it would have been best for her, but she would have hated it, wouldn't she?'

'Yes. And now she won't have to go through all that. It's just . . . oh, I'll miss her so much. She was such a friend to me. I know we only knew each other for such a little while . . . I can't explain.'

'I can see that you two hit it off. She was rather an extraordinary person, wasn't she? I wish I had had the chance to get to know her better, but I was always so aware of the family feud, whatever it was. She could be a tiny bit terrifying at times, though that may sound silly, a grown man saying that. Look, Kate, I'm sorry, I'm at the hospital. I have to go now. There's so much to do.'

'Yes, of course. Max, is there anything I can help with?'

'No, no, not at the moment, I don't think. There's no post mortem required thankfully, so I can get the death registered straight away. We'll need to plan the funeral together. I hope the vicar might be able to do it this week. It'll be a burial, won't it? Oh dear, I'd better go. Why don't I ring you this afternoon? Oh, you could do something for me, if you would – let Mrs Summers and Dan Peace know. Would that be all right?'

'Yes, of course. And, could you give me your number, please?'

Kate scribbled down his home and mobile numbers and Max rang off. She put the handset down but her hand shook so much it fell off its cradle. She picked it up but didn't replace it. Simon. She must speak to Simon. But his number was engaged so she left an urgent message for him to ring her. After a second she grabbed the phone again, thinking she would call Dan. He had given her his number once, but what had she done with it? Perhaps it would be better anyway to go round and find him rather than telling him on the phone.

The car practically drove itself to Seddington, thoughts of Agnes, of the diaries and Max all swirling incoherently round and round in Kate's head. She ought to tell her parents, she thought suddenly. And Marion. Hadn't Joyce given her the number? Who else was there?

She was on the edge of the village now. The cottage with the blue door near the pub, he'd said. There was the Fox, with all its flower baskets an obvious contender for Prettiest Pub in the County, and in the line of small detached flint cottages, unimaginatively labelled The Row, was one with a sky-blue door and a number 2 on it. She couldn't see any sign of Dan's van. She parked the car, got out and walked on shaky legs up to the door.

As her hand reached out for the dolphin-head knocker, Kate heard the sound of angry voices inside the house, and she froze, wondering what to do.

'Well, I'll get her then, if you can't be bothered,' snapped a female voice just the other side of the door and, before Kate had time to move, it flew open and a young woman stood before her.

'Oh,' said the woman, slightly crossly. Then she recovered herself. 'Hello.' She was taller than Kate, but very slim and fragile-looking in a tailored stripy shirt and pale blue denim Capri pants, her small pretty face framed by short fluffy blonde hair. She was dragging a folded buggy in one hand.

'Is D-Dan in?' Kate stammered, taking a step back.

'He's in the back. *Dan!* Someone wants you,' she shouted behind her. 'Go in, why don't you?' And without waiting for an answer, she squeezed past Kate, pulling her burden over to a scruffy Ford Escort parked across the road.

Dan's large figure shambled into the little hallway, but the gloomy expression vanished when he recognized Kate. 'Come in,' he said, casting a glance across the road to the woman now getting into the car. He shut the door behind Kate and gestured her into a little front room topsy-turvy with a mishmash of battered old furniture, toddler's toys and a great big television squatting in one corner, a pile of children's video boxes scattered around it.

'I'm sorry, I think I arrived at a bad moment,' said Kate.

Dan sighed. 'You're right – I'm in trouble again,' he said. 'Linda's always asking me to look after Shelley, but Shelley's got her own dad – that's where she is now, Linda's gone to fetch her.

282

Shelley gets very confused – calls both of us Daddy.' He stopped, seeing the emotions cross Kate's face.

'I'd love,' she whispered, 'to hear all about it. But there's a reason I've come, I'm afraid.' And as she told him about Agnes, she finally broke down in tears.

Dan swept some toys and an empty yogurt pot off the sofa so she could sit down, and grabbed a wadge of tissues from a box with teddy bears on it. After a while, Kate recovered sufficiently to look up and smile weakly at him.

He squeezed her shoulder briefly and she saw that he, too, looked immensely sad.

'I should have gone to see Agnes, I should have made the effort. And now I'll never know . . . Oh Dan, I'm sorry, I'm a complete mess this morning.'

'No, you're not. I'm not surprised you're so upset. Don't worry. It's best to get it all out.' He paused and said in a low voice, 'I'm so sorry she's gone. She was a part of my life for five years. Going up to help at the house was a lifeline when I got back from London, not knowing what to do with myself. She took such an interest in me.'

'And in me. And now everything will change.' Kate's voice broke. 'The house will go to Max and he'll sell it I expect, and there'll be strangers living there and all the lovely things will go.' Dan nodded. 'And in a silly way I feel it's part of my history. I suppose it's the first time there's really been a place in my life that feels like a link with the past, like home.'

'I know what you mean.' Dan looked round the tiny, untidy room. 'This has always been home for me,' he said. 'I know it's small, but it always seemed just right and I can't imagine living anywhere else. Dad inherited it from his parents – they died before I was born. I think that's why he didn't want to move after Mum died – there were other memories that held him here.'

'Dan,' Kate remembered suddenly, 'Marie doesn't know yet. We've got to tell her.'

'I'll do that now, if you like. Maybe you'd make us some coffee.'

While Dan was on the phone comforting Mrs Summers, Kate went into the little kitchen, boiled the kettle and found the mugs and the coffee powder. The kitchen was clean and modern, but when Kate peeped into the second reception room, obviously used as a breakfast-room-cum-study, with a computer in one corner, it was in the same cheerful mess as the front room.

Through the window she could see the back garden, a pretty square of grass bordered by flowering shrubs. There was a climbing frame on the lawn and a sandpit in one corner. Various plastic tricycles and a scooter lay scattered about. At the bottom of the garden was a large shed with a garage behind. The Dormervan and a motorbike were parked just by.

It looked a perfect house for a couple and a small child.

In the hall, Dan hung up the phone to Marie Summers. 'She's very upset, of course,' he said. 'She wants to know when you hear about the funeral.'

'I will ring you both as soon as I've spoken to Max this afternoon,' she promised.

Kate couldn't settle to doing anything for the rest of the day. When she got home it was late morning. Simon hadn't called despite the urgency of her message – she supposed he was now getting on a plane. She immediately rang her parents to tell them about Agnes. Her mother answered the phone.

'Oh, that's sad,' she said. 'A link with the past. Still she'd reached a great age. It must be very lonely living so long, seeing all your friends and family die before you.'

Barbara didn't know if they would be able to come to the

funeral. 'It's a bit far,' she said, 'and Ringo isn't too good at the moment. I can't really leave him with anybody and of course he wouldn't like the journey. He came with us to Sevenoaks on Thursday and he wasn't very happy.'

Which brought Kate on to ask, 'How was Thursday? I'm sorry I didn't get to speak to you.'

'Oh, it was fine. The weather wasn't too bad. The rosebush your father planted is blooming nicely, though we had to have a word with the groundsman about the weeds.'

'I suppose it doesn't get any easier, going?' Kate asked, feeling she was entering uncharted waters.

'No,' admitted her mother. 'But it's the only thing we can do for her, isn't it?'

'We could, I don't know, talk about Nicky more, remember her. We never talk about her.'

'It's your father – he finds it all hard,' said her mother in a too-brisk voice.

That's what Dad says about you, Kate thought to herself, but she couldn't say it out loud.

'Well, I hope it's a nice service,' said Barbara. 'I wonder if my cousin Marion will go. Her sister Frances is up in Newcastle now, so maybe she'll think it a bit far.'

'I'll ring Marion anyway, Mum,' said Kate.

Cousin Marion wasn't in when Kate called the number Joyce had given her so she left a message, then tried Simon's mobile again but it passed her on to voicemail. She put the receiver down and was halfway into the sitting room when the phone rang.

'Simon?' she said, when she scooped up the receiver.

'Darling, it's Liz,' said her friend. 'I'm in a taxi. Just thought I'd see how you are. I'm sorry I haven't rung before. Tony's being such a pain about the figures . . .'

'And there's a new nanny, I gather?'

'Oh, don't mention nannies. I had to stay at home on Monday to show her the ropes. She's already burned the bottom out of a saucepan and bumped the car – only ever used an automatic, she says now. Listen, I can't talk for too long, just hoped you were OK.'

Kate quickly told her about Agnes's death and gave an edited version of how things were with Simon. When she explained about him wanting to move back to London, Liz's tone turned glacial. 'I don't believe it! After he's made you drop everything and dragged you all out to the sticks. What did you say? I know what the hell I'd say.'

'I don't know what to do, Liz, I just don't know. I can't sort out how I feel about anything at the moment. It's all too fresh, him and Meredith. And there are so many other problems here at the moment. I don't want to keep ripping up roots and going off at a moment's notice any more.' Kate explained about her friendship with Agnes and the situation with the school.

'In a way, it could be the time to make the move, then,' Liz said. 'The school not working out and losing your cousin. You know what they say about some doors closing and others opening.'

'Yes,' said Kate shortly. 'Maybe I should just agree with Simon and throw in the towel. But I can't.'

'We're there. I've gotta go . . . I'll ring you again, Pussycat. Lots of love.'

Kate put the phone down and glanced at the clock. Half past twelve, time for some lunch. She made herself a sandwich and sat eating it slowly, flicking through the pages of Joyce's lifestyle magazine, trying to empty her whirling mind by taking in other people's worries from the problem page and studying fetching holiday swimsuits for the older woman. When she had finished the sandwich, she sought the comfort of a chocolate bar from their hiding place in a top cupboard – Sam could eat half a dozen on the trot if they were left in the biscuit tin – and splashed boiling water onto a peppermint teabag. This lasted her all the way through the romantic short story which, with wretched coincidence, was about a woman who started life anew in the country after her divorce. Of course, this woman immediately bumped into a tall dark handsome farmer with a tragic past. If only life were like fiction. Certainly, if fiction were too like life, no one would read it. There would be so many boring bits.

Kate was ruminating on this point and wondering whether she could make a career of writing women's magazine stories, like the mother in *The Railway Children*, when a familiar silver Range Rover squealed to a halt outside the cottage.

Kate got up from the table and went to the door as masculine footsteps marched up the path and, through the peephole, a distorted view of Max came into view. She opened the door to find herself face to face with a very angry man.

'What's the matter?' she enquired. 'You'd better come in.'

'Mmggh,' he muttered, which might have been 'thank you'. She showed him into the living room but he refused her offer of a seat.

'I just came to say,' he managed to impart, his voice strangled with fury, 'that I've just discovered what you've done, and I think it's despicable. Utterly despicable.'

'What are you talking about?'

'Don't pretend you don't know. The will, of course.'

'What do you mean?'

'Agnes's will. The house should have been mine. It was always going to be mine.'

'Yes, that's what I imagined. Why, isn't it?'

'No, it damned well isn't – *as you very well know.*'

'Max, I have no idea what you're talking about.' Kate stared into his eyes, appalled at the force of his anger. He was almost crying, his sensitive face pinched with white and red blotches, his normally sleeked-back hair falling across his forehead. They stood there, challenging one another for what felt like minutes but was probably seconds. Then she said, 'I really have not an inkling about what is going on.'

He considered her words, not taking his eyes from her face, and then, slowly, she saw the passion go out of him to be replaced by frustration and disappointment. 'You don't, do you? You really don't know. Not even with all your sweet talk about not having a proper home and being glad to have found a friend like Aunt Agnes. Well, she's changed her will, that's what's happened, and I'm out of it. And you, little Miss Innocent, are in.'

'What do you mean?' Kate could hardly take it in.

'Seddington House. It looks like it's yours,' he said, giving a stagey shrug of his shoulders. 'It's complicated. I will get something, but basically, Kate Hutchinson, your wheedling your way into Agnes's affections all these months has worked very nicely for you.' He turned away to look out of the window, his hands shoved deep in the pockets of his navy trousers.

Kate sat down on the sofa. 'That's not what happened. You can't mean it,' she whispered, feeling hot and cold with shock. Seddington House, the dream house, was hers?

'I wish I didn't,' he said, pacing the room, looking merely defeated now, 'but unfortunately, I do. The bloke from Horrocks and Spalding will no doubt be in touch shortly to give you the full rundown.' He made as though to leave, but Kate broke in.

'Max, this is as big a shock to me as it must be for you. I really *don't* know anything about Agnes changing her will. There must be a mistake somewhere.'

'Well, there isn't.' He slowly walked back from the door and sank down into one of the armchairs, then took off his glasses and rubbed his eyes. He looked exhausted.

'It's not just the house,' he said, his voice earnest now, 'though the money from selling it would have been useful. I thought it would be symbolic,' he added, looking up at Kate. 'It would show that the rift in the family, whatever it was all about, was finally over. My grandfather never received a penny from Gerald Melton, his and Agnes's father, you know.'

A thought struck Kate. She said carefully, 'I think I might know what it was about. What was your grandmother's first name?'

'Vanessa,' he said. 'Why?'

Kate was silent for a moment, working it out. Finally she said, 'It was something Agnes mentioned. Vanessa was the name of her stepmother.'

Max stared at her, a look of distaste growing on his face. 'My grandmother was . . . my grandfather's stepmother, is that what you're saying? That's ridiculous. Like a soap opera.' He gave a short laugh. 'I'm not sure I believe you.'

Kate explained what Agnes had said about Raven damaging his father's marriage.

'I can't take it in,' breathed Max. 'But if it's true, I can see why they never spoke again.'

'Do you have family of your own?' she asked him after a moment.

'Two girls,' he answered. 'They live with their mother just outside Norwich. Grace and Emily are the reasons why I wouldn't have wanted to keep Seddington House and move over here.'

Kate nodded, trying to understand.

'Oh,' he said dully. 'And the funeral. The vicar can fit it in on Friday, eleven o'clock. He wants to see us about the service. Can you do this evening?'

Kate said she probably could.

After she had shown Max out, the shock of everything hit her and she sank onto a kitchen chair in a trance. The grief that she wouldn't see Agnes in this life again was still there, but a great flood of gratitude, like golden light, was also spreading through her. Her eye fell on the picture on the fridge. The dream house with the dream family. Could Agnes really have granted her this wonderful gift?

# Chapter 25

'She wanted the house to stay with the family, you see. That's what she told me when she asked me to come to the hospital.' Raj Nadir, a partner of Horrocks & Spalding, solicitors, was a cheerful, slightly tubby Asian man in his late thirties. Despite the plethora of comfortable leather armchairs in his book-lined room in the Georgian offices in Beccles, he chose to perch on a computer chair behind his desk, rocking it from side to side as he started to explain to Kate, sitting opposite, the contents of her cousin's will.

He had telephoned her late on the afternoon of Agnes's death and arranged an appointment for her to see him the following morning.

'When did she ask you to come?' Kate said now, taking in the details of the room – the golf clubs in one corner, the photograph of a slightly slimmer Nadir with his arm around a laughing woman in a blue sari, another of two solemn little boys in school blazers.

'Ah, it was soon after they moved her back to Halesworth, about two weeks before the will was finally signed on . . .' he checked one of the documents in his hand '. . . the sixth of June. One of the fastest wills our legal executive has ever drawn up,' he chuckled. 'Always snowed under, you see,' he added anxiously, as though Kate would think he was being unkind.

Kate realized with a pang that the will had been signed on her birthday. So the gift of the pearls really *had* been symbolic. She opened the copy of the will that Raj now passed across the desk and quickly looked over it. It ran to six pages and on the last she saw that one of the nurses had acted as witness.

'I – I'm sure I'll want to read it all through myself,' Kate said, feeling a bit stupid, 'but if you could just give me an outline of what it all means . . . the legal language looks complicated.'

'Of course. As I was saying, Miss Melton was anxious to change the will because, she said, she felt she had finally met someone of her blood to whom she could entrust the family home. Yes, there's a letter somewhere . . .' He reached for a pink folder and drew out an envelope and passed it to her. *Kate Hutchinson* it read. *To be opened on the death of Agnes Lavender Melton.*

The letter was short, written in ballpoint pen in shaky handwriting:

*My dear Kate*

*By the time you read this letter I will be reunited with many of the people I have loved most in this world – so do not grieve for me but rejoice that I am with them, at peace in the everlasting arms.*

*Kate, Seddington House is yours. I know that you already love the house and I would like to think of you living there with your lovely family, having your own home at last, which, in turn, you can hand on to your children. My nephew, I can read him well, doesn't understand its importance. He will only want to sell it.*

*I have one piece of unfinished business in my life, Kate, and*

*that is that I had a child, but he was taken from me. I have
searched and searched for him but have never found him. From
the bottom of my heart I plead with you to continue this
search. You will need to read the diaries hidden in the safe in
the library to understand. Marie Summers has the key.*

*Kate, may God's blessing be upon you. Thank you for your
gift of friendship.*

*Yours truly,
Agnes Melton*

Kate read the letter through twice. So Agnes really had given
birth to a child – a son, the sealed envelope in the safe had
revealed – and had lost him. But not to death, if the phrase
'taken from me' was to be read literally. What a terrible thing,
even so. How had it happened and why? And how frustrating
that Agnes had been so close to sharing her secret with Kate.
Once again the young woman cursed herself for not visiting
Agnes last week.

Slowly, she handed the letter over to the lawyer. Raj Nadir
read it quickly, nodded, and returned it to her.

'She didn't tell you about this matter then?' he asked. 'She
told me nothing more either, I'm afraid. Just how she wished to
frame the will.'

'She started to say something the last time I saw her,' Kate
said. The letter indicated that Agnes's original intention had
been for the diaries to be read *after* her death. She must have
changed her mind. And yet so far there had been nothing in
the old exercise books about this mysterious child or quite
what had caused the split in the Melton family. It was all deeply
mysterious.

Nadir's voice pulled Kate out of her reverie. 'Basically, the will leaves the house, its land and its contents to you, Mrs Hutchinson, without condition. You are free to sell the contents in order to raise the money necessary for the upkeep of the property. That is the arrangement enshrined here. But then follows the problem. All Miss Melton's financial assets – and I should say that these are not inconsiderable – are to transfer free of tax to this unknown person, her missing child. If the child or its heirs are not found living six months after Miss Melton's death, or if it is discovered before then but is incapable or deceased and without direct heirs, the money automatically passes to Maximilian Charles Jordan. It's an unusual arrangement, but there is no doubt that Miss Melton was clear in her mind when she directed the will to be drawn up.'

Nadir scootered his chair over to his computer and tapped the keyboard briskly. 'Ah yes,' he said. 'The previous will . . . It was dated December 1984.' He manoeuvred the chair back and flipped through some folders in a box behind him, eventually dragging one out. He unfolded the document. 'On that occasion everything was left to Max's mother, Elizabeth. She was Agnes's niece by her brother Raven. Or to Max on the event of Elizabeth's death. Mmmm, yes, just refreshing myself on the details.' He peered over the top of the document at Kate. 'In this old version, if a proven child of Agnes Melton be discovered alive at the time of her death, it could have claimed £200,000 of the estate. So, Sammy must have known about the child. That puts an interesting light on the matter.'

'Who is Sammy?' asked Kate, wondering whether she had fallen down a rabbit-hole like Alice, she felt so confused and disorientated by the turn of events.

'Samuel Horrocks. Former senior partner here. He oversaw the Melton family's affairs for forty years – until his death last year, in fact.'

'Why is that significant?'

'Well, it isn't. Except that if this mysterious child was mentioned in the previous will and is now found, so that Max ends up with nothing, it might be more difficult for him to contest the new will on the basis of his great-aunt being mentally incapacitated. It wasn't some scheme she just dreamed up in hospital.'

'Do you think he would contest it?' Kate said. 'I suppose I could see his point.'

'He might be successful if he could demonstrate that Miss Melton was mentally fragile at the time of drawing up the will, or that it was in some ways blatantly unfair. But I will be able to reassure the authorities that she was as sharp as a tack. Plus Miss Melton assured me that documentation exists in which her father set out his reasons for excluding Raven Melton and his line from inheriting. It might be hard for Max to overturn that. Still, he could try.'

'Is there any information in any of the files about this missing child?'

Nadir shook his head. 'I have been through all the papers,' he said. 'There is some correspondence between Miss Melton and Mr Horrocks arguing the clauses of the 1984 will. Mr Horrocks was a traditionalist and advised her to leave the house to her brother's family. He didn't like this talk of a love-child at all, oh no.' He laughed. 'Miss Melton would have had a far harder time persuading *him* to draw up the new will. Quite a tough cookie, was Sammy. Lucky for her and for you it was me this time!'

He picked up the copy of the new will. 'There are minor bequests,' he said, frowning as he flicked through the pages. 'Five thousand pounds free of tax for Marie Summers, twenty-five hundred for Daniel Peace, sums to various charities . . . Ah, and the executors. They are to be myself, you and Mr Jordan.'

'That's going to be a little difficult, isn't it, with Max? What would happen if he did contest the will?'

'Yes, but Miss Melton insisted on his name appearing. There would have to be some dispensation of his duties in that situation,' said Nadir. 'Let's hope it doesn't come to that. There is, also, another possibility . . .' He stopped. 'No, it's not very likely,' he said.

'What? I think you must tell me,' Kate said.

'If Agnes's child or his descendants are found, it might be that they could successfully sue for a bigger part of the estate. But,' he shrugged, 'there are too many ifs and buts to worry about *that* happening. My guess is that it's going to be very difficult, if not impossible, to track down this heir, dead or alive. There are no clues, you see. The first thing we must do is advertise.'

'You mean "Any who may have an interest in the last Will and Testament of Agnes Melton should contact her solicitor"? Like a Victorian novel.'

'Like a Victorian novel, yes. And, like a Victorian novel, we shall probably receive a number of enquiries from fortune-hunters. Thank goodness for DNA testing!' And he smiled.

That afternoon, with an hour to spare before she had to pick up the children, Kate took Bobby out along the winding path she had walked that evening back in April when she had seen Seddington House and its inhabitant for the very first time.

The air was warm, the path almost dry despite the recent shower, though the hedges glittered with raindrops. But this time, when after twenty minutes she reached the little door in the wall, it was to find it locked against her. Someone had been taking their security duties seriously – the same person, presumably, who had locked the front gates. Conrad, she supposed.

She whistled to Bobby, who was snuffing at some interesting

smell wafting under the door, then set off again along the foot-path, which followed the wall, wending gently downhill to the road. There she clipped on Bobby's lead and walked along the worn verge under the poplar trees until she reached the drive of Seddington House.

The gates were closed, but today there was no padlock and the latch lifted easily. Bobby dragged her inside, forcing her to drop the lead. He bounded off towards the house and round the corner, out of sight.

Kate relatched the gates and stood for a moment, looking up at the house. It seemed different, knowing it was hers. Like a lover whose love was finally fully requited, she studied it as it slept in the sun, loving the imperfections – the chipped rooftiles, the ragged gardens sparkling with rain – as much as the graceful sweep of the drive, the elegant dimensions of the building and the Gothic shapes of the diamond-paned win-dows. Slowly, she walked up the drive to the front door and tapped the knocker lightly in case Conrad was there. But no one came.

She walked around past the kitchen, across the terrace and down through the Italian garden. Bobby was rolling ecstatically in something over near the little door in the wall, but jumped up and barked when he saw her and tore off in the direction of the rose garden.

Kate stood by the silent fountain and studied the back of the house, shading her eyes against the light. Funny to think Simon had still never seen it. He had been almost speech-less when she had told him her news the previous evening. A little cloud passed across the sun, casting a cold shadow over the garden and she shivered. A sudden movement in an up-stairs window caught her eye. She stared but it was gone. It could have been a reflection, she thought. Was that the cry of a peacock? The sun came out from behind the cloud and the moment passed.

She looked down at the fountain – three scalloped stone bowls, the topmost the smallest, all covered with lichen. A pipe emerged from the ground just by the small basin beneath and Kate wandered over to the battered greenhouse to see if she could find where it went. There she found it joined a network of pipes and taps, which she turned experimentally one by one. After a moment, she heard the fountain pipe bang into life and when she looked up, it was to see the water spluttering out into the bowl. A fierce gush of joy tremored through her.

Agnes had loved this house. When she was born in the Edwardian era it must have been at its heyday. But as the family had faced tragedy, war and betrayal, it languished and Agnes had only just kept it going.

Kate could bring this house alive again. It would be her sanctuary. She would nurture her children here and keep it for her grandchildren. She wouldn't move back to London; surely Simon would see how important this was to her. She had to persuade him. Somehow.

Later, when Kate arrived at school with Bobby to pick up Sam and Daisy, Gwyneth Smithson suggested she leave the children with their teacher for five minutes whilst she went through the agenda for Thursday night's meeting with Kate, Debbie and James, Sebastian's father. Kate, having settled Bobby in a corner of the headmistress's office, was hardly able to concentrate but took in that Mr Overden, the chairman, was to make the opening comments and that after Mr Keppel from the council had gone through his Powerpoint presentation, the committee should ask two or three key questions and then the discussion would be thrown open for questions from the floor.

She and the children got home to find Joyce waiting anxiously to hear what the solicitor had said. When, after frequent interruptions by Joyce, Kate had repeated the whole story, her mother-in-law smiled broadly.

'I'm so pleased for you, dear. It really solves so many problems, doesn't it? You'll all be able to live there, and there should be enough money to bring the place up to date. It's probably still a little too far from Diss for Simon, but I expect he'll get used to it. It's a shame for that kind Mr Jordan,' Kate had given Joyce an edited version of his anguished visit, 'but it sounds as though he'll inherit the money. A child, indeed. Who would have thought it? He must be in his late seventies by now or even dead! Well . . .' She patted Kate's hand. 'It's sad that the poor lady's gone, but it's a very happy outcome for you, isn't it?' Then: 'I'm sorry, dear, I'm prattling again, aren't I?'

'It's just I don't think it's going to be as straightforward as that,' Kate said quietly. 'We'll have to see what Simon wants.'

'But of course he'll want to live there! Especially when he realizes how important it is to you.'

'Joyce.' Kate hadn't been intending to tell her mother-in-law about the full nature of the differences between her and Simon, but she had to put her in the picture. 'We can assume nothing. Simon has asked me if we can move back to London.'

Joyce's face was a picture of surprised puzzlement. After a moment she said, 'You mean all this,' the sweep of her arm encompassed Kate, the children and Paradise Cottage, 'was for nothing? I – I don't know what to say. He can't keep chopping and changing his mind, can he? Are you just going to let him? I must have a little talk with him—'

'No, please, it's probably better to leave it,' Kate said firmly.

*

Simon rang from Frankfurt that evening, sounding harassed. Kate asked tentatively if he might be back for Agnes's funeral on Friday morning.

'I'm not going to be back in London until late Friday – so no, sorry.'

He was much more interested in Kate's visit to Raj Nadir. 'Well, what did he say? Is the house really yours?' His voice sounded sharp.

'I still can't believe it, but yes. There's going to be an awful lot of admin. Everything in the house must be valued. Raj and Max will go through the investments. Agnes had an accountant, and it appears that she kept all her share certificates and whatnot in the bank, so with luck there won't be too much to sort out there.'

'Who can you get to value the contents? Farrell's in Ipswich would be the obvious choice.'

'Yes, Raj suggests Farrell's, too' she said. 'They're auctioneers as well, aren't they?'

'What the hell do we do about the house?' Simon seemed to be speaking to himself rather than to her.

Kate took a deep breath.

'Simon, we have to keep it. We must.'

'We're talking about moving back to London, Kate. If we sell it and its contents, we'll be laughing. We could live in one of those huge houses in Putney, or—'

'We can't sell it, Simon. Don't you see? That's why Agnes left it to me – to us. So we'd live there. It would be the family home – we could pass it on to our children and our children's children.'

'Do you mean there's a condition in the will? That we're not allowed to sell it?'

'No, there doesn't seem to be. I suppose Agnes could have put one in, but perhaps she didn't want to tie me down that much. After all, there would be no point since Max would have sold it, too. No, I think she just felt that I would want to live there. And I do.'

There was silence. Then, 'It's a very nice idea, Kate, and of course it's a beautiful house, but is that what we want? I mean, we really ought to talk properly about the whole thing.'

'Of course we've got to talk.' Kate's voice was shaky. 'But I really really, want to live there. I must.'

That evening when she went to bed she picked up the diary she hadn't finished, and started to read.

# Chapter 26

*Summer 1928*

Agnes pattered up the wooden stairs of number 11 Fitzroy Street, her legs almost giving way under her with excitement. It was the fourth, no the fifth visit to Harry's apartment in three weeks and, in between, waiting for the endless time to pass before the next visit, she felt she floated on a different plane from other people around her, above the level of such ordinary activities as eating, gossiping or worrying about whether the butcher was supplying tough meat. Her main occupation was thinking about Harry, going over and over every tiny detail of each meeting, each word spoken, the softness of his lips on hers.

The first time she went to the flat, she hadn't announced her visit, but used an excursion to Peter Jones in Oxford Street as an excuse to Vanessa for her absence and a reason to herself for calling on Harry casually – on the spur of the moment as if she was just passing, feeling it was too forward to send him a note first. One lesson she had repeatedly learned from those tedious girls' lunches was that it didn't do to be seen to chase men.

In the event, she didn't have to test the unreliable middle bell – a man leaving the house held the street door for her as he passed through. The second floor, Harry had said. When he opened the door to his apartment, his expression was defensive, uncertain, and her heart plummeted into her little bowed shoes. But then his face lit up with a smile. He pulled the door wide and she stepped inside.

'Sorry,' he said as he closed the door behind her. 'Thought it was that damned woman from downstairs again. She's already been up twice today. Wants me to look after her horrid pug dog later – smelly animal.'

Agnes smiled weakly, suddenly shy. She had spent hours dressing for this afternoon, finally settling for a cream two-piece suit trimmed with lace, a hat the soft shades of a seashell, and a beige bag and shoes. Now, though Harry looked her up and down appreciatively, she felt overdressed next to his shabby Oxford bags and open-necked shirt.

'Well,' he said, pulling down his rolled-up sleeves as if aware of the sartorial comparison. 'You've come. I'm so glad you've come.'

They stood facing one another, but Harry's face was unreadable against the gold bars of light streaming through the windows. So instead, she looked around the untidy little living room.

Harry suddenly seemed to remember his manners and erupted into action.

'Sit down over here, do,' he said, pulling some newspapers and a cardigan off a sofa. 'I'll make some tea – would you like tea?'

But in the face of this brightness, Agnes lost what little courage she had.

'I'm sorry, I'm probably interrupting something. Your work . . .' she stuttered. 'I was just passing and remembered you lived here. I won't stay.'

Harry laid the cardigan carefully over the back of a chair, as if it were made of some precious material. Then he moved to her side and, hesitantly, lifted his hands and rested them lightly on her shoulders. She looked up shyly to see him studying her face.

Suddenly she understood. His feelings for her had not changed since the evening they had first met. They were there in his steady gaze, his slightly parted lips, the faint puzzlement in his brow. He was entirely present for her, sensitive to her every mood.

She smiled, slowly. He touched her cheek. Then he leaned forward and their lips met in a gentle kiss. He drew back and looked at her again, lazily, then kissed her once more, at first with soft, nibbling little kisses, then harder, more urgently, his tongue exploring her mouth as she leaned into him.

Breathless, she came up for air, then laughed, pulling away, suddenly overwhelmed by the situation, smoothing down her crumpled costume.

Seeing her confusion, Harry stepped back, like a sculptor scrutinizing his creation, a small secret smile on his lips.

'Come on,' he said. 'I'll show you where I work, where you might sit for me if you like. And then we'll have tea. Otherwise, I won't be able to keep my hands off you!'

Now it was three weeks on from that first delicious afternoon. As Agnes reached the first landing, the door of the apartment there squeaked open and a woman's face stared out. For a moment their eyes locked. Agnes had time only to take in the diagonal of short jet-black hair falling across a hard face whose paleness was only relieved by a carmine mouth before Harry's voice echoed down the stairs, 'Agnes?' and the door shut with a click. She continued her journey.

'Who is she?' Agnes asked later in the warm post-meridian light of the second bedroom, which Harry used as a studio.

She was half-naked, sitting three-quarters turned away but looking over her nearer shoulder towards him, a pose she was finding it uncomfortable to maintain. Several times he had growled at her to 'damn well keep still' as she had tried to ease her neck or arch her back.

'Mmm?' he said now, frowning at the break to his concentration.

'The woman in the flat below. She spies on me, you know.'

He shrugged, then put down his pad and charcoal and reached for a cigarette. 'All right, I've finished for today. Suzie Herbert? Just some woman. Schoolfriend of my sister's. She got me this place.'

'She seems very interested in us.' Agnes stretched like a cat, the smell of the newly lit tobacco giving her a sudden kick. She looked down out of the window to the street where a young man loitered with a newspaper. If he looked up, she thought daringly, he would see me like this. But he didn't.

Behind her she heard Harry take a deep drag of his cigarette then exhale in a long sigh. 'She's just lonely. She left her husband – a drunk who hit her, my sister says. She gets on my nerves a bit, always wanting little favours. But she's all right. I feel sorry for her really. Why? Jealous are you?' He moved closer. His nearness made her prickle with desire.

'No, not jealous.' Agnes slowly turned towards him, lifting her stockinged legs langorously across the daybed. He drew on his cigarette, but did not breathe out right away. Through wreaths of smoky dust motes she watched him watching her, as she arched her breasts towards him, the nipples hardening. She brushed her fingers against herself and desire leaped like a pain. The silky gown that nestled modestly round her hips felt apart

305

revealing her underwear, the suspenders digging into the pale flesh.

He rose as if in a dream and moved towards her, reaching out, touching her breasts wonderingly, then gently stroking them till she gasped. She pulled him towards her, grabbing his hair, bringing his face down to hers, kissing him in long deep kisses, her hands burrowing under his shirt, over his buttocks, pressing his hardness to her. In a practised movement he lifted her off the couch and fumbled her underwear undone, almost tearing it in his eagerness. Then he shuffled off his own clothes and pushed her down on the daybed and entered her.

It was painful, but it was a delicious pain. For a while he didn't move and she could feel herself enfolding him, drawing him in so deeply every slightest movement was a wave of delight. He raised his head to look at her, he stroked her breasts, nibbled her neck and whispered in her ear, 'Little love, you're so beautiful.' She closed her eyes for a moment, and when she opened them, she was awed to see his were full of tears. Then he lowered his lips to her breasts and began to move inside her, at first slowly, then with more urgency. She raised her hips towards him, crying out as waves of sensation spread through her. She was on a galloping horse, flowers falling around her, then Harry gave a gasp, a wordless cry and arched up inside her. The flowers faded like stars . . . Darling, wonderful Harry.

Later, as they lay together on Harry's bed, he got up and fetched a little box from the chest of drawers. He opened it and took out a locket on a silver chain.

'I found it in a curiosity shop,' he said. 'The girl – look.' He showed her. 'Something about her expression. It made me think of you.'

It was an oval piece, about the size of a half-crown with a

rough-hewn figure of a serene young girl on the front. On her open palm there perched a dove. Agnes slid a fingernail into the catch and opened the locket. Into one half Harry had slipped a photograph of himself.

'You must find a picture of you for the other half,' he said. Then, 'I love you, you know.' A look of deep sadness shadowed his face.

'Harry?' Agnes whispered. 'What's the matter?'

'Nothing,' he said after a moment, and the sadness was replaced by tenderness. 'No, nothing.'

And he leaned forward to embrace her once more.

When Kate woke panting in the darkness, her body pulsed with hot blood and her face was wet with tears. She lay awake for a long time in the darkness, wondering, until finally she slept again.

# *Chapter 27*

If Mr Keppel, the man from the council, had a byword – it was *efficiency*. It wasn't efficient to have a school where the roof was falling in and the playground had potholes in it. (The parents were with him on that one.) It wasn't efficient to have lots of very small schools in satellite villages when a large, bright new school building in the local town could be used by every-body instead. It wasn't efficient when the figures didn't work – as they certainly weren't doing at Fernley. The figures on his Powerpoint show certainly didn't look efficient when viewed in that light. Nearly £50,000 was required to repair and upgrade the school.

'It is impossible for the Education Department to find that sort of money when there are other viable, much cheaper alter-natives,' he said, switching his laptop onto standby. He sat down to a babble of angry voices from the 100 local people sitting on hired chairs who filled the little school hall to bursting point.

Mr Keppel's presentation had certainly been efficient, Kate said to herself fiercely from her seat facing the crowd. The bullet points zooming onto the screen had been all about statistics and budgets and rationalization. They hadn't been about fuzzy con-cepts like supporting local communities or tending to the needs of individual children and families. She shifted nervously in her chair and, as Peter Overden, a sweet-natured gentleman in his sixties, rose and waved a hand for silence, she unfolded a scrumpled piece of paper. On it was typed the question she had written out this morning and practised over and over in the mirror.

'Our first question, Mr Keppel,' intoned Mr Overden, 'has to be, why has the Department done nothing previously to maintain the school?' Kate noticed many heads nodding vigorously. 'We have been asking for repairs to be conducted for the last five years. Here is the file.' He waved a thick sheaf of correspondence as evidence. 'If the roof *had* been mended back in nineteen ninety-nine, we wouldn't have had all these further problems with rotten timber, damp walls and ceilings that you've just itemized. Can I put it to you that this neglect represents a deliberate attempt to wind down and close the school?'

Mr Keppel insisted that it wasn't and embarked on a complicated technical discussion with Mr Overden, who was a retired chartered surveyor, over maintenance problems in Victorian buildings.

When this was finally over, hands in the audience shot up. Here was Kate's chance. She shakily put her hand in the air and, seeing that she was the first committee member with a question, Mr Overden chose her to speak. In the end she felt so fired up she found she didn't need her notes.

'We hear a lot in the media at the moment about rural depopulation, the loss of traditional village life and political disempowerment. Do you regard it as important, Mr Keppel, that rural towns and villages maintain the institutions that enable them to function as living, thriving, self-governing communities?' Kate's voice strengthened as she got into her stride.

She was relieved when several people in the audience shouted 'Hear, hear!' and, 'Exactly!' in response.

Mr Keppel paced up and down in front of his audience. He didn't have a Powerpoint screen for 'life of rural communities'. After a moment, he cleared his throat and said, 'Yes, of course I do. But in these days of fragmentation it is far more efficient to see a rural community in the . . . ah . . . broader sense. Halesworth and the villages around it form a cohesive, active community.'

A young woman from the floor raised her hand immediately. She spoke with barely suppressed anger. They'd already taken away the library, hadn't they? And the post office had only just survived the latest decimation because of the village petition. Didn't the authorities want everyone to get out of their cars and use local services? So why take those local services away?

After that, Mr Keppel was besieged on all sides. Kate felt overwhelmed by how much people here cared about their community. Once galvanized into action, they seemed prepared to fight tooth and nail to keep their school. They might be reluctant to go to their polling station (and where would they go to vote if their polling station, the school, closed – the pub?) to vote for a national government. Maybe they felt powerless when it came to national politics – perhaps it was in local matters that the politicians should try to reach people instead. If the electorate truly felt that they had a stronger say in matters such as how their local schools and hospitals were run, could resist main roads cutting ugly swathes through their towns, or huge housing estates going up at the behest of a faceless administrator in Westminster, wouldn't they all become interested and more involved in the way their society was run? Kate rather thought they might.

As she listened to all the questions and Mr Keppel's blustering attempts at answers, an idea began to grow in her mind. Around her the buzz of voices rose as the room, despite Mrs Smithson ordering the doors at the back to be opened, grew hotter and hotter.

Eventually, overwhelmed by the opposition, Mr Keppel turned to Mr Overden and raised his hands in a despairing gesture. The noise abated slowly and Kate indicated that she wanted to speak again.

'Yes, Mrs Hutchinson?' said Mr Overden, who looked exhausted. 'This is the last question we'll take tonight, ladies and gentlemen.'

'Mr Keppel,' said Kate, 'you have seen demonstrated clearly and unequivocally tonight how much Fernley values its school. Could I ask you now, honestly: if the people of Fernley – and I say "if" because fifty thousand pounds is a huge amount of money – were able to raise some or a substantial part of the sum, would your Department reconsider its decision to close the school?'

The hubbub started to build again and Kate glimpsed people shaking their heads at the suggestion of such a commitment from local people. Many of them, she knew, held down low-paid jobs or seasonal work. Mr Overden rose and waved the room to silence.

After a moment Mr Keppel spoke. 'I must agree,' he said, 'that the feelings in this room appear to run high. Much higher than I anticipated. I cannot properly answer the question you ask without consultation with my colleagues, but I am inclined to say that "if" – and, ladies and gentlemen, that is a huge "if" – the monies or part of the monies are forthcoming from the community, there is a large chance that the Department would reconsider the . . . ah . . . efficiency of its current decision.'

He sat down. Everybody looked enquiringly at Kate as if to

311

say, 'Well, what are you going to do about that then?'

After the chairs were piled up and pushed to the sides of the room, ready for collection by the hire firm in the morning, Mrs Smithson invited those of the committee remaining for a glass of wine in her office. Mr Keppel had sensibly vanished, almost before Mr Overden had closed the meeting. As the parents began to disperse, they could hear his powerful car screech away outside.

'And good riddance,' said Jasmin. 'What a number-cruncher *he* turned out to be.'

'I thought Kate's last question pinpointed things nicely,' said another of the governors, a grey-haired lady in a dark wool suit. 'It does seem to come down to us meeting the cost of the repairs ourselves, but how could we raise that sort of money? Think how difficult it was to raise thirty thousand for the church repairs five years ago. None of us could look another cake sale in the face after that!'

'We could see what there might be available in grants and regional funding,' said Jasmin, fishing a piece of cork out of her wine glass. 'Maybe we could build in some special project – I don't know, like having a musician in residence or a young people's science lab to attract money.'

Everyone nodded with enthusiasm at that.

'We've some good ideas here,' said Mr Overden. 'Why don't we meet next week before school breaks up, and get some plans in place for the holidays?'

Fifty thousand pounds, thought Kate as she walked home afterwards. It was a huge, an impossible sum of money. It seemed that staying in Seddington was going to be a battle every which way she turned.

# Chapter 28

Although Kate was familiar with the profile of Seddington church, its short spire rising above the square-towered building on the little hill, the Friday of Agnes's funeral was the first occasion she had had to go inside. It was very like St Felix's, she thought, plain and dark, with the same simple Norman design, but whereas the church in Fernley had stained glass only in the window above the altar, the four arched windows on the south side of St Mary's Seddington cast a rainbow of soft jewelled light across the twenty-odd people waiting quietly in the old oak pews.

The coffin, completely covered with flowers, was in place by the altar rail and a thin elderly lady was squeezing some appropriately lugubrious sounds from the little organ. Kate selected an empty pew halfway down the church, then noticed Dan, distinguished in a dark suit, wave to her from his seat next to Marie Summers, so she slipped in beside him instead.

Just then, the vicar emerged from the vestry and swept over in his robes.

'We'll just wait a couple more minutes,' he whispered, nodding to Max who arrived to sit in a pew nearby. The Reverend Mike Davies was, on the face of it, a jolly man who would not have been out of place running children's parties, but since the Hutchinsons' move to Fernley, where he was also vicar, Kate had quickly noticed that he had a side to him of considerable depth and experience. He had been a management consultant until his early forties, he had told her, but his parishioners knew he was as patient of their personal problems as he was at the frustrating administrative side of running this large rural parish with its overwhelming financial burdens.

When she and Max had met up with Mike earlier in the week, it was to learn that he had come to know Agnes well in the seven years he had been in the parish, and he was able to reveal that she had had an active spiritual life and a very enquiring mind in theological matters.

'She would come up with questions I certainly couldn't answer,' Mike shook his head smiling, 'about the afterlife and what would happen there. And she had strong views on which bits of the Bible she believed in and which she didn't. We had some lively conversations, I can tell you. I will miss her.'

After Mike had moved away, Kate looked down at the Bible open on her lap and tried without success to calm her nerves. It was Mike who had suggested the reading to her as one from which Agnes had frequently found comfort, a passage from St Paul's Letter to the Romans about the workings of the Holy Spirit. *We know that all things work together for good for those who love God . . .* She had noted the connection with Mother Julian straight away: *All shall be well and all manner of thing shall be well.* The phrase was like an underground river, coursing through both their lives.

'Are you all right?' whispered Dan, close beside her. 'Not nervous?'

'A bit,' she said and smiled at him, then she caught Max's eye across the church. She wondered who the other people in the congregation might be. Some were surely villagers, but there was a neat, carefully made-up matron in a navy suit and pearl stud earrings near the back, sitting on her own, flicking through a pocket diary. Could that be her mother's Cousin Marion? She was Kate's first cousin once removed, Kate established, remembering Agnes's explanation of how it worked. She thought the woman looked vaguely familiar, though, to be honest, Marion was not the only relation who had come to her wedding but whose face had since dimmed to a hazy blur in her mind.

Marion had returned her call on Tuesday, and had immediately agreed to come to the funeral, 'for old times' sake' as she'd pronounced in her loud county tones. Marion was clearly a lady who knew where her duty lay. Kate's mother had been right about Marion's sister Frances, who had communicated through Marion that Newcastle was too far away to come for the funeral.

Raj Nadir, in a baggy black suit he probably reserved for client funerals, was talking in a low voice to a bony, very serious woman with an ash-blonde bob. She was nodding vigorously and using her hands a lot when she talked. Otherwise, there was a sprinkling of well-to-do elderly gentlemen in dark lounge suits, and a few assorted women, one in an ancient pudding-basin hat, who must be locals, quietly waiting for the service to begin.

The church door opened, and one of the undertakers slipped in and nodded at the vicar. Mike whispered to the organist and the lugubrious music ceased mid-bar. Finally, after a wheeze from the organ, the strains of 'Abide with Me' started up and the congregation rose.

> Swift to its close ebbs out life's little day;
> Earth's joys grow dim, its glories pass away;

Kate stood, too choked to sing, watching a fat tear plop onto her hymn book. She and Max had chosen this hymn because Marie Summers had thought it a favourite of Agnes's. Kate hadn't liked to say that it had been sung at her sister Nicola's funeral, too. She gave the skin of the hand holding the book a sharp pinch with the finger and thumb of the other hand to hold herself together.

The service was a simple one. Max read a passage from Psalm 121: 'I will lift mine eyes to the hills', before Kate took her place at the lectern. Her voice broke once or twice as she read the short passage, but she managed to keep going. Afterwards, the vicar spoke very movingly, giving thanks for the long life of a warm and brave woman.

'She had lost so many people she loved so early in life,' he said, 'and now we can thank God that she is reunited with them again.'

Kate sat, head bowed. Mike was right. This service should be the celebration of a long and full life, but that didn't stop Kate from missing Agnes.

The service over, they followed the coffin out into the warm sunshine and over to a corner of the churchyard dotted with Melton family gravestones.

'. . . in sure and certain hope of the resurrection to eternal life . . .' Mike's voice was strong, unwavering, as Kate scattered some rose petals from Agnes's garden over the coffin in the grave, whispered goodbye and turned away. After the ritual was finished, she walked amongst the other graves for a few moments, noting older, long-dead Meltons, then finding the faded headstone to Agnes's mother. Beneath the inscription to Evangeline and her dead baby was written *Gerald Maurice Melton, d.1943*. There was a vase of fresh roses on the grave – had Marie placed them there?

\*

Later, in the drawing room at Seddington House, two trestle tables groaned under the weight of sandwiches, savouries and cakes that Marie Summers had prepared.

Kate helped pour sherry then stepped out into the garden to talk to Marion. She was in her early sixties, Kate remembered her mother explaining, but looked younger, carefully coiffed and made-up. The inflections of her voice were also like her mother's, but whereas Barbara spoke softly, Marion was clearly used to view-hallooing in the hunting field.

'I was just hearing from Agnes's solicitor that you're getting the house,' she boomed. 'What a windfall. Mind you, rather you than me – it's quite a pile, isn't it? You're surely not going to live in it? I must confess myself a bit surprised she left it to you. I'd have thought that young man, her brother's grandson, would be first in line. Still, she always knew her own mind, did Agnes.'

Kate, at a loss as to what to say after this forthright speech, managed to change the subject to the safer ground of family reunions. Then wished she hadn't, as tact was not one of Marion's strong points.

'Of course, I haven't seen Barbara since your own wedding. It's a shame. We used to spend so many holidays together when we were little. Barbara and her poor brother Kenneth often came to stay with us at Woodbridge. Perhaps I shouldn't say this, but she changed after she married. Became quieter. A bit dowdy. Quite unlike when she was twenty. She was a scream then, I can tell you. But your father – I was surprised Barbara went for someone quiet like that.'

Kate gave the plate in her hand the gurn of dislike she was too polite to project at Marion, then looked up and studied the woman's face. How much did Marion really know of her parents' marriage? she wondered.

'Then there was the awful business of your sister,' Marion continued. 'They didn't seem to want to have much to do with us after that. Turned in on themselves. We invited them to Tiggy's wedding soon after yours – Tiggy is our eldest – but they said it was too far. It was only Suffolk.' She shrugged. 'There's Christmas cards, but that's it. How is she now, Barbara?'

Kate explained deliberately vaguely that she was very up and down. Out of the corner of her eye she noticed Dan in conversation with Max. The latter's arms were folded and Dan was half turned away, looking across the garden. What were they finding to say to one another?

'I don't think you can ever get over the loss of a child,' went on Marion, draining her sherry. 'Really awful.'

'Do you know,' said Kate, on sudden impulse, 'whether Agnes ever had a child?'

'Agnes?' Marion gave a skirl of a laugh. 'Good Lord, no. She was an old maid when I first knew her. Of course,' she added, 'there was talk of some man she had turned down once, an older man, but I can't imagine she did *that* with him. Still, people do surprise you, don't they?'

Kate watched Dan amble off into the house, head bowed, and Max came up to introduce himself to Marion, so she left them to spar with one another. She was immediately captured by Raj Nadir.

'Kate, I want you to meet Ursula Hollis – from Farrell's, the auction house.' Kate shook hands with the tall bony woman Raj had been sitting with in the church.

'I am so sorry about Agnes,' said Ms Hollis softly. 'She was a good friend of mine and a great source of advice. Her knowledge of English eighteenth-century miniatures was astonishing.'

'How long had you known her?' asked Kate.

'Twenty years – as long as I've been at Farrell's. My then boss – John Sands, he's long retired – introduced us.' She looked up at the house. 'I understand that this place will be yours?'

Kate nodded. Nadir was obviously telling everyone about the will. Now he broke in. 'I've been talking to Ursula about the contents, Kate. She'd be most happy for Farrell's to give a valuation.'

'Yes, indeed.' Ursula's eyes shone with interest. 'Agnes asked us to put a rough price on a number of pieces a couple of years ago, but we would obviously need to be more precise for the taxman. It would be a real privilege to help you with this treasure-house in any way we can.'

'Thank you,' said Kate, taking the business card Ursula Hollis passed her now. 'I'm sure we'll be in touch once all this,' she indicated the funeral party, 'is over. I know we couldn't expect Agnes to live forever, but it's all somehow been such a shock. Not least about inheriting this place.'

She smiled at Ursula and then moved on to talk to the other guests. There were three elderly gentlemen who turned out to be prominent figures in the arts and antiques world – one a Cambridge emeritus professor, one a retired expert from Sotheby's, the third an Italian dealer in paintings who had happened to be flying over to Britain on business and so was able to attend the funeral. Each of them cited Agnes as a close friend as well as a colleague and all of them congratulated Kate on inheriting the house. Kate was struck by the position of influence Agnes had held within her chosen field, and by the respect in which these people had held her. Suddenly she felt a weight of responsibility for the care of Agnes's collections.

People were starting to say their goodbyes. Kate gathered a

tray of glasses and went inside to give them to Conrad, who was washing-up in the kitchen. She asked him how his job interview had gone, but he shook his head sadly. On her way back through the house she came across Dan, studying a small painting in the hall. She turned on the picture lights and came to stand at his shoulder.

'It's Dunwich,' he said, gesturing to the representation of the ruins of a church on the edge of a cliff, against a stormy sky. He squinted at the signature. 'Local artist, looks like,' he added. 'Eighteen ninety. Might be worth a bit though.' He stood back and looked around the cluttered hall. 'You know, all this – you might be pleasantly surprised by how much it's worth.' He gestured at another painting, this time a huge still-life. The dead birds and the hares were beautifully drawn, so the fibres of each feather, the colours in each hair, reflected the light. 'Beautiful – if you like that sort of thing, of course. George Woodstow. His oils are fetching upwards of twenty thousand now.'

'No!' Kate breathed. Her head was beginning to whirl.

Dan turned and studied her face, then smiled. 'I'm glad that it will be yours.' Then he sighed. 'I miss Agnes already, you know. It seems to be a week for losing people.'

'What do you mean?'

'Linda,' he said simply,' and Shelley. They've moved out. You know when you came round on Monday? Well, when they got back, after Shelley had gone to bed we had this blazing row. They left in the morning.' He shook his head sadly. Kate couldn't see his face.

'I'm sorry,' she whispered. 'Poor you. And Linda. And Shelley. Where have they gone?'

'Back to her mum's.'

Just at that moment, someone called 'Kate?' and Max came

into the hall. He took in Dan and Kate at a glance but spoke just to Kate. 'The vicar is looking for you to say goodbye,' he said. Kate looked at Dan, who gave a tiny nod and stood back to let her pass. As she walked through the doorway, she felt Max's hand lightly press her back.

Later, when Max was leaving he said, 'I can come down for a day next week and we could start going through Aunt's papers. What do you think? Would Wednesday be all right?'

By the time they had finished clearing up and helped Conrad lock up, it was getting late. Kate hurried off to pick up the children from Debbie's. When she arrived, the house was in pandemonium.

'Have they been awful?' groaned Kate, staring at Debbie's living room, which had been turned into a big den with half the bedding from upstairs.

'Let's just say lively,' said Debbie, who looked exhausted. 'Getting into the holiday spirit a week too early.'

'Sorry.' Kate grimaced. 'But thanks so much for having them.'

'How did it go today?'

Kate told her all about the service and the party afterwards, and finished off by explaining just how valuable the contents of the house might be.

'I know there is going to be a lot to pay in tax, but we're still talking serious money here. I . . . I can't think why so much of it's coming to me.'

'You'll need it if you're going to live there,' said Debbie. 'The modernization will be expensive, for a start.' She was brushing some biscuit crumbs into a pile as she said carefully, 'How are things with Simon at the moment? Better?'

Kate nodded. 'I think so, but there's a way to go. And he's not convinced we should keep Seddington House.'

Debbie looked at her quizzically so Kate explained quickly about Simon's unhappiness living in Suffolk.

'I have to say, I'm gobsmacked, Kate. But he's really not seeing this woman any more?'

'No.'

Debbie nodded slowly, then gave Kate a hug. 'Oh, I so hope everything works out for you, and that you stay. I know how much you want that house, but don't let it become a matter of choosing between it and your marriage. A house is only a house, after all.'

'I . . . I know. But I always thought Simon and I wanted the same things. And now it turns out that we don't at all.'

That evening, after Kate had put the children to bed, she sat in the kitchen sipping a glass of wine while Joyce cooked supper.

'Have you had any more thoughts about moving, dear?' Joyce asked.

Kate slumped in her seat. 'Not really,' she said gloomily. 'I definitely don't want to go back to London. My life is here, especially now I have Seddington House. Whatever happens, we need to move soon – get out of your hair, Joyce. You've put up with us for so long.'

'I can't say that it's always been easy, but I've loved having you, dear. Though that isn't why I asked.' Joyce put a large help-ing of fish pie in front of Kate and sat down with hers. 'How are you and Simon going to sort this out? There I go again. Sticking my beak in.'

'Except we are camping here with you.'

'Kate, I don't mind, really. I just want the best for you all. You must take all the time you need.' Was Kate imagining a certain weariness in her tone?

'Thank you, Joyce, you're so kind. It must be so hard for you.

You never have your book club here or your friends round to supper.'

'Don't worry, they do understand, though I sometimes feel a bit guilty not returning hospitality. Still, it's not long before my holiday, and I can treat them all while we're away.' Joyce's reading group was taking a cultural cruise down the coast of Italy in two weeks' time. They were meeting tonight at Hazel's house to discuss their reading for the holiday.

'And when you come back, we'll have left for France,' said Kate. 'I've booked that gîte for the four of us, so you'll have the house to yourself for a few days.'

'It will be good for you all to be together as a family, and the gîte looks lovely. Simon has earned a rest and you just need some time away, don't you?'

'I suppose we do,' said Kate. Secretly she was dreading the holiday. Who was going to win this argument about where they were to live?

Simon rang from the airport at eight thirty. He sounded tired but on a high. 'Yeah, the deal's in the bag. We've been celebrating which is why we're so late. Should be back half eleven if the trains don't mess me about. Don't turn out, I'll call a minicab.'

Who's this 'we'? Kate thought crossly. 'We' had always been Simon and her.

'Oh, and I've got some news.'

'What?'

'Tell you when I get back.'

'Simon, I can't take any more surprises.'

'Oh, right. Well, my promotion's in the bag. Gillingham told me on the plane.'

'That's fantastic!'

'I know, isn't it? I've got to talk to him more about it next week, but they've been impressed with me over this East Europe thing. Kate, all the time I've put in, all these trips, have been worth it.'

She put down the phone with mixed feelings. Simon sounded so elated and she had to feel proud of his achievements. He had never succeeded so well in his career before. And yet at what price had this promotion been bought? And, even more to the point, what was there still to pay?

They would have to talk about it while they were in Normandy – which reminded her. She went to check the computer for confirmation of their tickets. The e-mail she'd been hoping for popped into the in-box, followed by one from Claire. She clicked on Claire's quickly.

*Hi, Kate. Sorry it's been a long time. You'll remember what it's like, this pregnancy lark, feeling too sick and grumbly to do anything at all. I keep having to go home to Mum. It's also been difficult with Alex. We're still seeing each other and he says he'll help with the baby when it comes, but it's not the same. He's so angry with me and blames me, though at least, with his Catholic upbringing, he has never suggested I get rid of it. I couldn't have faced it if he'd said that. So we're just soldiering on, though he says he doesn't want to be tied down – he must be free for his singing. His career is at such an important stage, I can see that. Have you heard from Liz at all, by the way? She's so busy at work these days. I wonder how you are and hope things are better with Simon. I'll give you a call sometime. Love to the kids. Claire xx*

Poor Claire, soldiering along. Kate was just clicking on 'Reply' when the computer, which had a mind of its own, disconnected itself. Then the phone on the desk rang and she picked up the receiver.

'Kate?' It was her father.

'Dad? I thought you might ring.'

'How did today go?'

'Very well, really. Though it's sad that there were so few people left who knew Agnes. Ninety-odd years on this earth and only a handful of friends at your funeral. It's very humbling.'

'Yes.' Kate's father sounded distracted.

'Is there anything the matter?' she asked.

'Your mother's a bit weepy, I'm afraid.'

'Oh, why?'

'It's poor Ringo.' Oh, the wretched dog. Kate sighed, remembering how much attention her mother vested in those dogs. 'We had to have him put out of his misery today.'

'Oh Dad, I'm sorry. I hadn't realized he'd got that bad.'

'He was practically in a coma when we got up this morning, it was the only thing to do. But your mother's upset. I've given her a pill and sent her to bed. I . . . I . . .'

'Dad, are you all right?' Her father sounded frail.

'Yes, just tired, my dear. I'll be all right after a bit of supper.' He cleared his throat. 'Just thought you ought to know about Ringo. The other dog's not too good either, if you want my opinion.'

'It's probably miserable about Ringo. Is Mum all right?'

'Yes, yes, tucked up nicely. I expect she'll appreciate a call tomorrow. She's keen to hear more about the house. She still can't take it in, that it's yours now, and this nonsense about Cousin Agnes and a baby. I must say, it all sounds very extraordinary. And bad luck on that other chap, her great-nephew. Anyway, I'm sure she'll want to hear all the news, it'll take her mind off Ringo.'

'I feel awful that I haven't been down to see you for a while,' said Kate. 'It's just it's a bit difficult at the moment. There's so much going on here . . .' She trailed off. Several times she had thought of explaining to her parents about her problems with Simon. They ought to know. And yet she had never found the right words. It was something else that would upset them deeply: wouldn't they think she had let them down?

'Yes, yes, I quite understand,' Kate's father said now. 'We're managing, though. Don't worry about us.' Desmond had recovered his usual bluff manner by the time they said goodbye, but behind the cheeriness Kate heard a quavering note of uncertainty.

At ten o'clock, Joyce arrived home with a long reading list of novels with Italian themes. She said with deliberate tact that she wouldn't wait up for Simon to return, she was tired and would go to bed. Kate wished her goodnight and sat up, flicking through the channels on the TV. The news featured a Labour minister who looked, she thought, a little like Marion, and, as she zapped the off button, she remembered their conversation at the funeral.

Marion, who had been in touch with Agnes since the younger woman was a child, didn't know anything about a baby, but had mentioned a suitor, an older man. Surely that didn't mean Harry? Where on earth was she going to search next for clues? There was the house itself, of course, and it wouldn't be long before she and Max would be going through Agnes's papers. But unless there was a date of some sort to go by, it would be pointless trying to seek evidence of the birth in the parish register or at the Register of Births, Marriages and Deaths up in London. Would there be anyone in the village who was old enough to remember anything? She supposed she could try asking some of the elderly inhabitants. There was, of course, the diary upstairs that started with Agnes's father, Gerald's, illness. She must read that properly, though when she had flicked through it, there had been no mention of babies. It was Harry, she thought, Agnes's affair with Harry, that she should try to follow up.

Suddenly she remembered. The letter accompanying the diaries! Now Agnes was dead, surely it would be all right to open the envelope? She hurried up the stairs two at a time, retrieved the sealed envelope from her bedside cabinet, and, sitting on the bed, read the direction: *To my son from his mother, Agnes Lavender Melton*. She carefully tore open the flap and pulled out a single page of yellowing foolscap, handwritten on both sides. It was dated May 1950.

*My darling child*
*It may be that we never meet in this world, but I want you to*
*know that I have missed you every day of my life, and that*
*every day I have prayed that you are safe and happy. I also*
*want to tell you that I love you, whoever you are, whatever you*
*are, wherever you are. I loved you from the moment I knew that*
*you were growing inside me; if ever there was a baby that was*
*wanted, it was you. It is the greatest tragedy of my life that,*
*against my will, you were taken from me before I even set eyes*
*on you. You were a part of me: I knew you, the shape of you, the*
*feel of your movements under my skin, although I never held*
*you in my arms and looked into your eyes. Darling, I am sorry,*
*so terribly sorry that the mistakes I made meant that you lost*
*your mother before you even knew her. It has always been my*
*prayer that you found loving parents and that you grew up*
*whole and happy, unaware of the void of separation that I have*
*lived with every moment since your birth.*

*I expect that, if you want to think about me at all, you will have many questions to ask, so I am leaving you my diaries, which tell my story, which is also your story.*

*Yours truly in this life and the next,*
*Your mother, Agnes Melton*

Kate lay back on the bed and squeezed her eyes closed. So Agnes had never even seen the child she gave birth to. Someone had separated mother and child without any concern for the consequences. How cruel.

Suddenly her eyes flew open. Perhaps the baby had, in fact, died, and Agnes had lived under an illusion all these years. Kate had often read of occasions in the past when midwives and doctors had thought they were sparing a mother pain by taking away a stillborn baby before the mother could even acknowledge her child and say farewell. They believed they were being kind, as if the mother would really forget that she had ever nurtured a child within her for so long and given birth, and would just get up the next day as if nothing had happened so long as she wasn't presented with physical evidence of the tragic end of her hopes and labours. Agnes strongly believed her child to be alive – why was that? Was it a delusion or had somebody told her that her living baby had been taken away – to where?

On impulse Kate reached into the drawer of her bedside table and took out the last diary. She turned to the first page. *1943*. Agnes's father was dying. Even Agnes was aware that this was the case as he lay coughing, his breath coming in long strangled wheezes, his chest heaving. Lung disease, the doctor had told her, the symptoms exacerbated by weakness following the gas attack in the Kaiser's war. And Gerald was losing the will to live.

*After Vanessa left, his spirits never really recovered. He has been diminished, shut inside himself, though he has taken comfort in the routines of hard work, the rituals of daily life. My mother broke his heart,* Agnes wrote. *Vanessa broke his spirit.*

The entry for 23 July, when Gerald was laid to rest in the churchyard of St Mary's, Seddington, beside his beloved wife Evangeline, revealed Agnes to be at the lowest point Kate had known.

And so I am alone, utterly alone. Raven has not even come to his father's funeral. It was a truly sad occasion, the rector clearly bowed down by the loss of a good friend. So many people were not there who should have been. Only Mr Armstrong travelled down from London on the last of his petrol ration, Father's other business contacts have only sent their condolences. Lister was there, naturally, and Mrs Duncan, all that are left of our small household now Ruby has gone to nurse. And, amongst local people, Diana and her mother, of course, and our neighbours at Fortescue Hall. Lady Fortescue looks so haggard and old what with the news of Paul being missing and their home being requisitioned for troops.

Kate turned the pages. Much of the rest of the diary was about ordinary routines, going through Gerald's possessions, sorting out the farm estates, details of Agnes's reading, of visits to Diana in a nearby parish where the curate who had won her was now vicar and she was bringing up four noisy children of her own, together with two evacuees. Gerald's illness had precluded the accommodation of children from the city at Seddington House. Then came a surprising entry.

*This morning, a letter from Vanessa. The first I have had from her, for she didn't even write on Father's death. It's about Harry. She thought I would want to know. He has died in an air-raid. The whole building was destroyed and set ablaze. I can't quite take it in.* The entry ended abruptly, though a few days later, she confided: *Harry's death is the death of all hope. Although my head told me that it was all over, we would never be together, underneath, my heart must have been singing a different song. But now it is, all, truly over.*

With the deaths of her father and her estranged lover following in such quick succession, Agnes was plunged into a deep depression. She wrote in her diary only rarely, and in stilted sentences that described how some days she used to walk endlessly around the lanes and fields, as if by physical effort she could fight off the demons, whilst on others she wrapped herself up in a quilt in her favourite attic and stared at the ceiling or slept. She had few companions in these months. Diana came when she was able to make the rare trip to Halesworth. Gerald's loyal business friend, Mr Armstrong, was an occasional visitor – an invaluable help with the complexities of Seddington business, which Gerald's lawyer was still winding up. On one of her walks she described walking through Wenhaston, a village some five miles away, and meeting their old housemaid, Ethel, with two of her children.

She said she and Alf had moved there when Alf's mother had become ill in the summer of 1928. They had lived in Alf's childhood home until the mother died and the house had become theirs. Alf, thankfully slightly too old to be called up, was gardener at a local hospital now, where the lawns had been carved up to grow vegetables. The children, a girl and a boy of about ten and eight, have Alf's unruly brown hair and Ethel's fine hazel eyes. The boy told me they have a sister at home, of nearly fourteen. I said we needed a maid at Seddington House so if the girl wanted a job when she left school, there was a place open. But Ethel seemed offended at that idea, which surprised me. Perhaps she has better ambitions for her children. Maybe there will be more opportunities for ordinary families in this strange upside-down world when the war is over.

By the beginning of 1945, Agnes seemed to be recovering from her mental turmoil. As the tide of war strengthened in the Allies' favour she began to plan her life. She was resolved to stay at Seddington House and her mind was once again on her collections. It would be a while before the devastated art market recovered, and so much had been lost to air raids, confiscation and looting, but she wanted to get involved.

In the meantime the mystery of the suitor Marion had mentioned, became plain. After his long and faithful friendship with both Agnes and her father, William Armstrong proposed marriage.

Of course, I had to say no. He is a good man and has been alone for so long, since his wife died. But I just can't think of him in that way; he doesn't inspire any passion in me at all. Not after Harry. Harry has spoiled everything. And I'm so used to my own company now. It would be exciting to have a lover, yes, but I feel too crotchety and selfish now to be a wife. Diana thinks it's a matter of meeting the right person. She says she's surprised William hasn't said something before and that there are many kinds of marriage – somebody quiet and steady might be just what I need. She knows about Harry, but she doesn't know the full story. She doesn't know why Selcott left so suddenly. Everyone has been waiting for William to say something to me for years, I know, but I thought they were wrong. He was never slushy and romantic with me, his manners have always been perfect, so I just

331

thought his visits were in friendship to my father. Poor William. I have begged him still to come to see me, that we must be friends, but I don't know whether he will. It's all a waste.

Kate reached the last page and closed the diary. So Agnes's suitor had been a dry old widower. And after that? Who knew. Perhaps Agnes had found patches of passion and happiness. She had certainly found success in her chosen life's work. But her heart had been shattered by Harry and by whatever had happened to part them. And there had been a child, a child born so secretly that even Diana didn't appear to know about it.

Kate picked up Agnes's letter once more. The answers to questions lay in the diaries, Agnes said, yet those Kate had found hadn't revealed the core of the secret. There had to be another volume somewhere. *But where?*

Kate was tired now. She wondered whether she would dream again tonight, dream of the house and the events she'd just read about. She remembered the first time she had dreamed of Seddington House. She had imagined it was something to do with the locket before she saw the picture of the house in her mother's album. What tricks our minds can play. Anyway, the locket had disappeared. She was sure she had put it in a box in the shed but several searches there had proved fruitless.

She went to her jewel box and riffled through the costume jewellery for the umpteenth time – the pearl necklace was hidden from burglars in a drawer under the bed. Yet again she looked behind the chest of drawers, checked the floorboards for holes but found no clue. She was still puzzling about it when she heard a car draw up outside.

She got up and opened the front door, waiting in her socks on the threshold, her hand on Bobby's collar, as Simon paid off the taxi driver and wheeled his suitcase down the path.

He dropped his heavy flight bag on the hall floor and kissed her. He tasted unfamiliar – of fast food and whisky – and this, coupled with his face, pale and excited with great shadows under the eyes – gave him the air of a stranger, a refugee.

He pulled off his jacket and tie and ripped open his top button, then rummaged in his flight bag.

'Bubbly,' he said, flourishing a bottle. 'Let's put it in the freezer for a bit.' He clattered about in the kitchen, fixing himself a sandwich. Kate sat at the table and watched him. Finally, he sat down opposite her and poured them each some champagne.

'Congratulations,' said Kate and took a sip. It was only cool.

'Christ, I've worked my socks off for this promotion,' said Simon, gulping down his drink as though it were lemonade, then pouring himself some more. 'But it's been worth it.'

There was something manic about his expression. Kate shivered.

'I'm really pleased for you, darling,' she said, and forced her face into a smile.

'Are you? Are you really?' He flung himself back in the chair and stared at her.

'What do you mean? Of course I am. I know how hard you've worked and how much you've wanted this.'

Simon seemed mollifed. 'It's the first time I feel I've really succeeded at something. Something I've worked hard at. Even Dad would be pleased with me now.'

'He would, darling,' said Kate, allowing him his moment of glory. Simon was studying her. His eyes glittered navy, his hair was ruffled and greasy from travelling. It struck her that he must have had a lot to drink over the evening.

'I know what you're thinking,' he said harshly. 'You're thinking Dad's opinion shouldn't matter. That the old boy's dead. But it does matter.'

'Well,' she shrugged, 'I still want my parents to be proud of me. It's silly, isn't it, once we get to our age. But I'm really proud of you, too.' She reached her hand across the table and squeezed his fingers. He didn't respond.

'I expect you're thinking I shouldn't spend so much time at work though.'

'You know I think that. But that doesn't mean I'm not proud of you. Just that there *are* other things to succeed at in life as well. Things that are even more important. Surely you see that.' Her eyes drifted across to the fridge and the picture of the dream family.

'You and the kids,' he mumbled, watching her. 'Yes, I know that. But that's different. That doesn't give me the same feeling of achievement. The excitement of the office, conflict, getting the deals done, the politics – it feels like living on the edge, urgent, important.'

'But we're important, too,' Kate said wearily.

'Of course you are. It's you and the kids I'm doing all this for.'

'Simon, no it's not. It's for you. Don't get me wrong, I know work is important – for me as well as for you. But not so it takes over your life in the way it's taking over yours.'

'It's only taking over my life because of the travelling. There won't be so many trips abroad for a while. And if I could cut out the travelling down here . . .'

'Now we are just going to start going round in circles again.'

'We've got to settle this one. And this house – how much d'you think it's worth then?'

'Simon, you must come and see Seddington House tomorrow. And then maybe you'll see what I mean, why I want us to live there.'

'Sure. If you like.'

Exhausted, they stared at one another like swimmers through murky water.

# Chapter 29

The next morning, Simon looked haggard. He was brisk with the children who, of course, wanted all his attention after his week's absence, and it was a relief when they could drop them off at a birthday party at the swimming pool.

Then Kate took Simon to see Seddington House. This time, although Marie Summers had given her a key, Conrad was there to let them in. Simon wandered around the rooms, glancing critically at everything, as if he were a prospective buyer who had only deigned to come and look at the insistence of an over-assiduous estate agent.

'It's the most extraordinary clutter, isn't it?' he said, touching a huge, squat mahogany cabinet inlaid with lapis lazuli, which occupied a space under the windows in the dining room. 'Who on earth would want it all? I can see that the pictures . . .' he gestured at a set of delicate watercolours of Suffolk scenes glowing in a dark corner of the room '. . . might be of interest, but do people really want this sort of stuff?' His gesture encompassed the great hulks of furniture, the miscellany of curios, the piles of books that crowded the room.

'The auctioneers seem to think so,' said Kate, annoyed at the way he was dismissing her precious inheritance. 'We'll know for certain soon.' There had been a letter in the morning post. Raj had fixed up for Ursula Hollis and her team to arrive on Tuesday week to spend several days valuing the contents of Seddington House.

They went outside.

'It's a lovely pile, there's no mistake,' Simon said grudgingly, as they strolled around the rose-blown gardens. The lawns were mown but the flowerbeds were overgrown with weeds and many of the shrubs required cutting back. 'It's too big for us, though. And it needs a lot of work, Kate. Plus it doesn't solve my travel problems, does it? We'd be better off selling it lock, stock and barrel, paying off the taxman and buying somewhere sumptuous in London on the proceeds.' He stood silent for a moment, clearly doing calculations. Then he said, 'I've no idea about the contents, but surely we'd walk away with pretty much three-quarters of a million on the house sale alone. Let's say that, after tax, you clear five hundred thou and add it to the two hundred we have in the bank. Factor in the contents and we'd be paying cash for a big London house somewhere central.'

'But that's just it,' said Kate stubbornly. 'I don't want to live somewhere central, or indeed anywhere in London. I want to live here, in Seddington House.'

'Kate, think about it, please. We're going to have to come to some agreement . . .' Just then the phone in his pocket bleeped and he took it out. He looked at the display. 'Sorry, gotta take this,' he said, and walked off through the Italian garden, the mobile clamped to his ear.

Kate watched him go. She couldn't hear what he was saying, but occasionally he laughed, and she wondered what could be funny about high finance.

She walked over to the little door in the wall through which she had once broken into the new world of this magical house.

She stood, trying to recapture the wonder of that evening, back in April, but her mind was too crowded with anxieties now. What if she and Simon could not agree on their future? Was there a compromise? To live much nearer London but out in the country – Hertfordshire or Hampshire. She supposed so . . . except she didn't want to. She wanted to live here. Anyway, their relationship was too uneasy at the moment to make any firm plans about something as committed as another new life somewhere else.

The argument drifted on until after the weekend. Simon had taken a couple of days off, but he seemed at a loss when it came to finding things to do. He spent hours on the computer, annoying Joyce who couldn't use the phone, kept taking Bobby off for long walks and didn't seem at all interested in Kate's suggestions of visits to Aldeburgh or Norwich.

On Sunday night he quarrelled with his mother after, Kate heard from Joyce later, she tentatively suggested he wasn't spending enough time with the children. 'I know, dear, it's none of my business, but it's so difficult to say nothing when I can see what's going on in front of me. Sam particularly wants input from his father. Boys need to do things with their dads, don't they? They go off the rails so easily these days.'

Secretly, Kate had to agree with her. When she had picked Daisy and Sam up from the swimming party at Saturday lunchtime, she had been concerned to find Sam had been crying. The birthday child's mother had taken Kate aside and said, 'I don't think he's enjoyed himself very much. He didn't want to go in the pool and was upset when everyone else did. I'm sorry, but I didn't know what to do.'

'What was wrong, Sam? You love swimming,' Kate had said on the way out to the car, Daisy skipping ahead.

'He's just a wuss,' Daisy said, spinning round to stick her tongue out at her brother.

338

'I wanted you and Daddy to have stayed,' Sam wailed, aiming a kick at Daisy.

This week, Sam had asked Simon on both Monday and Tuesday, 'Promise to c'llect me?' Simon had dutifully turned up at the school gates at three o'clock each afternoon, but once he had brought the children home he would vanish back into the study or out by himself, leaving Sam in anguish, searching for him. Simon might have been living on another planet, Kate thought crossly, for all the interest he took in domestic life. And yet it was her job to berate him about it, not Joyce's.

'He's very tetchy at the moment,' she said to her mother-in-law. 'He might take it better from me.' In the end, she didn't have the courage to start what would undoubtedly end up as another argument, and it was a relief when her husband went back to work on Wednesday morning.

That same Wednesday morning, after Kate had taken the children to school, she drove to Seddington House to help Max start tying up some of the loose ends of Agnes's life. In the library, there were two big writing bureaux and a filing cabinet full of papers. Upstairs, a preliminary search revealed a dozen dusty cardboard boxes of files, letters and memorabilia in one of the spare bedrooms. The contents of the boxes looked older than the papers in the bureaux, though. It was obviously the bureaux they had to tackle first.

As Max pulled out of the filing cabinet a folder labelled *Buildings Insurance* in Agnes's shaky handwriting, Kate asked him the question that had been hovering in her mind ever since her visit to Raj Nadir's office last week.

'Max, perhaps I shouldn't be asking you this, but I need to know how you feel – about the will.'

Max dropped the folder back in the drawer. 'Am I going to

contest it, you mean? I don't know. I'm taking advice from a colleague.'

'Do you still think that it's my fault? Agnes leaving me the house, I mean.'

He sighed, then smiled, a bit sadly. 'To tell you the truth, no,' he said. 'I can see you're not a fortune-hunter. And various people – Nadir and Dan and Mrs Summers – have taken pains to make me see that it was important to Agnes, leaving this place to you. Having a family here again to bring it back to life.'

'That's something then,' Kate said. But he had not quelled her unsettled feelings. Despite what Raj said about Max not having a strong case, wills did get contested and surprising judgements were sometimes made.

'I'm sure I'll get the money she's left me, though,' Max continued. 'This story of a child – it's got to be a load of codswallop. No one knows anything about it, do they? Unless there's something in here.' He tapped the nearest bureau with the toe of his brogue. 'Still, whatever happens, she was my aunt, and it's our duty as executors to sort everything out. Perhaps we'll find something that clarifies matters. Come on.'

They started making piles on the floor of the mishmash of folders and papers, writing a list of the myriad tasks that have to be carried out in the event of a death. Kate opened the top drawer of the second bureau and found it to be full of photographs. She picked out one of a beautiful young man with short black hair sleeked back in the style of the times.

'Must be my grandfather,' breathed Max. 'Raven. He looks like a matinee idol, doesn't he? It's been touched up, of course, but my grandmother used to say how good-looking he was.'

'Oh, did you know Vanessa well?'

'My grandmother died in nineteen eighty-five, soon after her eightieth birthday.'

'What was she like? Raven died in nineteen sixty, didn't he? It was a long time to be a widow.'

'She was very lovely when she was young. Mum left some photographs. Even at eighty there was something fragile and appealing about her. Dad said she made men want to look after her, made them feel manly and protective. I was only a graceless lout of a teenager, but I could see what he meant.'

'Did she marry again?'

'No, but she had lovers.'

Kate laughed suddenly. 'I can't believe you were a graceless lout,' she said, taking in his tall neat form, the blue cashmere sweater perfectly teamed with camel cords and a snow-white open-necked shirt.

'I used to dress all in black,' he said, 'and practise a sneer.' He gave one now, making Kate giggle.

'I bet you were the type of guy I was terrified of at uni,' she said. 'Impossible to impress and refusing to engage in any conversation that didn't come back to Post-structuralism.'

'I was all of that,' he admitted, 'but only because I was lonely. University was a bit of a disaster for me. It was only when I started work that I got some confidence. Then I met Claudia – she was a social worker involved peripherally in a case I was working on.'

'She's your ex?'

'Yes. She's from Norwich originally, and I had been brought up in Cambridge, so when she got pregnant we decided to go back to home ground. Her parents could help with the kids, you see.'

'What went wrong, then?'

'She seemed different at home amongst her family. They smothered her. It was "Mum says this," and "Dad says you shouldn't do that." We started to argue a lot. And then she bumped into an old boyfriend from school . . .' He shrugged, his face impassive.

Kate nodded in sympathy, then busied herself again with the contents of the bureau. She wondered whether she should confide in him about her own relationship problems, then decided it was more restful not to.

Two hours later, papers and files lay in neat piles around the library floor. Max and Kate sat drinking coffee and staring at the mess.

'It's like Raj said – most of the financial stuff must be with him or the bank,' said Max.

'Or the accountant,' agreed Kate. 'Raj said his predecessor wound up everything to do with the old farm estates, and made Agnes put things like the deeds and share certificates in the bank. Can't think why he didn't deal with the jewellery, though.'

'God, jewellery. I suppose we ought to see what's around the house. It all belongs to you now, of course'

'Yes, but I know where some of it is. In the safe over there.' Kate nodded in the direction of the fireplace and picked up her hand-bag to find the little key Agnes had given her. Then she walked over and started pulling the *Domesday* volumes off the shelf.

'A safe. So *that's* what you were up to with Dan that after-noon,' said Max, aggrieved, so Kate explained as she worked.

'There were some diaries Agnes wanted me to read, you see. To tell me about her child.'

'Diaries?' he said sharply.

'Yes, but there's nothing in them about the child,' she said hastily. 'Just a letter she wrote to tell him to read the diaries. There might be another volume that I've missed. I don't know, we must see.' She knew she ought to offer Max the chance to read the exercise books now that Agnes was dead, but she was jealous of them. They were her private bond with Agnes, with

342

the past. And anyway, she wanted to find and read that final volume first – if it existed.

The door of the safe swung open, and Kate removed the top box from the pile of jewel-cases. Max gasped when he saw the exquisite diamonds within. He grabbed at the other half-dozen boxes, opening them one by one, his eyes widening in amazement at the contents. As he pulled out the last box, Kate could see with disappointment that the safe was empty. No more diaries, then.

'These must be worth thousands,' Max breathed. 'They ought to be in the bank.'

'That's exactly what Dan said when he saw them—' Kate stopped, seeing Max's face change expression. 'What have you got against Dan?' she asked.

He shrugged. 'Nothing. Just that he always seemed to be hanging around my aunt, that's all.'

'I don't think that was for any sinister reason,' said Kate gently. 'Just that she helped him and he was fond of her.'

'He was very relaxed with her, very close. In a way I could never be.'

Suddenly Kate understood. 'It's a shame,' she whispered. 'I suppose there was too much baggage. Not your fault.'

'What do you mean?'

She looked at him, her gaze level, taking in his sensitive face, the nearly black hair, the intense expression.

'You are Raven's grandson, that's the problem. And you look so incredibly like him. Agnes wanted to forget the past, to bury it. And every time she looked at you, she must have been reminded of all her pain.'

By lunchtime, they had sorted through both bureaux and each of them had a long list of tasks. Kate's included sorting out the

343

buildings and contents insurance and advising a raft of different companies of Agnes's death. Max's involved taking the jewellery and the miniatures and a number of other bits and pieces to Agnes's bank in Halesworth. He turned down Kate's suggestion of lunch and arranged to meet her again the following week for the start of the auctioneers' visit. On the way out, they met Conrad parking his bicycle and explained what they were doing with the valuables.

As Kate drove through the village, her mind turned to Dan. Leaving the car by the church she walked down and tapped on the door with the little dolphin knocker of number 2, The Row.

When he opened the door, Dan was wearing a paint-spattered brown shirt and eating the last of a sandwich. He waved Kate into the living room, where the television was showing the lunchtime news. The room smelled stale, the cushions were crushed down the backs of the chairs, papers and glasses nestled against table-lamps and the waste-paper basket overflowed in a corner. But the toys and children's videos had all vanished.

'I couldn't remember which days you go to the gallery,' she said as he turned off the news.

'Usually this morning, but I wanted to finish something here.'

His face was tired and rumpled, Kate noticed, and he was unshaven – a complete contrast to his smart appearance at Agnes's funeral last week.

He seemed aware now of how he must appear.

'Sorry,' he said, drawing his fingers through his unkempt hair. 'You've not got me at a good time. No,' he put a hand on her arm as she embarked on an apology, 'don't get me wrong, I'm pleased you've come. Have you eaten?'

Kate said she hadn't so he took her into the kitchen and made her a great wedge of bread and Cheddar. 'What have you been finishing?' she asked through a mouthful, trying not to notice the piles of dirty crockery everywhere, the crumbs and smears on every work surface.

In answer, he opened the back door and she followed him out with her sandwich into the now overgrown garden and down the path to the shed.

She gave a gasp of surprise as he pulled open the door and stood back to let her go in first. Without, this was an ordinary garden shed smelling of creosote. Within, she was hit by a great waft of turpentine and linseed oil. White-painted plasterboard and a huge north-facing window in the roof, hidden from the garden, had transformed the interior into an art studio. Though cluttered with canvases and a mess of equipment, like Dr Who's Tardis, Kate thought, the inside seemed bigger than the outside.

'I've got to show it to someone sometime,' Dan said sheepishly as he turned an easel towards her, 'so it might as well be you.'

It was a painting of a woman sitting at a table – the little table in Dan's dining room – with a mug of coffee before her, and staring up, out of the window as if in rapture. In a corner of the painting, a small child sat on the floor absorbed in dressing a doll. The texture was fine, painterly, the line between the child on the ground, the woman's face and the object of the woman's gaze a natural arc, but what was breathtaking, Kate thought, was the light – that cold north light that would hit the dining-room windows in the same way it would enter Dan's skylight here. It rendered the figures as carven statues, serene, peaceful, lovely, all imperfections smoothed away by its silver touch.

'It's Linda,' she said after a moment. 'And Shelley. You've made them beautiful. No, they were beautiful before, but you've made them . . . like angels. Uplifted, not of this world.'

'Like before the Fall,' Dan said, nodding, and they stood and looked at the painting together.

'How long have you been working on it?' she asked.

'Six, seven months.' He shrugged.

'It's good,' she said, wondering if it was the right thing to say. 'Very good.' Something was tugging on the thread of memory. What? 'Does it have a title?' she asked.

'Have to think of one,' he said, as he led her out of the shed, locked it, and they walked back to the house. 'Titles are important. What do you think?'

'I can't name your painting for you,' she laughed.

She stood in the hall and peered into the room where the painting was set. Apart from the square-hatched windows it was unrecognizable as the same place. There was mess and dust everywhere, books sprawling across the floor.

'I've not done much about housework for a while,' Dan said. The implication was obvious – since Linda left.

'Dan, are you OK?' Kate asked in response to his bleak expression.

'Yes, I suppose I miss her. Linda – and Shelley. Well, I don't miss the fights with Linda, but I miss having them both about the place, you know. And Shelley's unhappy. Linda's mum says she misses me.'

'I'm sure she must do. You're like a dad to her, aren't you?'

'Yeah. But she's got a dad of her own. I can't take his place, can I?'

'Does she see much of him?'

'I think he would like to see more of her, but he's not good at looking after her. Forgets to feed her properly. Linda's still angry with him. He wasn't around for her when Shelley was born, you see, and she had a bad time.'

'And what does Linda think about Shelley seeing you?'

'I don't know. Linda won't talk to me at the moment. Her mum rings when Linda's out at work and tells me what's going on with Shelley.'

Dan looked so gloomy, Kate reached out and patted his shoulder, meaning it to be a comforting gesture, but he didn't seem to notice.

'I'd better go,' she said quickly. 'Thanks for the sandwich.' And smiling goodbye, she opened the door and slipped outside.

She sat in the car for a moment thinking about Dan's unhappiness and how innocent children become victims of grown-ups' misery.

She remembered Dan's painting and a phrase slipped into her mind. *One morning at the beginning of the world*. She had no idea where the line had come from. And then the thing she had been trying to remember drifted into focus: an image of another woman admiring a picture by another artist. A lifetime ago.

# *Chapter 30*

That evening, as Kate was getting ready to go to the Save the School meeting, Simon rang. He wasn't coming back until Friday, he said, but he had had his meeting with Gillingham that day and his new pay package was a generous one. He spoke to each of the children and promised Kate they would celebrate properly at the weekend.

The Save the School meeting began in optimistic mood.

There had been a letter to the governors from Mr Keppel. In view of their plans for fundraising, he had been able to secure the agreement of his management to delay the final decision about the school for a further academic year, but that was all.

'Twelve months to raise fifty thousand pounds,' muttered Debbie.

'It took years to raise the thirty for the church,' remarked Mr Overden, shaking his head.

'We'd better get our plans into place quickly then,' said Jasmin, pulling a small black notebook out of her handbag. The others watched her in fascination. 'I have here a list of possible benefactors we should be asking for donations. And here are some copies of a letter I've drafted.' She handed out some papers.

'This is a good list. And we must write to the MP and the Education Secretary, of course,' said the grey-haired lady secretary.

Debbie broke in, waving a piece of paper. 'Jonny's sorry not to be here, but he's given me several ideas for publicity to add to Kate's.'

Mr Overden cleared his throat and took the top off his pen, Mrs Smithson offered to take minutes and the meeting got under way.

After an hour of discussion, everyone in the group had a list of tasks to take away and pursue over the holidays. As Mr Overden looked at his watch and put the cap back on his pen, signalling that the meeting was over, Kate finally took her courage in her hands and said quickly, 'I can't promise anything at the moment about how much, but I am due to come into some money, and all being well should be able to make some sort of donation towards the fund.'

Everybody made suitably excited noises and the meeting came to a close. Kate realized her heart was thudding. With the voicing of her thought, a decision had been made and that decision was stated publicly. The fact that she was thinking of making a donation to save the school meant that she was committed to the family staying in Fernley. What had she done and what was Simon going to say?

In the end, she didn't have to discuss the matter with Simon at all. It fell by the wayside, unnoticed, in the thundering path of something much bigger.

When Simon arrived at Paradise Cottage on Friday evening at the remarkably early hour of seven o'clock, Kate could see at once that his mood had changed again. He seemed pale, wired, nervy. He endured the children dragging him into the living room, where they insisted on going through with him all the bags of worksheets, artwork and clay figures they had brought home with them on this, the last day of term, but he seemed unable to concentrate and snapped when Joyce rather inanely suggested that his promotion would mean he could relax at work now and come home every night.

At half past nine he said he was going for a walk and was out for an hour. When he came back he sat downstairs drinking whisky until after midnight. Eventually Kate coaxed him up to bed.

'What's the matter, for goodness sake?' she hissed, noticing that he had been reading the same page of his Dan Brown thriller for the last twenty minutes. 'Things haven't gone wrong with Gillingham, have they?'

'No,' he said dully. 'Nothing like that.' He turned off the light and rolled over, his back to her.

Kate sat, frozen, watching him for a moment. Finally, she turned off her own light, edged herself under the covers and silently wept into the pillow.

When she woke the next morning, Simon was up and getting dressed. He muttered something in response to her 'hello', but seemed absent – he didn't even look at her. He went downstairs and she heard Bobby bark, then the front door opened and closed and his footsteps went up the garden path and down the road. It was an hour before he reappeared.

It was a cloudy day, but warm and the rain held off, so they carried out their plan of a day in Southwold with Jonny and Debbie and the children. Whilst Debbie and Kate chatted, Simon was gloomy, though he took his turn with the children with Jonny while the women went shopping.

That evening, Kate was beside herself with misery. Joyce looked from her son to her daughter-in-law in anxiety, as both just toyed with their supper.

This time, when Simon whistled for Bobby and said he was going out, Kate slipped out after him. The sun was low in the sky and the flower-perfumed air filled with birdsong as she caught up with him just before the field.

'Simon,' she said, then louder: 'Simon.' She grabbed his arm, but he went stiff and she dropped her hand. 'Simon, what on earth is the matter?'

He was silent for a moment, staring into the distance, then he looked at Kate and said, 'I don't know.' He walked on, his wife stumbling after him. After a moment, he stopped. 'I suppose I feel we're stuck at the moment. In limbo. I want one thing, you want another. One of us is going to have to compromise. We can't go on living like this, can we? Having conversations that go round and round in circles. Where we're going to live, what we're going to do with our lives.'

'Well, no.'

'You want to live here, in Seddington House. I definitely don't want to live there – I'm fed up with commuting! Everything's going so well at the office, but I also want to see more of the children. I don't want a snatched family life at weekends when I'm tired.'

'But you must have known it was going to be like this. It was you who really wanted us to move, remember?'

'Because I thought it would be good for us all. You were so worn out. It wasn't working where we were. I thought it was worth a go.'

'But you haven't really given it a go. It's not giving it a go, staying with your mother and everything feeling so temporary.'

'It's given me enough of a flavour, all I need to know. I don't like being out here, Kate. I don't want to live my life on the train between Diss and Liverpool Street. God, I know every inch of that landscape now. Every blade of grass, every tree, every office block by every station.' He started walking again, Kate two paces behind, up the edge of the field, the wheat an old-gold colour in the dying light, desperate for harvesting. With every pace she felt her resentment grow. When they reached the stile at the top, he stopped again. Bobby threw himself on the ground, panting, looking up at them both as if to say, 'Now what?'

'Simon,' Kate said carefully, 'when we planned this move, we had it all worked out. Our reasons for coming here. That it would be better to bring up our children in the country. That it would be nice to be near your mother. That it would be better for me here, for the balance of family life. And we talked about your work. We did! I know you think you don't want to try something different, locally. I know your job is going well where you are. But have you considered all the options? Couldn't you work from home sometimes?' She was starting to feel desperate.

'Look, I've just been given a promotion, for goodness sake! They want more out of me, not less. You know how the City regards homeworkers – as slackers.'

'Oh, surely that's so outdated.'

'God, you're as bad as my mother. I have to be part of the culture, don't you see? Watch my back. Go out to the pub with the others. Be a company man. That's how it is, full stop.'

'That's how you're going to let it be, without challenging it, you mean,' she said bitterly.

'This is exactly what I'm talking about – our conversations going round and round.' Simon sat down suddenly on the stile, looking at the ground. Bobby was worrying a stone, which he dropped by Simon's feet. Simon scooped it up and threw it viciously hard, right into the middle of the cornfield. Bobby slashed through the wheat in pursuit, barking joyfully.

Kate tried to keep her voice calm, reasonable. 'For the first time in my life I feel I belong somewhere. I have a home, a house that's been in my family for generations. I'm part of a community, and the children are, too. I'm stronger, I don't feel so upset about things. Funnily, having moved away from Mum and Dad I actually feel closer to them, I can understand them better. Simon, I know this sounds weird, but I think being here, having Seddington House, is somehow meant.'

'Because you've dreamed about it, I suppose?' Simon's tone was sarcastic. 'Kate, you can't base your life on dreams. They're just something your mind makes up, plays with, when you're asleep.'

'I don't know why I dreamed of Seddington House, whether they were prophetic dreams, or some sort of visualization of my deepest desires fed by a childhood memory.' She had told him about her mother's photograph. He had seemed relieved at the time, that his wife wasn't fey or going crazy. 'But we all have dreams, whether waking or sleeping. And there was a time when you encouraged me to follow mine. And you brought us all here in the first place.'

'I came up with the idea, yes, but it was a joint decision, Kate, don't try and blame it all on me. We're both adults, after all – you could have said no. But yes, I have encouraged you. Don't forget what we've been through together, how I've put up with everything . . . your depression, for instance.

'That's low. We've both had our trials and tribulations.'

'I know, I'm sorry, but it hasn't been easy, you weeping all over the place for a year, and then after Sam.'

Kate stared at him. The wound was to the heart. A snide little voice inside her said, *Ah, but you didn't just put up with it, did you, Simon?* Which brought back the pain of his recent betrayal a hundredfold.

'Well, at least I never—'

'Don't say it,' he hissed, standing up suddenly, his face hard with anger. 'I'm never going to escape that one, am I? Never, never. No matter how hard I try with you, for evermore. There's always going to be that between us.' He stopped to draw breath. 'Kate, it's decision time. We've got to find some sort of compromise, or I don't see us going on together.'

'What do you mean?' she asked, disbelieving.

'Just that. I'm not going to live down here,' he declared. 'I'm just not. You've got to choose. The house or me.'

She couldn't believe what she was hearing. 'That's nonsense! We don't have to make any instant decisions. There must be some middle way.'

'Well, from where I am, I don't see it.' He was turned away from her now, ignoring Bobby, who was panting hopefully at his feet. But in another respect he was miles ahead, striding out of sight. She was left behind, pleading for him to wait.

She noticed suddenly that his shoulders were shaking. 'Simon, what's wrong?' She pulled him round to face her. He was crying. He pushed her away. Then he lunged at her, throwing his arm around her in a clumsy hug, burying his face in her shoulder.

'I'm sorry, so very sorry,' he cried, his voice strangled and his body heaving.

'What is it? What's wrong?' A growing sense of dread.

Simon crushed her tighter, still shaking and sobbing now. 'I can't help it,' he groaned. 'I'm just pulled both ways. It's no good, I'm torn in half. I don't know what to do.'

Then Kate suddenly saw everything, what all this was about.

'It's her, isn't it?' she shouted, shoving him away. 'She's still got you. Why can't she leave you alone? You said you told her.'

'I did,' he said, 'but she didn't accept it.'

'But she knew you belonged to me. To me and Daisy and

Sam. How could she? How could you let her?' She thought suddenly. 'Did she go to Germany with you?'

He nodded, not looking at her. 'She loves me,' he said simply. 'She really loves me.'

'But *I* really love you! What gives her the right, the nerve . . . ?' The tears were pouring down Kate's face now, but they were tears of anger. She was absolutely furious. Furious at his weakness, at Meredith's strength, at her seeming inability to change anything. This wasn't an argument about where to live. It was much bigger than that.

Anger finally gave her the strength she needed. Any respect she still had for Simon was suddenly gone. Where was the man she had looked to for support? Where was the soulmate in whose arms she had felt completely safe? Where was her rock? He had proved to be a man of clay. And in that moment of realization, the remnants of her love for him fled.

'You've ruined everything,' she whispered. 'How could you? I hate you.'

The tears still streaming down her face, she turned away and stumbled down the path, across the darkening field, back towards her sleeping children and the house that was not her home.

'Kate!' She heard Simon's voice, thin in the distance. She didn't even falter.

She was sobbing uncontrollably when she fell against the gate to Paradise Cottage, then a wave of rage crashed through her. She couldn't just walk in through the front door and pretend to Joyce that nothing was wrong. Where could she go? Her hand touched the car key in her pocket. She must get away. Somewhere. Anywhere.

She fumbled the key into the ignition of the Audi and the car rolled out into the near-darkness. The headlights swept over

Simon where he was dragging Bobby back up the road, but Kate ignored him and pulled the car out into the direction of the coast. Where was she going? She didn't know and she didn't care.

The vast East Anglian sky glowed gold and grey around her, but she was driving towards purple, indigo, midnight blue and, in the far distance, black. There was no moon, but faint stars already pricked the velvety sky. Hedges rose on either side and every now and then she passed through a comforting tunnel of trees, the headlights highlighting the details of every leaf and branch, reflecting the eyes of terrified creatures on the road. Slowing down to let them pass calmed her mind. She couldn't really be mad if, in the depth of her misery, she was still instinctively protective, could she?

When she came to the main road, she turned right towards the great silent church at Blythborough, then dodged down through the maze of dark, deserted lanes to the coast at Dunwich. There she parked the car and walked out alone onto the stony beach.

It was quiet now, apart from the rhythm of the waves; there was no harsh wind, just a cool zephyr from the sea. She walked up the beach, with the dark hulk of the crumbling cliff on her right and the whitish glowing dome of Sizewell nuclear power station in the far distance, then stopped and looked out to sea.

Deep under the black mass of water, she knew, lay the ruins of a city. Sometimes, people would say, one could hear the distant tocsin of bells from the drowned churches, the single ghostly remant of what had been a bustling port in medieval times, before the storms that had clawed great gobbets of the land into the murky depths. *That passed. This will too.*

Out here in the darkness, lulled by the gentle sound of the sea,

Kate was restored to herself again. Still racked with pain, afraid, but in control. She knew what she had to do now. Debbie was right – she *would* come through. But it would be without Simon.

She waited as a crescent moon began to rise over the water, bathing her in its peaceful light. Then she turned and made her way slowly back to the car.

'Simon, I want you to leave,' Kate said quietly. 'First thing tomorrow morning.'

She had returned to Paradise Cottage to find him waiting alone in the half darkness of the living room. Joyce had scurried off to bed. The house was in silence.

Simon was sitting in an armchair, arms wrapped around his chest, staring at the floor. Kate perched on the edge of the sofa, hands clasped and resting on her knees. Her position suggested she was counselling Simon, not dictating the end of their marriage.

He raised his head. His face was ravaged with emotion. 'Yes,' he croaked. He scraped one hand back through his hair. 'I know. But what about the children? I can't just leave them. Kate, whatever happens to us, I love my children. I want to be their father, to be there for them.'

A rush of angry retorts tore through Kate's mind at this. She rejected all of them as unhelpful.

'We will have to tell them together,' is what she finally said. 'I've no intention of depriving them of their father, whatever happens. It's a cheap form of revenge and would only hurt them. You need have no worries on that score.'

Simon's shoulders relaxed and he nodded.

'And we must tell your mother together.'

'Yup,' he said and sniffed.

She stood up, still calm. Her anger was ice-cold. 'I'm going to bed now. I can't bear to talk to you any more this evening.' She glanced at the sofa.

'Don't worry, I'll sleep down here,' Simon muttered, brushing away tears with the back of his hand, 'if you'll let me get a couple of blankets out of the cupboard.'

When she took some dirty cups through to the kitchen on her way to bed, Kate noticed the picture on the fridge. The dream house and the four smiling stick figures, the dream family. She put the cups down by the sink and, tearing the picture off the fridge door, ripped it to pieces.

The next morning, after breakfast, they told Joyce together as she and Kate were loading the dishwasher in the kitchen. Joyce immediately burst into tears.

'Sorry, I'm sorry. I could see it coming but I haven't dared think it would really happen. Oh, the poor children.'

Telling the children was much, much worse. Kate had had a sleepless night thinking about it. They were both old enough to realize something serious was happening. Daisy, at six, understood a little more than Sam, who just knew that his daddy was going away. Both of them cried. Sam clung to his father, weeping uncontrollably. Daisy's tears were angry. She kicked at Kate when her mother tried to comfort her in the armchair where she had buried herself.

Simon was crying as he took his suitcase out to the car, watched by the white-faced women and with Sam struggling in his mother's arms. Daisy wouldn't come out and say goodbye.

The following Thursday morning, a large manila envelope addressed ominously to *Ms Kate Hutchinson* arrived by registered mail. It contained a letter from a firm of City solicitors and informed Kate that Simon was requesting a formal separation. As well as demanding that Kate deliver the children to him every weekend, Simon was claiming a large proportion of the value of Seddington House and its contents.

# Chapter 31

Kate read the letter through twice, shock succeeded by disbelief. Let Meredith have her children? And every weekend? Never! Was Simon crazy? How could he leap from their civilized conversation of last weekend about sharing the children's upbringing to this – this intolerable demand! She threw the letter on the table as though it was burning her. And Seddington House! How could he just walk out on her, then turn round and grab for something that was hers, that was nothing to do with him. The injustice of it all!

She stared at the letter again, then in a sudden movement, snatched it up, balled it and stuffed it into the pedal bin. Then she swept up the breakfast bowls and banged them angrily into the sink. It was Simon who had had the affair, Simon who had gone off with someone else, leaving her without any immediate means of support and with two children to look after. Surely the law wouldn't uphold such unfairness. What kind of monster was he, to make these demands? What would Joyce say, when she heard what her son had done? But Joyce was in Italy with her reading group, and mercifully, could enjoy her holiday in ignorance of this further injury to family happiness. Thank goodness also, Kate thought, that she had cancelled France yesterday. They couldn't have gone on holiday, she and the children, with something like this hanging over them, could they?

She slumped down into a chair, the fire gone out of her. Now she felt so alone. Who could she speak to? Certainly not her parents – she had said nothing to them so far about her marriage problems, and when she plucked up the courage to do so, she knew she would have to comfort them rather than the other way round. And she so badly wanted comfort. And advice. Liz, she thought.

Kate checked that the children were still watching TV cartoons in the living room then rang her friend's office. Rosie, Liz's nice secretary, answered. Kate had forgotten Liz was away in Jersey for a fortnight. After she put down the phone, she retrieved the letter from the bin, straightened it out and read it again. A wave of misery and defeat rolled over her. How was she to fight this?

Would she, after all this searching, lose her dream house before it was truly hers? Was she, in fact, despite all the dreams, finding lost family, establishing connections with the past . . . never meant to have this wonderful place to call home? She had, it seemed, set her heart on something she had been convinced would bring happiness for herself and her family, but it wasn't working out that way. Maybe the dream was just that – a nighttime fancy, a trick of the mind, that melted away in the truth of daylight. Or a dark chimera that had led her astray, bringing in its wake only betrayal, envy, decay.

She had to talk to someone or she would go crazy. She picked up the phone once more and punched in Debbie's number.

Within five minutes of putting down the phone to Debbie, Kate had goaded Sam and Daisy to put on their shoes and shepherded them, both protesting, to the car. As she strapped them in, it occurred to her to wonder how long she would have the family car. Simon had left it behind, but it was a company car, not his own.

'I can't believe Simon would do something like this,' she raged to Debbie as her friend read the letter. They had retired to the kitchen, having ushered the five children into the living room, with a huge plate of chocolate biscuits and a new video Debbie had been hoarding for emergencies. 'It's not like him at all. It's cruel, and whatever else Simon has turned out to be, he's never ever been cruel.'

'Could this be to do with Meredith?' Debbie asked. 'Is she quite an aggressive person?'

'That's what I was thinking. It's the only explanation. I don't know what she's like, but she must be tough to be so successful in the City, and this whole thing smacks of the American legal approach – all guns firing.' Kate was surprised at how coolly her mind was working. Although she could feel a black sea of panic and distress surging away underneath, she was holding herself together.

'At least he's not asking to have the children full-time,' said Debbie.

'How could he? He works ten hours a day. And he must know the courts would be unlikely to find for him. But still, every weekend . . . It would be so stressful for them, never mind for me.'

'Jasmin,' said Debbie suddenly. 'She's a family lawyer, isn't she? She's not cheap, I've heard, but I'd put my money on her sorting things out. Ring her. I'll have the children while you go and see her.'

And that's how, later that day, Kate found herself sitting in Jasmin Thornton's bright modern office in Ipswich, a large mug of strong coffee in her hand and the Orwell River twinkling in the distance through the huge plate-glass windows.

'I've read about this guy.' Jasmin looked up from the crumpled letter and smoothed her severe black bob, frowning. 'He's from New York originally but married a British lawyer and retrained. Let's say he's brought some American legal manners with him. He goes for the jugular. Especially if there's someone like this Meredith egging Simon on.'

'But surely they don't have a leg to stand on.'

'All I can say is that we've got some tough negotiating ahead. But,' she said, smiling slightly, 'I'm in the mood for this, so they'd better watch out.' She leaned back in her chair and prepared to take notes. 'I am less worried about the access issue – you're right, the courts are unlikely to go for something that places too much stress on the children. It's the finances we have to sort out. Now, tell me about Seddington House. Where are you with probate?'

Kate spent an hour with Jasmin, who had cancelled another meeting to see her, going over what she could remember of Simon and her finances and her bequest. She gave Jasmin Raj Nadir's phone number and promised to make sure she was sent a copy of the will, together with various other documentation. By the time she drove back to Fernley, she felt much calmer, but utterly exhausted.

As she drove through Seddington village in the late-afternoon sunshine, she noticed Dan's bright van parked outside the church and was overcome by a longing to see him. She knew she ought to get back to relieve Debbie of the children, but she hadn't yet told him about Simon, so she parked her car behind his and went to knock on his door. There was no answer. As she waited she looked round the tiny front garden, decorated with tubs of geraniums and lobelia. Dan's house was so small, but it was usually loved and cared for, although she remembered with a pang of empathy that he wasn't feeling up to housework at the moment.

After a while, she walked down the lane that ran behind the cottages, but there was still no sign of him. She slumped against the fence, suddenly giving way to weariness. Just as she was gathering the strength to go, a motorbike roared up the lane behind her.

Dan pulled the bike up against the fence, killed the engine and lifted off his helmet, smiling hello. His toffee-coloured curls were crushed and beads of sweat stood out on his forehead. He smelled of leather and oil as he brushed past her to open the gate, then turned and quickly kissed her cheek.

'What's happened?' he asked, seeing Kate's wan expression.

She couldn't speak, so he drew her into the garden. She followed him down the path and watched mutely as he unlocked the back door.

'Put the kettle on, would you? While I get these off.' He gestured to his boots and leathers. He stomped through to the hall and she stood listening to the sounds of zips, thuds and scuffling as she stood in her misery watching the kettle. Finally Dan appeared in the doorway, combing his curls with his fingers, his bulk overwhelming in the small kitchen. He looked enquiringly at her.

'It's Simon,' she said.

'I thought as much.' And seeing the tears well in her eyes, he pulled her towards him and snuggled her into his chest. Kate sobbed against his comforting old sweater. After a while she grew calmer. Taking the hank of kitchen roll, he ripped a piece off for her to blow her nose.

'Hang on a moment,' Dan said, and reaching past her, he set about making the tea. Without letting her go, he grabbed both mugs in one hand and guided Kate into the living room where he threw a lot of papers, books and clothes into a corner and sat her down next to him on the sofa. Then she told him everything, about Simon leaving and the lawyer's letter. She was all cried out, and just sat there dully staring at a cobweb in the fireplace that was gently shivering in a gust of air from the chimney.

Finally she looked up and smiled weakly at Dan, wiping her eyes with her hand. 'Sorry, must look like the wreck of the *Hesperus*,' she said.

'You look lovely. As always.' He smiled with deliberate mock gallantry, but his eyes were serious.

She pressed her lips into a smile that didn't convince either of them. 'I ought to be getting back now. Could I go and wash my face?'

Dan got to his feet. 'Of course. The bathroom's at the top of the stairs.'

Upstairs was tiny – two bedrooms and a bathroom that might once have been a boxroom. Some toy building bricks spilled out across the doorway of the smaller bedroom, but the door to what must be Dan's room was almost closed. In the bathroom Kate dashed water over her hot face and rubbed at the flakes of mascara under her eyes with a damp tissue. The bathroom was as untidy as the rest of the little house, though at least it was clean. The tiles over the bath were hand-painted with fishes and seahorses and seaweed, and a plastic duck resting on its side looked dolefully up at her. The line-up of masculine toiletries was pitiful next to the clump of feminine bottles and jars that filled the shelves and the windowsill. Kate felt confused. Why had Linda not taken them with her? Or Dan not swept them away? She supposed because it was so difficult often to say a relationship was definitely over, that there was no bridge back, even if neither party actually wanted to cross it. She knew things were definitely over with Simon – she had decided that, the evening on the beach at Dunwich, and the lawyer's letter had nailed the lid on the coffin. But at the same time, so much of her wanted Simon back – desperately. How long would it take for this longing to pass? Months? Years? This was just the beginning for her and for Sam and Daisy – the start of a rocky path that twisted on up, out of sight. She could only hazard one step at a time and hope she wouldn't slip.

She dabbed her face dry with the corner of a towel and carefully descended the steep staircase. Dan stood watching as she picked up her handbag from the floor of the hall.

'Bye,' she said, her smile stronger this time. 'And thank you. I'll see you at the house later in the week, won't I?' Dan was due to assist with the valuation, to move pictures and furniture as required.

'Thursday, yes,' he said, and reached forward to flick back the door-latch. As she moved past him to the door, she felt his hand on her arm.

'Come and see me anytime,' he said simply, his eyes gentle. 'I'm here for you.'

# *Chapter 32*

It was the second day of the valuation when Kate recovered the final exercise book containing Agnes's diary. Robin, Farrell's book expert, a large ponderous man with a voice trained to a whisper by long service in the silence of the country's great libraries, had pulled out the Oxfordshire volume of the *Domesday Book* to find the the red notebook caught between its pages.

'Could this item be of any interest to you?' he asked Kate as she appeared with some coffee for him. 'It appears to be of an – ah – personal nature.'

She gave him the coffee in exchange for the book, and as he returned to his task, she sank into Agnes's chair, almost shivering with excitement. Even before opening it, she knew what the little book must be. How had it got there? Possibly it had got left out of the safe by accident and Agnes had found it and slipped it onto the shelf, meaning to add it to the others next time she opened the safe.

She turned to the first page. The volume started in August, 1928. Kate tried to remember. It must be a month after the previous volume had left off – after Agnes had first met Harry, and Raven had left home.

'Hi.' Max appeared in the doorway, a sheaf of papers in one hand. 'Do we have keys for the display case behind the door of the morning room?' He had been helping Ursula as she listed the porcelain and the silver. Kate pushed the diary under the cushion and jumped up to go and search for further caches of keys.

The rest of the day she had no time to do more than fit the red book into her handbag. Then, when she got back at tea-time to relieve Michelle, who had been looking after the children all day, she remembered that ages ago she had beaten the tourists and booked tickets to see the latest Harry Potter film at the tiny cinema in Southwold that evening.

Daisy was dancing around in excitement. 'We had a picnic with Coca Cola. And I lost my tooth, Mummy. The wobbly one. It finally finally came out without me doing anything. We've put it under my pillow already.'

Michelle, who was picking up her little pink handbag to go home, put it down again and said, 'And we found some treasure, didn't we, Daisy? I almost forgot.' Daisy nodded but stopped dancing and looked sheepish.

Kate followed Michelle into the kitchen and saw her take something off the dresser. Something on a silver chain. 'My God,' she said. 'My locket. Where on earth . . . ?' She turned it over in her hands, blowing dust off the photograph, which was so faded she wouldn't have taken it for Agnes, even now. Relief coursed through her. She looked up at Michelle who read her look of delight.

'It *is* yours, then. Daisy said it was but I thought it might be the other Mrs Hutchinson's.'

'Where did you find it?'

'When Daisy's tooth come out she went up and put it under her pillow straight away, but then she come down saying she had lost it, so I went up with her. We couldn't see it, so I lifted the mattress and it had fallen down onto the wooden bit. Then I saw the necklace.'

After Michelle had gone, Kate asked Daisy, 'What was it doing in your bed then?'

The little girl hung her head and said, 'It was ages and ages ago, in your bedroom. I only wanted to look at it. You're not cross, are you?'

'Daisy, you must have known I was looking for it.'

But Daisy merely made big round innocent eyes and shook her head. 'It wasn't really lost, was it? I mean, it was there all the time, but I forgot about it.'

'I am a bit cross, actually, Daisy. It is something special of mine, and it's to do with Aunt Agnes who's died. You shouldn't have taken it in the first place and you should certainly have given it back or said you'd had it.'

'I knew you'd be cross, that's why I didn't want to tell you when I couldn't find it,' Daisy wailed, and Kate sighed heavily. She wasn't really cross, just glad to have the locket back, especially now that she knew its origin – Harry had given it to Agnes. But why had it been torn in half? Suddenly she longed to stay at home and read the diary and find out, but she couldn't disappoint the children. She felt so sorry for them at the moment. They hadn't taken in what Simon's absence actually meant. She supposed they would when she delivered them to their father in London, whenever that might be. She hadn't heard anything since receiving his solicitor's letter – probably he was too scared to ring. And he was right to feel scared; she was furious with him.

It wasn't until after ten that she hauled herself shivering out of the bath, where she'd lain thinking about Simon until the water had gone cold, and retired to bed to read.

She was weary with grief, aching after the long day of shifting boxes and books. Her nose was blocked from the dust, while her head still jangled from the Harry Potter film with its whooshing magic brooms and nightmare encounters with celluloid evil spirits. But when the diary fell open halfway at a crumpled page and she read the first words scrawled there, she forgot everything else.

*I can hardly bear to consign my thoughts to paper,* Agnes had written. *The black ink on the white page is solid, undeniable. It makes what has happened to me real . . .*

Kate turned back to the first page and began to read.

*April 1929*

Agnes waited in the front seat of the Bentley as Lister lifted their cases out of the boot and Jane Selcott struggled to unlock the door to Seddington House. Apart from the soft light burning over the porch, it was pitch black on this moonless night, and cloud cover denied even the pale comfort of stars. Never before, thought Agnes, had home seemed so unfamiliar, so unwelcoming. She winced and clasped a hand to her swollen abdomen as the child within gave a sudden squirm, scraping against her spine. Even Mrs Duncan had gone home for the night; the house had been shut up for most of the last six months, and the cook was living in semi-retirement with her ailing maiden sister in the village.

Lister took the cases inside and Miss Selcott came back to the car to help Agnes out. The governess tried to take the girl's arm going up the few steps to the house, but Agnes shook her off and, one hand pulling her coat round her against the chilly night breeze, she staggered up by herself.

Lister refused to meet her eye as she stepped into the hall, as he had ever since meeting them off the last train just now, but his offer of hot milk was civil, though equally civilly refused.

'I'll go straight up to bed,' said Agnes. 'Bring my case up, please.' She was exhausted by the journey, by the advanced stage of her pregnancy. Moreover, she felt queasy and on edge – her skin crawled.

Halfway up the stairs she sank against the banister as another wave of tightness curled its way across her abdomen. It passed, leaving her breathless. Aware of the two servants watching her below, she recovered herself quickly and dragged herself up the remaining flight.

Later, alone in her room, she threw off her travel-stained clothes, pulled a nightdress over her head and slipped into bed where she lay on her side, grateful to be sinking into the coolness, alone with her thoughts at last.

The train journey with Miss Selcott had been an unpleasant interlude. Agnes's father had been supposed to accompany them, but at the last moment some business crisis had presented itself, and Gerald had said he must stay; he would follow them down to Seddington as soon as he could.

Miss Selcott had ordered the station porter to find them an empty compartment – no great task at this time in the evening – and as the train jolted and swayed its way down to Suffolk, Agnes bracing herself against each movement, the governess had pulled down the blinds and addressed her captive audience in a non-stop monologue.

'Your father is so brave. I don't know how he's survived everything you and your brother have done to him. To say nothing of that good-for-nothing wife of his. After the terrible sufferings he had already been through, poor man, all he's done for his children, just for you to throw it back in his face. And so shaming. I don't know where he's found the strength to raise his head in all this disgraceful, sordid affair.' She opened her bag and, drawing out a handkerchief, dabbed at the corners of her eyes before replacing it in her bag and closing it with a disapproving click. 'The sooner we get you down to that nursing home and finish your sorry part in the business, Miss, the better, if you ask me.'

As if anybody did ask you, you shrivelled old cow, thought Agnes, but she couldn't be bothered to say it. Since she had been forced by her father to spend so much time in Miss Selcott's chaperonage over the last few months she'd learned that the only way she could survive it was by ignoring the tiresome woman. So now she said nothing, instead snapping open the window blind and wiping the condensation from the window so she could peer out on the dark countryside flashing past. If only she could shut out the preaching voice.

Now, as she lay in the familiar darkness of her bedroom, memories of the last nine months crowded in.

It had been on a warm afternoon in the middle of August that Agnes had pulled shut the door of Harry's apartment and started down the stairs. When she reached the first landing, the door there opened and the woman, Susan Herbert, holding a fat rasping pug dog, came out and leaned against the lintel.

'Hello,' said Agnes uncertainly, as the woman looked her up and down, coolly. The dog struggled in her arms, so she let it down and it waddled back into the flat.

'I expect it doesn't like the heat,' Agnes said.

Mrs Herbert ignored her comment and said instead, 'Who are you?'

'Agnes Melton,' said Agnes, a little taken aback by the woman's rudeness.

Mrs Herbert thought for a moment and shook her head. 'No, I don't know any Meltons,' she said. Then, 'Where are you from?'

Agnes started to explain, but the woman cut her short, saying, as if to herself, 'Just as I thought.' To Agnes she said – was that a glint of sympathy in her eyes or was the woman just toying with her, 'You're very young, aren't you? What can your mother be thinking of? It's a shame someone doesn't take you in hand.' She looked up the staircase and listened a moment, whilst Agnes tried to frame a response. Then she looked directly at Agnes and said, cruelly, 'He's told you he's married, hasn't he?'

There was a silence. Agnes felt the blood suddenly pound in her veins. She opened her mouth but no sound came.

'No, I can see he hasn't. Wretched man. Yes, married. Of course, they're separated, but she won't be able to divorce him. There's no hope of that. They're Roman Catholics. The families would be appalled.'

Agnes still couldn't bring herself to speak. It couldn't be true. Susan Herbert was playing with her.

'You're lying,' she whispered. 'You're just jealous. You're lying.'

A look halfway between contempt and pity crossed the other woman's face. 'Well, you would think that, wouldn't you?' she said. 'Poor thing. I'm sorry for you. But men are all the same, you see. Pity you've had to learn the hard way.'

And with that, she went inside her flat and closed the door.

Slowly, dazed, Agnes made her way downstairs and out of the street door, out into the sunshine. For a long time – she didn't know how long – she walked, past lines of white terraces, through the gardens of the squares, now fading in the late-summer heat, wondering how complete joy could turn to utter desolation in one cruel stroke. Finally, she sat down on a bench in a garden where children played in the care of gossiping nannies, and cried.

After the storm came calm and false hope's false dawn. She would go back and see Harry, ask him if what that horrible woman said was true. Perhaps it wasn't. Harry loved her, she believed that as strongly as ever. Surely he would have told her something as important as that – that he was married, that he could never marry Agnes. Or perhaps there was something they could do?

And so she retraced her footsteps.

But there was no answer this time when she rang Harry's bell, and after waiting for a moment, she thought she saw a shadow at a window in the first-floor flat and a curtain fluttered, so she slipped away.

When Jeanette let her into the flat in Queen's Square, the mantel clock was chiming six and no one was home. This, however, was par for the course these days. Agnes had hardly seen Raven since his angry departure nearly six weeks before, but she knew Vanessa saw him regularly – she was too absorbed in her own affair to realise how regularly. Her stepmother assured her that Raven was happy. He had found a place at his friend Tom's newspaper, part devilling in the office, part writing pieces on routine matters that the regular journalists were too busy or too bored to cover. He was staying with a wealthy artist friend. Once or twice he and Agnes had met, but always in busy cafés or at crowded parties, and they had avoided the subject of Raven's quarrel with their father. Raven seemed to have changed; he was caught up with his work, his writing, his new friends. He hardly saw Freddy any more, he said. Their paths had just diverged. Agnes thought sadly that she, too, had been left behind in his slipstream.

Jeanette saw at once that Agnes was distraught. She sat her

down in the empty drawing room and went to make her some tea.

'Madame Melton, she waited for you but then she must go out,' the maid explained. 'She is worried, very worried. You must telephone her *chez son amie* Madame Marshall now to say you are safe.'

Agnes's father hadn't returned from work when Agnes went to bed that night after an early supper. She lay all night, it seemed, tossing and turning until by the morning she was running a temperature.

Her father woke her, bursting into her room at nine o'clock. He had received a letter in the morning's post from a Mrs Susan Herbert making certain allegations about his daughter's morals. Did Agnes realize what she had done?

It was a week before Agnes, confined to the flat by her father, received a letter from Harry brought in by Jeanette who clearly thought that Agnes's *affaire de coeur* was the most exciting and romantic thing to have happened for a long while. Although she was too careful of her job to assist the star-cross'd lovers to actually meet, she was happy to deliver this letter.

It confirmed the findings that Agnes's father had already revealed to her. Harry confessed that he had married the youngest daughter of a neighbouring Catholic family in Cambridgeshire five years before. He had met Laura at a hunt ball and fallen for her quiet dark beauty, her air of mystery. But after the marriage he had realized there was something damaged about her. Her mystery veiled not dark passions beneath, but a heart that was locked up. She could not seem to give of herself, and a man as passionate and creative as him desperately needed a soulmate to whom he could open up. He had been deeply unhappy.

There was no chance of a divorce. Laura had already borne Harry a child – a daughter – and both families had closed ranks around mother and child. The whole matter was never to be mentioned outside the family. But Harry was in disgrace.

*I can never forgive myself for becoming involved with you, my love, because I have hurt you so much, yet I cannot regret our love,* Harry wrote. *You are so natural, so impulsive and your love for me shone out of your eyes. I could not but respond in full. I adore you. You are the other half of my soul. I will always love you. I am not a whole person without you. But your father has made it plain to me that I should not see you and, thanks to La Herbert, my family threaten to ruin me if I bring further scandal by trying to force an end to my marriage. Shame, trouble and poverty are all I am ever able to offer you. Next to these the shining joy of my love would surely tarnish, corrode, grow worthless.*

If Agnes had received this letter only a week before, she would have been demented with grief, but by now, some steel had entered her soul. She knew Harry was right. She could not breach her ties with family, she could not endure public humiliation. Nor would she bring down misery upon Harry himself. She was only seventeen, she had no mother to show her how to behave and she was lost.

She took off the locket that she always wore and opened it. A photograph of herself in the front half now faced the little portrait of Harry. She held one half in each hand and, closing her eyes against the tears, twisted the two halves until the hinge gave way. The half with her picture she wrapped in a little silk square. Then she took some paper and wrote the following:

*I believe that you love me, truly, fully, and for us that must be enough. When you look on this locket, may you dream of me. When I look on your picture, may I dream of you. May God go with you always.*

Then she placed the silk package and the note in an envelope for Jeanette to deliver.

Two weeks later, Agnes began to suffer from bouts of nausea. After she fainted in the street, Gerald called a doctor. The baby was due in May.

Agnes must have slept, because the next thing she knew, an iron hand was squeezing her abdomen. As the pain receded, she heard the clock in the hall chime two. She manoeuvred herself in the bed until she could turn on the light and there came a hot rush of liquid between her legs. The next contraction gripped her and she gasped in pain. When she lifted the blankets she screamed. Her nightgown and sheets were soaked with blood and water.

A door across the corridor opened. Miss Selcott came into the room, her hair bundled up in a ridiculous nightcap. She was still tying her voluminous dressing-gown. Taking in what was happening, she rushed over to the bed and grabbed the corner of the blankets from Agnes, who gasped again as the next contraction took hold.

'You've started then?' Miss Selcott said briskly, glimpsing the soaked sheets. 'I'd better get some more linen.'

'It's early,' whispered Agnes in terror. 'Surely it shouldn't come for another month.'

'We'll just have to manage. We'll wait till morning, then I'll send Lister for the doctor.'

'Get the doctor now!' Agnes pleaded and panted through another wave of pain. The contractions were growing in strength and frequency, but she was learning to breathe through them.

'It's too soon for the doctor, girl! First babies always take a long time. That's what my mother said. Two days she was in labour with me. All the doctor will do is take one look at you and go away again.'

'I want a doctor. Or somebody! Not you!' Agnes cried out.

'I'll go and find Lister,' sighed Miss Selcott. 'But you can't expect it not to hurt. You should have thought of that before you went to the bad, Miss.'

'Just bring the doctor!' And Miss Selcott vanished.

And so Agnes entered a place filled with pain where time had no meaning. As the hours passed and the room gradually lightened, she fell into a half-doze from which each contraction wrenched her. Her half-waking dreams were filled with ghoulish figures – Gerald, Raven, Harry, Vanessa – all shouting at her and wailing.

She hadn't seen Raven and Vanessa since September, not since that terrible day when Gerald arrived home unexpectedly early on Jeanette's afternoon off to discover his wife and his son entwined in the marital bed, all unaware that Agnes, too, was asleep in her own room.

Agnes was wrenched out of sleep by shouting and screaming, then the slamming of doors. Then a low exchange of angry words as Vanessa and Gerald dealt one another the verbal blows that spelled the death of their marriage.

Gerald was inconsolable. He would hardly speak to Agnes, but spent long hours at the office, even sleeping there. After a fortnight, during which Vanessa sent a motor van round to collect her possessions, sorted and packed into boxes by the weeping Jeanette, Gerald summoned Miss Selcott from Seddington Rectory. Her instructions were simple: to be Agnes's constant companion, her chaperone and her carer. She was to make arrangements for Agnes's confinement in Suffolk and, in due course, for the adoption of the baby. Above all, nobody in Suffolk – none of the neighbours – and as few people as possible in London, were to learn of this terrible further disgrace that had struck the Melton family. Enough people were gossiping about Raven and Vanessa. Somehow, Agnes must be saved from shameful public humiliation.

Agnes, stunned by the hard reality of Vanessa and Raven's betrayal, which she had been up to then too naive to see clearly, and by the sight of her father once more brought to his knees by grief, felt only compassion for Gerald. She meekly complied. She would live a quiet, sequestered life, she would put up with the ministrations of Miss Selcott. The one thing she would not do was part with the baby.

'I will not let you give it away,' she sobbed at him. 'I love its father and I can't let the baby go. I will bring it up quietly, find somewhere away from you if that is what you want.'

'You couldn't look after yourself and a baby all alone,' he said gently. 'And, Agnes, what chance do you think you would have of a life of your own, with a child with no name? What man would look at you twice? And think of the child – it would be vilified. You must allow the baby to be adopted, my love, it is yours and his only chance for future happiness.'

'It will not be given away,' she said stubbornly.

Her father studied her gravely. 'Think about what I have said to you, my dear,' he said. 'I will not do anything without your consent, but I beg you to give me that consent.'

As the birth approached, Agnes believed more and more strongly that she must keep this child of her love. No matter what kind of life she might have to lead, she would find a way to mother this baby.

Gerald rented a cottage in Hertfordshire, and she and Miss Selcott lived there quietly. Miss Selcott had made arrangements with a small hospital on the Suffolk coast to admit Agnes when the time drew near for the baby to be born, and it was with a view to travelling on there that they were to stay at Seddington House for a few days over the Easter holiday. Now, of course, all their plans were thrown into confusion by the baby's early arrival.

As the morning sun strengthened, there was still no sign of the doctor. 'Lister's gone out now to see if he can find him,' said Miss Selcott vaguely.

Agnes felt a change shudder through her body, as if she were being sucked into a vortex, then a terrible, burning pain as the baby began to push down inside her. She gasped and grunted, kicking off the tangle of hot, restricting bedclothes that Miss Selcott had modestly replaced each time Agnes had freed herself of them.

Miss Selcott rose from her chair, clutching her handkerchief uselessly, then, forgetting delicacy, cried out as she saw that the baby was coming. She caught it as it slithered out and Agnes fell back on the bed, exhausted.

Agnes was to go over and over this birth as the days, weeks, months and years elapsed, and each time, the certainty became rooted in her more strongly that, throughout the whole event, Miss Selcott's behaviour had been strangely furtive. And now that the baby was born, Miss Selcott must have busied herself cutting the cord and wrapping the child in a towel. It didn't cry, and the governess immediately left the room with her bundle.

Briefly occupied as she was with the further contractions that racked her body, and the shocking liver-like placenta that slipped out from between her thighs, part of Agnes's mind was crying out for the baby. Where had Miss Selcott taken her child?

She called out, but could do nothing but lie there and wait for the strength to return to her limbs.

A few minutes later, Miss Selcott opened the door quietly and came and stood by the bed. Her face was grave.

'How are you now, Agnes?' she asked.

'I'd like to see my baby,' Agnes said, ignoring the question.

'I'm afraid I have bad news for you, dear. The little boy did not survive. I am sorry.'

'I don't believe you.'

'It's true, my dear. It must be terrible to take in. The child is dead. I have given him to Lister who will make the necessary arrangements.'

'I must see him.'

'No. It's not right. It will just upset you more.'

'I must see him!'

'You cannot. Lister has already taken him away. And he will bring the doctor. We are told the doctor was busy all night. There were more deserving mothers who needed his help you know.'

Agnes tried to pull herself up. 'I don't believe you. I don't believe any of this. You've taken him, haven't you? You've taken him.' Her voice rose to a scream. 'I want my baby!

'It's a dreadful thing to have happened, but you will come to see that it's for the best,' the woman told the hysterically weeping girl. 'You'd have had a wretched life bringing up a child of shame, and you're a selfish, stubborn girl refusing to let a married couple give it a respectable home. Just think, every time your father saw the boy it would have been a reminder of your wickedness. With the child dead there's a chance now that some kind man might marry you, and you'll have more children – but in the right way this time. God has been kind.' Miss Selcott's eyes almost glittered as she delivered this sanctimonious speech and she leaned in towards Agnes so the girl had to brush the spittle from her face.

'*Give me my baby!*' Agnes screamed.

*

381

The scream Kate heard was her own, as she was wrenched out of sleep in Paradise Cottage, the perspiration pouring down her face, her heart thudding in terror. Something was lost. A baby. Her babies. Sam. Daisy. She threw back the duvet and was halfway across the room before she recognized the familiar shape of the chest of drawers, the homely smell of pine and polish, and realized that she and her children were safe in Paradise Cottage. Pulling open the door, she padded out across the landing and into their room. They were both deeply asleep. Kate stroked a strand of hair from Daisy's forehead and straightened Sam's pillow, dropping a gentle kiss on his downy cheek before returning to her own bed.

She was too alert now to sleep. She lay waiting for the terror of her dream to dispel, and thought of Agnes and everything she had gone through. After a minute, she turned on the light and started to leaf through the diary once more.

The earlier entries covered the traumatic events of August and September 1928. Agnes had charted the progress of her affair with Harry and its break-up, then, in several long entries, the discovery and aftermath of Raven and Vanessa's betrayal. She had been furious at herself for not recognizing what was going on under her nose. Perhaps she could have done something . . . ? The entries for the months leading up to her giving birth were a testimony to Jane Selcott's petty power games, the loyal governess's warped determination to restore peace and respectability to the Melton family, or what was left of it.

Then, between the last four weeks of her pregnancy and the following May, Agnes had laid down her pen.

The account of the birth of her baby, which she set down in one single entry, was therefore informed by the advantage of hindsight and overlaid by a cold hatred of Jane Selcott. Two things further Kate learned. One was that in the days after the birth Agnes came to realize that her half of the locket was missing. The other was that the day before Agnes sat down to write the account of the birth and disappearance of her child, Gerald Melton had had enough. Jane Selcott had been asked to leave at once.

*He can bear no more of her fawning, her petty rages, her tyrannical behaviour towards the other servants. Mrs Duncan, whom Father had persuaded to return to cook for us, has threatened to leave once more and Father has chosen between them. And now Diana tells me the old witch has quitted her parents' house with rent unpaid. She has left no forwarding address and carries no reference. And good riddance. May God preserve all other children from her ministrations.*

Kate closed the diary and lay back on the pillows, gazing at the whorls of plaster on the ceiling. Outside an owl hooted. So Agnes must have lain in Seddington House over seventy years before, having consigned her passion to the page, feeling her life was over before it had properly begun.

'I'll try and find what happened to him, Agnes, I promise,' Kate whispered, turning out the light.

*If you don't lose the house to Simon or even to Max if he sues*, said the little voice in her head. *Or you could lose it to Agnes's son or grandchildren, if you find them. They, too, might sue for the family home.*

Yes, that was a risk. But Seddington House was partly important to her because of what Agnes meant to her, and the young woman's terrible grief at the loss of her only child was key to understanding Agnes. Kate had promised her to look for him, and she would not betray that promise.

But if the baby *had* survived, what on earth had happened to him? And what an appalling, wicked thing for Miss Selcott to have done! Kate supposed the woman to have been deranged. Her actions had apparently been motivated by her desire to protect Gerald from further shame. Presumably she expected his gratitude and possibly a financial reward for spiriting away his illegitimate grandson.

There were so many unanswered questions! First, it seemed that Lister must have been involved in the deception. Then, surely, if a doctor had examined Agnes he would have wanted to know what had happened to the child. If told it had died, he would have needed to see it in order to issue a certificate giving the cause of death. And Agnes would surely have protested to Gerald about the loss of her baby. Someone *must* know what had happened to that little newborn baby! Kate shuddered at the thought of having Sam or Daisy taken from her at birth like that. How had poor Agnes endured it?

But now Kate had learned the full secret of Agnes's past. Who knew, but perhaps in death Agnes had been reunited with Harry, the lover she could not have and hold in life. *All shall be well and all manner of thing shall be well.* And Kate sent up a prayer that this should be so.

# Chapter 33

The following day Kate was due at Seddington House at ten o'clock, but the children slept late. Kate dropped Daisy off at Debbie's easily enough. The trouble came with Sam. The little boy was due to play at Sebastian's house, but he hadn't been there before, and when Kate pulled up outside their thatched farmhouse, he refused to get out of the car.

'I don't want to go,' he whined from his slumped position in the back seat.

Kate sighed. Sam had been very quiet this morning but she had hoped he was just tired. She got out and opened the back door. Sam merely rolled over and buried his face in the seat, so she lowered herself down next to him and gave him an awkward hug.

'Would you rather come with me, then?' she asked. 'It won't be very interesting, darling. I have to be looking at pictures and papers at Aunt Agnes's.'

Sam stiffened, then lifted his head. 'Don't want you. Want Daddy,' he said, and rolled back into the seat. But he turned his face in time to watch his mother's rictus of pain.

Fortunately, Sebastian's face appeared at the other door. He was holding a large white cat. Sam sat up, suddenly alert.

'This is Rosie,' Sebastian said to him through the open window. 'And Mummy says we can go on the computer. Are you coming?'

All troubles forgotten, Sam shoved the door open and, without looking back at his mother, rushed off towards the farmhouse after Sebastian and Rosie. Kate felt guilty at the force of her feeling of relief.

She didn't arrive at Seddington House until eleven. The same team was there as the day before, with the addition of an expert in eighteenth-century genre painting. Max had some business to catch up with in Norwich but Dan had arrived to help sort some of the material stashed in bedrooms and attics, and it wasn't long before Kate was able to talk to him alone. They were standing in one of the attic rooms.

'I wanted to ask your advice, you see,' she said, having pieced together for him the story she had gleaned from the diaries. 'And I'd love you to read them sometime. It might be that you would recognize some of the names from the village or suggest how I can follow up matters locally. What happened to the family of Agnes's friend Diana, for instance, who the governess lodged with after Gerald's marriage to Vanessa? They should be easy to trace since Diana's father was rector.'

'His name and dates will be up on the board in the church, won't they? There might even be a family grave if they died in the parish. You could start there, at least.' He thought for a moment. 'And it should be possible to get the name of the local doctor then. There's a little museum at Halesworth station. They might have a sort of archive. Or ask the council.'

'What about Lister the butler and the cook, Mrs Duncan. Are they names you recognize?'

Dan shook his head. 'No. Mind you, you don't know what else you'll find in this house,' he said.

386

'I am sure that Agnes herself would have made all the same enquiries, many years ago, and over and over again.' Kate felt discouraged.

'Come on, I'd better get this lot out and blow the dust off it.' Dan nodded at a stack of framed pictures leaning against an old sofa in the attic where they stood. Kate helped him take them downstairs to be tagged and catalogued. The valuer decided to take several away with him for further scrutiny.

Upstairs, fishing a last shabby print out from behind the sofa, Dan's hand brushed against something underneath and he pulled out a photograph. He glanced at it and passed it to Kate. She found herself looking at a family portrait – an Edwardian gentleman and his wife, two very young children, one only a baby, all solemnly staring back at her.

'Do you think the baby could be Agnes?' she asked Dan, passing it back to him.

He squinted at it. 'Could be. It would be the right period, wouldn't it?'

'And the boy does have very dark hair and the look of Raven. You know, this could be the attic where Agnes had her den,' she said. 'There might be something else of interest here.' At the back of her mind was the vain hope that the missing half of the locket might emerge, but Agnes herself must have looked everywhere over the years. Now, the search revealed nothing, except an old copy of Keats's complete poems that had lost its cover.

Kate perched on the seat of the dusty old sofa, flicking through the book reading out some of the heavily underlined passages.

*'Into her dream he melted, as the rose*
*Blendeth its odour with the violet, –*

> Solution sweet: meantime the frost-wind blows
> Like Love's alarum pattering the sharp sleet
> Against the window-panes: St Agnes' moon hath set.'

Dan listened, then sank down onto the cushion next to her as she slowly shut the book. After a moment he reached out and touched her arm. 'You look sad. How are you?'

She smiled at him. 'Numb,' she said. 'And I haven't heard from Simon for days. Sometimes I kid myself that it's just another ordinary week with him away again, but then I remember. And the kids miss him. They keep asking when he's coming home, even though they've been used to him being away.'

He nodded.

She sighed, pulling her fingers through her hair. 'Yeuch,' she said, finding it lank with grime. 'I don't know why everything here's gone so wrong,' she said gloomily.

'You mean Simon?'

'Simon and the school and Agnes dying, then it looks as if I might lose the house, if Simon has his way. This process will probably go on for ever, won't it? Listing the contents, sorting out probate, the stress of waiting to see who actually gets the place.'

'It will all work itself out in time.'

'This move to Suffolk was so important to me, Dan, don't you see? Everything was going to be wonderful. A beautiful house, my own home. Simon and I watching our family grow up in a lovely place away from the rat race. Creating the love and security I never had when I was little. But nothing seems worth it now without Simon. Even this place.'

'Houses are just bricks and mortar without the people you love, aren't they?' Dan said quietly. 'Even one as lovely as this.'

'Everything was going to be so perfect,' she said, almost to herself.

'But life never is perfect, Kate. I don't think humans have the ability to stand perfection anyway. We smash it up somehow.'

Once again, Kate's eyes swam with tears.

Dan snaked an arm around her shoulders and squeezed her gently. She felt herself moving towards him, burying her face in his torn Oxford shirt. He smelled of dust and polish and something faintly musky. After a moment, he raised her face towards his and smiled sleepily at her in a way that made her blood thud in her veins. Then he leaned forward slowly and planted a kiss on her mouth. She closed her eyes. He kissed her again, this time the tip of his tongue probing its way along her teeth. Her body was turning to liquid, electricity pulsed through her.

And then, suddenly, she came to her senses. What was she doing? Exactly what Simon had done.

Dan, sensing the life go out of her, dropped his hands and moved away. 'I'm sorry,' he said hoarsely, unable to meet her eyes.

'It's too soon,' she said miserably. 'I can't.'

Dan stood up, then came to crouch in front of her. His face was shining, tender. 'I've wanted to do that for so long,' he whispered. 'Forgive me, I thought you wanted it, too.'

Kate looked up at him. 'I don't know what I want at the moment, Dan. Everything's stirred up, raw.'

'You're very special to me, Kate. Well, I hope there might be a time when both of us . . .' He stopped and gestured uselessly, then stood up, ducked through the doorway and was gone. She heard his footsteps crashing down the staircase.

*Come back,* she wanted to shout, but the words wouldn't form in her mouth. She picked up the photograph from the arm of the sofa and gazed at little Agnes, happy and secure on her mother's knee.

*

389

That afternoon, Kate sat drinking tea in Debbie's kitchen whilst the children played in the garden. She hadn't told Debbie about Dan. That was a secret she had been thinking about since he kissed her, re-enacting it in her mind for the twentieth time. Despite her guilt, the part of her that craved physical comfort and security had welcomed his passion like manna in the desert. Sternly, she told herself to think of something else; she couldn't unravel her marriage that quickly. And it was madness to fall into the arms of the first man who came along after Simon.

'Everything seems a mess,' she muttered as she picked at a toffee muffin. 'I don't know what to try and tackle first.'

'You've got a huge amount to deal with, that's for sure,' Debbie agreed, 'but things will sort themselves out. It's a journey to another stage of life. There are relationships to be reforged and practical arrangements to be made, but you can do it. Just don't expect everything to happen right away.'

'I've been thinking about something Dan said earlier. It was about a house not being a home if the people you love aren't there. Seddington House *is* lovely and it *was* my dream house, but now that Simon has gone, I feel I shouldn't fight for it so hard. If it's meant to be mine it'll come to me, but if Simon or Max or this mysterious child of Agnes's should take it away from me, then that's got to be all right, too. We'll survive, we'll be happy again. Home will be with the people I love. That's with Sam and Daisy at the moment – I've got to get used to the fact that it won't be with Simon.'

Debbie nodded. 'Jonny and I were broke when we met. We rented a flat in London that was on a big junction. Bus passengers could look in through the grime on our windows as they swung round the corner inches away. But we were so happy there.'

Kate laughed wistfully, then said: 'I've got to start thinking about getting a job, too. Any ideas?'

'Plenty, actually. But do you have to yet? You're not broke, are you?'

'Jasmin's trying to sort that out. Both our names are on the bank account holding the money from the London house, thank goodness, but I'll need something regular from Simon soon or the children will be going back to school without shoes!'

'But I don't understand why you can't come down here and talk about it . . .'

That evening, Joyce was on the telephone to Simon in the kitchen. The door with its dicky latch had swung ajar, and the words drifted up to Kate, stopping her dead on the landing between the children's bedroom where Daisy was changing into her pyjamas and the bathroom where Sam gurgled like a sea monster in the bath, catching plastic farm animals in his mouth.

Kate knew she shouldn't listen, but the horrific fascination of hearing her husband and her mother-in-law discussing their marriage was too much to resist. She stood slowly turning Sam's pyjamas inside out, a frown on her face.

'You're throwing it all away, Simon. You'll live to regret it – yes, you will. Poor little Kate. How can you do this to her?'

Kate closed her eyes as a bolt of fury shot through her. Did Joyce really think this approach was going to work with Simon? Downstairs, the woman must have been aware that her voice was carrying, because the kitchen door closed again.

This was an impossible situation. Since her return from Italy two days before, and learning about Simon's demands, Joyce had been beside herself with shock and frustration. 'It's wrong, it's so wrong, I don't know why he's doing it,' she sobbed to a grim Kate one moment, the next she would be on the phone wheedling her son to think again about his actions, Kate listening in, mortified.

This evening, however, she could take it no longer.

'Joyce,' she said hesitantly, as they cleared up in the kitchen later on, 'when I say this, I don't mean that you shouldn't be talking to Simon, but please, please, don't try and act as go-between. It won't work and it's possibly making things worse. It's a particularly sensitive matter at the moment because of the legal situation.'

Joyce dabbed absent-mindedly at a stain on the pine table and looked up, her face etched with misery. 'I have to support my son. I can't just say nothing.'

'You'll be supporting him more if you don't tell him what to do or give away details about how I'm managing. I'm sorry, I know it's awful for you. I've been thinking. It's high time we moved out, found somewhere nearby.' If she could just work out the money situation with Simon.

'No,' Joyce said firmly. 'I thought you might say that and I don't want you to. I want to help you, you and my grandchildren. Please don't go.'

Kate studied Joyce's face and was shocked to realize how she had aged over the last few weeks. Under the slight tan from the cruise she was pale; her eyes were red and rheumy, with great dark shadows underneath. Her usually upright figure seemed slightly stooped. Kate reached across and hugged her.

'This is as miserable for you as it is for us, isn't it?'

'I think,' Joyce said, hugging Kate in return, 'that you're being incredibly brave, dear. If only Simon would act in a more civilized fashion.'

After that conversation, Joyce came gradually to accept that Kate and Simon should sort out their own affairs and that her role must be restricted to providing practical help and support. But there was one more damaged relationship that was on Kate's mind.

After her encounter with Dan in the attic of Seddington House, Kate avoided being alone with him. She didn't trust herself in her present confusion, and she feared hurting him. But she couldn't help thinking about him often; indeed, on many lonely nights now, she lay and imagined what it would be like to make love with him. However, when they *did* meet at Seddington House, amongst the Farrell's staff, or with Max or Conrad, their conversation was stilted. Was it her fault, or had Dan at some level withdrawn from her? That thought made her angry. Had Dan only been interested in her in that way, and not in her friendship?

Ten days passed and she could endure the stand-off no longer. Plus she needed to ask Dan some more questions about Agnes, so on the Monday morning, armed with the diaries, Kate plucked up courage and walked into the Waveney Gallery in the High Street to find him. It would be best, she thought, to see him on neutral ground. Part of her wondered guiltily whether Max should have seen the diaries first, but she brushed that thought aside.

Dan was on the phone, but smiled and mouthed at her to wait, so she spent five minutes walking around and gazing at the paintings. Dan's portrait of Linda and Shelley graced one wall, Kate noticed, and when she peered at the label, she realized with a little stab of satisfaction that he had chosen the title she had eventually suggested – *One Morning at the Beginning of the World*. It was so apt, she thought again now, studying the sharp purity of the silver light. He had portrayed a state of innocence seen through the eyes of love. But all that was sullied now. Dan and Linda had parted acrimoniously and Shelley, by all accounts, was a very sad and confused little girl.

When Dan put down the phone and came and stood beside Kate, she told him again how much she loved the painting and asked him how Shelley was now.

'I've seen her a few times. Linda's mum brings her over, and I've taken her out to the beach once, but Linda's edgy about it. She came round yesterday and took the rest of her stuff. Hardly spoke to me. She's got a new boyfriend, but I'm told he doesn't like kids much. It's a shame – poor little Shelley. I'll be there for her as much as I can. I can't be her dad, but why should she suffer because Linda can't sort her life out?'

Kate nodded, glad that he had decided to help the little girl, then, showing him the diaries she said, 'I'm sure you're busy now, but I wanted to give you these.'

Dan took them from her and opened the cover of the top volume. He stared at the title page as though weighing something up, then closed the book and looked at Kate.

'It's quiet today,' he said. 'Have you got a moment for coffee? Grant's round the back. He'll cover for me here.' When Kate nodded, Dan shouted to his partner in the office that he was going out and they wandered into a busy coffee shop several doors down and ordered cappuccinos.

Now that they were sitting down together, face to face, Kate felt self-conscious, so she showed Dan the order in which to read the diaries then asked him again if he knew anyone who might remember the old days.

'There is a neighbour of mine, lives three doors down,' he said. 'He's always telling me how his parents ran the village shop until after the war. I'll ask him if he'd have a chat with you, if you like.'

'That would be great. Thanks,' said Kate.

There was silence for a moment and then both of them started to talk at once. 'No, you go on,' said Kate.

'I'm sorry about the other day,' he said, stirring his coffee slowly.

'Don't be.' Kate reached out and rested her hand on his for a moment. 'It was . . . nice. No, that's a silly thing to say. It was wonderful. It's just the time's not right. And I can't promise it ever will be.'

Dan looked sad, but he nodded. 'Don't not see me though,' he said. 'I couldn't bear that. We've become good friends, haven't we?'

Kate couldn't stop herself breaking into a smile at that. After a moment, Dan smiled back. They sat there in silence smiling at one another, blind to everything going on around them.

When they parted, Dan said, 'I'm going away next week for a fortnight. Friend of mine has a place in Umbria. I'll give you these back,' he indicated the diaries, 'before then.' He kissed her quickly on the corner of the mouth and let her go. The time was wrong for them, but she still had to force herself to walk away.

# *Chapter 34*

*September 2004*

Agnes In the event, Sam and Daisy did go back to school in September with new shoes. They also began a new routine, for Jasmin was as good as her reputation. After several rounds of sassy bargaining, she sorted out regular payments to Kate and relegated Simon's demands for custody of the children to fortnightly weekends in London and Sunday visits to Suffolk, plus parts of the school holidays. In the meantime, Simon came down twice to Paradise Cottage to spend time with Sam and Daisy. Once Kate made sure she was away for the night, going to the theatre in London with Liz; the other occasion she went over to stay with her parents.

The first weekend of the new arrangement, Kate delivered Sam and Daisy to Simon on Liverpool Street station on a Friday evening. She had been dreading that Meredith would be there, although they had agreed that the children shouldn't meet his new partner yet, and was relieved when they walked out through the ticket barrier to see that Simon was alone. He looked tense, his face greyish and tired.

Sam dropped his little rucksack and ran to his daddy's arms.

Daisy, on the other hand, looked up at her mother as if asking permission.

'Go on,' whispered Kate, and took her time picking up the rucksack. When she straightened, it was to see the three of them regarding her anxiously, as if waiting for instructions.

'I'll meet you here three o'clock on Sunday,' she said to Simon, making no pretence at the nicety of saying hello. 'Sam's toothbrush is in the pocket here and he's only allowed one drink at bedtime.'

Simon took the rucksack, nodding briefly then saying humbly, 'Don't worry, I'll look after them.'

Jasmin was right, Kate reflected. The American lawyer had to have been Meredith's idea.

It took an immense effort of will for Kate to kiss her children goodbye and walk away. After a moment, she turned and looked back. They were weaving through the oncoming crowd towards the Underground, two diminutive figures so dear to her, the man between them holding their hands so familiar-looking it was painful to remind herself he belonged to her no longer. Then just before they reached the steps, Daisy half turned, saw her mother and waved. Kate relaxed. It was time to go.

She was travelling straight back home again. Next time she might stay in London with Liz for the weekend, but for now, after the long holidays, she wanted a couple of days for herself, not to be on the edge of another family's happy life.

The early-evening train was full of tired commuters and when she found her booked seat, a large florid-faced man was already in it, head back, eyes closed. She was just mustering the courage to nudge him and ask him to move, when someone said, 'Kate?'

She turned to see a man half rising from a nearby window seat. It was Max. He gestured to the empty seat beside him, so she went over.

'No one's turned up,' he said, peering at the white 'reserved' ticket on the top, so Kate abandoned the sleeping seat-stealer and joined him. Immediately, there was a judder and the train started to slide away from the platform.

'Not first class for you, then?' she teased as she took in his formal suit, conservative tie, the small silver laptop waiting open and ready.

'Not when it's a Legal Aid client,' he said good-humouredly as he closed the lid of the computer. 'What have you been doing up in Town then? No shopping bags?'

Reassuring herself that their fellow travellers opposite – a young man plugged into an iPod and an elderly lady absorbed in a Danielle Steel library book – were not listening in, Kate took a deep breath and dived into an edited version of her separation from Simon.

'I'm sorry. And it's hard for the children, too, I know,' Max said. 'Grace particularly – she was Daisy's age – blamed me for going away, as she put it. She was angry for weeks. And even now, Emily says "When you come home, Daddy . . ." It's heartbreaking.'

They moved on to the matter of Seddington House, where Farrell's had almost completed their job and expected to deliver a full report for probate in the next couple of weeks. In the meantime, Raj, together with Agnes's accountant, had trawled the old lady's finances with some input from Max. Kate had been happy to let them get on with it.

'Has Raj had any more responses to his advertisements?' Kate asked eagerly. Large announcements requesting any close relations of Miss Agnes Melton to apply to Horrocks & Spalding, solicitors, had appeared in the local papers and the legal newspaper, the *London Gazette* for the previous few weeks.

'I spoke to him yesterday. Only the usual round of tryers-on and loonies.' Max shook his head. 'Have you had any leads?'

Kate had told Max about finding the final volume of the diary, and now she explained how her recent enquiries had gone.

'Basically I've drawn a blank.' She shrugged. 'I really need to go up to London and search the birth and death certificates, but I haven't had a chance yet, and frankly, it'll be like looking for a needle in a haystack.'

She told Max how, by visiting the parish where Diana's husband had been vicar and then working through a local telephone directory, she had tracked down Diana's youngest daughter, Angela, who lived at Lowestoft. Now herself an elderly widow, Angela had nursed her mother until she died fifteen years before. She didn't know anything about Miss Selcott, just that her mother had mentioned being taught by a strict governess who had later lodged with them. And Angela knew Agnes, of course, though Diana hadn't seen much of her in later years. 'Mother always said Agnes had changed – became very depressed – and thought it was a love affair that had gone wrong. She felt very sorry for her.'

The current rector, Mike, had helped Kate look through the Seddington parish records. He was almost as intrigued by the mystery as Kate. The idea of the very correct elderly spinster he had known being a woman of mystery, with an illicit affair and a love-child in her past, both amused and touched him in equal measure. They had read through the baptisms for 1929 and copied out some names, but it was difficult to make judgements about what to do next. After all, you could hardly visit families still in the area and ask if there was any possibility that Grandad was born the wrong side of the blanket. Mike promised, however, that he would make some tactful enquiries amongst elderly parishioners he visited regularly. They were only mildly cheered by the fact that there had been no infant funerals during April.

'What would have happened to a stillborn baby? It would have died unbaptized. Weren't there rules about that?' Kate asked Mike suddenly, remembering there were sometimes complications about who could be buried in consecrated ground.

'Strictly speaking, there was no duty to bury them in the churchyard,' mused Mike. 'But it was usually left to the local clergyman, who would often be sympathetic to the bereaved family. If the mother had died, too, as in Evangeline's case, then mother and baby would be buried together. Sometimes I've heard of a dead newborn being slipped into the grave of an unconnected person being coincidentally buried at the time. The clergyman concerned might or might not have made a note of that in the records.' However, that clue, too, bore no fruit.

'I think what must have happened,' said Mike, closing the heavy leather volume of burial records, 'was as Agnes believed. Her baby was secretly given away for adoption to some local, unidentified couple. It might well be that he never had a birth certificate, let alone adoption papers. Children were still considered relatively less important in that period, and all too often, uncomfortable questions would not be asked. The matter might have been brushed under the carpet.'

'But what would have happened when the child grew up and applied for a passport, or when the Welfare State came into effect and everybody was given National Insurance numbers?'

'Today, yes, everything is regimented, but then, especially in the muddle after the war, when so many documents had been destroyed or gone missing, or people were displaced, I suppose officials just had to make strategic decisions. As for a passport, remember that foreign holidays are relatively new. Many people never needed to apply for one.'

Max had been listening intently to Kate's report. Now he

said, 'What about asking round the village yourself? Is there any famous old character who's a repository of local history?'

'I went to see a neighbour of Dan's who was born in Seddington in 1928. He's lived in the village all his life – don't you think that's amazing, these days? Anyway, he chattered on about everything as though it was yesterday. His parents ran a local greengrocery, which closed down when they retired in the early nineteen fifties. He remembers where Mrs Duncan, the Melton cook, lived with her sister, but they're long dead and neither of them had children, so that link's no good. And he said a Doctor Lymington used to come when his mother "took bad". The Lymingtons moved away, though. He doesn't know where. And the doctor would be dead now anyway. The only other point of interest is that he didn't remember Miss Selcott, though he delivered groceries for Diana's family and remembers them all right, but not a lodger. So Miss Selcott definitely can't have stayed on at the rectory. And that's it. I've run out of leads now, unless Mike comes up with something.'

'Sounds to me as though you've been as thorough as you can,' said Max. 'You've done your duty by Agnes, Kate. More than.'

Although Kate was aware that Max's legacy depended on them *not* tracing Agnes's heir, she said stubbornly, hoping he'd understand, 'I want to go further. I must find out what happened.'

'Why? And what good would it do? Suppose the person doesn't want to be found, anyway? Or doesn't even suspect that they were adopted? You might cause them terrible distress.'

Kate remembered the vivid nature of her dream, the young Agnes's pain – anguish she still felt deeply, seventy years later. Some wounds, like the loss of a child, never heal. Then Kate thought of her parents, still living a half life after nineteen years.

'Well I wouldn't want to force the knowledge on them, if they didn't want it,' she said carefully now. 'But there's the letter from Agnes – they might want to see that – and the money . . . I'm sorry, Max, I'm so stupid and tactless.'

'I'm not thinking of the money,' Max said coldly. 'Or rather, I'm *trying* not to think of the money. Since I honestly don't believe you're going to find Aunt Agnes's son, frankly I'm not very worried that I'll lose my part of the inheritance. I just think you sound a bit obsessed, that's all. Agnes is gone, Kate. You can't make yourself responsible for her unfinished business. You've done all you can reasonably do, why don't you leave it?'

'It's partly that I feel there is some wrong to be righted, Max. If you had read the diaries . . . Why don't you? I'll give them to you.' Suddenly, she felt it was time. Dan had brought the diaries back to Paradise Cottage before his holiday and left them with Joyce as Kate had been out. 'It's such a terribly sad story.'

'I would like to read them. Thank you,' he said. 'I want to learn about my grandfather, too, though I wish I could read what happened from his point of view.'

'And about your grandmother, Max,' Kate said softly. 'You'll need to understand what their love did to Agnes and her father. It ruined their lives. Love conquers all, indeed, but at what cost?'

They were silent for a moment, then Kate said, 'You've never told me much about your parents.'

'They're both dead now,' he said. 'My mother, Elizabeth, five years ago, my father two years before that. He was a professor of natural sciences at Cambridge and a bit older than my mother. When he was in his late sixties he developed Alzheimer's. He died in a nursing home eight years later.'

'That must have been awful.'

'He had been a brilliant man and it was shocking to see his decline. And we had always been a tight little unit. My mother was Raven and Vanessa's only child, and they had little contact with Vanessa's side of the family as well as Raven's. She had a lonely childhood, I would imagine.'

The train was slowing as it drew into Diss station. Max said, as he got up to help Kate with her coat, 'I'll come and pick up the diaries soon. Then when I've read them, perhaps you'd have dinner with me?'

His face behind his spectacles looked so earnest, so hopeful, Kate nearly laughed. Instead she kissed his cheek and replied solemnly, 'Of course. Give me a ring and we'll fix it.'

When she arrived home, a meeting of Joyce's book club was going on in the living room.

'You can come in and join us,' Joyce said in a stage whisper as she came into the hall to greet her.

'Thanks, but I'm exhausted,' sighed Kate. 'I'll have a bath and an early night.'

Joyce's face disappeared and Kate wearily trudged up the stairs. Talking to Max on the train had helped her forget that she'd just left her children to strange new experiences in a big city. She stopped at the half-open door of their bedroom and pushed it wide. The knowledge that Sam and Daisy weren't there, tucked up safe in their beds, couldn't stop the cloud of desolation descending and she took in the drawn-back curtains, the neatly made beds, the unnatural tidiness of the room. The rows of sightless eyes of the soft toys on Sam's bed glinted at her malevolently in the darkness. Don't be silly, she told herself, shutting the door. They're probably having the time of their life with their dad. She hurried into her own room, switched on all the lights and tuned the radio to Classic FM.

As she pottered about tidying up, her eye fell on her locket on the bedside table. She picked it up and a thought struck her.

Apart from the diaries, it was the only real clue she had to Agnes's past. This was obviously the half that Harry had been sent after they were forced to part. How had it ended up in that little shop in Norwich?

Kate mused over her plans for the weekend. The following morning, she intended to visit Seddington House to sort through some more papers. Later she would have supper with Debbie and Jonny. But, as it turned out, she would do neither of these things. The next day, while she was eating her breakfast, the telephone rang. Joyce answered it, and after a second, passed her the handset with an anxious look on her face.

'Your father,' she said.

# Chapter 35

Now she had negotiated the traffic past Ipswich and it was a straight run across to the M25, Kate at last allowed her thoughts to wander. The reason for her father's phone call had still hardly sunk in, and it had been a relief to concentrate instead on the endless twists, turns and roundabouts that had constituted the route so far.

'It's your mother, Kate.' Her father's voice had been quavery. An old man's voice. 'I'm at the hospital. It's happened again. The doctors don't know if she'll pull through this time.' And then, the simple cry of need, 'Please come.'

She had been in the car and on the road in fifteen minutes flat, leaving Joyce with a flurry of instructions.

Now, as she peered through the drizzle and swung into the outside lane to overtake a long straining line of trucks, she tried to remember her father's broken sentences. Barbara had been hoarding her anti-depressants, it seemed. When Kate had been down to see them a few weeks ago, she had been struck by her mother's low mood, but had connected it to the news that she had brought them – that she and Simon were separating.

Yet it was her father who had seemed to take it more to heart. Kate had been surprised.

'I can't help feeling that this is partly our fault,' he said to her sadly when she sat with him after breakfast in the morning, whilst Barbara was getting dressed upstairs. 'We've been so caught up in ourselves, in ... what happened.' He looked around, then, at the many faces of Nicola, smiling happily at them across the room. 'We haven't made enough time for you all.'

Kate had been left fighting for words. In the end, she said carefully, 'I'm still not sure what was at the root of Simon's drifting away. I think it's not the first time he's been unfaithful to me, but I can't see that that's remotely connected with anything you or Mum have done. In the end, he was not prepared to put me and the children first. Oh, it's all a great muddle at the moment, it doesn't make proper sense . . .' She drifted off and, feeling the tears prickle, leaned forward to pet Benjy who, himself bereft, had come to press himself in uncharacteristic friendliness against her leg.

Had it taken the breakdown of her marriage to start this sea-change in her relationship with her parents, or were other elements in play? Her father, now seventy, seemed suddenly less certain. As chinks appeared in his bluff exterior she could see how fragile it was, this brave face he presented to the world. This time, when she left, she hugged him and gently kissed her mother, and it wasn't an effort of will.

It was lunchtime before she reached the hospital, eventually found a parking space and followed instructions to the intensive care unit. A nurse took her into a room where her father sat gazing at his hands next to a bed in which a slight figure lay unconscious, an oxygen mask over her face, a drip feeding into one hand, her vital signs spelled out on several instruments on the further side of the bed.

'Kate!' Her father was suddenly animated, eager. He grabbed her hand and squeezed it. Then they stood together looking down at Barbara.

After a moment, Kate pulled up another chair and sat down by her father, once more taking his hand.

'What happened?' she said.

He sighed heavily. 'The doctor had been giving her something for the depression since the last time.' That was six months ago, Kate calculated. 'I counted out the pills for her every day. But sometimes she must have hidden them. Then, yesterday evening, when I was round at the Scotts' playing bridge, she must have taken them all. I found her when I got back. She was on the bed, but she'd been sick. That might be what saved her, the doctor says.

'Anyway, I called an ambulance and they brought her up here. When I rang you, they weren't sure if they were in time, but they say she's a bit stronger; she could be coming up for air soon.'

'Poor Mum. I – I hadn't realized she was that bad again.'

'She was going downhill over the summer. Kept saying she was very tired and there wasn't any point in anything. And . . . she felt with me, that we're somehow to blame for your marriage going wrong.'

'But you're not, Dad.'

'Yes, we are.' He shook his head sorrowfully. 'We've been old fools. We've not helped you enough.'

It was several hours before Barbara started to surface. She opened her eyes and there was such a look of anguish in them, Kate was glad when she closed them again. A quarter of an hour later, her eyelids flew open once more. This time she moved her head, as though irritated by the mask over her mouth. Later still, she gently squeezed her husband's hand as he whispered her

407

name and crooned words of comfort. Kate was intensely moved to see him lay his head on the pillow next to Barbara's and kiss her cheek and stroke her hair. After all these years, he was still devoted to her.

Kate pulled her chair up to the bed. 'Mum?' she whispered. 'It's me.' She watched in dismay as tears zigzagged their way across her mother's cheeks and she made little moaning sounds through her mask.

Major Carter's sister Maggie arrived late afternoon, summoned by phone soon after Kate arrived at the hospital. She arranged a large bouquet of scented lilies in a vase she had brought with her and ordered Kate to take Desmond home.

'He's been up all night and I bet he's hardly eaten.' It was true that Kate's father had barely touched the sandwiches Kate had bought him. He had just sat there in the café endlessly stirring his tea, looking around him in bewilderment. Kate was alarmed to see him so vulnerable, so alone.

'I'll stay here and make sure she's comfortable, Des, you mustn't worry,' his sister told him. 'I'll call if there's anything, I promise.'

They got home at eight for Kate to find there was little food in the house. 'I'd been going to go shopping today,' her father said tiredly as he sank onto the sofa.

'Well, never mind, there are eggs and some bits and pieces. I'll make an omelette.' Kate poured her father a couple of fingers of malt whisky and went off to cobble together a meal for them both, which she coaxed him to eat.

'Why don't you sit down while I clear up,' she said afterwards, 'then I'll bring you some coffee.' But when she came through into the living room, he wasn't there. She heard him moving about upstairs and went up after him.

She had hardly been into her parents' bedroom in this new house. When she knocked on the door and peeped in, it was to see her father sitting on the old walnut double bed that had followed them across continents, a small suitcase open beside him.

He smiled at Kate weakly. 'Just thought I'd pack her a few things,' he said. 'But I suddenly feel tired.'

'I'll help you,' she said, giving him his coffee. 'Tell me what to do.' And she went to drawers, bringing out a nightgown and underwear, spare slacks and a blouse, then through to the bathroom to collect some wash-things. When she returned, her father was riffling through the drawer of her mother's bedside table.

'This is where she kept the pills – look,' he said, indicating a few crushed tablets in the bottom of the drawer. 'And I just didn't notice.' He moved over to a little armchair and sat down, nursing his coffee in a morass of gloom.

Kate carefully pulled out the drawer and started sorting through the muddle of items, intending to clean away the powdery mess. Amongst the tangle of long bead necklaces, an eye bath, some plasters and some half-eaten packets of mints were a pottery hedgehog and an enamel brooch Kate had once made, two little boxes covered in velvet and some homemade cards. She placed the hedgehog on the bedside cabinet and opened one of the boxes. In it were what looked like small grey and white bits of gravel – she knew at once what they were as she had started her own collection with Daisy – a child's milk teeth. She opened the other box – another set. Shutting the lids, she turned each box over. Under one was a sticker on which was handwritten *Nicola*. Under the other, *Kate*.

The cards were tatty and handmade. They included a drawing of a Father Christmas from Nicola to Mummy and Daddy, and a Valentine's card saying, *Mummy, I love you from Kate xxx*, which Kate vaguely remembered having made when she was nine or ten. Hidden amongst the cards were several photographs. Three were of Kate: one as a toddler, then one of her aged ten, and the last one of her in a cerise party dress at fifteen; only one was of Nicola. Under everything else in the drawer were two little polythene sachets. Each contained a curl of dark hair.

Kate sat in a dream, absorbing the fact of these items. Her mother, who had always seemed so emotionally distant, had carefully kept Kate's baby teeth, a curl from her first haircut, had hoarded the precious cards, little presents Kate had given her, all these years. Her mother loved her.

Her hands started to tremble slightly as she went about replacing everything in the drawer. Then she became aware that her father was watching her intently.

'I – I didn't know Mum had kept all these,' she said shakily. 'I thought she threw them away, the things I made. That she didn't like them because they got crumbly and old, made a mess probably.'

Her father put down his coffee and leaned towards her.

'She might not have shown it very well, but she always treasured what you gave her.' He sighed. 'She wasn't always like this, you know,' he said gruffly. 'Sad, I mean. She was so full of life when I met her, always laughing. She loved dancing. It was at a dance that I first met her.' He fell silent, remembering.

'It was at Sandhurst, wasn't it?' Kate waited for him to go on.

He nodded. 'Yes. A schoolfriend invited me. He introduced me to Barbara. Oh, she was so beautiful. I couldn't take my eyes off her. In a silvery dress, she was, it shimmered like water. And she was kind. She could see I didn't know anybody much there. I still don't know what she saw in a quiet type like me.'

In that moment, seeing her father sitting straight and proud, a light in his eyes, Kate knew exactly what Barbara must have seen in him – solidity, gentleness, faithfulness. This was a man who would never let her down, who would protect her from the world, who would stand by her whatever happened. And Barbara had been right.

'I was only able to dance with her twice that evening,' he went on, 'but I persuaded Bob to set us up as a foursome with his girl. Bob had a car and we had some great times, driving down to the coast, dancing, the flicks. We all got on so well. It turned out that Bob's girl – Janey, her name is – had known Barbara's brother. Your mother had had some sadness in her life, with Kenneth being killed in Egypt, as you know, and I think I reminded her of him a bit. Anyway, she was my girl, and I was so proud when she agreed to marry me.'

Kate waited.

'It all went well until her first pregnancy. I don't know whether she's ever told you, Kate, but she lost the baby.'

'No!' This was new. Out of the blue.

'One morning, she woke me and said, "I can't feel it moving." She still had three months to go and they made her wait weeks until it was born of its own accord. It was a little boy. It was terrible, going through all that, knowing the baby was dead. And they wouldn't even let me be with her.'

'Was this in Hong Kong?'

'We were still stationed in Kent then. We went to Hong Kong soon after. She was still depressed, quiet and thin. But Nicola started very soon after and we thought things would get better.'

'And did they?'

'No. Nicola was beautiful, so beautiful when she was born. I cried when I first held her, after all that had happened, but Barbara, she was like a broken spring. It was an easy birth, I was told, but Barbara was terrified the whole time that the baby

411

would die, and she couldn't bond with Nicola, was frightened she would lose her. I thought it would help to get her involved more with the regiment, looking after the NCO wives, some secretarial work. Anything to get her out of the nursery. But nothing seemed to help. She went to the doctor, and he said it was baby blues but that she must pull herself together. She would recover once she realized the baby was thriving and start enjoying motherhood. But she never really did. And then you came along, so small and pretty, a little Bright Eyes. She has always loved you, you know, your mother. Don't ever doubt that. But she has never been able to show it in the usual ways.'

Kate looked down at the little drawer of mementoes, now neatly arranged, and bit her lip. She could hardly take all this in.

'It sounds like what I had, doesn't it?' she said, meeting her father's eyes. 'Post-natal depression.'

'I think that's what a doctor today might say,' her father agreed, 'but of course no one talked about that sort of thing then. Especially not ex-pat army doctors. And in those days, you just put a brave face on such things.'

'Then, losing Nicola . . .'

'Was a terrible blow for both of us, all of us. But for your mother – she felt so guilty, that she'd been so inadequate as a parent. She felt she had lost her chance forever.'

Kate was surprised by a sudden bolt of anger. 'She had lost her chance with Nicola, yes. But not with me. She still had me. You . . . she . . . you forgot me. All you could think about was Nicola, Nicola, Nicola.' She went on passionately, 'Dad, did you never consider after Nicola died that *I* might be hurting too? That *I* needed comfort? Not just Mum, not just you. She was my sister. Instead, you buried yourself in your grief. You both forgot about me – maybe you blamed me for not dying instead of her, I don't know! And now it is photos of Nicola you have downstairs, not pictures of me and my family. The dead, not the living. You hardly see Sam and Daisy or even remember their birthdays.'

Her father buried his face in his hands. Kate saw that he was trembling. Was he crying? After a moment, he looked up at her with a strained white face. 'I must take a lot of the blame for that,' he said. 'I've been so careful to guard your mother. She loves you, I know she loves you. It's not her fault, it's a sort of illness with her. And the drink, this terrible self-harm, it's her way of dealing with it all.'

'Have you never talked to a doctor about it all? Found a specialist for her?'

'We've never found anyone who's done more than give her the anti-depressants.'

'Well, Dad, you've got an opportunity now. It's really important that you push the doctors until you get Mum to see a psychiatrist and that you explain everything to them – the whole history and that you get Mum to do what they recommend. The counselling is an essential part of it all these days – it's her best chance. Otherwise, she'll go on doing this until she succeeds.'

Weary now, she went over and, putting her arms round her father, hugged him. Then she picked up the little drawer and slotted it back into the cabinet before turning her attention to her mother's overnight bag. On impulse, she hurried downstairs and picked up the single photograph of Sam and Daisy – the one take several years before – and returning to the bedroom, placed it in the little holdall by the washbag and zipped the bag closed.

The next morning, Maggie rang to tell them that Barbara had been moved to a recovery ward. Now that she was settled, Maggie was going home.

When Kate and her father arrived, Barbara was fully conscious, but very tired. Kate sat on the chair by the bed while her father fussed about with flowers and the contents of the holdall, showing his wife the photograph of Sam and Daisy before balancing it on the bedside cabinet.

'How do you feel now, Mum?'

'My throat hurts,' Barbara whispered. 'And I've got a headache.'

'Why did you do it? Please tell me.'

But her mother turned her face away, her expression closed.

'Mum, Dad's been talking to me and I understand a bit more now, about why you hurt so much. But Dad and I, and Sam and Daisy, we love you. And we want you to get better. So you mustn't do this again. You must get some help. Dad's made me promise that you will get some expert help. We'll pull you through this, we must. Sam and Daisy need you, they need their granny, do you understand?'

Her mother's face was still turned away, but she nodded almost imperceptibly. And that was enough.

Kate rang Joyce from a payphone at the hospital. Her mother-in-law had insisted she would go up on the train and fetch the children on Sunday night, but Kate was grateful to hear that Simon had volunteered to bring them down to Diss himself. He would meet Joyce at the station.

Kate remained at the hospital all day, helping her father talk to the doctors, arranging for her mother's future care. When, the following morning, she set off for Suffolk once more, her father hugged her as he never had before.

'You're a brick, my girl,' he said, and though she saw that his armour, his bluffness, his army correctness, were returning, there was something akin to a twinkle in his eye. It was still the

414

beginning of things, but the bond between the three of them had been reforged.

When Kate met the children out of school on Monday evening, Sam ran to her and wrapped himself around her as though she were the only solid object in an unstable world.

'What's the matter, sausage?' she whispered, holding him tight.

'I love you, Mummy,' was all he said. 'Don't go away again.'

Later, as they sat down to fish fingers, Daisy said, almost conversationally, 'Mummy, is Granny Carter going to die?'

Sam sat up and watched his mother's face, his eyes wide.

Kate could hardly breathe for a moment and then she said, 'No, darling. She's been very ill, but she's going to get better.' How could she and Joyce and Simon have been so caught up in their troubled adult lives that they hadn't taken enough care of the children's fears?

She explained to them now that Granny Carter was still in hospital but that the doctors and nurses were helping her and soon she would go home. She then moved on to ask them about their stay with Simon. Had they enjoyed themselves?

Sam resumed eating his fish fingers and nodded slowly. 'We went to see the ships,' he said, 'and where people had their heads chopped off.'

'Daddy forgot to ask Sam to clean his teeth,' Daisy said in adult tones, and then clearly regretted the indiscretion because she quickly added, 'but it didn't matter, because he made Sammy brush them twice in the morning.'

They are already learning the knack of protecting me and Simon from one another, Kate thought sadly.

'Mummy, do we have to go up to London next weekend?' Daisy asked.

'No,' Kate said, wondering what the reaction would be.

'Oh good,' said Daisy. 'It's a long, long way. I'm going to ask Daddy to come back and live here.'

Kate had to hide her feelings, but she could have wept.

# Chapter 36

*October 2004*

'I am so sorry, Kate. Have you been waiting ages?' For all his sharply creased cords and spotless jacket, Max looked flustered as he put down the package he carried and unwound the scarf from his neck.

It was three weeks later, a surprisingly warm Saturday evening in October, and for the last twenty minutes Kate had been sitting in the bar of the Swan Hotel in Southwold nursing a glass of mineral water and watching the door in between reading a long progress report Jasmin had compiled for the next Save the School meeting. Really, that woman was amazing, Kate told herself, as she totted up the number of people Jasmin had approached and from whom she had received offers of money. She was also pleased that her own interview with a journalist on the local paper had paid off; there had been a large feature printed recently about the plight of the school, and she was sure this had helped Jasmin's efforts.

'Only a few minutes. Traffic, was it?' she asked, smiling, and bundled her report back into her handbag.

'No. Claudia was late picking up the children.'

Their table, at the back of the restaurant, was ready, so they went and sat down. When they had ordered, Max passed across the package he had brought. 'The diaries,' he said. 'I finished the final volume last night.' He shook his head slowly. 'It's an incredibly moving story, isn't it? I'm gobsmacked really. I had no idea about any of it. No wonder the two sides of the family didn't speak.'

'It's just not the kind of thing anyone can say "sorry" about and "let's all have Christmas together this year", is it?'

'I don't even know if Raven and Vanessa told my mother the full story,' Max said. 'She didn't say much about it to me. I knew Vanessa had been married before and that her divorce was scandalous, but I just assumed it was because divorce *was* a scandal in the nineteen twenties.'

'And the story of the baby?'

'Heartbreaking. And cruel. Poor Agnes.'

'Do you think I've missed anything, Max? It's so useful having another perspective. Did you spot any clues that I haven't?'

'Nothing leaped to the eye, no. Except the missing locket, I suppose. Was it just a coincidence it disappeared at the time of the birth?'

'Agnes didn't say it was exactly at the time of the birth, did she? Perhaps Miss Selcott took it out of spite.' Then Kate remembered. 'Max, there's something I haven't told you! It's something I only realized, though, when I found the last bit of the diary.' And she went on to tell him about buying Harry's half of the locket in the curio shop in Norwich.

He was amazed. '*Really?* I'd love to see it.'

'Well, you can.' And Kate delved in her handbag and handed it across the table.

He studied it carefully, turned it over and frowned at the faded photograph. Then he handed it back. 'It's not exactly pretty, is it? But interesting, very distinctive. I know the shop where you found it, actually. I bought Claudia a Lea Stein brooch once there. They have some later pieces, as well as the Art Deco stuff, you know. That you should walk in off the street and find it is an incredible coincidence.'

'Only if you view the situation with hindsight,' said Kate, carefully stowing the necklace in her bag again. 'If you look at it chronologically, I think it was the locket that helped draw me into this situation in the first place.'

She had told nobody about her dreams, not even Agnes. Not since Simon had ridiculed her visions of the 'dream house'. Although she knew she must have seen the photograph of the house when she was a child, but had buried it in her subconscious all these years, why should it have emerged in her dream precisely after buying the locket? Perhaps it was time to give the locket a proper place in the narrative. And Max, after all, had some right to know: Agnes's story was partly his story, too. So she told him, stumbling with embarrassment at first, about how she had dreamed about Seddington House, and about her vivid dreams after reading the diaries.

She remembered the words of the last letter that Agnes had sent Harry, together with his half of the locket. *When you look on this locket, may you dream of me . . .*

'I know it sounds complete tosh, Max,' she finished, 'but whether it's to do with the locket, the diary or Agnes herself, there's some sort of psychological connection going on here. I can't explain it any further.'

Max, who had left his terrine untouched to concentrate on Kate's story, said nothing for a moment. Then he took a gulp of wine and put his glass down.

'When I was at school,' he said, 'I used to dream sometimes about places I hadn't been to. And then – it might not be for ages afterwards – I'd visit somewhere and think: I've been here before!

**419**

They would be quite ordinary places – once it was an old house in Cambridge that had been turned into a museum. I was certain I'd been there once, but not when it was a museum. And yet my father assured me he and Mum had never taken me there.' He shook his head, remembering. 'Another time it was a beach. I have never told anybody this,' he confided, 'but at the time I almost started to believe that perhaps I *had* been to these places before – *but in another life*. Sounds ridiculous now, doesn't it?' He broke into a smile. 'I expect it was adolescent hormones playing tricks. Anyway, what I'm saying is that I don't disbelieve you.'

'Thank you.' It was such a relief to have told someone about her dreams and for that person not to have laughed at her.

'I'm not sure where all this leaves us now, though,' said Max, finally taking his terrine as Kate started to spoon her soup. 'Assuming the baby didn't die, but that Selcott, probably with the help of Lister, sent it away somewhere . . . God!' He put down his fork. 'That's horrible. You don't suppose they would have killed it, do you? Killed it and buried it?'

Kate's spoon dropped in the bowl, splattering soup over the white cloth. 'Surely not. I know the governess was cruel to Agnes, but she believed herself to be an upright Christian woman. That would have been against all her beliefs, killing a child. No, I can't believe it, even of her.'

'Let's hope you're right. OK, so she and Lister gave the baby away. Where do you go in a little country village to give a baby away?'

'It implies local knowledge, doesn't it? Kate said thoughtfully. 'Knowing someone who had lost a child, or wanted a child, who would take the baby right away, no questions asked, and keep its origins secret.'

'Selcott might have known someone like that, more likely it was Lister.'

'I suppose it might not even have been in Seddington. I wonder where Lister lived, when he wasn't at Seddington House, I mean.'

'I've no idea how we find out,' Max said.

As the waiter came and removed their plates, discreetly arranging a napkin over the spilled soup, Kate watched Max, who seemed lost in thought. Their main courses arrived and their glasses were refilled. Max looked up.

'Looks delicious, doesn't it?' They had both chosen locally caught fish. 'What's so funny?'

'I'm just amused by how interested you're getting in this mystery now. Having accused me of being obsessed, I mean.'

'It's a mystery about our own family, that's why. And my aunt's anguish comes across so strongly in her writing. Yes, I can see why you want to make things right, Kate.'

They had started eating, but after a couple of mouthfuls, Max put down his knife and fork and steepled his fingers.

'Kate,' he said, his expression serious, 'there is one thing those diaries have really made me see, and that is why Agnes left you Seddington House and not me.'

'Oh,' she said, relieved but not sure what to say.

'I know my aunt tried her best to be friendly to me these last few years, and I know she was a fair person, too. She didn't blame me for the actions of her brother, but at the same time, it would have been a difficult thing to flout her father's memory, wouldn't it? To leave the house to a child of the son who had betrayed him so fundamentally, and whom he had cut out of his own will. And you're right – I *do* look like Raven. What I mean to say is, that I accept the way she wanted things. I will not be challenging her will.'

'Thank you,' Kate said simply. Then wondered if she should tell him about Simon's claim. She thought she would. He was a lawyer. It wasn't his specialist area, but she would still be interested in his opinion.

Max listened quietly as she related how Simon's lawyer was now using Seddington House as a bargaining point to enable Simon to keep the capital from the sale of their Fulham house as well as other savings and any claim on his pension.

'It's very difficult to untangle before the will is proved,' Raj had sent all the forms off to the probate office last week and it was now a waiting game, 'but Jasmin's point is that the inheritance was left to me, not to Simon, and that anyway, I hadn't received it at the point separation proceedings were initiated. Jasmin thinks that Simon hasn't got a viable claim on the bequest, but that my future wealth would be taken into consideration when it comes to the division of property from our marriage.' Kate shrugged as she put her knife and fork together on the plate.

'It must be incredibly stressful for you, all this.' Max reached over and gently squeezed her hand.

'It is, and yet I'm trying to be philosophical about the house,' she said, withdrawing her hand. 'It's the children who are most important to me at the moment. Sam in particular gets very upset when I take them up to see Simon. He seems to enjoy being with his father once he's there, but he finds going very stressful. Daisy thinks it's quite exciting, having two homes, but once the excitement wears off, she might become resentful. At least Simon is reasonable over the children. I think a lot of the financial stuff is to do with his lawyer rather than him. Jasmin keeps telling me not to take it all too personally, that this is what lawyers do.'

Kate paused, then went on, 'And I've been thinking a lot about the house. I love it, but there's a huge amount to do to it, to make it right for modern family life. It'll be very expensive, and it's going to be a big job dealing with all the contents. And we still don't know, do we, exactly who is going to get what.'

'Agnes's descendants have to declare themselves within six months of her death, don't they? Which is mid-January, I believe – two and a half months away.'

'It seems ages. I feel for you, too, Max, not knowing.'

'I feel for me, too,' he grinned. 'If someone comes out of the woodwork and claims to be Agnes's lost son, I don't get a penny.'

'And yet you seem quite caught up in the story.'

'Yes, I am, but I must be truthful and say I'm just not going to try too hard to find the answer to the mystery. You're on your own there, Kate.'

'I don't blame you.' She smiled.

'Coffee for both of us,' Max told the waiter, as Kate declined the dessert menu. When the coffee came, he slowly took off his glasses and cleaned them on his handkerchief. He said to Kate, very casually, 'I've really enjoyed this evening. Shall we do it again sometime?'

Their eyes met. Kate noticed the boyish lock of hair that fell across Max's forehead, how vulnerable he looked without the barrier of his spectacles, the contrast of the strong jaw and the sensitive mouth. Now that she had got past his brusque exterior there was something very familiar about him. Aren't women supposed to fall for men who remind them of their fathers, their brothers? she thought. But she had never had a brother, not even a close male cousin. The son her mother had lost – perhaps he would have been like Max. She felt affection for Max, but it wasn't desire. She and Max should be close, but not like that. So in the end she said, 'Why don't you bring the little girls over for lunch one Sunday when Sam and Daisy are home. They'd love to meet their – what are they?' Kate stopped and drew a little family tree on a scrap of paper she pulled out of her bag. 'Your girls and I are third cousins, so they are my children's third cousins once removed.' She pushed the paper over to Max with a flourish.

Max replaced his glasses and peered at the paper for a moment. Then he nodded and smiled. 'Let's just say cousins. Anyway, it's a brilliant idea to let them meet,' he said. 'Let's do that.'

# *Chapter 37*

*December 2004*

A warm wet autumn gave way to a warm wet winter. One night in early December Kate lay awake in darkness listening to heavy rain beating on the roof of Paradise Cottage. It was a sound she had taken a while to get used to when they first came to live with Joyce, and even now she loved to remember that only a few thin layers of plaster and thatch separated her upturned face from open sky.

The grandmother clock downstairs gently pinged five o'clock, an irritating time to be awake in the darkest part of winter. Too early to get up, too late to go back into a deep sleep and be dragged awake at seven with a thick head when there was a busy day ahead. Kate and Joyce were helping Jasmin with the costumes for the school nativity play in which Daisy was a snowflake and Sam a king. First fittings were due to start at nine o'clock.

So Kate lay and turned over in her mind the news she had received yesterday. Jasmin had telephoned and read out a letter from Simon's Rottweiler lawyer that had made Kate almost drop the phone with relief.

Simon had finally conceded Kate's right to her inheritance. Seddington House was not to be taken into account in any settlement. In addition, she would receive a large part of the capital sum accrued from the sale of the Fulham house. The chattels they must divide up between them.

Kate knew that the details had still to be battled out, but at least a basic financial agreement was now in place, she was beginning to realize what great stress she had been under. She didn't feel elation, or even peace of mind. The devastation of Simon's betrayal and desertion was too recent for that. Every time she saw him, when she delivered the children, was a painful reminder of her loss. But, rather like the survivor of a shipwreck who has struggled his way to the shore, battered but alive, she felt a deep exhausted gratitude for her survival and a tiny flutter of hope. Now she could begin to move on.

Shortly after Jasmin's call, Raj had rung Kate.

'Farrell's has sent a list of the paintings they recommend we sell,' he said. 'I'm putting it in the post to you.' Two weeks before, he, Kate and Max had met with the probate officers. The will would be proved and the executors granted authority to act, once inheritance tax had been paid. The sum seemed huge, but after consultation with the accountant they had decided not to contest it. It would mean selling right away a dozen of the most valuable of Agnes's pictures, together with the jewellery.

'We are lucky,' went on Raj. 'Sometimes discussions about the value of a large estate can go on for months. Farrell's have helped make it very simple for us. Once we have settled this tax bill we can start paying out the bequests.'

Debbie and Dan had been right. Back in the summer when Kate had felt so overwhelmed by the changes in her life, the end of her marriage, the loss of Agnes, the burden of putting the old lady's affairs in order, they had both told her that things would work themselves out. And instead of being overwhelmed by depression she had found inner resources of strength and determination she hadn't known she possessed. And gradually she was coming through the worst of it.

Her greatest pleasure was that, despite these seismic events, or perhaps partly because of them, the long winter of her own relationship with her parents was finally thawing, and here and there were signs of a long-awaited spring.

Kate had taken Daisy and Sam to visit her mother and father two weekends before and was astonished. Barbara was now regularly seeing a consultant psychiatrist, a young woman with particular expertise in the area of depression. The combination of new medication and sessions with a cognitive therapist were already making a marked difference.

Major Carter had confided to Kate, 'Doctor Alton seems to take us seriously. We've not had all this attention before – they just fobbed your mother off with pills. I always thought this therapy stuff was so much baloney, but it makes sense the way Doctor Alton explains it. Helps you pull yourself together. And something certainly seems to be happening. Your mother's taking an interest in things. Talks about places we went when we were courting. Do y'know, she wants me to look up our old friends Bob and Janey in Yorkshire? Haven't seen them for years. Now she wants us all to get together. So I've written to them, asked them to come and stay.'

'Good for you, Dad,' said Kate.

Her mother was making more effort with Sam and Daisy, too.

'I sent Grandad to get you some toys,' Barbara said, pulling out a large box of puzzles, games and cars from a corner of the living room, and Grandad brought in a handsome-looking doll's house he had made and a plastic garage he had acquired in a charity shop. There were even the children's favourite biscuits to eat and chocolate-chip ice cream at tea instead of the usual tinned fruit cocktail. 'Grandparents are meant to spoil their grandchildren,' said Barbara. 'Just don't give Benjy any biscuits, Sam. He's tubby enough already, the naughty boy.'

The greatest symbol of the change in Barbara was the fact that only one photograph of Nicola now adorned the room. It was the large studio portrait taken the winter before she died. Kate studied it with sadness. Nicola's smile was gentle, but a twinkle danced in her eyes, betraying her love of life. Around it on the bookcase and the piano were now scattered half a dozen pictures of Daisy, Sam and Kate, a black and white wedding portrait of Desmond handsome in his officer's uniform and Barbara a beautiful, vivacious original of her dead daughter. A snap of Aunt Maggie with her beloved tabby cat completed the family circle.

Major and Mrs Carter were coming up for a couple of days at Christmas, but this time they would stay at Paradise Cottage.

'It'll mean you sleeping with the children, Kate,' Joyce warned.

'And that will mean precious little sleep on Christmas morning.' Kate laughed. 'But I don't mind. It'll be lovely for Mum and Dad to see the kids open their stockings. Thank you so much, Joyce.'

Moving on.

And now, drowsy as she was, Kate's thoughts drifted to Dan.

She had not seen him alone since they had had coffee together back in August, the day she had lent him the diaries. First he had gone away on holiday and then the routine of school, of the children's weekend visits to Simon, her mother's illness, myriad tasks, had kept Kate occupied and she was glad of the diversion.

She had bumped into Dan very occasionally, once at Seddington House with Max, and once at the adventure playground, he with Shelley, she with her children, and she found herself longing to see him. But lately, suspicion had been hardening into certainty that he was deliberately avoiding her.

Was this because he was no longer interested in her, or because he *was* interested – but was trying to avoid being hurt? Either way, whenever she thought of him, it was with a swelling tenderness like pain, as if she were repressing deep emotion.

Her feelings about Simon were still raw, but she was starting to accept that he was gone from her. And thinking about Dan was like a salve to her wounds. Was that a good thing or a bad thing? Were her feelings for Dan 'on the rebound'? She didn't know.

All she did know was that she was ready to move on. As she went about her business she looked for him, at the shops in Halesworth, as she drove through Seddington, whenever she went to place flowers on Agnes's grave. He had told her back in August that he valued their friendship – so why didn't he call?

The clock downstairs struck six, interrupting her thoughts. Immediately, the bedroom door whispered open and a little figure slipped into the room. Sam climbed onto the bed and burrowed down under the duvet, snuggling up into his mother like a warm puppy. There Joyce found them at quarter to eight, deeply asleep.

It was two days later that Dan finally rang. At first Kate could hardly speak for relief. He asked her about her mother, about the progress of Agnes's will, then, almost casually, how the children were getting on with their new routine, and Kate, divining the true motive behind his question, let fall how matters stood between her and Simon.

After a while she waited for him to speak.

'Are you busy next Thursday evening?' he said.

No, she nearly said, then remembered you were supposed to pretend to men that you were busy. 'I'll just look at the calendar.'

'I know it's a bit near Christmas, but the gallery is throwing a launch party for our new exhibition. Alison Rosa – do you know her paintings?'

'Sorry, I don't,' Kate confessed.

'She has to go into hospital after Christmas, so we thought we'd have a party for her now instead. And a few of us are having dinner afterwards – it would be great if you would come.'

'I am free Thursday, but . . .' she watched Joyce bustle past '. . . I'll need to find a babysitter.' It crossed her mind that Joyce might feel ambivalent about babysitting for her daughter-in-law to allow her to go out with another man, then she pushed the thought away. There would be other people present; she wouldn't be alone with him. Anyway, she could always ask Michelle.

'Can I let you know?'

'Yes. I hope you can come,' said Dan softly into the phone and Kate's heart did a little dance of joy.

When she hung up, she stood for a moment as if in a dream. As she turned, slowly, to go up to her room, it was to see Joyce standing in the entrance to the kitchen, drying a tea-cup. The woman was smiling at her, but sadly.

'If that is who I thought it was,' she said quietly, 'then, yes, I will babysit for you next Thursday.'

'Thank you,' Kate said soberly, and watched as her mother-in-law turned her face away. At that moment she knew. She and Sam and Daisy would have to leave Joyce and Paradise Cottage as soon as she could find somewhere for them to go.

# *Chapter 38*

The following Thursday evening Kate dressed carefully in black velvet flared trousers, a white silk shirt with silver buttons and a little black cardigan in soft cashmere.

She wondered whether to try Agnes's pearls, which she had hardly dared wear they seemed so precious, but in the end the locket seemed to hang at just the right length and, she thought, it added a suitably arty touch to her outfit.

'You are pretty, Mummy,' Daisy said solemnly, 'and you smell lovely too,' and as a reward for her flattery she was allowed to spray scent on Mummy's wrists and on her own, then try some lip gloss.

When Kate slipped in through the door of the gallery, she was hit by a wall of heat and noise. She was just wondering whether she recognized anybody at all when Dan pushed his way through the crowd.

'Hi,' he said, kissing her gently, his warm cheek against her cold one. 'Are you OK?'

She nodded and they smiled at one another. This was a new Dan, Kate thought with appreciation, as she took in the fact that his gold-brown mane was neatly styled and he wore a sharp suit. He took her hand and drew her into the throng. Soon, warming her fingers on a glass of mulled wine, she found herself talking to Jacqui, a lively Irishwoman with a head of ginger curls who turned out to be the girlfriend of Dan's business partner, Grant; together they walked round to look at the exhibits.

The paintings were large, bright landscapes in oil, technically assured but the colours too harsh, unnatural, for Kate's taste. Other people clearly thought differently, because red 'sold' spots already appeared by two of the larger works; and when Kate looked round for Dan, she saw him apparently haggling with a bearded man at a desk and punching figures into a calculator.

An older woman who knew Jacqui joined her and Kate, and began to talk about some local theatre project they were both involved in. Kate drifted in and out of the conversation, all the time keeping an eye on Dan. He appeared to have reached an agreement with the man with the beard, who was now filling in a form. One hand resting on the desk, Dan was fielding questions from a middle-aged couple. After a moment, he led them across to a tall thin nervous woman Jacqui had previously pointed out as the artist, Alison Rosa, before returning to the desk to conclude his sale.

Dan seemed utterly self-possessed, Kate thought. His temples were glowing slightly with perspiration, but he spoke to everyone who approached him, kept an eye on the young waitress serving canapés and tiny mince pies, and introduced loners to groups, occasionally telegraphing to Grant who was suavely working the room. Every now and then Dan would spot Kate watching him and give the very slightest of smiles.

At one point he brought the nervy Alison over to meet Kate and the two women talked about their love of the Suffolk landscape and what it was exactly that drew so many artists to the area. 'It's the quality of the light that attracted me,' said Alison.

'And the ever-changing skies. Every mood of the sky transforms the landscape.'

By nine o'clock there was only a small group of people left and it was then Kate noticed that Dan's painting *One Morning at the Beginning of the World*, had been sold. When she asked him who had bought it, a smile spread across his face and he said, 'It was through a London dealer. And he wants to show what else I've done.'

'Dan, that's fantastic. Congratulations.' She wanted to hug him, but felt too self-conscious.

'Shall we move across to the restaurant, folks?' called Grant. They hastily helped the waitress collect up the few remaining glasses before Dan locked up shop.

The group for dinner turned out to be a small one – Grant and Jacqui, Alison, a woman called Deirdre who was the editor of a small but prestigious regional arts magazine, and Dan and Kate – but the restaurant was busy with Christmas bookings and they were asked to squash onto a table in a corner. Jacqui and Kate and Dan opted to share the banquette against one wall, the others sitting opposite.

They ordered their food and more wine and toasted Alison on the success of the party. She said little and her face was grey with exhaustion. It must be her illness, thought Kate, remembering that the artist was due to go into hospital.

The restaurant was stuffy, and it was while Kate was peeling off her cardigan that Dan's eye fell on the pendant.

'I noticed that earlier,' he said, and Kate, who was already intensely aware of his presence close beside her, gave into the temptation to lean towards him. She lifted the locket to show him and he studied the front before turning it over in his fingers.

'I think it's Agnes,' she said as he squinted at the faded

photograph, and seeing the interest of the others in the party, she briefly explained the story of the lovers.

'That's just so sad,' said Deirdre. 'But beautiful. What happened to the other half, do you suppose?'

Kate shrugged. 'Lost,' she said.

'Could I have a better look?' said Dan, so Kate took off the locket and handed it to him. After studying it for a moment or two, feeling its weight in his palm, he frowned and passed it into Deirdre's outstretched hand.

'My guess is it's influenced by the Arts and Crafts movement,' she said after a moment. 'At the end of the nineteenth century these artists wanted to get back to simple values. This is lovely, though not, perhaps, by one of the more skilled craftsmen. You can see the design is a little rough-hewn.'

The pendant was passed around the table and exclaimed over, then Dan asked to see it again. He seemed reluctant to return it but finally, wordlessly, he fastened the chain back around Kate's neck and turned his attention to his dinner.

The conversation moved back to Alison's exhibition and how well Dan and Grant thought the opening had gone. Then, after they had all eaten vast bowls of pasta, Grant went off in search of cigarettes, and Jacqui and Alison engaged in low-voiced conversation, Kate gathered, about Alison's hospital treatment. Deirdre took the opportunity to ask Kate about Agnes and Seddington House.

'I went there once when I was researching a piece,' she said. 'Miss Melton had some paintings I needed to see. An extraordinary treasure house. Did you say it's all yours now? That's incredible.'

'I can't quite believe it myself.'

'What are you going to do with everything?' asked Deirdre. 'It's such an Aladdin's cave.'

'It is,' Kate agreed. 'I don't know – sell a lot of it, I suppose.' She glanced at Dan as she said, 'And then I would like to move in with my children as soon as I can. But we're going to have to rent somewhere first until it's ready.'

Kate had plucked up the courage to talk to her mother-in-law about this last weekend. Joyce was still insisting that they share Paradise Cottage with her until Seddington House was ready for them, but Kate was determined that after Christmas, she would look for somewhere for herself and the children. It was important to make the break now, to forge her own path and leave Joyce to her own life, which included rebuilding her relationship with her son.

'I haven't got my head round it yet, though,' Kate told Deirdre now. 'Nor what to do about Seddington. There's just so much stuff, for a start, and apart from it having been Agnes's, most of it doesn't mean anything to me. What would I do with a nineteenth-century silver wool-holder or a stuffed pug dog or even a porcelain eye-bath? It would be like living in a museum!'

Deirdre laughed loudly.

'Does that sound awful, Dan?' Kate appealed to him. 'I don't mean to be disrespectful to Agnes, but these things were her passion, not mine.'

'I think she would have understood that,' Dan said. 'It was the house itself that she wanted to pass on to you, the family home. She would want you to make it into your home, filled with your family's things.'

'I think so, too,' Kate sighed. 'But it seems so cold, so unfeeling, to send everything away.'

'I know what could work well,' said Jacqui, who had tuned into the conversation. 'A people's auction.'

'And what might that be?' asked Dan, draining his glass.

'It's a country-house sale, really,' explained Deirdre. 'Made into a big community event. Sounds a great idea, Jacqui.'

'The Melton family were so well known,' went on Jacqui, 'that there'd be a huge amount of local interest.'

'What, buy a piece of the Meltons?' Alison joked.

'Why not?' said Deirdre. 'Of course, you'd get Farrell's to do it all for you. They would publicize it to the big dealers, too. And if you timed it right, you'd get the London green welly brigade down here on their summer hols, as well.'

Kate listened, resting her chin on her hand, her eyes shining with amusement.

'Don't let them bully you,' Dan whispered in her ear.

'Oh no, don't worry, I won't. It's something to think about, though, isn't it?' she replied. 'A people's auction. You know, I reckon that would rather have appealed to Agnes.'

At the end of the evening, Dan helped Kate into her coat and walked her back to her car. He didn't say much, he seemed to have something on his mind. They stood in the poorly lit car park while Kate fumbled for her key.

'Goodbye, Dan,' she whispered and kissed him gently on the cheek. He let her, without responding.

'You take care,' he said as she got into the car, then, as she started the engine, he waved before slipping away into the darkness.

Overwhelmed by a sudden sense of desolation, Kate let the engine stall. She sat in the car park watching the shadows and thought.

She knew now that she loved Dan. She still hurt about Simon, hurt abominably, just as she supposed that Dan must hurt about Linda. But she felt she was herself with Dan. He was rock-like and that was important to her. She could rely on him, she just knew it. And her body longed for his. Did he feel like this about her? She had thought he did this evening, had just felt it to be so, that they were dancing that same slow dance together, but now he had said goodbye, so abruptly, had left her almost without hope.

This was silly. She was acting like a teenager, she thought, starting the engine with such a savage movement that the starter motor roared.

## Chapter 39

'I know it had to have happened sooner or later, but why couldn't he have asked me first? I could have explained to the children about it then.'

It was the following Monday and Kate, who had had another bad night, stomped round the kitchen banging cupboard doors and slamming drawers as she cleared up after breakfast. 'And giving them presents, too. I mean that's just craven, buying their affection. Look out, you're losing everything.'

Joyce was sitting at the table, tidying out her handbag to look for a receipt she had lost, fluffy paracetamol and elderly rolls of lipstick rolling on to the floor.

'Thanks, dear. Oh, it must be here somewhere . . . I don't blame you for being cross, Kate. But they don't seem very traumatized by meeting Meredith, do they?'

'You mean it's just me?' Joyce was diplomatically silent and Kate slumped into a seat and glowered.

'Well, of course you're upset, dear. Anyone would be in your position. But children take things in their stride more.'

'Especially if a big red fire engine and a portable CD player are involved.'

Suddenly everything Liz said two nights ago made sense.

Liz, Claire and Kate had met up on Saturday evening at Claire's little flat in Greenwich overlooking the high street after Kate had left the children with Simon. It was a short weekend for Daisy and Sam to share with their father – he had been off travelling again the previous week and he looked strained and exhausted.

Claire, also, seemed tired and hollow-eyed. Seven and a half months into her pregnancy, she was still an astonishingly neat figure in her bootleg-cut maternity jeans and jacket, her bump entirely presenting to the front like a football.

'Look at you.' Liz almost wept with envy. 'I was a beached whale by this stage with the twins. You've hardly put on any weight at all. Are you eating, you wretched girl?'

'I still feel so nauseous sometimes,' Claire moaned. Kate privately thought anxiety over Alex couldn't help. They were still seeing one another but Claire confided in them, 'He's just not interested in the baby. Part of him is pretending it's not happening. Of course, he can't ignore it entirely.' She giggled suddenly. 'You should have seen the look of horror on his face the other evening when I was in the bath and this little foot pushed up out of my belly and started wriggling. He thought it was a rerun of *Alien*.' She sighed. 'But he won't talk about names or show any interest in buying things for the baby.'

'What's the due date again?'

'Tenth of February, but they might have to induce before then. I've been getting a bit of high blood pressure, you see, and the baby is slightly small for the dates. The consultant says I've got to be careful and rest, so I've been cutting down on my work a bit and getting taxis. Anyway, I don't feel too bad. My sister's pestering me to go and stay with them, but I'd rather be here. She'll come to the hospital with me when the time comes, that's the important thing.'

As they tucked into a vegetarian lasagne, Liz surprised them all by saying she thought she'd be handing in her notice soon.

'They're pushing the magazine to places it shouldn't go,' she said. 'It's a mistake to aim too squarely for the mass market. *Desira* has always had an edge, a smallish but defined market. It can't compete out there with *Cosmo* and *Company*. It just won't work and I won't do it.'

'So what will you do?' Kate asked her, as they cleared the table and moved to the little sitting room with their coffee.

'I might spend some time at home for a bit. Freelance and hope something comes up. I need to take a leaf out of your book, Kate, see a bit more of the children. Lottie's having some problems at school. She always feels she comes second to Lily and has difficulty making friends. I need to be meeting her out of school for a while, seeing that she's OK. What about you, Kate? Have you had any thoughts about work? Or can you afford to just lie back and be châtelaine?'

'I wish. But there's still so much to sort out. I'm putting off the evil work decision for a bit till we're more settled.'

Later on, Liz said, 'By the way, Ted came round the other night for supper. Do you know, I think he might finally have cracked things on the girl front? His new girlfriend's Czech. She was a teacher there and has come over to learn English. He met her at an evening class. They're absolutely starry-eyed over each other.' She shook her head in amusement. 'Laurence's mum is practically knitting matinée jackets for their unborn children. Why is it that mothers always want their children married off?'

'Especially when it then all goes wrong,' said Kate gloomily.

'Ah, yes,' said Liz and was uncharacteristically quiet for a moment. Then she said, 'Ted told me something interesting about Meredith.'

Kate tried to look as though Liz was talking about the price of tomatoes.

'She was in a relationship for five years, apparently. And it broke up because they tried to have children and it didn't happen. They even started fertility treatment, but the whole thing was too much of a strain. The bloke got married to someone else who promptly got pregnant. Awfully sad for Meredith.'

'Strangely enough, I have difficulty finding much sympathy for her,' said Kate.

'But it does explain her interest in Daisy and Sam,' Liz said. 'Ted says she's always talking about them.'

'She hasn't met Daisy and Sam,' snorted Kate. 'Simon and I agreed. I said he's got to wait until they're used to us being apart.'

'From what Ted says, I think you'll find he hasn't waited,' said Liz gently.

So when she collected the children the following afternoon she mouthed at Simon fiercely, 'I'll ring you.' And when she casually asked the children on the train home, they chattered away about the treats they had had with 'Daddy's friend' and the presents she had given them to keep at the flat.

'I think you've just got to get used to it, Kate,' sighed Joyce now. 'We've got to move on.'

*We've got to move on.* The words echoed in Kate's mind. Yes, she knew they all had to move on, but other people were moving on faster than she was. Simon was moving on, the children were moving on, even Joyce appeared to be accepting what had happened and moving on to the new. Kate was left behind, still mourning. Maybe it was time for her to look forward too.

Suddenly, as she worried about this, a strange thing

**441**

happened to Kate. It was as though a physical weight around her neck, like the Ancient Mariner's dead albatross, was cut away and fell into darkness. It *was* her turn to embrace a new life. It wouldn't always be easy, she was ready for that, but she was equally certain that all sorts of good things lay before her.

'Ooh, look, here's the receipt,' exclaimed Joyce. 'It was in the bag with the jacket all the time. I'll go for the navy one this time, don't you think? Much smarter for Hazel's seventieth.'

Twenty minutes later, Dan rang. Kate couldn't keep the joy out of her 'hello'.

'Are you very busy this morning?' Dan asked, and Kate's newfound joy deflated slightly. He sounded so odd.

'Nothing that can't be put off. Why?'

'I'm just on my way home from Halesworth. Can I pick you up in a few minutes? I want to talk to you about something.'

'Well, OK.' Then, after a moment. 'Is everything all right?'

'Yes, everything's fine. I'll see you in five. Oh, something important. Can you bring your locket with you? And the diaries.'

'Why?'

'I'll tell you when I see you.'

Kate hurried upstairs, dragged a brush through her hair, fastened the locket over her turtleneck sweater and picked up the packet of exercise books. Mystery or not, she was seeing Dan and she was content.

'Goodbye,' she shouted to Joyce, who asked, 'Shall I see you at the dress rehearsal?' because they were on nativity costume duty after school.

'Yes, unless I'm back before,' she called out, as she put on her coat, then she closed the door firmly on Bobby's accusing face, and hurried down to the main road. Dan's van drew up straightaway and she climbed in.

'Hello,' she said, busying herself with the seatbelt so she didn't have to decide whether to kiss him or not. 'Where are we going then? Your place?'

'No.' Then, after a moment. 'You haven't met my dad, have you?'

His dad? Kate shook her head. 'We're going to see him? He's in Wenhaston, isn't he?'

'Just outside the village, yes.'

'Oh.' Dan fell silent and inscrutable, so she sat back and let him drive.

The man who opened the door of the modern bungalow to Dan and Kate was instantly recognizable as Dan's father. Like his son, he was tall and rangy, though slightly stooped. His cropped curls were iron grey, but the startling blue eyes and sudden warm smile were Dan to a T. Patrick Peace was a partner in a small plumbing business, Dan had once told Kate. He was practically retired now but filled a few hours a week dealing with the company paperwork. His wife, Sally, was a secretary at Halesworth Town Council.

Mr Peace gestured Kate through to the living room. As she handed him her coat, his eye fell on the locket around her neck and his eyes widened slightly, but he said nothing. She followed Dan's invitation and sat down on the sofa while Patrick Peace made them coffee. Dan disappeared into the kitchen and she heard their voices, then footsteps going upstairs.

There was a row of photographs on the brick mantelpiece over the gas-effect fire. They were mostly of children and teenagers who had to be Sally's but she smiled at a picture of a slighter, younger Dan proudly staggering under the weight of a huge fish. She looked for a picture of Dan's mother but, perhaps in respect to the second wife, there was none.

Just then Patrick appeared with a tray of coffee mugs and

Dan came in on his heels carrying a battered shoebox, which he placed on the coffee table. Patrick sat stirring sugar into his coffee and cleared his throat.

Kate waited for somebody to say something. Finally, Dan and his father both spoke at once. Dan motioned for his father to continue.

'Dan's very interested in your locket, Kate,' Patrick said, harumphing. 'Would you let me take a look?'

'Of course,' Kate said, puzzled, and passed the pendant to him. As Dan had done the other night, he turned it over in his hands, stroking the image gently with his thumbs and squinting at the faded photograph. Then he nodded, reached for the shoe-box, opened it and drew out what Kate first of all thought was a fifty-pence piece.

She watched, amazed, as Patrick fitted the coin to the back of the locket and, with a tiny pair of pliers that Dan handed him, fiddled with the hinge.

Then he looked up and flashed her a smile before passing the locket back. She sat staring at it, amazed. The locket was complete. She slid her thumbnail into the catch and opened it. There, facing the picture of Agnes, was a yellowed portrait of a good-looking young man with sleek dark hair. For the first time she gazed on the face of Harry Foster. Joy and astonishment shot through her. She looked from Dan to his father, to see their smiles meeting her own.

'Where did you get this?' she whispered in wonderment.

'I keep this shoebox in the loft,' said Patrick. 'It has a few things Joanna left – Dan's mother, you know.'

Dan's mother? Kate's mind was working overtime, but she couldn't yet make it compute any answers.

Dan sat listening as his father went on. 'Dan's told you, has he? Jo died – when he was ten. Twenty-five years ago now. She

**444**

was only thirty-two. The cancer had spread right the way inside her.' Kate could see the pain in the man's eyes, even thinking of it now.

'Joanna's own mother died young, too, of the same disease. Before I met Jo.' He rummaged in the box for a moment then drew out two photographs and passed them to Kate. One was of a tall, quiet-looking girl with fair hair, just approaching womanhood. She was standing in a garden against the wall of a cottage. The second showed the girl again, at seven or eight with a boy of about four and a woman holding a baby. They were on a beach and there were other children playing in the background. 'Her name was Esther. Esther Howells, before her marriage, I remember Joanna said. There are still Howells round this way.'

He took a mouthful of his coffee, cleared his throat again and went on. 'This piece of the locket was Esther's.'

Kate sat bolt upright, startled. 'Why? How?'

'I don't know exactly,' Patrick said. 'Jo said her mother kept it in her jewel box. That her own mother had given it to her. Esther had no idea who the photograph was of, just that her mother had said it was special, that she was to look after it.'

Just then, Dan broke in. 'And I remembered it, when I saw your half of the locket the other night. It's the decoration round the rim – look.'

Kate put down the photographs and picked up the locket from the sofa beside her, studying the swirling pattern etched into the edges of both halves.

'I saw Mum's half once before. Dad had showed it to me years ago, when we were clearing out Mum's things, weren't we, Dad? But we weren't sure what it had been part of. It could almost be a section from one of those old photograph trees.'

Patrick nodded.

'What else is there in the box? If I'm not being rude, asking.'

'No, you're not. Mostly mementoes of Jo. Some bits of jewellery, her birth certificate, some letters.'

Kate looked through the things that Patrick passed her, but there seemed to be no further clues to the mysterious Esther, who was merely mentioned as 'housewife' on the birth certificate. She put everything back in the box. Patrick sat back in his chair, and Dan took up the thread.

'Dad found Mum's half of the locket on Friday, and over the weekend I did a bit of research,' he said. 'I saw the vicar here, asked around in the village. Dad's right about the Howells. Esther's brother's and sister's families have moved away – we lost touch after Mum died – but her cousins' children still live here. It turns out that Esther's parents were Alf and Ethel Howells and that they used to work at Seddington House.'

'Alf and Ethel. They were the gardener and the parlourmaid. That's extraordinary. But hang on, they left a couple of years before Agnes even met Harry. So why would they have had Agnes's half of the locket?'

'Well, this is where we're down to conjecture. Let's look at those photographs again.' He picked up the box and passed the pictures of Esther over.

Kate pored over them, then she said, 'If that's her mother, on the beach, she doesn't look much like her, does she? Esther doesn't look much like her brother or sister either, come to that.'

'We don't know for definite that that woman's Ethel, though, do we?' Dan put in.

'Why don't we look through the photos at Seddington House?' Kate rushed on. 'There might be pictures of the servants from that period.'

Dan nodded. Then: 'There is another important thing, though. Dad, tell her.'

'Yes. Jo said once that her mother had never had a birth

**446**

certificate. Ethel and Alf had always claimed that it must have got lost, but when her mother needed to get a copy once, for a passport or something, there wasn't one even in Somerset House.'

'There's one thing wrong with all this, isn't there?' cried Kate. 'We are looking for a boy. Agnes had a boy.'

'Did she ever say she saw the baby?' asked Dan quietly.

'No, Miss Selcott took it away before she saw it. But she told Agnes it was a boy.'

'Suppose she was lying, Kate. Trying to put Agnes off the scent. If there was a hue and cry, everyone would be looking for a baby boy, not a girl. Perhaps it was a girl, and the girl was Esther.'

'But that would make you Agnes's great-grandson, Dan. It would have been you we were looking for all along!'

'Esther Howells,' said Kate. 'Esther must have been Agnes's lost child.' It was an hour later, and she and Dan were sitting still in their coats against the cold on a sofa in the library of Seddington House, a dozen photograph albums and piles of unmounted photographs on the floor around them. In the end it was Dan who had found what they were looking for. The photo showed the staff of Seddington House standing out on the steps. *1926* was pencilled on the back. Kate had peered at the faces.

'That is obviously Lister.' A severe-looking butler stood slightly aloof. 'The older lady must be Mrs Duncan. That's the gardener, and that gangly chap must be Alf. And there's Ethel – she's awfully pretty isn't she? She's definitely the woman holding the baby in your dad's photo, but she doesn't look at all like Esther. She's dark and petite. And Alf's got dark hair, too. Esther does look a bit like Agnes, don't you think? You know, Dan,' Kate's eyes were shining, 'I think you're right. You've got to be right! But how did it all happen?'

She picked up the envelope of diaries and, drawing out the first two volumes, searched through for references to Alf and Ethel. 'This is interesting. It says that Ethel lost her first baby. Maybe she thought she couldn't have another, maybe she was desperate for a child.'

'She did have further children of her own, though, didn't she?'

'But she and Alf loved Esther – I feel they did. They didn't even tell her she was adopted. Some of their relations must have known, but I suppose they kept quiet about it for Ethel and Alf's sake, because her parents wanted her to be the same as their younger children. Oh, at least she was loved.'

'What do you reckon happened on the night of the birth, then?'

Kate closed her eyes. 'I think,' she said slowly, opening them, 'that Lister took the baby and gave it to them. He knew about their disappointment, you see, and they lived far enough away for no one to make the connection. It would be very difficult for Agnes to find the child.'

'What about the locket?'

'I'll just find the bit about Agnes losing her half of the locket.' Kate flicked through the pages of the last volume she had read. 'It doesn't say when the locket went missing, just that it did. You know,' she said, shutting the exercise book, 'suppose Lister or Miss Selcott decided to give it away with the child? It was what mothers would do when they were forced to part with their babies. They would leave little mementoes with the child to identify it.'

'Or to give the child a part of themselves, I suppose,' Dan agreed.

'I wonder what happened to the letter,' Kate said softly.

'Which letter?' said Dan.

'Agnes's lover wrote her a letter. She copied some of it out into the diary.'

Dan shrugged. 'There's nothing in the shoebox like that.'

'Lost, then.'

'I suppose there's a chance it's somewhere in this house.' Dan stood up, his hands in his coat pockets, and began to walk around the chilly room, looking at the shelves. Occasionally he would reach for a volume or draw his finger across the rim of a chair. Kate watched him, her thoughts running in a babbling stream. She hadn't yet worked out their own relationship to each other in the complex Melton family tree.

Did knowing he had a right to be here in this house give him that new lift to his shoulders, or was that just her interpretation? In his long sweeping overcoat and black boots and with his wavy mane of gold-brown he looked, well, authoritative, like some lord of the manor. He didn't look at Kate, but seemed caught up in some world of his own as he paced about the room.

After a moment, he wandered over to the door and, opening it, went out into the hall. Kate listened from her seat on the sofa, the photograph of the servants still in her hand, hearing his footsteps on floorboards around the lower part of the house, doors opening and closing as he prowled.

Minutes passed and Kate got up and went in search of him. She found him in the dining room, his hands gripping the back of a chair as he stared at an empty space on the wall, where a fine eighteenth-century portrait of a soldier on horseback had been.

'Shame that that one had to go,' he said.

'Yes. Fourteen are being sold in the end. Farrell's have been very firm about which ones they can get buyers for right away at good prices.' She shrugged. 'Have we done the wrong thing, do you think?'

He turned to where she stood at his elbow and said, 'No,' and smiled. His eyes swept her face briefly and she felt the warmth of his breath.

'You look sad,' she said.

He curled his lips in a smile, but it didn't reach his eyes. Releasing the chair, he put his hands in his pockets, walked over to the window and peered out into the garden. Then he turned to face her.

'I do feel incredibly sad. And angry really.' She waited for him to go on. 'I've had a few days to get used to this idea – that I'm Agnes's great-grandson – and now I'm aware of just how much I've missed. Of what my mother missed, come to think of it, and most importantly of all, *her* mother before her – Esther. Agnes's child. I don't mean,' he gestured at the contents of the room, 'money or this house, though I can't pretend those don't have a place. No, I mean not to have known Agnes as our own. Not to have known about my great-grandfather, even. Harry. That he was an artist – like me. Everybody always wondered where my ability to draw came from. But it's all too late now. Too late.'

'At least you did know Agnes,' said Kate, faltering.

'But she didn't know me as her great-grandson, did she? I was the hired help, the charity case.'

'She never thought of you like that. She was very fond of you. You were a friend, a good friend.'

'But it's not enough for me, don't you see? And then there's this place. If she'd known, she would never have left it to you, would she?'

'No, I suppose not.' Kate looked down, focusing hard on her lap, fighting the tears that threatened. She had never seen Dan angry before, and now he seemed angry at her. When it wasn't her fault. 'There's the money, though. Oh God, we're going to have to tell Max.'

'There is the money,' he said quietly. 'But no recognition, no name.' Suddenly the anger seemed to rise in him like milk coming to the boil. 'Kate, you must excuse me. I have to get out of here.' And he pushed past her to the door.

After a moment the front door slammed and she heard urgent footsteps on gravel. To her surprise, he walked past the van and marched down the drive.

There seemed a vacuum in the room. Kate slumped into a dining chair and, falling forward onto the table, cried until her coat sleeves were soaked.

She cried for Dan, thrown into such turmoil, she cried for Agnes and everything she had never had, and she cried for herself because she thought she had lost this wonderful man whom she loved.

After a while she looked at her watch. It was past one, but she didn't feel hungry. Anyway, she realized, she had been reliant on Dan for a lift. She'd have to walk home if he didn't turn up again.

In the kitchen she found some coffee and a packet of biscuits. Conrad, though he sometimes slept here still, had a daytime job now, stacking shelves in a supermarket. Really, the sooner the place was ready for her and the children to move in, the better from the security point of view.

She took her coffee into the drawing room where she turned on an electric fire and, kicking off her shoes, drew her legs up under her and wrapped herself in a blanket someone had left there. With the hot drink inside her and the room warming up nicely she began to feel better. It was peaceful, in fact, sitting here in a comfortable armchair, the smell of beeswax mixing with old wood and the pungent whiff of burning dust from the fire. The grandfather clock tocked contentedly in a corner. She supposed Conrad had kept it wound – either Conrad or the ghosts.

She sighed. She felt so at home here – and yet not at home. Everything had changed again. Perhaps it should really be Dan's home. What would Agnes have wanted? She had a strong feeling that Dan was right: if Agnes had realized Dan was the grandchild of her own lost baby, she would have left the house to him, not to her. Could she, Kate, happily live here, now that she knew who Dan was, and that, by rights, the house should be his? She squeezed her eyes tight, trying to imagine it.

The trouble was, this wasn't just any old house. She felt tied up in its history because, well, in her dreams she had been here. However, she couldn't live here if she believed that in a moral, if not in a legal sense, she had stolen it from its rightful owner. Maybe she would feel Agnes's spirit hovering here, accusing her. No, that had to be rubbish. Agnes had been a loving person, would not have wished her harm. But all the same. *Come on, think, Kate, think.*

What was home? Home was more than a house. It was being with the people you loved in a place where you felt secure and happy. She had a home with Joyce. Despite everything that had happened since they had moved to Suffolk, Paradise Cottage had been a wonderful haven and Joyce had sacrificed so much for them and seen to their every physical need.

She had a sort of home with her parents now. Kate remembered what a contrast the recent weekend there with the children had been, compared to previous visits. She knew her parents wanted them to feel that they had their own bedrooms in that house. Her father had talked about Daisy and Sam helping him choose new beds and decoration for the single bedroom and the boxroom. He would send all those old magazines to the recycling, he had said; he didn't need them taking up the space.

She and the children would make their home here, some-where around Fernley. She could buy a small house – like Paradise Cottage maybe – because there were only the three of them. And they could get a dog. It would be home because they made it home and because they had so many friends here-abouts.

Kate huddled herself up warm in the blanket, the thoughts turning over and over in her mind. Emotionally exhausted, but with things finally clear in her mind, she dozed off.

There was a banging sound. Kate woke up, instantly alert. The banging came again. Someone at the door. She struggled out of the blanket and padded into the hall in her socks.

When she opened the door, Dan was standing there.

'Hello. I wasn't sure you would still be here.' His anger was gone, but he still didn't smile. Kate hurried back into the draw-ing room, where she hastily pulled on her shoes and ran her fingers through her hair, squinting at her creased-up face in the mirror over the fireplace. It was three o'clock. At this rate Joyce would have to cope with the dress rehearsal without her.

'Cosy in here,' said Dan, coming in and closing the door. He peeled off his coat and dropped it onto the chaise longue before coming over and sitting on the sofa in front of the fire in the already darkening room. He sat in complete stillness for a moment, his forearms resting on his knees, fingers entwined.

'Where did you go? I wasn't sure whether to wait.' Kate knew she sounded grumpy but she didn't care.

'Sorry. Everything just seemed too big to deal with. I walked round the village a bit then went up to the church. Visited Agnes's grave, in fact. Was it you who left the chrysanthe-mums?'

'No. Maybe it was Marie, or Max. I don't know.'

'Oh. Well, if you don't think I'm crazy, I talked to Agnes. Cleared my head.'

'I won't tell anyone you're a fruitcake. What did you say to her?'

'Just that I was . . . fond of her, and that wherever she was, she must know the truth now and I hoped she was glad it was me. And I wanted to reassure her that her daughter probably had a good life, that she was loved.'

'You know,' Kate broke in. 'I've just remembered. In one of the diaries, Agnes talks about meeting Ethel during the war. It was something about asking if her daughter wanted a job in this house and Ethel turning her down. How weird.' Kate got up. 'I'll go and find . . .'

Dan pulled at her sleeve. 'No, wait,' he said. 'It'll keep.' She sank back into the chair. 'I've been thinking.'

'So have I,' she rushed in. 'I realize now, you're absolutely right.'

'About what?' he said, puzzled.

'What you said earlier. About what Agnes would have wanted. I've made a decision, Dan.' She took a deep breath, felt a dizziness in her head. 'If Agnes *had* known you were her great-grandson she would definitely have left you the house. *Definitely.* So it's right that you should have it. You must have it.'

'But . . .'

'So it's yours. I don't need it, not really. We can find somewhere else nice to live. I will need some money, though, a bit from selling some of the stuff in this place – but perhaps we can talk about that. Then the children and I will get ourselves somewhere locally and I'll find a job. But we'll be OK. Oh, and maybe Max can have his money, too.'

'Kate. Kate, listen!' Dan's expression was soft. 'Do you mean that? Do you really mean that?'

454

'Yes,' she said. 'I do. I wouldn't feel happy here, knowing it should be yours, do you see? I'd feel like an imposter. It wouldn't feel like home.'

He shook his head in amazement, then reached out a hand and squeezed hers. 'Thank you,' he whispered. 'You're incredible. You really are.' He released her and stared in concentration at the carpet.

'But you see, when I was talking to Agnes and thinking about things, I reached absolutely the opposite conclusion.' He seemed agitated now, and got up and started to wander round the room. He picked up a porcelain bird from the mantelpiece, rubbed some dust off it and carefully set it down again. He turned towards Kate.

'This discovery hasn't fundamentally changed me, who I am. It's like looking at myself with a new filter, in a sharper focus, that's all. But I'm still the same old Dan with the same moodiness and the same ambitions. I've made mistakes in my life, I'll probably make more. But I'll get some things right and good things will happen. And I'm not unhappy really. I've got a home of my own. Yes, it's small, but I love it and I can work there. I've got a business that's going well. And someone's interested in buying my paintings – and painting is what I really want to do.

'Seddington House is lovely and it's the family home, but I don't need it. Do you see? It's important to me because Agnes loved it and she wanted it to go to a Melton. But I really, genuinely think, that she would be happy for you to have it still. And so you must have it, Kate. It's yours.'

Kate laughed, a little bark of a laugh. 'Now who's being incredible, Dan? You're extraordinary.'

Feeling suddenly overwhelmed, she too got up and went over to the French windows. Outside, the garden was drab, sodden. Moss grew over the flagstones of the terrace. But soon the weather would be warmer. Little green shoots would appear, pushing their way up through the earth's shroud, and before you knew it, the garden would be dotted with snowdrops, then early daffodils and crocuses. The spring air would throb with birdsong.

She faced Dan once more. 'Is that truly what you want?'

Dan didn't look at her. He was tracing the lines of an exquisite Chinese vase with his finger, from the lip down into the waist and round the voluptuous billowing curve of its base. Then he took a small step towards her, followed by another. Finally he stood before her at the window, straight and sure.

'What I really really really *really* want, Kate, darling Kate,' he said, lifting his hand and tracing the line of her cheek with his forefinger as he had caressed the vase, 'is you.'

'Oh Dan,' she said. And, 'Oh *Dan . . .*'

And this time, when she moved into the circle of his arms and their mouths and bodies entwined, there was nothing to hold her back.


Kate never did make it to the nativity play rehearsal, but they managed without her. Instead, Dan led her up to the top of the house, to the attic where the sun streamed in and where, long ago, little Agnes had watched and waited and dreamed, and there they lay together on the old sofa and loved each other and talked about everything under the sun.

And Kate knew for certain that after a long journey through a howling wilderness, she had finally come home.

# Chapter 40

*Six months later*

'Half an hour to go. How are you feeling? Nervous?' said the usher, a cheeky young man in a dark suit. They were standing near the door of the marquee, during a short lull in the rush of visitors.

'Terrified,' said Kate, cool in a pale green shift dress and jacket, and fingering Agnes's pearls. 'I never thought it would be so exciting.'

'It's a big day,' he said gravely then he called out, 'This way if you would, ladies and gentleman,' to a party of three ambling in a vague fashion up the matted path towards them. 'Lovely weather, isn't it? Yes, two catalogues admit the three of you. That's right, madam, over there to register.'

The first day of the people's auction had finally arrived, a beautiful morning in late June. It had taken six months of hard work, precision planning and carefully laid publicity, but now everything was in place and the bidding for a substantial part of the contents of Seddington House would start at 10 a.m. sharp.

'Darling, hello! We've been looking for you simply

everywhere.' Liz emerged from the crowd inside, with Laurence, clutching their catalogue, close behind, and kissed her.

'We're determined to buy something witty – maybe the doggy fire irons,' she said, 'though it's fun just to be here, soaking up the atmosphere.'

'It's lovely to see you. I hope the children weren't too angry about being left behind in London? Though if they're with Leo, I'm sure they'll be fine.'

'Oh, they're having an even more exciting time than we are,' Liz said. 'A male au pair. It's the answer to every freelance woman's dream.' Kate smiled as Laurence rolled his eyes. 'Anyway, it's ages since we had a few days off by ourselves, isn't it, Laurence? It's one of the great things about me not having to be in the office all the time now.'

'She'd never allow me any holiday when I reported to her,' said Laurence, a twinkle in his eye. 'Now, if you'll forgive me, I just want to have another quick look at those prints of Blythborough. Oh fantastic – look, it's Claire. And Alex and Mina!'

Kate spun round to see them enter the tent. Claire came first, petite in a long skirt and loose blouse, both of course black, and lugging a huge pink bag with teddies all over it.

'It's amazing that you've come. Thank you!' Kate hugged her before greeting Alex. A dark, heavy-set man, Alex wore a baby sling over his chest and, inside, the tiny shape of sleeping Mina pressed against her daddy's heart. Kate reached out and stroked her silky head with her fingertips, but she didn't stir.

'Claire's just fed and changed her, so with any luck we'll get some peace and quiet for a bit,' Alex grumbled, one large hand gently rubbing the baby's back through the sling.

'She's just started on the mashed banana and baby rice,' said Claire proudly. 'And it certainly makes her sleep well.'

Kate studied what she could see of Mina's little face in wonder. It seemed only a short few months ago that she had first seen her in an incubator, a fragile little doll with tubes strapped to every visible part of her. In January, Claire's blood pressure had shot right up and she was taken into hospital for an emergency Caesarian. When Mina was delivered she weighed only 4 pounds and her first month in the world was touch and go.

Just as moving for Kate as seeing the tiny baby struggling to thrive, was meeting Alex for the first time. When she arrived in the baby unit, Claire was out taking a shower, but there was a man sitting by one of the incubators whom Kate recognized instantly from the opera programme Claire had shown her on Walberswick beach. His clothes were crumpled and he looked drawn from lack of sleep, but his eyes were full of joy and tenderness as he gently stroked his daughter's chest with two fingers through a hole in the glass. When he became aware of the visitor he looked up.

'Hello,' he said, offering her his other hand. 'You must be Kate. Come and meet Mina.' Just then, the baby opened her eyes. Her navy-blue gaze was unfocused, but Alex slowly rose and moved into her area of vision, and it seemed as though she looked right back at him.

Later, Kate went down to the café with Claire. 'It's incredible,' Claire said. Despite her obvious tiredness, she seemed elated. 'He's been completely different since the birth. He was with me in the end, came in the ambulance and held my hand during the operation. He was brilliant. And the thing is, once he realized I was all right, he has hardly been able to take his eyes off Mina. Babies must be born with a dose of magic, you know.'

'Some secret potion that makes people fall in love, you mean. It should be patented.'

'He's asked me to marry him!' Claire whispered, her eyes sparkling.

'I'm so pleased,' Kate said, squeezing her arm.

'I told him I'd think about it,' Claire said with mock hauteur.

'You didn't!'

'OK, I didn't. I said yes, please.'

Kate watched Claire and Alex go inside the marquee now, hand-in-hand.

'And they lived happily ever after,' said Laurence wickedly as he started to follow them in.

'Course they will,' said Liz, swatting at him. 'They deserve to, don't they? Catch up with you later, Kate.'

And here's my happy ever after, thought Kate, watching Dan come up the path in the sunshine, one hand in Daisy's. She waved and hurried out to meet them.

'Hi,' she said, kissing each of them in turn. 'Is Sam all right?'

'He was painting,' said Daisy, who wore a superior air, being allowed to miss school to attend this grown-up event for which Sam was Too Young. 'Making an awful mess.' Sam had got his own back by being sick the night before and Joyce had offered to look after him. It was fun to go to Granny's. The rented modern bungalow Kate had moved them into just after Christmas was nice because it was so close to Debbie and Jonny's family, but the garden was a small square of weed-infested grass and there was no Bobby.

'The next Jackson Pollock,' said Dan, smiling. 'Joyce was spreading newspaper all over the floor when we left.'

Paradise Cottage had not quite returned to its pristine pre-child state because the children were round there so often, but Joyce didn't complain. It was clear to both parties, without anyone saying so, that their relationship was all the better for them being queens of separate castles, and Joyce's great fear, that she would see too little of the children, had been quickly laid to rest. Paradise Cottage was the children's third home – after Simon and Meredith's London flat, of course – followed closely by 2, The Row, Dan's home, where they often visited and occasionally met Shelley. They took all this extended family in their stride.

'Come on, Daisy.' Dan ruffled her hair. 'Let's leave Mummy to say hello to people and go in and find our seats.'

'They're near the front, Dan. You'll see the cards. Mum and Dad are in there somewhere, so are Debbie and Jonny. I'll be with you in a minute.'

When they had gone, Kate went and picked up a spare catalogue from the table where two women from Farrell's were busy registering the financial details of would-be buyers and supplying them with numbered paddles with which to make bids during the auction.

She flipped to the timetable. At ten o'clock was the picture sale, to be followed by books. During the afternoon, furniture and antiquities would go under the hammer.

Tomorrow it would be the turn of the silver, the ceramics and the textiles.

She flicked through the catalogue thoughtfully. It had been a difficult job deciding what to sell and what to hold on to. In the end, her rule of thumb had been to keep what she really liked and anything she knew would have been of particular sentimental value to Agnes. So, for instance, the lovely painting of Dunwich remained in the hall, some of the more useful and attractive items of furniture, the grand piano and the faded suite, the miniature that had been the start of Agnes's collection, the big dining table and chairs. But the catalogue, with its meticulous listing of each object for sale, accompanied by photographs, still ran to two hundred pages. Today was Monday, and during the

Thursday and Friday of the preceding week, hordes of visitors had swarmed into the grounds to view the contents of the auction, some of it displayed downstairs in the house, much of it in two great marquees that Farrell's had erected in the grounds. It had been a huge operation, effortlessly masterminded by Ursula and her team.

Ursula herself approached Kate now. 'Have you seen the local paper yet?' she asked, passing her a copy. Kate unfolded it and stared in amazement at the front page. *Treasure to be Auctioned Today* the headline blared under a colour photograph of Seddington House. On pages two and three was an article with pictures of some of the artefacts, together with a short interview that Kate had given the journalist last week.

It was only the latest in a whole wave of publicity generated by the event. Not only had the local paper flagged the auction over the previous few months, but *The Times* and the *Telegraph* had both sent journalists down and Farrell's had made sure that the sale had been fully written up in all the relevant journals, magazines and websites for the art and antiques trade.

'Everything's ready now,' said Ursula, who was today dressed in a severe navy trouser suit in readiness for her role as chief auctioneer. 'We've record numbers for registration and the big players are all in place.'

Kate knew that long-distance telephone bidding from key dealers would decide the fate of some of the more valuable pieces.

'We've just run over all the equipment again to make sure there will be no technical hitches. You've found where you're sitting? Good. Well, I'll see you in a few minutes, then. And don't worry, Kate. It's going to be terrific.' And Ursula hurried off in the same direction as Dan and Daisy.

Kate stayed to welcome the vicar, who had arrived with his

wife, the belly-dancer, a lively woman with a mane of fair curls cascading over her shoulders and an Indian print dress. Close behind was Peter Overden, the chairman of the school governors. And there was Raj, hurrying over from the refreshments tent, a Styrofoam coffee cup held out before him. She had spoken to him earlier, when he joined her conversation with a collector.

'This is one of the most important sales of miniatures outside London that there's been for some time,' the man was saying.

'Miss Melton was a most wonderful person,' Raj told him. 'An expert in her field. She would be happy to think that her collection would be admired and valued by others, wouldn't she, Mrs Hutchinson?'

'Most definitely,' Kate agreed. 'And you know, part of me feels that she's here with us today. I wanted this sale to be in memory of her.'

It was Kate who had suggested the preface to the sales brochure, which commemorated Agnes's life and work. Farrell's had even unearthed a photograph of Agnes from years before to accompany it. The picture had illustrated an article she had written for a magazine and showed her in lively conversation with the then director of Christie's.

'Have you seen Max?' Kate called to Raj now.

'He was looking for his ladyfriend,' said Raj. 'Look, here they come now.' Max appeared from the direction of the house deep in conversation with a slender dark-haired woman.

'They look so much like brother and sister, those two,' Raj said, amused.

And it was true. The doctor Max had met at a Christmas party in Norwich had small round glasses and the same earnest expression that he did. As Kate and Raj watched, the couple stopped and Olivia brushed a leaf off Max's dark sheen of hair, then kissed him quickly.

'But she's much prettier than he is,' Kate told Raj and giggled. Max's two daughters were delicate female versions of him, too. Grace and Emily had been to visit the Hutchinsons several times now, and Sam and Daisy were enchanted to have acquired two cousins, though, 'I wish Emily was a boy,' sighed Sam.

Despite briefcase and coffee, Raj managed to squint at his watch. 'Five to ten, Kate. Time to sit down.'

'And the maiden bid is two hundred and eighty. Am I bid two ninety, three hundred, yes, the gentleman over there, three twenty, three fifty, four hundred, five hundred, six hundred. Six hundred, are you all done? Seven hundred, eight hundred. At eight hundred against you all, eight hundred. Thank you, the lady here by the aisle . . . Now, Lot 46 . . .'

Kate could hardly breathe as she listened to the sale of the miniatures. There was particularly fierce bidding for a portrait of one of Bonnie Prince Charlie's descendants and a little girl in an Empire-line dress, both of which made more than ten times the estimated value. The picture of the girl eventually went to a local lady who, one of Ursula's colleagues told Kate as she gulped down a lunchtime sandwich, had reason to be convinced it was of one of her ancestors.

Nearly all of the paintings had also reached prices well beyond Farrell's estimates. Kate was gobsmacked when a delicate watercolour by a fringe member of the Bloomsbury group sold for £30,000 instead of the estimate of £5,000. 'This can happen at these country-house auctions,' Ursula had explained earlier. 'There's such a mix of interests – international dealers, local people bidding for sentimental reasons. Caution will sometimes be thrown to the winds. It's quite impossible to predict in advance how things will go.'

By the end of the first day, it was clear that almost twice the

464

total estimated figure had been reached. Virtually everything had found a buyer.

By the end of the second day, only a few lots were unsold and Ursula was ecstatic. 'We're looking at over a million,' she confided to Kate and Dan, when they cracked open the champagne early that evening, 'though I would need to confirm that with you, of course.'

'That's amazing,' said Kate. 'Thank you. Thank you so much, Ursula.' She turned to Dan, her eyes shining. 'It means I can do everything I promised.'

They had worked it out between them, Max, Dan and Kate, over the previous six months. All three were to receive equal payments from the Melton estate – both Kate and Dan were determined Max wouldn't lose out because of the discovery of Dan's ancestry, proved, incidentally, by the DNA test Raj had gently insisted on. There was one further donation Kate intended to make. In her bag was an envelope with a cheque for £25,000 made out to the Save Fernley School appeal. £25,000 had already been promised from other sources, mostly through Jasmin Thornton's efforts. When Mr Overden came to say goodbye, Kate gave him the envelope. His look of astonishment when he opened it made her laugh out loud.

'I still can't imagine myself actually living here,' said Kate as she and Dan strolled through the gardens of Seddington House in the golden light of evening.

'It'll be a mess for a while with the builders and decorators,' said Dan, 'but you'll make it yours all right.'

'It's not just a matter of interior decoration, Dan. It's that I've seen the place for so long through Agnes's eyes. Her spirit is part of it all. Do you believe in ghosts?'

'I suppose I think that Agnes was ready to die when she did, and that she's happy wherever she is now. So there wouldn't be any reason for her to hang around here, would there?'

'I just wondered – because of the dreams. I wondered whether I might have some special connection to her.'

'You'll remember her, won't you? And you'll tell your children and grandchildren about her. That will be your thanks to her. She will live on through our memories.'

'You're right, I'm just being fanciful.' Kate stopped and turned to face him. 'Dan, will you think about what I said? Would you come and live here, too? The children are so fond of you. I think it would work. And it's a great idea to keep your house as your studio.'

Dan shoved his hands in his pockets and shuffled the gravel with his shoes. 'It would have to more than work,' he said, his voice gruff. 'And what about you? Are you "fond" of me, too, Kate?' he said, teasing her.

Kate's answer was to wrap her arms around him and kiss him passionately. After a long moment, he raised his face and looked at her. His face was suddenly serious.

'How about this? Will the lady in the big house,' he said, stroking her hair, 'take the man in the little house, to have and to hold?'

'She will. But the lady in the big house,' she said, trying not to smile, 'would give up the big house without a single regret, to come and live in the little house with the man.'

'The lady in the big house might find it a bit of a squash for her children,' he said. 'Especially if we have any more.'

'Oh! We haven't talked about that one yet.'

'We've plenty of time to talk,' he said, laughing. 'And for everything else.'

And, taking her hand, he led her into the house that was to be their home.

## Acknowledgments

Many friends have been supportive during the writing of this book. I would particularly like to thank Juliet Bamber and Dr Hilary Johnson for their sensitive comments on the manuscript, Dr Ann Stanley for advice on medical matters, and Bob and Janet Mitchell for photography, laptops and encouragement.

In the publishing world, great thanks to my agent Sheila Crowley and to Suzanne Baboneau, Melissa Weatherill, Joan Dietch and the team at Simon & Schuster. Also, thank you to Nick Sayers for advice.

Finally, it would have proved impossible to write this novel without the loving support of my family. I am particularly indebted to my husband David who helps in so many ways, and to Felix, Benjy and Leo, who occasionally allowed me use of 'their' computer.